THIS TENDER LAND

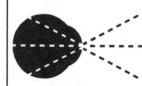

This Large Print Book carries the
Seal of Approval of N.A.V.H.

THIS TENDER LAND

WILLIAM KENT KRUEGER

THORNDIKE PRESS
A part of Gale, a Cengage Company

Farmington Hills, Mich • San Francisco • New York • Waterville, Maine
Meriden, Conn • Mason, Ohio • Chicago

GALE
A Cengage Company

Copyright © 2019 by William Kent Krueger.
Thorndike Press, a part of Gale, a Cengage Company.

Thorndike Press® Large Print Basic.
The text of this Large Print edition is unabridged.
Other aspects of the book may vary from the original edition.
Set in 16 pt. Plantin.

LIBRARY OF CONGRESS CIP DATA ON FILE.
CATALOGUING IN PUBLICATION FOR THIS BOOK
IS AVAILABLE FROM THE LIBRARY OF CONGRESS

ISBN-13: 978-1-4328-6934-2 (hardcover alk. paper)

Published in 2019 by arrangement with Atria Books, an imprint of Simon & Schuster, Inc.

Printed in the United States of America
1 2 3 4 5 6 7 23 22 21 20 19

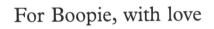

For Boopie, with love

Sing in me, Muse, and through me
tell the story.

— HOMER, *THE ODYSSEY*

■ ■ ■ ■

- PART ONE -
GOD IS A TORNADO

■ ■ ■ ■

PROLOGUE

In the beginning, after he labored over the heavens and the earth, the light and the dark, the land and sea and all living things that dwell therein, after he created man and woman and before he rested, I believe God gave us one final gift. Lest we forget the divine source of all that beauty, he gave us stories.

I am a storyteller. I live in a house in the shade of a sycamore tree on the banks of the Gilead River. My great-grandchildren, when they visit me here, call me old.

"Old is a cliché," I tell them, with mock disappointment. "A terrible trivializing. An insult. I was born along with the sun and earth and moon and planets and all the stars. Every atom of my being was there at the very beginning."

"You're a liar." They scowl, but playfully.

"Not a liar. A storyteller," I remind them.

"Then tell us a story," they plead.

I need no goading. Stories are the sweet

fruit of my existence and I share them gladly.

The events I'm about to share with you began on the banks of the Gilead. Even if you grew up in the heartland, you may not remember these things. What happened in the summer of 1932 is most important to those who experienced it, and there are not many of us left.

The Gilead is a lovely river, lined with cottonwoods already ancient when I was a boy.

Things were different then. Not simpler or better, just different. We didn't travel the way we do now, and for most folks in Fremont County, Minnesota, the world was limited to the piece of it they could see before the horizon cut off the land. They wouldn't have understood any more than I did that if you kill a man, you are changed forever. If that man comes back to life, you are transformed. I have witnessed this and other miracles with my own eyes. So, among the many pieces of wisdom life has offered me over all these years is this: Open yourself to every possibility, for there is nothing your heart can imagine that is not so.

The tale I'm going to tell is of a summer long ago. Of killing and kidnapping and children pursued by demons of a thousand names. There will be courage in this story and cowardice. There will be love and betrayal. And, of course, there will be hope. In

12

the end, isn't that what every good story is about?

CHAPTER ONE

Albert named the rat. He called it Faria.

It was an old creature, a mottle of gray and white fur. Almost always, it kept to the edges of the tiny cell, scurrying along the wall to a corner where I'd put a few crumbs of the hard biscuit that had been my meal. At night, I generally couldn't see it but could still hear the soft rustle as it moved from the wide crack between the corner blocks, across the straw on the floor, grabbed the crumbs, and returned the way it had come. Whenever the moon was just right and bright beams streamed through the high, narrow slit that was the only window, illuminating the stones of the eastern wall, I was sometimes able to glimpse in the reflected light the slender oval of Faria's body, its fur a dim silver blur, its thin tail roping behind like an afterthought of the animal's creation.

The first time I got thrown into what the Brickmans called the quiet room, they tossed my older brother, Albert, in with me. The night was moonless, the tiny cell as black as pitch, our bed a thin matting of straw laid on the dirt floor, the door a great rectangle of rusted iron with a slot at the bottom for the delivery of a food plate that never held more than that one hard biscuit. I was scared to death. Later, Benny Blackwell, a Sioux from Rosebud, told us that when the Lincoln Indian Training School had been a military outpost called Fort Sibley, the quiet room had been used for solitary confinement. In those days, it had held warriors. By the time Albert and I got there, it held only children.

I didn't know anything about rats then, except for the story about the Pied Piper of Hamelin, who'd rid the town of the vermin. I thought they were filthy creatures and would eat anything and maybe would even eat us. Albert, who was four years older and a whole lot wiser, told me that people are most afraid of things they don't understand, and if something frightened you, you should get closer to it. That didn't mean it wouldn't still be an awful thing, but the awful you knew was easier to handle than the awful you imagined. So Albert had named the rat, because a name made it not just any rat. When I asked why Faria, he said it was from a book, *The Count of Monte Cristo*. Albert loved to read. Me, I liked to make up my own stories. Whenever I was thrown into the quiet room, I fed Faria crumbs and imagined tales about him. I looked up rats in the worn *Encyclopaedia Britannica* on the school library shelf and discovered that they were smart and social. Across the years and the many nights I spent in the isolation of the quiet room, I came to think of the little creature as a friend. Faria. Rat extraordinaire. Companion to misfits. A fellow captive in the dark prison of the Brickmans.

That first night in the quiet room, Albert and I were being punished for contradicting Mrs. Thelma Brickman, the school's superintendent. Albert was twelve and I was eight. We were both new to Lincoln School. After the evening meal, which had been a watery, tasteless stew containing only a few bits of carrot, potato, something green and slimy, and a little ham gristle, Mrs. Brickman had sat at the front of the great dining hall and told all the children a story. Most dinner meals were followed by one of Mrs. Brickman's stories. They usually contained some moral lesson she believed was important. Afterward, she would ask if there were any questions. This was a conceit, I came to understand, to make it seem as if there were an actual opportunity for dialogue with her, for the kind of conversation that might exist between a reasonable adult and a reasonable child. That evening, she'd related the story of the race between the tortoise and the hare. When she asked if there were any questions,

17

I'd raised my hand. She'd smiled and had called on me.

"Yes, Odie?"

She knew my name. I'd been thrilled at that. Amid the sea of children, so many that I didn't believe I would ever be able to learn all their names, she'd remembered mine. I'd wondered if maybe this was because we were so new or if it was because we were the whitest faces in a vast room full of Indian children.

"Mrs. Brickman, you said the point of the story was that being lazy is a terrible thing."

"That's true, Odie."

"I thought the point of the story was that slow and steady wins the race."

"I see no difference." Her voice was stern, but not harsh, not yet.

"My father read that story to me, Mrs. Brickman. It's one of Aesop's fables. And he said —"

"*He* said?" Now there was something different in the way she spoke. As if she were struggling to cough up a fish bone caught in her throat. "*He* said?" She'd been sitting on a stool that raised her up so everyone in the dining hall could see her. She slid from the stool and walked between the long tables, girls on one side, boys on the other, toward where I sat with Albert. In the absolute silence of that great room, I could hear the *squeak, squeak* of her rubber heels on the old floorboards as she came. The boy next to me, whose name I didn't yet know, edged away, as if trying to distance himself from a place where he knew lightning was about to strike. I glanced at Albert, and he shook his head, a sign that I should just clam up.

Mrs. Brickman stood over me. "*He* said?"

"Y-y-yes, ma'am," I replied, stuttering but no less respectful.

"And where is *he*?"

"Y-y-you know, Mrs. Brickman."

"Dead, that's where. *He* is no longer present to read you stories. The stories you hear now are the ones I tell you. And they mean just what I say they mean. Do you understand me?"

"I . . . I . . ."

"Yes or no?"

She leaned toward me. She was slender, her face a delicate oval the color of a pearl. Her eyes were as green and sharp as new thorns on a rosebush. She wore her black hair long, and kept it brushed as soft as cat fur. She smelled of talcum and faintly of whiskey, an aromatic mix I would come to know well over the years.

"Yes," I said in the smallest voice I'd ever heard come from my own lips.

"He meant no disrespect, ma'am," Albert said.

"Was I talking to you?" The green thorns of her eyes stabbed at my brother.

"No, ma'am."

She straightened herself and scanned the room. "Any other questions?"

I'd thought — hoped, prayed — this was the end of it. But that night, Mr. Brickman came to the dormitory room and called me out, and Albert, too. The man was tall and lean, and also handsome, many of the women at the school said, but all I saw was the fact that his eyes were nothing but black pupils, and he reminded me of a snake with legs.

"You boys'll be sleeping somewhere else tonight," he said. "Come along."

That first night in the quiet room, I barely slept a wink. It was April, and there was still a chill in the wind sweeping out of the empty Dakotas. Our father was less than a week dead. Our mother had passed away two years before that. We had no kin in Minnesota, no friends, no one who knew us or cared about us. We were the only white boys in a school for Indians. How could it get any worse? Then I'd heard the rat and had spent the rest of those long, dark hours until daylight pressed against Albert and the iron door, my knees drawn up to my chin, my eyes pouring out tears that only Albert could see and that no one but him would have cared about anyway.

Four years had passed between that first night and the one I'd just spent in the quiet room. I'd grown some, changed some. The old, frightened Odie O'Banion was, like my mother and father, long dead. The Odie I was now had a penchant for rebellion.

When I heard the key turn in the lock, I sat up on the straw matting. The iron door swung open and morning light poured in, blinding me for a moment.

"Sentence is up, Odie."

Although I couldn't see the contours of the face yet, I recognized the voice easily: Herman Volz, the old German who oversaw the carpentry shop and was the assistant boys' adviser. The man stood in the doorway, blocking for a moment the glare of the sun. He looked down at me through thick eyeglasses, his pale features soft and wistful.

"She wants to see you," he said. "I have to take you."

Volz spoke with a German accent, so his *w*'s sounded like *v*'s and his *v*'s like *f*'s. What he'd said came out, "She vants to see you. I haf to take you."

I stood, folded the thin blanket, and hung it across a rod attached to the wall so that it would be available for the next child who occupied the room, knowing that, like as not, it would be me again.

Volz shut the door behind us. "Did you sleep okay? How is your back?"

Often a strapping preceded time in the quiet room, and last night had been no exception. My back ached from the welts, but it did no good to talk about it.

"I dreamed about my mother," I said.

"Did you now?"

The quiet room was the last in a row of rooms in a long building that had once been the outpost stockade. The other rooms — all originally cells — had been turned into storage spaces. Volz and I walked along the old stockade and across the yard toward the administration building, a two-story structure of red stone set among stately elms that had been planted by the first commandant of Fort Sibley. The trees provided the building with constant shade, which always made it a dark place.

"Pleasant dream, then?" Volz said.

"She was in a rowboat on a river. I was in a boat, too, trying to catch up with her, trying to see her face. But no matter how hard I rowed, she was always too far ahead."

"Don't sound like a good dream," Volz said. He was wearing clean bib overalls over a blue work shirt. His huge hands, nicked and scarred from his carpentry, hung at his sides. Half of the little finger on his right hand was missing, the result of an accident with a band saw. Behind his back, some of the kids called him Old Four-and-a-Half, but not me or Albert. The German carpenter had always been kind to us.

We entered the building and went immediately to Mrs. Brickman's office, where she was seated behind her big desk, a stone fireplace at her back. I was a little surprised to see Albert there. He stood straight and tall beside her like a soldier at attention. His face was blank, but his eyes spoke to me. They said, *Careful, Odie.*

"Thank you, Mr. Volz," the superintendent said. "You may wait outside."

As he turned to leave, Volz put a hand on my shoulder, the briefest of gestures, but I appreciated what it meant.

Mrs. Brickman said, "I'm concerned about you, Odie. I'm beginning to believe that your time at Lincoln School is almost at an end."

I wasn't sure what that meant, but I didn't think it was necessarily a bad thing.

The superintendent wore a black dress, which seemed to be her favorite color. I'd overheard Miss Stratton, who taught music, tell another teacher once that it was because Mrs. Brickman was obsessed with her appearance and thought black was slimming. It worked pretty well, because the superintendent reminded me of nothing so much as the long, slender handle of a fireplace poker. Her penchant for the color gave rise to a nickname we all used, well out of her hearing, of course: the Black Witch.

"Do you know what I'm saying, Odie?"

"I'm not sure, ma'am."

"Even though you're not Indian, the sheriff

asked us to accept you and your brother because there was no room at the state orphanage. And we did, out of the goodness of our hearts. But there's another option for a boy like you, Odie. Reformatory. Do you know what that is?"

"I do, ma'am."

"And is that where you would like to be sent?"

"No, ma'am."

"I thought not. Then, Odie, what will you do?"

"Nothing, ma'am."

"Nothing?"

"I will do nothing that will get me sent there, ma'am."

She put her hands on her desk, one atop the other, and spread her fingers wide so that they formed a kind of web over the polished wood. She smiled at me as if she were a spider who'd just snagged a fly. "Good," she said. "Good." She nodded toward Albert. "You should be more like your brother."

"Yes, ma'am. I'll try. May I have my harmonica back?"

"It's very special to you, isn't it?"

"Not really. Just an old harmonica. I like to play. It keeps me out of trouble."

"A gift from your father, I believe."

"No, ma'am. I just picked it up somewhere. I don't even remember where now."

"That's funny," she said. "Albert told me it

24

was a gift from your father."

"See?" I said, shrugging my shoulders. "Not even special enough to remember where I got it."

She considered me, then said, "Very well." She took a key from a pocket of her dress, unlocked a drawer of the desk, and pulled out the harmonica.

I reached for it, but she drew it back.

"Odie?"

"Yes, ma'am?"

"Next time, I keep it for good. Do you understand?"

"Yes, ma'am. I do."

She gave it over and her spindly fingers touched my hand. When I returned to the dormitory, I intended to use the lye soap in the lavatory there to scrub that hand until it bled.

CHAPTER TWO

"Reformatory, Odie," Albert said. "She wasn't joking."

"Did I break a law?"

"That woman, she gets what she wants, Odie," Volz said.

"The hell with the Black Witch," I said.

We left the shadow of the elms and headed toward the great yard, which had once been the parade ground for Fort Sibley. Directly south across the huge, grassy rectangle were the kitchen and dining hall. Spaced along the rest of the perimeter were most of the other school buildings: the dormitories for the youngest children, the laundry and maintenance facility, and the woodworking and carpentry shops, one above the other. Set back a bit were the dormitories for the older children and the general classroom building, which were newer constructions. Everything had been built of red stone from a local quarry. Beyond these lay the athletic field, the water tower, the garage where the big pieces of heavy equipment and the school bus were parked, a warehouse, and the old stockade. Edging the whole property to the north ran the Gilead River.

The morning was sunny and warm. The boys who'd drawn grounds duty that day were already at work mowing the grass and trimming along the walkways. Some of the girls knelt on the sidewalks with buckets and brushes, scrubbing the concrete clean. Who cleaned sidewalks that way? It was a useless chore, one we all knew was meant to drive home to the girls their complete dependence and the school's absolute control. They glanced up from their work when we passed, but none risked conversation, because the watchful eye of the groundskeeper, a sloppy, sullen man named DiMarco, was always on them. DiMarco was responsible for the welts on my back. When a boy required a beating at Lincoln School, it was usually DiMarco who delivered it, and he enjoyed every swing of that leather strap. It was late May and school no longer in session. A lot of the kids at Lincoln had gone home for the summer to their families on reservations in Minnesota or the Dakotas or Nebraska or even farther. Children like Albert and me, who had no family or whose families were too poor or too broken to take them back, lived at the school year-round.

At the dormitory, Albert cleaned the welts

on my back, and Volz gingerly applied the witch hazel he kept on hand for just such occasions. I washed up, then we headed toward the dining hall. In the stone above the entrance was still chiseled MESS HALL from the old days when soldiers had been fed there. Under the stern command of Mrs. Peterson, who was responsible for feeding all the kids, nothing could have been further from the truth. The floor of the great hall, though terribly scuffed, was always swept clean of every crumb. After each meal, the rows of tables were wiped down with water and a bit of bleach. The kitchen and bakery were run with a rigid hand. I'd heard that Mrs. Peterson complained there was never enough money to buy proper food, but she managed to stretch whatever she had. True, the soups contained more water than solids and often tasted like something ladled from a ditch, and the breads were hard and heavy enough that they could have been used to break rock (she claimed yeast was too expensive), and the meat, when there was some, was mostly gristle, but every child ate three meals a day.

When we stepped inside the dining hall, Herman Volz said, "I have bad news for you, Odie. But also some good. First, the bad. You have been assigned to work in Bledsoe's hay-fields today."

I looked at Albert and saw it was true. Bad news, indeed. It almost made me wish I was back in the quiet room.

"And also, you have missed breakfast. But you already know this."

Breakfast was served promptly at seven. Volz hadn't sprung me from the stockade until eight. Not his fault, but Mrs. Brickman's doing. One last punishment. No breakfast that day.

This in advance of one of the hardest work assignments a kid at Lincoln School could draw. I wondered what the good news was.

Almost immediately, I understood. Donna High Hawk appeared from the kitchen, wearing a white apron and a white headwrap, and carrying a chipped, white bowl filled with Cream of Wheat. Donna High Hawk, like me, was twelve years old. She was a member of the Winnebago tribe from Nebraska. When she'd come to Lincoln School, two years earlier, she'd been scrawny and quiet, her hair long and worn in two braids. They'd cut the braids and run a nit comb through what hair was left to her. As they did with so many of the new kids, they'd stripped off her shabby clothing and washed her all over with kerosene and put her in the uniform dress of the school. She hadn't spoken much English then and had hardly ever smiled. In my years at Lincoln, I'd come to understand that this was not unusual for kids straight off the reservation.

But now she did smile, shyly, as she set the

bowl on a table for me, then brought out a spoon.

"Thanks, Donna," I said.

"Thank Mr. Volz," she said. "He argued with Mrs. Peterson. Told her it was a crime to make you work without food in your belly."

Volz laughed. "I had to promise to make her a new rolling pin in my carpentry shop."

"Mrs. Brickman won't like this," I said.

"What Mrs. Brickman don't know won't hurt her. Eat," Volz said. "Then I take you out to Bledsoe."

"Donna?" It was a woman's voice calling from the kitchen. "No dawdling."

"You better go," Volz advised.

The girl shot me one last enigmatic look, then vanished into the kitchen.

Volz said, "You eat, Odie. I'll go make nice with Mrs. Peterson."

When we were alone, Albert said, "What the hell were you thinking? A snake?"

I began to eat my hot cereal. "I didn't do it."

"Right," he said. "It's never you. Christ, Odie, you just took a step closer to leaving Lincoln."

"And wouldn't that be terrible."

"You think reformatory would be better?"

"Couldn't be any worse."

He gave me a steely-eyed glare. "Where'd you get the snake?"

"I told you, it wasn't me."

30

"You can tell me the truth, Odie. I'm not Mrs. Brickman."

"Only her servant."

That one got to him and I thought he was going to slug me. Instead he said, "She takes her singing seriously."

"She's the only one who does." I smiled, remembering her wild dance when the snake had slithered over her foot. It was a black racer, harmless. If it had been a prank, it would have been a bold one because of the beating that would surely result. Even I would have thought twice about it. I suspected the creature had simply found its way in from outside the dining hall by accident. "I bet she wet her bloomers. Everybody thought it was funny."

"But you're the one who got the strapping and spent the night with Faria. And now you'll be working Bledsoe's fields today."

"The look on her face was worth it." That wasn't exactly true. I knew that by sundown I'd regret being blamed for the snake. The welts on my back from the beating DiMarco had given me were still tender, and the hay dust and the salt from my own sweat would make the wounds hurt even worse. But I didn't want Albert, that smug know-it-all, to see me worry.

My brother was sixteen then. He'd grown tall and lanky at Lincoln School. He had dull red hair that was plagued by a perpetual cowlick in back, and like most redheaded people, he freckled easily. In summer, his face was a rash of splotches. He was self-conscious about his appearance and thought of himself as odd-looking. He tried to make up for it with his intellect. Albert was the smartest kid I knew, the smartest kid anybody at Lincoln School knew. He wasn't particularly athletic, but he was respected for his brains. And he was honorable to a fault. It wasn't something in his genes, because me, I didn't give a crap about what Albert called ethics, and our father had been a bit of a con man. But my brother was stone hard when it came to doing the right thing. Or what he saw as the right thing. I didn't always agree with him on that point.

"Where are you working today?" I asked between spoonfuls of cereal.

"Helping Conrad with some machinery."

That was another thing about Albert. He was handy. He possessed a mind that could wrap itself around a technical problem that had others scratching their heads. His work assignment was often with Bud Conrad, who was in charge of facility maintenance at Lincoln School. As a result, Albert knew about boilers and pumps and motors. I figured he'd grow up to be an engineer or something. I didn't know what I wanted to be yet. I just knew whatever it was it would be far away from Lincoln School.

I'd almost finished my meal when I heard a child's voice call out, "Odie! Albert!"

Little Emmy Frost ran toward us across the dining hall, followed by her mother. Cora Frost taught homemaking skills — cooking, sewing, ironing, decorating, cleaning — to the girls at the school, as well as teaching reading to all of us. She was plain and slender. Her hair was reddish blond, but to this day, I can't recall clearly the color of her eyes. Her nose was long, bent at the end. I always wondered if it had been broken when she was younger and badly set. She was kind, compassionate, and although not what most guys would have called a looker, to me she was as lovely as any angel. I've always thought of her in the way I think of a precious gem: The beauty isn't in the jewel itself, but in the way the light shines through it.

Emmy, on the other hand, was a cutie, with a thick mop of curls just like Little Orphan Annie in the funny papers, and we all loved her.

"I'm happy they've fed you," Mrs. Frost said. "You have a very busy day ahead."

I reached out to tickle Emmy. She stepped back, giggling. I looked up at her mother and shook my head sadly. "Mr. Volz told me. I'm working Bledsoe's hayfields."

"You *were* going to work for Mr. Bledsoe. I've managed to get your assignment changed. You'll be working for me today. You and Albert and Moses. My garden and orchard need seeing to. Mr. Brickman just gave me approval to use all three of you. Finish your breakfast and we'll be off."

I gulped down what was left and took my bowl to the kitchen, where I explained to Mr. Volz what was up. He followed me back to the table.

"You got Brickman to change his mind?" the German said, clearly impressed.

"A little flutter of the eyelashes, Mr. Volz, and that man melts like butter on a griddle."

Which might have been true if she'd been a beauty. I suspected it was the goodness of her heart that had won him over.

Volz said, "Odie, that don't mean you don't work hard today."

"I'll work extra hard," I promised.

Albert said, "I'll see to that."

At mealtime, the children entered the dining hall through different doors, the girls from the east, the boys from the west. That morning, Mrs. Frost led us out through the boys' entrance, which could not be seen from the administration building. I figured this was because she didn't want Thelma Brickman to spot us and maybe countermand her husband's decision. Everyone knew that although Mr. Brickman wore the pants, it was his wife who had the balls.

Mrs. Frost drove her dusty Model T pickup

down the road that followed the Gilead River into the town of Lincoln, half a mile east of the school. Emmy sat up front with her. Albert and I sat on the open flatbed. We passed the square where the Fremont County courthouse stood, along with the band shell and two cannons that had been fired by the First Minnesota Volunteer Infantry Regiment in the Civil War. A number of automobiles were parked around the square, but this was 1932 and not every farmer could afford a vehicle, so there were a few wagons with horse teams tied to hitching posts. We passed Hartman's Bakery, and I could smell warm bread, the kind with yeast, so it didn't break your teeth when you bit into it. Even though I'd already had cereal, the aroma made me hungry again. We passed the city police station, where an officer on the sidewalk tipped his hat to Mrs. Frost. He eyed Albert and me, and his hard look brought to my mind Mrs. Brickman's threat of the reformatory, which I'd pretended to shrug off, but which in truth scared me a lot.

Beyond Lincoln, all the land had been turned with plows. The dirt road we followed ran between fields where green corn sprouted in straight rows out of the black earth. I'd read in a book that this had all been prairie once, the grass higher than a man's head, and that the rich, black soil went fifty feet deep. To the west rose Buffalo Ridge, a long stretch of low, untillable hills, and beyond that lay South Dakota. East, where we were headed, the land was flat, and long before we reached them, I could see the big hayfields that belonged to Hector Bledsoe.

At the Lincoln Indian Training School, boys were fair game for Bledsoe, or most any other farmer in the area who wanted free labor. It was justified as the "training" part of the school. We didn't learn anything except that we'd rather be dead than farmers. It was always grueling, dirty work — mucking out cattle yards or slopping hogs or detasseling corn or cutting out jimsonweed, all of it under an unrelenting sun — but haying for Bledsoe was the absolute worst. You spent the whole day bucking those big bales, sweating bullets, covered in hay dust that made you itch like you were being chewed on by a million fleas. You got no break except for lunch, which was usually a dry sandwich and water warmed by the sun. The kids assigned to Bledsoe were the bigger, older ones or, like me, those who'd created a problem for the staff at Lincoln School. Because I wasn't as strong as the older boys, it wasn't just Bledsoe giving me crap. It was also the other kids, who complained that I didn't pull my weight. When Albert was there, he stood between me and trouble, but Albert was a favorite of the Black Witch and seldom worked for Bledsoe.

Mrs. Frost drove into the field where the alfalfa, cut and dried, lay in rows that seemed to stretch to the horizon. Bledsoe was on his tractor, pulling the baler. Some of the boys were throwing hay into the machine with pitchforks; others followed behind, lifting the bales from the ground and loading them onto a flatbed truck driven by Bledsoe's son, a big kid named Ralph, every bit as mean as his old man. Mrs. Frost parked ahead of the tractor and waited for Bledsoe to reach her. He cut the engine and climbed down from the seat. I glanced at the guys from the school, shirts off, sweating like pack mules, black hair turned gold from all that hay dust. On their faces, I saw a look I understood — partly relief that they could rest for a few minutes, and partly hatred because Albert and I weren't suffering along with them.

"Good morning, Hector," Mrs. Frost said cheerfully. "Is the work going well?"

"Was," Bledsoe said. He didn't take his big straw hat off in the woman's presence, which most men did. "You want something?"

"One of your young men. Mr. Brickman promised him to me."

"Whoever it is, Brickman promised him to me first."

"And then changed his mind," she said.

"Never called me to say so."

"And how would he have reached you out here in your fields?"

37

"Could've called the missus."

"Would you like to take a nice long break, and we'll go to your farmhouse and ask Rosalind?"

Which would have eaten up a good half hour. I saw the Lincoln kids, slumped against the baler, looking hopeful at that prospect.

"Or would you be willing to accept my word as a lady?"

I could see Bledsoe's brain going over the rough ground of the question. Unless he was willing to call her a liar, he had to give in. Everything in his black, shriveled, little heart was dead set against it, but he couldn't challenge the word of this woman, this schoolteacher, this widow. It was easy to see how much he hated her for that.

"Who is it?" he demanded.

"Moses Washington."

"Son of a bitch!" Now he took off his straw hat and threw it to the ground in utter disgust. "Hell, he's the best of the lot."

"And now he's part of my lot, Hector." She looked to a kid who'd been standing on the baler, feeding it hay. "Moses," she called to him. "Put your shirt on and come with me."

Mose grabbed his shirt and jumped nimbly from the machinery. He trotted to the Model T, easily hopped aboard the flatbed, and joined Albert and me where we sat with our backs against the cab. He signed, *Hello,* and I signed back, *Lucky you, Mose.* He responded with *Lucky us,* and drew a circle in the air that indicated me and Albert and him.

Mrs. Frost said, "Well then, I guess I have what I came for."

"Guess you have," Bledsoe said and leaned down to retrieve his hat.

"Oh, and if you'd like, here's the note of permission Mr. Brickman wrote for me." She held out the paper to Bledsoe.

"You could've given me that at the beginning."

"Just as easily as you could have accepted my word. Good day."

We drove from the field and watched as Bledsoe remounted his tractor and began again moving down the long row of dried alfalfa while the boys from Lincoln School bent again to their miserable labor.

Beside me, Mose made a grand gesture of gratitude toward the morning sun and signed again, *Lucky us.*

CHAPTER THREE

Cora Frost's property lay two miles east of Lincoln, on the south bank of the Gilead River. There was an old farmhouse, a small apple orchard, an enormous garden, a barn and some outbuildings. When her husband had been alive, they'd planted a good acreage in corn. She and Andrew Frost had both worked at Lincoln School, Mr. Frost as our sports coach. We'd all liked Mr. Frost. He was half Sioux and half Scotch-Irish and was a terrific athlete. He'd been sent to the Carlisle Indian School in Pennsylvania and knew Jim Thorpe personally. When he was eleven, he'd been in the stands the day that sports great had helped his team of Indian kids shock the hell out of the world by beating Harvard's football elite. Mr. Frost had been killed in a farming accident. He'd been sitting atop his disc harrow with little Emmy in his lap, guiding Big George, the Frosts' enormous draft horse, across the plowed field, breaking up the newly turned clods of black soil. As he approached the end of the field and turned the horse, Big George disturbed a nest of hornets in the grass along the fence line. The horse reared and took off in a panicked gallop. Little Emmy was bounced from her father's lap and thrown clear of the machinery. Andrew Frost, reaching for her as she flew, fell from his seat into the path of the sharp, eighteen-inch blades of the harrow, which sliced right through him. In her fall, Emmy hit her head on a fence post and was in a coma for two days.

By the summer of 1932, Andrew Frost had been dead a year. His widow had mustered on. She'd leased the arable land to another farmer, but there was still the orchard to see to and the garden. The old farmhouse was always in need of repair, as were the barn and outbuildings. Sometimes Mose and Albert and I were asked to help with that, which I didn't mind. I figured it couldn't be easy raising Emmy alone, trying to see to the farm chores while continuing her work at Lincoln School. Although Mrs. Frost was a kind woman, she always seemed under the shadow of a great cloud, and her smile seemed less bright than it had once been.

When we arrived at her place, we piled off the back of the truck, and she put us to work immediately. She hadn't freed me and Mose from Bledsoe's hayfields just out of the goodness of her heart. She gave Mose a scythe and instructed him to cut the grass that had grown high between the trees of her orchard. She set Albert and me to building a rabbit fence around her garden. Because the pay she received at Lincoln School was barely enough to live on, the garden and orchard were important to her. To supplement her diet and Emmy's during the long winter, she canned the vegetables and preserved the fruit. While we worked, she and Emmy hoed the garden.

"You're lucky you got your harmonica back," Albert said.

We'd just finished digging a hole, and I was holding up the fence post we'd put in while Albert backfilled around it and tamped the dirt down firmly.

"She always threatens to keep it for good."

"She carries through with her threats."

"If she kept my harmonica, she wouldn't have anything to threaten me with. I don't mind the quiet room."

"She could order DiMarco to give you more strappings. He'd like that."

"It only hurts awhile, then the hurt goes away."

Albert had never been on the receiving end of a strapping, so he wouldn't know. DiMarco's beatings hurt like hell, and afterward a kid usually moved gingerly for a day. But it was true; that kind of pain passed.

"If she knew how much the harmonica

really means to you, she'd break it while you watched."

"So she better never find out." I said this with some menace.

"You think I'd tell her?"

"These days I don't know what you'd do."

Albert grabbed a handful of my shirt, and pulled me close. He'd already freckled a lot, and his face looked like a bowl of soggy cornflakes.

"I'm all that stands between you and reformatory, goddamn it."

Albert almost never swore. Although he'd spoken quietly, Mrs. Frost heard him.

She straightened up from her hoeing and said, "Albert."

He let me go with a little shove. "Someday you're going to do something I can't save you from."

It sounded to me like that was a day he might be looking forward to.

We took a break for lunch. Mrs. Frost gave us ham salad sandwiches, which were wonderful, and applesauce and lemonade, and we ate together under a big cottonwood on the bank of the Gilead.

Mose signed, *Where does the river go?*

Mrs. Frost said, "It joins the Minnesota, which joins the Mississippi, which flows fifteen hundred miles to the Gulf of Mexico."

Long way, Mose signed, then gave a low whistle.

43

"I'm going down it someday," Albert said.

"Like Huck Finn?" Mrs. Frost asked.

"Like Mark Twain. I'm going to work on a riverboat."

"I'm afraid that era has passed, Albert," Mrs. Frost said.

"Can we go canoeing, Mama?" Emmy asked.

"When the work is done. And maybe we'll swim, too."

"Will you play something, Odie?" Emmy pleaded.

I never had to be asked twice. I pulled the little harmonica out of my shirt pocket and tapped it against my palm to clear the dust. Then I launched into one of my favorites, "Shenandoah." It was a beautiful tune, but in a minor key, so there was a sadness to it that settled on us all. As I played on the bank of the Gilead, the sun glancing off water the color of weak tea, the shadows of the tree branches lying shattered all around us, I saw tears come into Mrs. Frost's eyes, and I realized I was playing a song that had been one of her husband's favorites, too. I didn't finish.

"Why'd you stop, Odie?" Emmy asked.

"I forgot the rest of it," I lied. Immediately, I launched into something more rousing, a tune I'd heard on the radio, played by Red Nichols and His Five Pennies called "I Got Rhythm." I'd been working on it but hadn't

44

played it for anybody yet. Our spirits picked up right away, and Mrs. Frost started singing along, which surprised me because I didn't know there were words.

"Gershwin," she said when I finished.

"What?"

"Not what, Odie. Who. The man who wrote that song. His name is George Gershwin."

"Never heard of him," I said, "but he writes pretty good songs."

She smiled. "That he does. And you played it well."

Mose signed and Emmy nodded in agreement. "You play like an angel, Odie."

At that, Albert stood up. "There's still work to be done."

"You're right." Mrs. Frost began packing things back into the picnic basket.

After he'd finished scything the orchard grass, Mose joined Albert and me to help with the rabbit fence. When the work was done, Mrs. Frost, as promised, sent us boys down to the river for a little free time and to wash off the dust and dirt while she prepared supper. We stripped off our clothes and jumped right in. We'd been sweating all afternoon under a hot sun, and the cool water of the Gilead felt like heaven. We hadn't been in the river long when Emmy called from the bank, "Can we canoe now?"

We made her turn around while we climbed out and put our clothes on. Then Albert and

Mose lifted the canoe from the little rack at the river's edge where Mr. Frost had always kept it, and they slipped it into the Gilead. I grabbed the two paddles. Emmy got into the middle with me, while Albert and Mose each took a paddle and their places in the bow and stern, and we set off.

The Gilead was only ten yards wide and the current was steady but gentle. We canoed east for a while, under the overhang of the trees. The river and the land on both sides were quiet.

"This is nice," Emmy said. "I wish we could go on like this forever."

"All the way to the Mississippi?" I said.

Mose laid his paddle across the gunwales and signed, *All the way to the ocean.*

Albert shook his head. "We'd never make it in a canoe."

"But we can dream," I said.

We turned around and headed back upstream to the Frost farmstead. We set the canoe on the rack beside the river, stowed the paddles underneath, and headed toward the farmhouse.

That's when we got the bad news.

CHAPTER FOUR

We all recognized the Brickmans' automobile, a silver Franklin Club Sedan. It was covered with dust from the back roads and sat in the middle of the dirt lane like a big, hungry lion.

"Oh, brother," Albert said. "We're in for it now."

Mose signed, *Run.*

"But Mr. Brickman gave his okay for us to work here today," I said.

Albert's mouth was set in a hard line. "It's not Mr. Brickman I'm worried about."

They were seated in what Mrs. Frost called the parlor, a small sitting room with a sofa and two floral upholstered chairs. On the mantel above the little fireplace sat a framed photograph of Mr. and Mrs. Frost with Emmy between them, all of them looking as happy as any of us who had no family thought a family ought to be.

"Ah, there you are at last," the Black Witch said, as if we'd been gone a dozen years and our return delighted her no end. "Did you enjoy your boat outing?"

Albert said, "Emmy wanted to go, and we couldn't let her be on the river alone."

"Of course you couldn't," Mrs. Brickman agreed. "And how much more enjoyable boating on a river instead of working in a hayfield, yes?" She turned her smile on me, and I expected any moment to see a little forked tongue slip from between her lips.

"The boys worked very hard for me today," Mrs. Frost said. "Moses cut all my orchard grass, and the three of them together put up the rabbit fence around my garden. I would have been absolutely lost without them. Thank you, Clyde, for allowing me to have them for the day."

Mr. Brickman glanced at his wife, and the thin smile that had come to his lips quickly died.

"My Clyde is nothing if not softhearted," Mrs. Brickman said. "A failing, I fear, when dealing with children who need to be guided with a strong hand." She put down her glass of iced tea. "We should be off or the boys will miss their dinner."

"I had planned to feed them here before taking them back," Mrs. Frost said.

"No, no, my dear. I won't hear of it. They'll eat with the others at school. And it's movie night. We wouldn't want them to miss that, would we?" She stood, rising from the parlor

48

chair like a curl of black smoke. "Come, Clyde."

"Thank you, boys." Mrs. Frost gave us an encouraging smile as she saw us out.

"Bye, Odie," Emmy said. "Bye, Mose. Bye, Albert."

My brother held the car door open for Mrs. Brickman, then he and Mose and I climbed into the backseat while Mr. Brickman settled himself behind the wheel of the Franklin. Mrs. Frost stood in the lane, Emmy beside her, small lips turned down in a worried frown. From the sad waves they gave us as we drove off, you'd have thought we were heading to our own execution. Which wasn't far from the truth.

For a long time, no one said a word. Mr. Brickman kept his foot heavy on the accelerator so that we raised a cloud of dust behind us. Albert and Mose and I were furiously signing to one another.

Mose: *We're dead.*

Albert: *I can fix this.*

Me: *The Black Witch will eat us for dinner.*

"Enough back there," Mrs. Brickman ordered, and I thought she must have had eyes in the back of her head.

When we arrived at the school, Mr. Brickman pulled the car into the drive of the superintendent's home, which was located a short walk from the administration building. It was a lovely two-story brick house, with a

49

lawn and flower beds kept beautiful by the hard work of kids from the school. We all got out, and Mrs. Brickman said pleasantly, "Just in time for supper."

Meals were rigidly scheduled: breakfast at seven, lunch at noon, dinner at five. If you missed the beginning of a meal, you missed the meal altogether, because no kid was allowed in once everyone else had been seated. I was hungry. We'd worked hard that day, though not as hard as we would have if we'd been in Bledsoe's hayfields. I was buoyed by the Black Witch's comment. Despite what she'd said to Cora Frost, I'd figured we had as much chance of eating that night as Custer had of walloping the Sioux at the Little Bighorn.

Turned out, I was right.

"Clyde, I think we need an object lesson here. I think these boys will go without dinner tonight."

Albert said, "It was my fault, Mrs. Brickman. I should have double-checked with you before we left."

"Yes, you should have." She smiled on him. "But because you realize that, I think you will not miss your supper."

Albert glanced at me but said nothing. In that moment I hated him, hated every little toady thing about him. Fine, I thought. I hope you choke on your food.

"Boys," Mrs. Brickman said, "is there

anything you would like to say?"

Mose nodded and signed, *You're a turd.*

"What did he say?" the Black Witch asked Albert.

"That he's very sorry. But Mrs. Frost told him to leave the hayfield with her, and it would have been impolite to say no to a teacher."

"He signed all that?" she said.

"More or less," Albert said.

"And you?" she said to me. "Is there nothing you have to say?"

I signed, *I pee in your flower beds when you're not looking.*

She said, "I don't know what you signed, but I'm sure I wouldn't like it. Clyde, I think our little Odie will not only miss supper. He will also spend tonight in the quiet room. And Moses will keep him company."

I hoped maybe Albert would jump to our defense, but he only stood there.

I signed to him, *Just wait. When you're asleep, I'll pee on your face.*

They'd taken away my supper, but they'd left me my harmonica. As the sun went down that evening and all the other kids were gathered in the auditorium for movie night, I played my favorite tunes and Mose's in the quiet room. He knew the words to the songs and signed along with the music.

51

Mose wasn't mute. When he was four years old, his tongue had been cut off. No one knew who'd done it. He'd been found beaten, unconscious, and tongueless, in some reeds in a roadside ditch along with his shot-dead mother, not far outside Granite Falls. He had no way of communicating, of saying who might have done these terrible things. He'd always claimed to have no memory of it. Even if he'd been able to speak, he had no idea about his family. He didn't have a father he knew of, and he'd always called his mother simply Mama, so no idea what her real name was. The authorities insisted that they'd done their best, which because he was an Indian kid, simply meant they'd made a few inquiries of the local Sioux, but no one claimed to know the dead woman or the child. At four, he'd become a resident of Lincoln School. Because the boy couldn't speak or write his name, the superintendent, in those days a man named Sparks, had given him a whole new name: Moses, because he was found in the reeds; and Washington, who happened to be Sparks's favorite president. Mose could make sounds, scary guttural things, but not words, and so generally he just kept silent. Except when he laughed. He had a good, infectious laugh.

Before Albert and I had come to Lincoln School, Mose had communicated in a kind of rudimentary sign language that got him

52

by. He'd learned to read and write, but because of that missing tongue he never participated in class discussion and most teachers simply ignored him. After Albert and I arrived, we taught him to sign in the way we'd been taught. Our grandmother had contracted German measles while she was pregnant, and as a result, our mother had been born deaf. Our grandmother, who'd been a schoolteacher before marrying, learned American Sign Language and taught her daughter. That was how my mother communicated, so even before I could speak, I could sign. When Mrs. Frost saw this facility, she insisted that we teach her and her husband as well. Little Emmy soaked it up like a sponge. Once she could communicate with Mose, Mrs. Frost became his tutor and brought him up to speed in his education.

There was something poetic in Mose's soul. When I played and he signed, his hands danced gracefully in the air and those unspoken words took on a delicate weight and a kind of beauty that I thought no voice could possibly have given them.

Just before the light died in the sky and the quiet room sank into utter darkness, Mose signed, *Tell me a story.*

I told the story I'd thought up the night before when I was alone in the stone cell, except for Faria. This is what I said.

This is a story about three kids on a dark night

one Halloween. *One kid was named Moses, one was named Albert, and the last was Marshall.* (Albert was never impressed when I put him in a story, but Mose loved it. Marshall Foote was another kid at Lincoln School, a Sioux from the Crow Creek Reservation in South Dakota, a kid in whom meanness ran deep.) *Marshall was a bully. He liked playing cruel jokes on the other two boys. That Halloween, while they were walking home late at night from a party at a friend's house, Marshall told them about the Windigo. The Windigo, he said, was a terrible giant, a monster that had once been a man but some dark magic had turned him into a cannibal beast with a hunger for human flesh, a hunger that could never be satisfied. Just before it dropped on you from the sky, it called your name in a voice like some eerie night bird. Which did you no good, because there was nowhere you could run that the Windigo wouldn't catch you and tear your heart out and eat it while you lay there dying and watching.*

The other two boys said he was crazy, there was no creature like that, but Marshall swore it was true. When they reached his house, he left them, warning them to watch out for the Windigo.

Albert and Moses walked on, joking about the beast, but every sound they heard made them jump. And then, from somewhere ahead of them, came a high, thin voice calling their names.

"Albert," it cried. "Moses."

Mose grabbed my arm and signed into my hand, *The monster?*

"Maybe," I said. "Just listen."

The boys began to run, scared out of their minds. When they came to where the branch of a big elm tree hung over the sidewalk, a black shape dropped and landed in front of them. "I'll eat your hearts!" it cried.

The two boys screamed and nearly crapped their pants. Then the black shape began to laugh, and they realized it was Marshall. He called them girlies and sissies and told them to get on home so their mommas could protect them. He walked away, still laughing at his prank.

The two boys went on in silence, ashamed, but also mad at Marshall, who, they decided, was no friend after all.

They hadn't gone far when they heard something else. Marshall's name, called from the sky above in an eerie voice like a night bird. And they smelled a terrible smell, like rotting meat. They looked up and saw a huge black shape cross the moon. A minute later, a terrible scream came from far behind them, a scream that sounded like Marshall. They turned and ran back. But he was nowhere to be found. And no one saw him again. Ever.

I let our lightless cell fall into a deep, ominous silence. Then I screamed bloody murder. Mose gave out a scream of his own, one of those guttural, wordless things. Then he was laughing. He grabbed my hand and signed into my palm, *I almost crapped my pants. Like the kids in the story.*

We lay down after that, both of us deep in our own thoughts.

At length, Mose tapped my shoulder and took my hand. *You tell stories but they're real. There are monsters and they eat the hearts of children.*

After that, I listened to Mose breathe deeply as he drifted into sleep. In a while, I heard the little scurrying sounds from Faria as he came out from hiding to see if I had any crumbs to offer him. I didn't, and not long after that, I was asleep, too.

I woke in the dark to the scrape of a key turning in the lock of the iron door. I was up in an instant. The first thought I had panicked me: *DiMarco.* I didn't think he'd try anything with two of us there, especially if one of us was Mose. But like the Windigo, DiMarco was a being of huge, unsavory appetites, and we all knew the things he did to children in the night. So I tensed and prepared to kick and scratch and claw, even if he killed me for it.

The light of a kerosene lantern shown through the door. Mose was awake now, too, crouched and ready, his whole body taut in a way that made me think of a bowstring about to let an arrow fly. He glanced at me and nodded, and I knew we would not go down to DiMarco's depravities without a good fight.

But the face that came into the lantern light was not DiMarco's. Herman Volz smiled at us, a finger to his lips, and motioned us to follow.

Just west of the school grounds lay a vast open field full of rock slag and tall wild grass, and beyond that was the huge pit of an abandoned quarry. We crossed the field using a path that had been worn over the years by kids and others who'd sneaked away seeking solitude or to throw rocks into that deep-gouged hole or, if you were Herman Volz, for another reason. There was an old equipment shed at the edge of the quarry and inside was a secret only Volz and Albert and Mose and I knew about. Volz kept a heavy padlock on the door.

A small fire burned near the shed, and I smelled sausage cooking. When we got closer, I saw Albert holding a skillet, his face aglow in the firelight.

Volz grinned. "Couldn't let you boys starve to death."

"Sit down," Albert said. "Food'll be ready soon."

There were not just sausages in the skillet but scrambled eggs, too, and diced potato and onion. Albert was a good cook. When it was just him and my father and me traveling all over hell and gone, Albert had done most of our cooking. Sometimes it was over an open fire like this, or sometimes on the wood-stove of some little motor court in the middle of nowhere. But he wasn't a magician. He couldn't just conjure food. I figured our meal had come from Volz's pantry.

I felt bad now for hating Albert when the Black Witch hadn't sent him to the quiet room with Mose and me. I wondered if even then he'd been planning to find a way to feed us. Or maybe this was all Volz's idea. Either way, I couldn't be mad anymore.

"What was the movie tonight?" I asked when we sat on the ground near the fire.

"Something called *Fighting Caravans*. A western," Albert replied.

A western, of course. Which was fine with me. I liked shoot 'em ups. But I always thought it was odd at Lincoln School to show movies where Indians were mostly terrible people and killing them was the best solution.

I picked up a stick and poked at the fire. "Any good?"

"I wouldn't know," Albert said. "I didn't see it."

Mose signed, *Why not?*

"Right after supper, Mrs. Brickman put me to work washing and waxing her Franklin."

"That woman and her cars," Volz said, and shook his head.

Every year, Mr. Brickman bought a new car for his wife. In justification, they claimed that it was important she have decent transportation, because she spent a good deal of time driving around and raising funds for the school. Which was true. But it was also true that the lives of the kids at Lincoln School never got any better as a result.

"She buys herself a slick set of wheels while the children wear shoes no better than cardboard." Volz waved his hand, the one with only four and a half fingers, toward the general darkness beyond the fire. "Mr. Sparks, he must be turning in his grave."

Mr. Sparks was the Black Witch's first husband. He'd been superintendent of the school but had passed away long before Albert and I arrived. Though he'd been dead for years, everyone still spoke of him respectfully. Mrs. Sparks had taken over as superintendent. Shortly after that, she'd married Brickman and her name had changed. I thought it was interesting that both names fit her well. When she was angry, the sparks flew. But when she was quiet, you had the sense that she was just waiting for the right moment to come down on you like a ton of you-know-whats.

"I hate that witch," I said.

"Nobody's born a witch," Albert said.

"What's that mean?" I said.

"Sometimes when I'm working for her, after she's had a drink or two, she lets something else show through, something sad. She told me once that when she was eight years old, her father sold her."

"That's a lie," I said. "People can't sell people, especially their own children."

"You should read *Uncle Tom's Cabin,*" Albert said. "I believed her."

"Sold her to a carnival to be part of the spook house, I'll bet."

I laughed, but Albert looked at me seriously. "We lost our dad because he died. Hers sold her, Odie. Sold her to a man who, well, you know what DiMarco does to kids."

Which should have made her more like us. But for me, it made her even blacker because if she knew the pain of a strapping — or worse — she should have been more understanding, yet she still delivered kids into the hands of DiMarco.

"I'll hate that woman till the day I die."

"Careful," Albert said. "Maybe it's that kind of hate that's made her heart so small. And one more thing. When she's been drinking, I can hear a little Ozark slip in."

"You're saying she's got some hillbilly in her?"

"Just like us."

We'd been raised in a little town deep in a hollow of the Missouri Ozarks. When we first came to the Lincoln School, we still spoke with a strong Ozark accent. That twang, along with a lot of who we were, had been lost over our years at the school.

"I don't believe it," I said.

"I'm just saying, Odie, that nobody's born mean. Life warps you in terrible ways."

Maybe so, but I still hated her black little heart.

When the food was ready, Albert set the skillet on a flat rock, then produced the crusty end of a loaf of dark bread and a tin of lard. He gave us forks, and Mose and I tore the bread apart and slathered the pieces with the lard and dug into the eggs and sausage and potatoes.

Volz went to the old equipment shed and returned with a corked bottle of clear liquid — grain alcohol, which he'd made himself from his secret still inside the shed.

He'd built the still with Albert's help and Albert's expertise. Long before he began running bootleg liquor for other men, my father had been a moonshiner himself. Growing up, Albert had worked with him constructing many an illegal distillery, a skill in particular demand after the Nineteenth Amendment was ratified. Once Volz had Albert's trust and knew that he could trust Albert in return, the still was, as Albert liked to say, a foregone conclusion. We knew that Volz not only made alcohol for himself but also sold it to supplement the paltry salary he was paid by the school. With anyone else, this would have been a dangerous piece of knowledge for us to possess. But Volz had been like a godfather to us, and we would have undergone torture before divulging his secret.

Mose and I ate. Volz drank his liquor. Albert watched to the east to be certain we hadn't been seen.

When we'd finished our meal, Mose signed to me, *Tell them your story.*

"Some other time," I said.

"What did he say?" Volz asked.

Albert said, "He wants Odie to tell us one of his stories."

"I'm game." Volz held up his bottle, as if in encouragement.

"It's kids' stuff," I said.

Mose signed, *Scared the crap out of me.*

"What did he say?" Volz asked.

"That another time would be fine," Albert said.

"All right." Volz shrugged and took a swallow. "Then how 'bout you give us a tune on your mouth organ, Odie?"

I was fine with that, so I pulled my hobo harp from my shirt pocket.

"I don't know about this." Albert looked where a waxing half-moon lit the sky, and the buildings of Lincoln School stood black against that dim yellow glow. "Someone might hear."

"Then play soft," Volz said.

"What would you like?" I asked. But I knew what it would be. It was always the same tune when Volz had been drinking.

" 'Meet Me in Saint Louis,' " the old German said. Which was where he'd met his wife, who was long dead.

Volz never got drunk. Not because he was immune to the effects of alcohol but because he understood well how much depended on not being drunk. He drank until he felt a warm fuzziness, a soft distance between himself and his troubles, and then he stopped. When I finished the tune, he was in that place. He corked the bottle and stood up.

"Time to get you two back to the hoosegow."

He returned the bottle to the shed and secured the heavy door lock. Albert put the fry pan and plates and forks into an old Boy Scout pack and doused the flames with water from a canteen. He stirred the ash and embers and poured on more water until the fire was truly dead. Volz relit his kerosene lantern, and we left the quarry, walking single file toward the half-moon.

"Thanks, Mr. Volz," I said before he closed the door of the quiet room. Then to my brother I said, "I'm sorry I told you I would pee on your face. I wouldn't really do it."

"Yes, you would."

He was right, but under the circumstances, I didn't want to admit it.

"Get good a night's sleep," Albert said. "You'll need it tomorrow."

The door closed gently. The key turned in the lock. Once again, Mose and I were alone in the dark.

I lay on the straw matting, thinking about how much I'd hated Albert when I believed that he'd toadied out on us. And I thought about how much I loved him right at that moment, though I would never have told him so.

I heard the little rustle of tiny paws along the wall, and I reached into my pants pocket for the last bit of dark bread, which I'd saved for Faria. I tossed it into the corner. I heard the furious scurrying as he gathered up his prize and raced back to the hole in the stone wall.

I was ready to sleep, then Mose touched my arm. His hand slid down to my own hand and opened my fingers. On my palm he spelled out in sign, *Lucky us.*

CHAPTER FIVE

It wasn't Volz who woke us in the morning but the head boys' adviser. Martin Greene was a large, taciturn man, balding, with perpetually tired eyes and huge ears. He moved with a lumbering gait that, because of those big ears, always reminded me of an elephant. He walked us to the dormitory, the whole way talking about how he hoped we'd learned our lesson and maybe time in the quiet room wouldn't be in our future again. He hit hard on "the three *r*'s" that were always stressed at Lincoln School — responsibility, respect, and reward.

"Pay attention to the first two, and the last will come your way," he said.

We cleaned ourselves up and got ready for work. I didn't see Albert anywhere, or Volz, and that made me a little nervous. I hoped nothing had happened to them because of their kindness the night before. At Lincoln School, nothing good seemed to come from kindness. Ralph, Bledsoe's son, was waiting with a pickup, and Mose and I piled onto the truck bed along with all the other boys who'd drawn duty in the hayfields.

It was hard work, but it wasn't long that day. On Saturdays, in spring and summer, we were required to put in only half a day for a farmer. This was because we were expected to attend the baseball games our school team played in the afternoon. Hector Bledsoe fed us a lunch of dry bread and thin, tasteless cheese, then drove us back to Lincoln School himself. As we jumped from the pickup bed, he called to us, "Rest up this weekend, boys. Monday's supposed to be a scorcher." I thought he laughed gleefully but that could have been my imagination.

Some of the boys, like Mose, had to hurry off because they were scheduled to play. The rest of us went back to the dormitories. A few minutes before the game was to start, Mr. Greene marched us down to the field. We saw the girls coming from their dormitories, led by Lavinia Stratton, the music teacher and head girls' adviser. Miss Stratton was a spinster of indeterminate age. She was tall, with elongated features — long legs and arms, and her face, too, which was also very plain and always worried-looking. Her hands were slender, and her fingers, like everything else about her, were long and delicate. When she played the piano, she closed her eyes, and her fingers became things with a mind of their own. Sometimes her music was so lovely it lifted me out of my life at Lincoln School and took me for a little while somewhere else, somewhere happy. In those wonderful moments, I thought the world was beautiful and she was beautiful, too. When she stopped playing, the worry came back into her face and she was plain again, and my life went right back to being the uphill slog it had always been.

We sat on wooden bleachers. Some of the town folks were there, mostly to watch Mose pitch. In the same way that Miss Stratton's fingers on a keyboard could create something lovely, Mose, when he stood on the mound and hurled that horsehide, offered a beauty every bit as moving. That day we were playing a VFW-sponsored team from Luverne. The guys were already on the field, warming up. I looked for Albert, who was not athletic in the least and almost always sat on the bench. I didn't see him anywhere, and I began to worry. I spotted Mrs. Frost and Emmy sitting at the far end of the bleachers. They usually came to the games and cheered us on. When Mr. Greene was busy talking to Miss Stratton, I slipped away and found a seat beside Emmy.

"Hi, Odie," she with a bright smile.

"Well, good afternoon, Odie," Mrs. Frost said. "It's good to see you. I was afraid Mrs. Brickman might lock you up in the quiet room forever."

"Just for the night," I said. "But no supper."

Mrs. Frost went livid. "I'm going to speak to that woman."

"That's okay," I said. "Albert and Mr. Volz managed to slip some food to Mose and me. Have you seen them?"

"Isn't Albert out there?" She scanned the ball field, then looked back at me. "You haven't seen him?"

"Not since last night. And not Mr. Volz either."

"Is it possible they're just working on some carpentry project together?"

"Maybe," I said, thinking the project, if that was what had taken them away, was more likely Volz's still. I hoped it was that rather than some of the darker possibilities the Black Witch was capable of conjuring.

Then I saw Volz making his way among the bleachers. He caught sight of us and came over.

"Good day, Cora," he said to Mrs. Frost. "Hey there, little Emmy. You're looking lovely today."

Emmy smiled and her cheeks dimpled.

"Herman, have you seen Albert?" Mrs. Frost asked.

He shook his head, then checked the field. "What would keep him from playing?" He looked at me. "Have you seen him, Odie?"

"Not since last night."

"Not good," Volz said. "Let me see what I can find out. But, Odie, you should get back with the other boys."

"Can't he sit with us? Please?" Emmy said.

Volz frowned, but I knew he would give in. Nobody could resist little Emmy. "I'll take care of it," he promised.

When Andrew Frost was alive, he'd coached the baseball team and had whipped them into good shape. They had a reputation, and even the lackluster guidance of the current coach, Mr. Freiberg, whose main job was driving the heavy equipment, hadn't tarnished the efforts of Cora Frost's late husband. Mose pitched a great game, the fielding was flawless, and we won four to nothing. It would have been fun, except the whole time I was watching for Albert, or for Volz to return with word of Albert. But when the game ended, neither of them had shown.

After the game, and before dinner, we had an hour of rare free time. I lay on my bed in the dorm, reading a magazine, *Amazing Stories,* which I'd taken from the school library. Everything in Lincoln School library was donated, and I don't think Miss Jensen, the librarian, ever really checked the donated magazines carefully. I was always finding interesting publications — *Argosy, Adventure Comics, Weird Tales* — among the *Saturday*

Evening Posts and *Ladies' Home Journals*. We weren't supposed to take anything away from the library, but it was easy to sneak a magazine out under my shirt.

During the school year, the younger boys were in one dormitory and the older boys in another. But in the summer, when so many of the students had gone home, all the boys were herded into a single dorm. While I read, one of the younger kids was sitting alone on his bunk not far from mine, staring at nothing, looking sad and lost, which wasn't unusual, especially among the newer kids. His name was Billy Red Sleeve. He was Northern Cheyenne from somewhere way west in Nebraska. He'd come to Lincoln School from another Indian school, one in Sisseton that was run by Catholics. We all knew about the Sisseton school. Eddie Wilson, a Sioux kid from Cheyenne River, had cousins who'd been sent to Sisseton. He told us stories his cousins had told him, about beatings worse than anything we got at Lincoln, about nuns and priests who came into the dorms at night and took kids from their beds and made them do unspeakable things. At Lincoln School, there were a couple of staff we all knew sometimes did things to kids, most notable among them Vincent Di-Marco, but we did our best to wise up new kids fast, so that they could stay out of harm's way. Those who came from other schools, like Billy, wouldn't talk about what had been done to them, but you saw it in their eyes, in the frightened way they regarded everyone and everything, and you felt it every time you tried to reach out to them and met that invisible wall they'd erected in the desperate hope of protecting themselves.

I was deep into a story about a guy fighting Martians in the Arctic when I glanced up and saw DiMarco standing in the doorway. I slid the magazine under my pillow but realized I didn't need to. He wasn't even looking at me. His attention was focused on Billy. DiMarco walked down the dormitory, between the rows of bunks. There were a couple of other boys in the dorm, and they sat up straight and were as mute as posts while DiMarco passed them. Billy didn't notice him at all. He was busy mumbling to himself and fumbling with something he held in his hands. DiMarco stopped a couple of bunks away and just stood there, glaring. He was big and heavy. His arms and hands and knuckles were black with silky hair. His cheeks were dark with a perpetual stubble. His eyes were little beetles, which at the moment, crawled all over Billy.

"Red Sleeve," he said.

Billy jerked as if somebody had shot a few thousand volts through him, and he looked up.

71

"You were talking Indian talk," DiMarco said.

Which was a terrible transgression at Lincoln School. No kid was allowed to speak his Native tongue. It was a strict tenet of the Indian boarding school philosophy, which was "Kill the Indian, save the man." Getting caught speaking anything other than English usually resulted, at the very least, in a night in the quiet room. But sometimes, especially when DiMarco did the catching, a strapping was also part of the punishment.

Billy shook his head in feeble denial but said not a word.

"What do you got there?" DiMarco grabbed at Billy's hands.

Billy tried to pull away, but DiMarco yanked him to his feet and shook him hard. Whatever Billy had been holding fell to the floor. DiMarco let the kid go and picked up what had dropped. I could see it then, a corncob doll with a red bandanna for a dress.

"You like playing with girlie things?" DiMarco said. "I think you need some time in the quiet room. Come with me."

Billy didn't move. I figured it had to be because he knew — all of us in the dorm knew — what going to the quiet room with DiMarco might really mean.

"Well come on, you little sissy redskin." DiMarco grabbed him and started to drag him out.

Before I knew what I was doing, I was up off my bunk. "He wasn't talking Indian."

DiMarco stopped. "What did you say?"

"Billy wasn't talking Indian."

"I heard him," DiMarco said.

"You heard wrong."

Even as I was speaking these words, inside my head a voice was screaming, *What the hell are you doing?*

DiMarco let go of Billy and came my way. The sleeves of his blue work shirt were rolled up to his biceps, which seemed enormous to me at that moment. The kids in the dorm were statues.

"I suppose you're going to tell me this is yours?" DiMarco held out the doll.

"I made that for Emmy Frost. Billy just asked to see it before I gave it to her."

He didn't even glance at Billy to see if some different truth registered on his face. He glared at me, not like a lion, whose appetite was understandable, but like the monster Windigo of the story I'd told Mose the night before.

"I think you'll both go to the quiet room with me," he said.

Run! the voice inside my head desperately advised.

But before I could move, DiMarco had me by the arm, his fingers digging into my skin, delivering bruises I'd carry for days afterward. I tried to kick him but missed, and then he grabbed me by the throat and I couldn't breathe. I saw Billy looking horrified, probably thinking his turn would come next, and beyond him the other boys standing stone still, terrified and helpless. Although I tried to fight, DiMarco's choke hold was doing its job, and things began to go gray and vague.

Then I heard a commanding voice: "Let him go, Vincent."

DiMarco turned with me still in his grip. Herman Volz stood just inside the dormitory doorway, flanked on either side by my brother and Mose.

"Let him go," Volz said again, and it sounded to me like the blessed voice of the soldier angel Michael.

DiMarco released his grip on my throat but exchanged it for a viselike clamp on my shoulder, so that I was still his prisoner.

"He attacked me," DiMarco said.

"Did not," I tried to say, but because of what he'd done to my throat, it came out like a frog croak.

"Red Sleeve was speaking Indian," DiMarco said. "I was going to punish him. You know the rule, Herman. Then O'Banion here jumps in and attacks me."

"Billy wasn't speaking Indian," I said, still raspy but understandable.

Volz said, "I think there's been a misunderstanding, Vincent. I think you will not be taking these boys with you."

74

"Listen, you Kraut —" DiMarco began.

"No, you listen. You let go of that boy right now and you leave this dormitory. And if I hear that you have harmed Odie or Billy or any other boy, I will find you and beat you within an inch of your life. Do you understand?"

For a long moment, DiMarco's hand still dug painfully into my collarbone. Then, with a rough shove, he let me go.

"This isn't over between us, Herman."

"Go," Volz said. "Now."

DiMarco walked past me. Volz and my brother and Mose stepped aside to let him exit, then closed ranks again.

In the quiet after DiMarco's departure, I heard Billy Red Sleeve sniffling. I picked up the corncob doll and returned it to him.

"Best keep that out of sight," I said. "And don't ever let yourself get caught alone with Mr. DiMarco, you understand?"

He nodded, opened the trunk at the end of his bed, and dropped the doll inside. Then he sat down with his back to me.

"You okay, Odie?" Albert was beside me now. "Christ, look what he did to your throat."

I couldn't see it, of course, but I could tell from the expression on his face that it must be bad.

"That man," Volz said. "A coward, and worse. I'm sorry, Odie."

75

Mose shook his head and signed, *A bastard.*

I'd been strapped before enough to raise welts and leave bruises, but there was something about being choked almost to death that was different. It wasn't punishment, which everyone knew DiMarco enjoyed meting out. This was a personal attack. I'd hated the ugly gorilla before and been afraid of him. Now there was no fear, only rage. I swore to myself that DiMarco's day would come. I'd see to that.

"Where were you all day?" I asked Albert.

"Busy" was all he said, and it was clear he didn't want me pressing the issue.

I turned back to Billy Red Sleeve. "You okay?"

He didn't reply. He sat slumped, staring at the floor, gone deep inside himself.

I had Albert and Mose and Mr. Volz. I thought maybe Billy Red Sleeve believed he had no one, and I couldn't help thinking what a lonely place that must be.

But for Billy it would only get lonelier, because the next day he vanished.

CHAPTER SIX

Sunday mornings after breakfast we were required to attend the worship service, which was held in the gymnasium. We had two sets of clothing at Lincoln School, one for everyday wear and one just for Sundays and for whenever someone outside the school, usually someone well moneyed, was coming to look at the operation with an eye to donating. We sat in our Sunday clothes on bleachers. The service was conducted by Mr. and Mrs. Brickman, who occupied chairs behind a podium. The music was supplied by a portable pump organ, which Miss Stratton played. Mr. Brickman claimed to be a minister, though ordained in what church I never knew. He did the praying and preaching. His wife read the Bible lessons.

Christianity was the only religion allowed observance at the Lincoln Indian Training School. Some of the kids had gone to church on the reservations, Catholic more often than not, and a few of the girls wore little crosses on chains around their necks, the only form of jewelry tolerated at the school. But the Catholic kids didn't go into town to the Catholic church. They sat in the bleachers along with the kids who'd grown up in isolated areas where the spirits they honored had Indian names.

Many of the staff were in attendance. Mrs. Frost was there every Sunday with Emmy, looking clean and fresh. I don't think it was because she found the services particularly comforting in any spiritual way, but more that she wanted as much as possible to be a part of the lives of the children at Lincoln. I, for one, appreciated her there. Her presence was a reminder that the Brickmans were not everything, and that maybe even in the fires of Hell there might be an angel walking around with a bucket of cool water and a dipper.

When he preached, Mr. Brickman was something else, a great storm of vengeful wrath, strutting and gesticulating, beating the air with his fists, pointing an accusing finger at some kid unlucky enough to catch his eye and prophesying that kid's doom. But that kid stood for us all, because in Mr. Brickman's view we were, each and every one of us, a hopeless cause, a bag of flesh filled with nothing but sinful thought and capable of nothing but sinful deeds. I figured he was right on the money where I was concerned, but I knew most of the other kids were just lost and trying their best to survive Lincoln School and stumble toward what their lives would be afterward.

To begin his sermon that Sunday, Mr. Brickman read the Twenty-third Psalm, which was odd. Normally he drew his inspiration from some Old Testament passage that had a lot of smiting in it. After the psalm, he talked about God as our shepherd, which led to him and Mrs. Brickman and how, like God, they thought of us as sheep that needed their tending and they did their best to take care of us, which led to our need to be grateful to God for the salvation of our souls and to the Brickmans for the salvation of our bodies, for giving us a roof over our heads and food in our bellies. The whole point of the sermon, in the end, was that we needed to show our gratitude to Mrs. Brickman and him by not being such pains in the ass. I knew that the selfish way he twisted that beautiful psalm was a load of crap, but I did want to believe that God was my shepherd and that somehow he was leading me through this dark valley of Lincoln School and I shouldn't be afraid. And not just me, but the other kids, too, kids like Billy Red Sleeve. But the truth I saw every day was that we were on our own and our safety depended not on God but on ourselves and on helping one another. Although I'd tried to help Billy Red Sleeve, I

79

thought it wasn't enough, and I vowed to do better, to be better. I would try to be the shepherd for Billy and all the kids like him.

After the service, Mrs. Frost and Emmy stopped Albert and me and Mose on our way out of the gym. The Brickmans had already disappeared, and Mr. Greene, who was marching us back to the dormitory, said it was okay if we stayed behind for a bit. Like many of the men at Lincoln School, he was sweet on the kind, young widow.

When we were alone in the gym, Mrs. Frost said, "I want to talk to you boys about something."

We waited, and I looked down at Emmy, who was smiling as if it was Christmas. I thought that whatever Mrs. Frost had in mind, Emmy had already cottoned to the idea.

"How would you boys like to come and live with me and Emmy for the summer?"

She couldn't have surprised me more if she'd said, "I'm giving you a million dollars."

"Could we really do that?" Albert asked.

"I've been considering it for a while," Mrs. Frost said. "I finally talked to Mr. Brickman yesterday after the ball game. He agreed that it could be done, if you're all willing."

Mose signed, *What about the Black Witch?*

"Clyde said he would talk to Thelma, but he figured she would have no objection." She looked at me. "Not having to worry about you anymore, Odie, is a big selling point in Mr. Brickman's thinking."

"But why?" I asked. "I mean, I'm happy about it and all, but why?"

She reached out and put her hand gently against my cheek. "Did you know that I'm an orphan, too, Odie? I lost my parents when I was fourteen. I understand what it's like to be all alone in the world." She turned to Albert and Mose. "I want to farm my own land again. If I'm going to do that for real, I'll need a lot of help this summer and well into harvest time. You two are almost of age. You'll be leaving Lincoln School soon anyway. I don't know what your plans are, but would you be willing to stay on with me?"

"What about Odie and his schooling?" Albert asked.

I didn't care about my schooling, but Albert was always looking ahead.

"If it works out, maybe he can attend school in town. We'll have to see. Would that be all right with you, Odie?"

"Heck, yes." I felt like dancing, like wrapping my arms around Mrs. Frost and just dancing. I couldn't recall the last time I'd been so happy.

"So what do you all say?" she asked.

"I say yippee!" I threw my arms up in celebration.

Albert responded more soberly: "I think that would work."

Mose grinned ear to ear and signed, *Lucky us.*

Mrs. Frost cautioned us to say nothing to anyone. She had to put some things together, and until all the arrangements were in place, we should just sit tight and — she eyed me particularly — "Don't get into any trouble."

After she'd left, Albert turned to me. "Don't get your hopes up, Odie. Remember, she's dealing with the Black Witch."

Back in the dormitory, we changed out of our Sunday clothes. Albert and Mose and I kept looking at one another, and it was clear we could hardly believe our good luck. I wanted to shout hallelujah, but I kept it bottled up. Volz came in and spoke quietly to Albert and the two of them left together. Then Mr. Freiberg came in and took Mose and a couple of the other boys to clean up the baseball field and get it ready for the next game.

I had some time before lunch, and I lay on my bunk and stared up and imagined what it might be like living with Cora Frost and Emmy.

I barely remembered my mother. She'd died when I was six. Albert told me it was from something inside her that had just eaten her away. I had this final impression of her lying in bed, looking up at me out of a face like a dried and shriveled apple, and I hated that picture of her. I always wished I had a real photograph so that I could hold on to a different image, but when we'd come to Lincoln School, they'd confiscated everything, including a photo that Albert had kept of us all together, him and me and my mother and my father, taken when I was quite small and we lived in Missouri. So, in a way, Mrs. Frost had become the idea of a mother to me, and now it looked as if it might be that way for real. Not that she would adopt me or Albert or anything. But who knew?

My reverie was interrupted by Mr. Greene, who suddenly loomed over me and asked, "You seen Red Sleeve?"

Kids ran away from Lincoln School all the time. If they were off a reservation, they usually headed back that way, so it wasn't hard for the authorities to locate them trying to hitch a ride. Very few made it to the rez before getting caught. If they did reach home, they just got sent back anyway. The hardest to locate were the kids who had nowhere to go, nothing to return to. There were a lot of those. When they ran, God alone knew what was in their heads.

Mr. Greene questioned all the boys, but none had seen Billy take a powder. Just out of curiosity, I checked the trunk at the end of his bed. That little corncob doll was gone.

On Sunday afternoons, one of the most ironic gatherings at Lincoln School took place, our weekly Boy Scout meeting. Our scoutmaster was a man named Seifert, a banker in town. He was round and bald, with a bulldog face and a perpetual sheen of sweat on his pate, but he was a decent guy. He did his best to teach us all kinds of things that might be useful if we ever found ourselves lost and alone in the forest. Which was funny because there weren't any woods around Lincoln. We met in the gymnasium, where we got demonstrations on how to hone an ax or knife blade to a razor edge, how to identify plants and trees and birds and animal tracks. Outside on the old parade ground, we were shown how to pitch a tent, how to lash together branches into a lean-to for shelter, how to construct a fire and how to start it with flint and steel. In summer, when fewer activities were scheduled because of the reduced student population, all the boys were required to attend. If the situation hadn't been so tragic, I'd have found it funny, this heavy white man showing a bunch of Indian kids things that, if white people had never interfered, they would have known how to do almost from birth.

Albert was our troop leader, a position he took seriously. No surprise there. Mr. Seifert had donated two copies of the official Scout handbook to the school library, but I think Albert was the only one who ever read them.

That afternoon we learned about knots.

Which turned out to be interesting. There were all kinds of knots — who knew? — and they all served different purposes. I was pretty quick in picking up most of them, but there was one called a bowline that gave me no end of misery. It involved thinking of the rope end as a rabbit coming out of a hole and around a tree and back into the hole, or something like that. It was a knot favored by sailors, Mr. Seifert had told us, so I finally figured the hell with it. I was never going to sea.

At the end of the meeting, Mr. Seifert sat us all down and looked at us like he was ready to cry.

"Boys," he said, "I've got some bad news. This is my last meeting with you as your scoutmaster."

He didn't get much of a response, but he was probably pretty used to that by now. Most of us accepted everything he offered with stone faces.

"The bank I work for is transferring me to Saint Paul. I leave next week. I've been trying to get someone else to act as your new scoutmaster, but I confess I'm having a little trouble in that regard."

He took a clean, white handkerchief from his pocket, and I thought he was going to wipe off the shiny coating of sweat on his bald head and brow. But he blew his nose instead and wiped at his eyes.

"I hope I gave you all a few things you might take with you into the rest of your lives. I'm not talking about knots or putting up tents. I'm talking about a respect for who you are, maybe a sense of what you can accomplish if you set your minds to it."

He looked us all over and seemed for a moment too choked up to speak.

"You are every bit as good as any other kids in this country, and don't believe anyone who tells you different. The Scout oath is not a bad code to live by. Will you join me in it now, boys?"

He held up his right hand in the official Boy Scout sign, and we all did the same.

"On my honor," we repeated with him, "I will do my best to do my duty to God and my country. To obey the Scout law. To help other people at all times. To keep myself physically strong, mentally awake, and morally straight."

He let his arm drop to his side.

"I wish you all the best of luck."

He turned to Albert, who stood next to him, and they shook hands. Then Mr. Seifert walked slowly out of the gym, looking like a man who'd lost something he valued greatly.

We sat in silence after he'd gone.

Then Albert said, "All right, everybody back to the dorm."

Volz and Mr. Greene were waiting at the gym door to escort us. As we filed out, I asked them both, "Any word about Billy?"

"Nothing," Mr. Greene said.

"He will turn up," Volz assured me. "They always do."

On the way back, I walked with Albert and Mose.

"Transferring him, my ass," Albert said.

Mose signed, *What do you mean?*

"Mr. Seifert refused to foreclose on farmers behind in their mortgage payments. The people in Saint Paul are turning the bank over to someone who'll do that."

"What's *foreclose* mean?" I asked.

"The banks take the farms away."

"Can they do that?"

"They can. They shouldn't but they can. It's all because of the Crash."

I knew about the Crash on Wall Street but didn't really know what that meant. When I first heard it, I imagined Wall Street like this giant castle wall, and the banks and all their money were hidden behind it. And then one day — they called it Black Friday, and when I imagined it I saw it happening under a dark, threatening sky — that wall came tumbling down, and all the money the banks had stashed away just kind of went up with the wind and vanished. On the edge of the Great Plains, it didn't interest or really affect me. Out there, nobody had money.

That night in bed after lights-out, I listened to one of the younger kids crying. Sometimes a new kid cried at night for months. Even the old-timers occasionally gave in to an overwhelming sense of despair and let the tears flow. Despite the good news of that morning, Cora Frost's proposal and the prospect of leaving Lincoln School, I was feeling kind of down myself. I was thinking about Mr. Seifert, who was a good man, but it had got him nowhere. Thinking about all the kids who'd been taken from their homes and everything that was familiar to them. And thinking especially about Billy, who was weighing heavily on my mind. I'd vowed to be the shepherd for kids like him, but until Mr. Greene had asked about him, I hadn't even noticed that Billy had gone missing.

"Think they'll find him?" I whispered.

Albert's bunk was next to mine. We weren't allowed to talk after lights-out, but we could get away with it if we spoke quietly enough.

"Billy Red Sleeve? I don't know."

"I hope he's okay."

I heard Albert turn on his bunk, and even though I couldn't see him clearly, I knew he was facing me. "Listen, Odie, don't you go caring too much about other people. In the end, they just get taken from you."

"Are you thinking about Pop?"

"Don't forget Mom," he said. Because more and more I did.

"Are you afraid I'll get taken from you?" I asked.

"I'm afraid I'll get taken from you, and who'd look after you then?"

"Maybe God?"

"God?" He said it as if I were joking.

"Maybe it really is like it says in the Bible," I offered. "God's a shepherd and we're his flock and he watches over us."

For a long while, Albert didn't say anything. I listened to that kid crying in the dark because he felt lost and alone and believed no one cared.

Finally Albert whispered, "Listen, Odie, what does a shepherd eat?"

I didn't know where he was going with that, so I didn't reply.

"His flock," Albert told me. "One by one."

CHAPTER SEVEN

Monday morning, Mose and I were assigned to work Bledsoe's hayfields. At breakfast, Volz stopped by our table in the dining hall to give us the word. Albert and several other boys had been assigned to the German to help him slap a new coat of whitewash on the old water tower.

The water tower was legendary. Long before we came to Lincoln School, a kid named Samuel Kills Many had run away. Before he left, he'd painted across the water tower tank in bold black letters WELCOME TO HELL. Kills Many was one of the few kids who'd fled and had never been caught, and he'd become an important part of the mythology at Lincoln. They'd covered his parting sentiment with a coat of whitewash, but over the years the coating had faded and those bold, black words beneath, which resonated in the heart of every kid at Lincoln School, had begun to reemerge, ghostlike.

The morning was still and already hot, the

air so sultry that it was like trying to breathe water. I knew the day would be a bastard, just as Hector Bledsoe had predicted, but I was worried less about that than the whereabouts of Billy.

"Any word on Red Sleeve?" I asked.

Volz shook his head. "It's only been a day. Give it time, Odie."

We rode in the bed of Bledsoe's pickup, Mose and me and the others condemned to baling and bucking hay all day. We were quiet, as befitted a group of boys heading out to work under the control of a heartless farmer who would treat us like beasts. I thought maybe Billy Red Sleeve had the right idea. If I'd bolted with him, when we were caught, my punishment would most likely have been a night in the quiet room, and a pretty good strapping in the bargain, which, all things considered, might have been better than a whole day in the hayfields under an unrelenting sun, sucking in hay dust until it nearly choked me.

At noon, we broke from the work and jostled for a place in the shade under the hay wagon. We ate the dry sandwich Bledsoe's wife had made for each of us and shared a water bag, and all of us lay dripping sweat and silently cursing Bledsoe and the day we were born. All of us, that is, except Mose, who could work hour after hour without complaint. It wasn't because he had no voice to do the complaining — his fingers were plenty eloquent — but he seemed to revel in physical labor, in the way it challenged his body and spirit. Nobody faulted him for being the only one not miserable, because he was always quick to step in and help whenever one of the other boys needed a hand. Often, because of Mose's mute acceptance, Bledsoe lay the hardest work on his shoulders.

I sat next to him under the wagon, staring west, where the sky was beginning to look threatening. Clouds had gathered above Buffalo Ridge. Not the white puffy kind of a normal summer day, but a charcoal wall that mounted out of the southwest and spit lightning. Hector Bledsoe and his son Ralph sat in the shade of their pickup, eyeing the sky.

Mose tapped my arm and signed, *Storm. Quit early maybe.*

I shook my head and said, "Bledsoe's a son of a bitch. If we don't hay, he'll probably make us muck his cattle yard in the rain."

I heard an automobile and saw Mrs. Bledsoe driving their Model B down a hay row. She stopped at the pickup, got out, and spoke to her husband, gesturing toward the west. Bledsoe shook his head, but the woman put a hand on her hip and wagged her finger at her husband. Bledsoe again studied the sky, which was quickly being gobbled up by those ugly storm clouds. He took a deep breath, left his pickup, and walked our way. He pulled a wrinkled handkerchief from his pocket to blow his nose clean of hay dust.

"Wife says the storm's gonna be a corker, boys. That's all she wrote for today. I'll pick you up again when the hay's dried out. Load yourselves onto the truck."

You never saw boys move so fast. We were on the bed of that pickup before Bledsoe finished wiping his nose. Mose elbowed me and nodded toward Mrs. Bledsoe, who stood waiting by her car as if to be certain her husband did as he'd said he would.

Thank her, he signed.

"Thank you, ma'am," I called out.

She lifted her hand and watched as Bledsoe hauled us away.

By the time we got to Lincoln School, the clouds had turned dark green and swirled like witches' brew in a cauldron. The wind was up, and as we climbed off the truck, small hailstones began to fall. Nobody had expected us and so no one was there to herd us along. It wasn't necessary. We all ran for the dormitory. The building was deserted, which wouldn't have been unusual on a normal day. Lunch was long over and all the kids would have returned to their work assignments. But a threat like this should have brought them back inside. We all stood at the windows of the dorm and watched that storm sweeping off Buffalo Ridge. The hail got heavier, the sound of it on the roof deafening, so that we had to shout to make ourselves heard. A window shattered and a hailstone the size of a plum hit the floor near Mose's feet. A couple of minutes more and the hail stopped as suddenly as it had begun, but the storm wasn't finished. A mile away, we saw a long gray maelstrom of cloud slowly descend. It came down from the great green wall that had swept over Buffalo Ridge, and it looked to me like the finger of God reaching toward earth. The moment it touched ground, it turned raging black.

"Tornado!" someone shouted. "Run!"

None of us moved. We stood riveted at the windows as it came. My whole body tingled as if with electricity. That long crooked finger of cloud was a terrible thing to behold, but it was also mesmerizing. The air around it was filled with black pieces of debris like a flock of frenzying crows, things torn asunder by a power nothing earthly could resist. It was near enough now that I saw it uproot trees as it crossed the Gilead River. It came at the water tower, and I suddenly remembered Albert and Volz, who were whitewashing the big tank. I pressed my nose to the window glass, straining to see if they were still up there. The job was only half-done, WELCOME TO HELL still visible under the old whitewash, but as nearly as I could tell, the tower was deserted.

94

The tornado ripped across the ball field, and I watched the bleachers disintegrate in splinters. We should have moved, run to find shelter, but it was too late now. We stood paralyzed, watching our doom approach. Then, by some miracle, the tornado turned and began to follow the river. It tore up the ground north of the school, sliding past all the buildings and the Brickmans' fine home, heading toward the town of Lincoln itself. We ran to the windows along the east side of the dorm and watched the tornado skirt the south end of town and move into the farmland farther out along the river.

And I realized where it was headed.

Mose did, too. He grabbed my arm and signed, *Mrs. Frost and Emmy.*

When we ran outside, we saw Volz and Albert coming from the dining hall. Behind them, others trickled out, and I figured they'd all huddled inside that great stone building to ride out the storm. Mose and I raced across the old parade ground.

"Mrs. Frost and Emmy," I hollered. "Have you seen them?"

Volz shook his head. "Not today."

"That tornado's headed straight for their place."

"Shouldn't they be here somewhere?" Albert said.

"Let's try her classroom," Volz said.

She wasn't there.

"Mrs. Brickman," Volz suggested next. "She will know."

We hurried to the Brickman home and pounded on the door, but no one answered. Albert went to the garage and peered through a window.

"The Franklin's gone," he said.

Volz pounded more and the door finally opened. Clyde Brickman stood there, as white as a ghost.

"That damn tornado almost got me," he said.

"Cora Frost," Volz demanded. "Was she at school today?"

Brickman scowled and thought a moment. "I don't know."

"Mrs. Brickman," Volz said. "Does she know?"

"Thelma left for Saint Paul this morning, Herman. She's gone all week."

"Damn."

Volz looked east, down the track of destruction left by the storm. We all looked that way. In my whole life, I had never been so afraid.

"Wait here," Volz said. "I get my automobile."

He drove us all, Brickman included, toward the home of Cora and Emmy Frost. At the south end of Lincoln, we saw that the wooden buildings next to the grain elevators lay in rubble. We followed the dirt road that lay beside the river, driving through the aftermath of capricious destruction. Here, a barn had been torn in half while not twenty yards away the farmhouse stood untouched. There, a silo had lost its top, but inside the cattle pen still intact next to it, cows browsed as if nothing had happened. I saw a big sheet of corrugated metal bent around a cottonwood trunk like Christmas wrapping paper. For the first time in forever, I found myself praying sincerely, desperately asking God to spare Cora Frost and her daughter.

When we arrived at the farm, all my hope died. Where only a few days before, Mrs. Frost and the Brickmans had sat in the parlor sipping tea, nothing remained now but splintered boards. The barn had been obliterated. Many of the orchard trees had been torn out by their roots and lay thrown in an abysmal jumble. Mrs. Frost's truck lay flipped on its top like a dead turtle. Over everything lay utter silence.

We dug among the ruins, lifting debris, calling their names. I was sure we wouldn't find them alive, and because of this, didn't really want to find them at all. I could see how easily the storm had twisted and torn things of solid construction, and I didn't want to look on the actuality of what it must have done to something as fragile as flesh and bone. So mostly I just stood numb atop the broken roof beams that had once sheltered Cora and

Emmy Frost, and that, for a brief time, I'd let myself believe would shelter me, too.

I'd lost my mother and my father. I'd been beaten, degraded, thrown into isolation, but until that moment, I'd never lost hope that someday things would be better.

Then Mose signed, *Hear that?*

I listened, and I heard it, too.

Mose started pulling up boards and broken beams. The rest of us joined in. We worked feverishly, clearing the debris above the little cries we heard. We finally reached the outside entrance to the cellar, where the door was still blocked by two heavy sections of broken joists. We cleared those, and Mose yanked open the door. Staring up at us from the dark inside stood little Emmy Frost, her face and clothing covered in dust, the curls of her hair tangled stiff with grit, her blue eyes blinking at the sudden light. Mose bounded down the stairs and swept her up in his arms and brought her out, and signed to her, *Your mother?*

"I don't know." Emmy was crying hysterically. She shook her head wildly and said again, "I don't know."

"Was she with you down there?" Volz asked.

Again the headshake, and dust flew from her hair in a cloud. "She put me there and then she left me all alone."

"Where did she go, Emmy?" Albert asked.

"Big George," she said. "She was going to

let him out of the barn."

After her husband died, Cora Frost had chosen to keep the draft horse, though feeding such a great beast was a costly chore. Volz and Albert had already checked the pile of rubble that had been the barn, but they ran back and began going through the debris again.

"Where's Mama?" Emmy cried. "Mama?"

"Hush, girl," Brickman said. "It does you no good to cry."

She paid him no attention. "Mama!"

Mose sat down on the rubble of the house and took Emmy onto his lap and held her against his chest and she cried and cried. After a while, Albert and Volz returned and simply shook their heads.

"I will take her back to the school," Volz said.

"I'll go with you," Brickman said.

I crossed my arms and stood firm. "I'm not leaving until we find Mrs. Frost."

Volz didn't argue. "All right, Odie. Albert, Mose, will you stay also?"

They both nodded.

"I will send someone back for you. Clyde, let's get this little girl out of here."

They tried to pull Emmy away from Mose, but she clung to him fiercely, and finally Volz said, "You come, too, Mose."

They walked away, Mose carrying little Emmy, but Brickman lingered a moment and surveyed the destruction. Under his breath he said, "Jesus."

"You were wrong," I told him.

He looked at me and squinted. "Wrong?"

"You said God was a shepherd and would take care of us. God's no shepherd."

He didn't respond.

"You know what God is, Mr. Brickman? A goddamn tornado, that's what he is."

Brickman simply turned and walked away.

After they were gone, Albert and I stood alone. The sky above us was clear and blue, as if it had never hurled at us the hell of the last couple of hours. I heard a meadowlark sing.

"It was going to be perfect," I said. "Everything was finally going to be perfect."

Albert turned in a full circle, taking in the whole of the devastation around us. When he spoke, his voice was as hard as I'd ever heard it. "One by one, Odie," he said. "One by one."

CHAPTER EIGHT

They found Cora Frost's body later that day, a mile distant, cradled in the branches of an elm in a farmyard where the tornado had done no damage at all but had, as it dissipated, deposited a lot of debris. Big George, the draft horse, was found unharmed, not far from the destruction of the Frost farm, placidly munching grass along the bank of the Gilead River.

When she received the report of what had happened, Mrs. Brickman returned from Saint Paul immediately. She magnanimously declared that Emmy Frost would not be motherless for long. It was her intention to adopt the little girl just as soon as she could.

Mose, when he heard this, signed, *Black Witch her new mother?* Then he signed something that Mrs. Frost, had she been alive, would never have approved of.

Albert said in a low, resigned voice, "What the Black Witch wants, the Black Witch gets."

To me it seemed just one more unfair thing

in a long line of terrible unfairnesses. I could live with all the disappointment and destruction that a heartless God had sent my way. Maybe I even deserved it. But Emmy Frost? All she'd ever done her whole brief life was bring happiness to the rest of us. And Mrs. Frost? If ever there'd been an angel on this earth, it was her.

The funeral service was held on Thursday in the gymnasium. All the kids at school were there, except Billy Red Sleeve, who hadn't been picked up by the authorities yet. We were dressed as if for Sunday, and the podium Mr. Brickman always preached from stood on the gym floor with chairs behind it for him and Mrs. Brickman, and one for Emmy, who sat there slumped like a lifeless doll. We hadn't seen her since that terrible day of the tornado. She wore a new dress and shiny new leather shoes. The grit and dust and plaster had been so thick in her hair that they couldn't wash it out, and they'd simply cut back all her curls to within an inch of her scalp. Without the dress, she could have passed for a boy.

Miss Stratton sat at the pump organ. She played "Rock of Ages" and we all mumbled along. Mr. Brickman gave the eulogy. For the first time I could recall, he spoke to us in a respectful tone with no bombast whatsoever. I'd never liked him, but I was grateful for the kind — and true — things he said about Cora Frost.

Then the Brickmans got a surprise.

Miss Stratton announced, "Odie O'Banion and I have something we'd like to offer in Cora's memory." She nodded to me, and I stood.

"What are you doing?" Albert whispered. He eyed the Brickmans, who sat with looks on their faces that were far from Christian.

"Just listen," I said.

Mose signed, *Make it sweet, Odie.*

I stood beside the pump organ and pulled my harmonica from my pocket, and Miss Stratton and I played together the song we'd been practicing in secret.

I'd promised myself I wouldn't cry. I wanted to deliver the only gift I had to offer in the memory of Cora Frost. But as I started blowing the first notes of "Shenandoah," the tears began to run. I played on anyway, and Miss Stratton followed, and the music itself seemed to weep and not just for what we'd lost that week. It was for the families and the childhoods and the dreams that were, even for those of us so young, already gone forever. But as I continued, I went to that place only music could take me, and although Cora Frost was dead and about to be buried along with my fleeting hope of a better life, I imagined she was listening somewhere, with her husband at her side, and they were both smiling down on me and Emmy and Albert and Mose and all the others whose lives, at least for a while, had been better because of them. And in the end, that's where my tears were coming from.

When I finished, everyone was crying, even Mr. Brickman, who had a heart, I could see, though a small one. But the Black Witch had no heart, and she shed not one tear. She was giving me and Miss Stratton the evil eye. I tried to return to my seat on the bleachers, but Miss Stratton took my hand and held me where I stood.

Mr. Brickman closed with a prayer, and the kids all began to file out. Mrs. Brickman leaned to Emmy and said something, then she stood and walked to the pump organ.

"A lovely tune" were the words she said, but her voice said something entirely different. "And quite unexpected."

Miss Stratton looked as if she believed the Black Witch was going to pounce and devour her whole.

I said, "It was my idea, ma'am. I knew it was Mrs. Frost's favorite song. Miss Stratton was just being nice, that's all."

"Nice. Of course. But, Lavinia, next time you decide to be nice, I'd like to know in advance. And I have to tell you that I find it strange you bend so easily to the whims of one of our students."

"It won't happen again, Thelma."

Mrs. Brickman trained her eyes on me. "You played well, Odie."

"Thank you, ma'am."

"Enjoy that harmonica while you can." She walked to Emmy, took her by the arm, and led her out. Emmy glanced back at me once. I knew that lost look well, and it broke my heart to see it on her face.

Miss Stratton stared where they'd gone and said quietly, "That tornado took the wrong woman."

Idle time at Lincoln School was rare, and that day was no exception. We all had our work assignments. The haying was finished in Bledsoe's fields, but I'd drawn another unpleasant assignment — grounds work under DiMarco's iron gaze. I had no intention of working for DiMarco that afternoon. While the others followed Volz and Mr. Greene to the dining hall, I slipped away.

It was three miles to the devastated Frost farmstead. When I arrived, I saw that everything was pretty much as we'd left it on that terrible afternoon of the tornado, all untouched rubble. The leaves of the torn-up orchard trees were already drying out, turning brown and brittle. The truck still lay flipped on its top and still reminded me of a dead turtle. I saw a rabbit munching on the young shoots in Mrs. Frost's big garden. It eyed me and made no move to run. The destruction of the farmstead was total, but less than a hundred yards away, the trees along the river had been left untouched.

I walked down to the rack where Mr. Frost had always kept his canoe. The sturdy little craft still lay cradled with the paddles stored beneath. I sat down on the riverbank and remembered the last time I'd been there, the last good day. I'd cried some when I played "Shenandoah," but now I wept a river of tears. I hated Albert for being so right. I shouldn't have let myself get close to Mrs. Frost and Emmy. One was dead and the other, it seemed to me, was as good as. I felt terrible about the little girl's fate, but what could I do? It was just like with Billy Red Sleeve. I would never be the good shepherd I wanted to be.

I stood up, wiped my eyes, and went back to the destroyed farmhouse to begin going through the rubble, trying to find what it was I'd come for. I knew the general area I needed to get to, and I worked much of the afternoon lifting and pushing and crawling and sifting. When I'd sneaked away from Lincoln School, I'd known that my chances of succeeding on this little mission were slim, but the longer I dug the more discouraged I became.

I spotted a familiar dust-covered tin, the one in which I knew Mrs. Frost had kept gingersnaps. I salvaged it from the wreckage and popped it open. There were still half a dozen cookies inside, grit free because of the tight-fitting lid. I took them all and divided them between my pockets and kept digging. Five minutes later I saw what I'd come for. The corner of a silver picture frame peeked from beneath a section of roof beam. To get at it, I had to come from underneath, pulling free the debris from below. Carefully I slid the frame clear. The glass had been shattered, but the photograph inside was still intact. I took the photo out, slipped it inside my shirt, climbed from the rubble, and walked away.

When I got to the dorm, it was almost dinnertime and the other boys were washing up. Volz saw me and quickly came my way.

"You're in a big pot of trouble, Odie," he said. "DiMarco is steaming. He's going to flay you alive. Where did you run off to?"

"I had something to do," I said.

Albert and Mose came out of the lavatory, and they both eyed me like Mrs. Frost wasn't the only one who was going to be dead and buried that day.

"DiMarco's been looking for a chance to come down on you, Odie," Albert said. "And goddamn it, you gave it to him in spades. Where the hell were you?"

"Language," Volz cautioned my brother.

Mose looked scared and signed, *He'll take the skin off your back, Odie.*

"I don't care," I said. "It was important."

Albert grabbed my shoulder and dug his fingers in no less harshly than DiMarco had a few days earlier. "Where were you? What was so important?"

Before I could answer, I heard DiMarco cry behind me, "O'Banion!"

I pulled out the photograph I'd taken from the rubble and quickly gave it to Albert. "Don't let him see it." Then I turned to face DiMarco.

He came like a bull, and I swear the floorboards shook. In his right hand, he held the leather strap familiar to us all.

"Vincent," Volz began.

"Fincent?" DiMarco said, mocking the German's accent. He held up his hand in warning. "Not a word, Herman. This time I've got him." He snatched me by the shirt collar and started to haul me off. "Let's go, mister."

"I'm coming, too," Volz said quickly.

DiMarco paused and rolled this over in his head. Me, I was grateful as hell, because I knew that alone, DiMarco would probably do a great deal more to me than whip my back. He said, "All right, we'll do this here. I want all these boys to see what happens when one of them disobeys the rules. Shirt off, O'Banion, and turn around."

I slowly unbuttoned, turned, and handed my shirt to Mose, who looked at me as if he were the one about to get a strapping. I shook my head and signed, *It's okay.*

"Albert and Moses, you two hold him," DiMarco said.

"Please, don't," Albert began.

"Hold him or you get the strap, too. Then maybe I start on some of the other boys. You want that on your shoulders? This is exactly what you all knew was coming."

Which was true and why Volz stood by looking helpless, and why Albert took one arm and Mose the other, and I braced myself.

I'd been on the receiving end of the strap many times, but DiMarco had never thrown himself into a beating the way he did that day. I'd vowed I wouldn't give him the satisfaction of making a sound, but on the tenth bite from the leather, I finally cried out and burst into tears. DiMarco gave me two more brutal lashes, then Volz commanded, "Enough!"

I was relieved when the old German accompanied DiMarco as he marched me to the quiet room. I'd been afraid DiMarco might have more punishment in mind.

"Get a good night's sleep, O'Banion," DiMarco said. "I've got a special duty assignment for you tomorrow. If you think you hurt now, just wait." He turned to Volz. "Don't try to interfere with this, Herman. Clyde Brickman told me to do whatever was necessary to keep this hooligan under control. I own him now."

"You hurt this boy any more, Vincent, I don't care if they fire me, I will beat you bloody."

"We'll see who's still standing at the end of all this, Herman. O'Banion, give me that damn harmonica."

He'd taken much from me already, my dignity, my firm resolve not to break down when the strap bit into my back again and again, but that harmonica was the hardest thing to lose.

"We will see about this," Volz said.

"It's Brickman who wants the mouth organ, Herman. He says they're at the end of their rope with O'Banion. And listen, you lousy Kraut, if you're thinking of coming here in the middle of the night to offer this kid some food or comfort, think twice. Because if you do, I'll make sure the Brickmans know about that big secret of yours out by the quarry. You'll lose your booze supply, your job, and anything good you think you're doing for all these miserable little vermin."

DiMarco took my harmonica, put it to his own vile lips, and blew a shrill note. Then he closed and locked the door.

CHAPTER NINE

From the *Encyclopaedia Britannica* article I'd read years before, I understood that rats had a life span of three years at most. I'd known Faria for four already. Within the protection of the former stockade, he'd grown older than old. The speed and agility that had marked his early years were gone now. When he crept from the wide crack in the masonry, he didn't exactly scurry so much as sidle along the wall. He would have been an easy meal for any barn cat. But to me, he was an old friend, and I hoped the crumbs I was able to offer repaid him just a bit for keeping me company on so many otherwise lonely nights in the quiet room.

That evening he came from hiding early. When I saw his little whiskered nose poke from the wall crack, I was surprised. I'd never known him to come out without the cover of dark. He emerged a little farther and looked at me. Whenever I'd seen his eyes in the moonlight, they were shiny little things, but now they seemed dull. I reached into my pocket for the gingersnaps I'd pulled from the wreckage of the Frosts' destroyed farmhouse. They were broken, but I tossed some of the pieces toward the far corner to entice Faria into the open. He didn't move and that was odd. Me, I could have eaten a horse by then. I'd saved those gingersnaps especially for Faria, and it concerned me that he didn't seem interested. I tossed more crumbs much closer to him, but still he didn't respond. Finally, I threw them at the wall crack itself, where they scattered about his feet.

He sniffed at my offering, but didn't nibble, just sat there, looking at me.

We communicate in myriad ways — with our voices, our hands, our writings, even with our bodies themselves. But how do you talk to a rat? I wanted to ask, "What's wrong, Faria? Not feeling well, old friend?" I wanted, maybe, to be able to tell him a story to take his mind off whatever little misery had beset him. Or to commiserate because I was feeling pretty miserable myself after the beating DiMarco had delivered. I did talk, low and soothing and on and on, and Faria just sat there, not moving at all. Finally I realized the truth. The little creature was dead. Right there in front of me, no more than half a dozen feet away, he'd given up the ghost.

I know it must seem ridiculous that I wept over a rat in much the same way I'd wept for

Cora Frost. Love comes in so many forms, and pain is no different. The hurt from the welts on my back was nothing compared to the hurt I felt when I realized Faria was gone.

One by one, Albert had said. And I wanted to scream at him and at God.

I placed the creature's little body on a mound of hay and vowed that I would bury it in the morning. When night came, I lay down, wishing I had my harmonica, because only music, it seemed to me, could offer any solace. But DiMarco had done Brickman's bidding and left me no comfort at all that terrible night.

I woke in the dark to the sound of a key scraping in the lock of the iron door. I sat up, grateful to Volz for ignoring DiMarco's threats. Although I'd lost much, I still had friends, and that counted for a great deal. The door slid open, but Volz didn't carry a lantern this time and the only light that entered the quiet room came from the moon, which was nearing fullness. A black figure stood silhouetted against the moonlit sky.

"Mr. Volz?"

"The Kraut ain't coming tonight, O'Banion."

DiMarco. Oh, God. I slid across the floor and pressed myself against the far wall.

"Mr. Brickman wants to see you," he said.

"Now? What for?"

"Cora Frost's girl. She's run away. He thinks you might know where she's gone."

I didn't know, but even if I did I wouldn't have told them. Still, this was better than the other reason I thought DiMarco had come, so I followed him outside. He started walking, but not toward the Brickmans' home.

"Where are we going?" I asked.

"Brickman went to check the quarry, thought she might have gone that way. He's waiting for us there."

I wondered if DiMarco had told him about the still Volz kept hidden in the shed. Once I knew that DiMarco was wise to Volz's secret, I supposed it was only a matter of time before he ratted out the old German, who would be forced to leave Lincoln School. It made sense to me that it should happen now, when so much else had already been taken away.

We stumbled across the empty acreage between the school and the quarry, our way lit by moonglow, me in front and DiMarco close behind. When we reached the shed at the quarry's edge, a lantern sat on the rock where only a few days before Albert had put the pan in which he'd cooked the illicit meal for Mose and me. I didn't see Mr. Brickman or anyone else. What I did see sent a chill through my bones. On the rock next to the lantern was the leather strap DiMarco had used on me that day, and lying next to it was the little corncob doll I'd thought Billy Red

Sleeve had taken with him when he ran away.

"Red Sleeve cried like a baby," DiMarco said.

I didn't want to know, really, but I asked anyway, "Where is he?"

"Where no one will ever find him. Same place you'll be when I'm done with you."

He took up the strap, and it hung loose in his hand. He stood between me and Lincoln School, blocking any escape in that direction. At my back was the gaping hole of the quarry. He grinned in the lantern light, and then he lunged, but I was not like Billy Red Sleeve, dulled and broken. I dodged his attack and ran. The edge of the quarry was strewn with great pieces of shattered rock, and I leapt and zigzagged. I could hear DiMarco cursing at my back, and I knew what would happen if I stumbled. I ran between two enormous chunks of stone twice as tall as I was and spun into the black of the shadow cast by one of them. I crouched against the rock, trying to make myself as small as I could. DiMarco sped past but stopped almost immediately and turned.

"Got you now, you little bastard," he said.

I felt around desperately on the ground for something, anything I could use against him. The whole edge of the quarry was strewn with rock, but my hands couldn't find a single useful goddamn stone to throw, and now there was nowhere left to run.

In the bright wash of the moon, I could see that DiMarco's lips were curled in a hungry grin. I thought of the Windigo. That creature had been a fiction, a ghoul out of my imagination. But the thing staring at me from the quarry's edge was real and the horror in its heart worse than anything I could ever have imagined.

On impulse, I ran straight at him, closing the distance between us in three swift strides, lowering my shoulder to put the force of my whole body into the charge. But DiMarco simply sidestepped, and before I could stop myself, I was at the cliff edge, my arms flailing to keep myself from plunging into the abyss. But to no avail.

To this day, I have nightmares about that fall, about the black pit opening below me, ready, in those awful dreams, to grind my bones with its ragged teeth. But to my amazement, I fell only a few feet. I found myself sprawled on a small jut of rock, a little stone tongue sticking out, almost invisible in the shadow of the cliff wall.

I drew myself up, my head not quite level with the top of the quarry, and pressed myself against the wall, into the dark of the shadow there. DiMarco appeared above me, standing at the quarry edge. That long leather strap, instrument of so much pain, hung loose at his side. Without thinking, I reached up out of the shadow, grabbed the strap, and pulled on it with all my might. DiMarco must have been caught completely by surprise, because he yielded without a sound, his body rushing past me in its fall to the depths below.

No death is insignificant, and I believe now that no death should be celebrated. But for a moment, just a moment after killing Vincent DiMarco, the man who'd brought only misery into my life and the lives of so many other kids, I felt a kind of elation.

Then the full realization of my crime hit me, and my legs went weak. I leaned against the quarry wall for support. I'd wanted Di-Marco dead, had fantasized killing him dozens of times. But that had been imagining. This was real. This was cold-blooded murder.

A hand touched my shoulder and I jerked as from a jolt of electricity. But it was only Mose, standing above me at the quarry's edge.

He signed, *You okay?*

"Where did you come from?"

You weren't in the quiet room, he signed. *We went looking for you.*

"You and Albert?"

And Volz. We split up. He knelt at the lip of the quarry and peered down. *I saw him go over but I don't see him now.*

"Maybe he's not dead."

Two hundred feet onto hard rock. He's dead,

Mose signed.

The full weight of my crime settled on my shoulders. I'd killed a man. It wouldn't matter the circumstances. I could tell them exactly what had happened, but it would be the word of a known troublemaker, a known liar. I had no idea if Minnesota had a death penalty, but if it did, I was sure I'd get the chair.

Mose signed, *Let's go.*

He helped me up from the small jut of rock that had saved my life, and I walked away. But not all of me.

CHAPTER TEN

"Where were you?" Albert asked.

"Faria's dead," I said. Then I said, "Di-Marco, too."

Albert's eyes went huge. "How?"

"He just died."

"DiMarco just died?"

"No, Faria. I killed DiMarco."

We had found Albert and Volz standing in the old parade ground. They'd looked all over hell and gone and had been worried sick about me.

Once again, all the strength drained from my legs, and I had to sit down on the grass. Mose signed to them what had happened, and Albert interpreted for Volz.

Volz knelt and looked into my face. "Vincent killed Billy Red Sleeve?"

I nodded, still feeling sick and empty.

"He would have done the same to you, Odie, if you had not killed him."

I looked up into the kind face, the understanding eyes. "I wanted him dead. I stood there and I was happy he was dead."

Albert said, "We can't stay here."

"We just tell them the truth," Volz said.

"Who's going to believe a kid like Odie?" Albert said. Which had been my thinking exactly.

"We show them Billy's body."

Mose signed to me, *Know where Billy is?*

I shook my head, and Albert said to Volz, "He doesn't know what DiMarco did with Billy."

The German rubbed his chin with his four and a half fingers and squinted in the moonlight. "Maybe you're right. But it won't look good, you just running off."

"No choice," Albert said.

Mose signed, *Run where?*

"If we hit the roads, they'll find us in a heartbeat," Albert said.

"Maybe you could catch a railcar," Volz said. "Ride it far away."

"They'll put the word out and every railroad bull between Sioux Falls and Saint Paul will be watching for us," Albert said.

We knew about bulls. A kid named Benji Iron Cloud had run away a year earlier. He'd hopped a freight train and been caught by a bull, a private railroad cop, who'd beat him half to death before turning him over to the proper authorities.

"I can drive you somewhere myself," Volz offered.

120

"No," Albert said. "This is our trouble, not yours."

"My trouble," I said.

Albert stared me down. "Our trouble. We're family."

Mose nodded and signed, *Family.*

I looked away from them across the field of grass that had always been carefully clipped by boys under DiMarco's watchful eye. The moon was above the dining hall and a river of frosty light flowed across the old parade ground.

"The Gilead," I said.

Albert gave me a confused look. "What?"

"Remember what Mrs. Frost said? The Gilead River connects to the Minnesota and the Minnesota connects to the Mississippi. We can take Mr. Frost's canoe all the way, as far as we want."

Mose signed, *Tornado destroyed it.*

I shook my head. "I saw it when I was there today. It's still sitting on the rack. What do you think, Albert?"

"That you're not as dumb as you look. It could be our best chance."

"I will drive you to Cora's place," Volz said.

"Not without my harmonica."

"The Brickmans have your harmonica, Odie," Albert said. "You have to leave it."

"I'm not going anywhere without my harmonica."

"Don't be stupid."

"You go," I said. "I'll get my harmonica back somehow and meet you."

Albert looked at Volz and Volz looked at Albert, and some silent communication passed between them.

Albert said, "There may be a way."

In those days, folks in Lincoln, Minnesota, didn't lock their doors. I suspect it was the same in most small towns, where everyone knew everyone else. But the front door of the Brickmans' home was locked. The back door, too.

"Get us in the old way, Odie," Albert said, and handed me his official Boy Scout pocketknife, which had been a birthday gift from Mr. Seifert.

"The old way?" Volz said.

"Don't ask," Albert told him.

I took the knife and went to one of the basement windows. In the years we'd traveled with my bootlegger father, Albert and I had learned about jimmying locks. The lock on the basement window gave me no trouble, and I was quickly inside. Although the basement was terribly dark, moonlight poured through the narrow casement at my back, and after a minute, my eyes fully adjusted. I made my way to the stairs and up to the first floor, where I smelled fried chicken. Missing dinner had been a part of the official punishment DiMarco had levied, and I was starved.

Although I was tempted to detour to the kitchen, I went straight to the front door and opened it to the others. Albert and Mose came in, but when Volz tried to follow, Albert blocked his way.

"You can't be a part of this," he whispered.

"I am already a part of it," Volz said quietly.

"Not officially. Listen, Herman. If you get blamed for any of this, the Brickmans will have your ass. Think about all the kids here at Lincoln School who depend on you to keep the worst from happening. You owe it to them to look clean."

I was surprised to hear Albert call Volz by his first name. I understood that the familiarity between them went deeper than I'd imagined, and I was hurt in a way. I felt left out of a part of both their lives.

I could tell it pained Volz to give in, but he nodded and remained outside.

"I will wait for you. If anything goes wrong, I will be here," he promised.

Albert closed the door softly and led the way. I'd never been inside the Brickmans' home, but it was clear that Albert was familiar with the layout. We walked through the living room, which was lit by moonlight through the windows and smelled of leather furniture. The lamps looked ornate and expensive, and the rugs we crossed felt plush under my feet. Albert led us to the kitchen, where the smell of the chicken became overpowering and my stomach growled.

"Hush," Albert whispered.

"No dinner," I said. "I'm starved."

Albert opened the refrigerator, and a light went on inside. The Brickmans ate like royalty, I saw, which made me wonder how the Black Witch managed to keep herself bone thin. From a plate of cold fried chicken, Albert grabbed a drumstick and handed it to me. I sank my teeth in immediately. Although I hated everything about the Brickmans, my God did I love their fried chicken.

Albert slid open a kitchen drawer and reached inside. A moment later, a flashlight beam cut the dark. He turned it off right away and signaled Mose and me to follow. He led us up the stairs to the second floor, down the hallway, stopped at a closed door, and signed, *Let me talk.* He reached for the knob and flung the door open. At the same moment, he hit the switch on the flashlight.

The beam lit up the bedroom's four-poster, the biggest bed I'd ever seen. Brickman sat up instantly. The sheet covered him from the waist down. Above that, he was bare-chested. He wasn't alone, and I thought this was odd because Mrs. Brickman had driven their silver Franklin to Saint Paul that afternoon and wasn't due back for a couple of days. Then I saw that his bed partner's hair was blond. She sat up slowly, holding the sheet against her bosom. Miss Stratton stared doe-

124

eyed into the flashlight beam.

"What the hell's going on?" Brickman blustered.

"We need your assistance, Clyde," Albert said.

Brickman must have recognized Albert's voice. "O'Banion —" he began.

"We just want Odie's harmonica, that's all."

"Harmonica? What the hell are you thinking?"

"That if we don't get the harmonica, Mrs. Brickman will get the lowdown on you and Miss Stratton."

Though it was far too late, the music teacher drew the sheet up, so that it covered the lower part of her face.

"You can't threaten me."

"I just did."

"Who's that with you?"

"My brother. And Moses Washington. And moral rectitude."

Whatever the hell that was. I had no idea. But was I impressed with Albert. My brother stood there, just a kid really, in a face-off with Clyde Brickman, who wielded as much authority at Lincoln School as a king in a castle, and by God, Albert had the upper hand.

"The harmonica?" Brickman said. "That's all you want is the harmonica?"

"And to say goodbye to Emmy," I threw in.

125

That clearly puzzled Brickman. "Good-bye?"

"We're leaving Lincoln School," Albert said.

"You bet your ass you are," Brickman said.

"I figured that would make you happy. So, the harmonica?"

Mose signed, *And Emmy.*

"And Emmy," Albert said.

"I need to get dressed. You boys wait outside."

"We'll wait right here."

Brickman threw off the covers and stood up, buck naked. He drew on his pants, which lay on a chair next to the bed, and thumbed the suspenders over his shoulders. He turned to the woman in his bed and said, "You stay right where you are. I'll take care of this."

Brickman moved through us into the hallway and down to another door. He reached into his pocket and drew out a key.

"You lock her in?" I said.

"Just tonight." He looked back toward his own bedroom, and I got it. Even so, I hated the thought of Emmy locked up anywhere.

When he swung the door open, he called out, "Emmy, there's someone to see you."

He reached for the wall switch and the light came on. Emmy sat in a chair in the corner, dressed in overalls and a shirt and new-looking shoes, as if she'd been expecting us. When we appeared, she gave a little cry, leapt up, ran across the room, and hit Mose at a

126

run, then she threw her arms around me, and finally Albert.

"I knew you'd come to get me," she said.

"We're just here to say goodbye, Emmy." Albert turned to Brickman. "A moment alone with her."

Brickman moved back into the hall to give us some privacy.

"You try anything, Clyde, and I'll make sure the Black Witch knows everything."

Brickman didn't even wince at that derogatory nickname, but he gave my brother a taciturn nod of agreement.

When we were alone with her, Emmy looked up, her little face scrunched in horror, tears glistening in her eyes. "Goodbye?"

Mose signed, *We have to go.*

"I know," Emmy said. "And I want to go with you."

"You knew?" Albert asked. "How?"

"I just did. And I'm going with you," she demanded tearfully.

"You can't." I petted her cut-short hair. "But I have something for you. The picture, Albert."

On the way to the Brickmans', Albert had slipped back into the dorm and retrieved the photograph I'd given him earlier. It was the one that had sat on the mantel in the Frosts' parlor, a picture of them together, Mr. and Mrs. Frost and Emmy, all of them looking happy. Albert handed it to me and I gave it to Emmy.

"I lost my mother when I was a kid like you, Emmy. I can't even remember now what she looked like. I don't want you ever to forget your mother or your father. So I brought you that. Keep it somewhere safe, somewhere the Brickmans will never find it. Your folks were good people. They deserve to be remembered."

Emmy held the photograph to her heart. Then she pleaded, "You can't leave me with them. They're mean. Please take me with you."

"We can't, Emmy," I said.

It was Mose who stepped in. He tapped my shoulder and signed, *Why not?*

"She's six years old," Albert said. "How do we take care of her?"

Mose signed, *Better off here?*

I hadn't even considered bringing Emmy along, but now I thought, Why not? It made perfect sense. Leaving Emmy with the Black Witch and her husband was sure to give me nightmares. Could worrying about how to take care of her if we brought her along be any worse?

"Mose is right," I said. "We take Emmy."

"That's crazy," Albert said.

"This is all crazy," I shot back.

"Please, please," Emmy said and put her arms around Albert's waist.

He remained rigid for a moment, then I

saw him relax. "All right," he said and stepped away to eye her pants and shirt. "Looks like you're already dressed for it."

"What's taking so long?" Brickman called from the hallway.

We trooped out with Emmy, and Brickman looked as if he was having a heart attack.

"You're not taking her," he said.

"We are, Clyde."

"That's kidnapping."

"Not if she wants to go."

"I can't let you take her. Thelma will have my hide, and yours."

"She'll have to catch us first. Where's the harmonica?"

"No." Brickman crossed his arms and stood blocking the hallway.

"What do you think the Black Witch will give you the hardest time about?" Albert said. "Us grabbing a child who hates her anyway? Or knowing that you and Miss Stratton share a bed whenever she's not around?"

Brickman didn't give a hoot about Emmy, we all knew that. But his cushy life with Mrs. Brickman? That was something else altogether. Still, he hesitated.

"And don't forget the moonshine, Clyde," Albert said.

Which was something I didn't know about but was the final straw for Brickman. He turned on his heels and said, "This way."

We followed him back downstairs and into

another room. He turned on a desk lamp, and I saw that we were in a study or a library. Shelves of books ran along every wall. The books in the school library were all donated, well used, spines broken, pages falling out. These looked barely touched. Brickman walked to a corner where a big safe stood. He knelt and turned the dial this way, then that, yanked the handle down, and opened the safe door. His body blocked our view of what was inside. He reached in and came up with a gun.

I knew the Black Witch would have shot us in a heartbeat, and then shot us again. But Mr. Brickman was clearly hesitant.

"You boys leave now and say nothing about this to anyone."

"Or what?"

I turned, and there was Volz standing in the study doorway.

"You would really shoot them, Clyde? Then you would have to shoot me, too. Them, you could explain. Me, not so much."

Brickman looked panicked, and I knew that wasn't good. Even a mouse when cornered will fight back. That gun in his hand made him a lot more dangerous than a mouse.

It was Mose who took care of the situation. On the desk sat a stack of documents held in place by a big round paperweight of some dark, polished stone. Mose grabbed it and threw a perfect pitch. The paperweight caught

Brickman on the side of his head, and he crumpled to the floor. Albert jumped and grabbed the gun and trained it on Brickman. Which was unnecessary, because the man didn't move, didn't appear to be breathing at all.

Dead, I thought. Another murder. I glanced at Mose and could see the devastation on his face. Even though we all hated Brickman, the thought of killing him was probably unbearable for Mose's good heart.

My brother put a hand to the man's neck. "He's got a pulse."

I saw Mose breathe out a deep sigh of relief.

Albert knelt at the safe. From where I stood, I could see it was full of papers and letters and such, bound up with twine or ribbon. There was also money, two thick stacks of bills.

"Odie," he said. "Get the pillowcase from Emmy's bed."

I ran upstairs and down the hallway to her room. I pulled the cover off her pillow and started back. As I passed the Brickmans' bedroom, Miss Stratton called, "Odie?"

I stepped into the doorway. Without the flashlight, I could hardly see a thing.

From the bed, she said, "Will you tell on me?"

If we did, it would mean her job and her reputation, and I didn't know if she had anything else.

"No, ma'am. I promise."

"Thank you, Odie." Then she said, "If I could, I would leave, too."

And I realized there were prisoners at Lincoln School who weren't children.

"Good luck, Miss Stratton."

"God be with you, Odie."

I returned to the study, handed Albert the pillowcase, and he bent to the safe. The first thing he did was return my harmonica to me. Then he began throwing everything into the pillowcase — the money, papers, a leather book of some kind, and a couple of stacks of letters bound with twine.

"What do we need all that for?" I asked.

"If the Brickmans put it in here, it's worth something."

When he'd cleaned out the safe, Albert considered the gun he'd taken from Mr. Brickman.

"Leave it," Volz said. "It will only bring you more trouble."

Albert threw it in the pillowcase anyway and stood up.

"Time to go," he said.

CHAPTER ELEVEN

We regrouped on the old parade ground under a glaring white moon. The buildings of Lincoln School rose square and black around us and cast great shadows. They should have felt familiar after all these years, but that night, everything felt different, huge and menacing. The air itself seemed unsettled, full of raw threat.

God be with you. That was the last thing Miss Stratton had said to me. But the God I knew now was not a God I wanted with me. In my experience, he was a God who didn't give but only took, a God of unpredictable whim and terrible consequence. My anger at him surpassed even my hatred of the Brickmans, because the way they treated me was exactly what I expected. But God? I'd had my hopes once; now I had no idea what to expect.

"You all wait on the other side of the dining hall," Volz said. "I get my automobile and pick you up."

"There's something I have to do first," I said.

"What now?" Albert said.

"Can I have the key to the carpentry shop, Mr. Volz?" I asked.

"What for, Odie?"

"Please."

"Just give it to him, Herman," Albert said. "We're wasting time."

Volz took a small ring of keys from his pocket, detached one of them, and handed it to me.

"Behind the dining hall in fifteen minutes," I said.

The carpentry shop, when I unlocked and opened the door, was a confusion of smells — varnish, sawdust, oils, turpentine. I turned on the light and went to a wooden cabinet along one of the walls. Inside were paint cans, arranged and stacked by color and purpose. I grabbed a can of black paint and pulled one of the brushes from the shelf above. I turned out the light, locked the shop, and hurried away.

The water tower, whose whitewashing had been interrupted by the tornado, was now fully painted, Samuel Kills Many's parting sentiment completely obliterated. I stood at the base of one of the long legs, where the ladder was affixed, and stared up at the tank, which was clean and frost white in the moonlight. It was like the face of a naïve child turned toward heaven with nothing but pure expectation. I hooked the handle of the paint can into the crook of my arm, stuffed the brush into the waist of my pants, and began to climb. The catwalk that circumscribed the tank was a hundred feet above the ground. When I reached it, I paused a moment and looked down for the last time on Lincoln School. There was nothing but hardness in my heart. All I saw were the black shadows the buildings cast and how those shadows seemed to eat the earth where they fell. That was how it had been for me, too. Four years of my life eaten by darkness.

When I finished what I'd come there for, I left the paint can and brush and climbed down.

The others were waiting for me behind the dining hall, Volz with his automobile running.

"What was so important?" Albert asked, clearly irritated at the delay.

"Doesn't matter," I said. "It's done. Let's go."

It took us no time at all to reach the destroyed farmstead of Andrew and Cora Frost. Volz parked near the rubble of the house and we climbed out. The rest of us started for the riverbank and the canoe rack, but Emmy held back. She slipped her little hand inside the bib of her overalls and brought out the photograph I'd salvaged from the debris. She studied it, then stared at the pile of splintered wood where her life had once been but would never be again.

I put my arm around her and said as gently as I could, "We're your family now, Emmy. We won't ever leave you."

She looked up at me, her tears in the moonlight glinting silver down her cheeks. "Promise?"

"Cross my heart," I said, and I did.

Under the trees on the bank of the Gilead River, Mose and Albert already had the canoe on the water. They steadied it while Emmy got into the center. Before I joined her, I offered my hand to Herman Volz, and he enfolded it gently with his four and a half fingers.

"Thanks," I said. "Thanks for everything, Mr.Volz."

"You take care of this little girl, Odie. And you take care of yourself."

"I will."

Volz handed me four folded blankets he'd brought from Lincoln School, the same thin kind on all the bunks in the dormitory. Along with them, he gave me a filled water bag made of canvas, the kind we'd drunk from when we worked in Bledsoe's fields. VOLZ — CARPENTRY had been painted indelibly in white across the side.

"If we get caught with this, they'll know you helped us," I said.

"If you get caught, Odie, I defend your

honor and mine to the death," he pledged.

I got into the canoe behind Emmy, gave her two of the blankets to sit on, and put the other two under me. Albert tossed in the pillowcase he'd filled with the contents of the Brickmans' safe.

"They'll put the screws to you, Herman," he said.

"I think not so much, Albert. You and me, we got the goods on Clyde Brickman." He smiled and took Albert's hand in both of his own. "I will miss you. I will miss you all."

Mose shook the old German's hand, too, then stepped carefully into the stern of the canoe while Albert took the bow. With their paddles, they pushed us into the easy current of the Gilead, and we left Volz, probably our last friend in the world, standing in ragged moon shadow on the riverbank.

As we headed away he called out a parting sentiment: "May God watch over you."

But the God Volz was talking about wasn't the God I knew now. As we began our journey into all the unknown ahead, I thought about my own parting sentiment, which I'd painted in bold black on the water tower, one I was sure all the kids still imprisoned at Lincoln School understood in their hearts: GOD IS A TORNADO.

■ ■ ■ ■

- PART TWO -
ONE-EYED JACK

■ ■ ■ ■

CHAPTER TWELVE

That first night, we paddled by moonglow. The farmland around us was empty of any artificial light, and it felt to me as if we were in our own world. Cottonwood branches arched over the river, and we floated in and out of shadow, the only sound the occasional rustle of leaves in the night breeze and the dip and splash of the two paddles. Railroad tracks paralleled the river, crossing it from time to time along its crooked course. On the bank beneath one of them, we spotted the red glow of embers, and I figured it was from a fire built by someone who, like us, was on the move — in those days there were so many — and Mose and Albert stowed their paddles and we kept silent as we drifted past.

Little Emmy finally lay down on the blankets Volz had given us and fell asleep. Me, I couldn't have closed my eyes if I'd tried. Although killing DiMarco had taken something from me — maybe the last breath of my childhood — as the river and Albert and

Mose pushed us along through the dark, all I could think about was what I'd gained, which I thought of then as freedom, and I didn't want to miss a moment of it. The air I breathed felt cleaner than any I'd breathed before. The white satin ribbon that was the moonlit river and the silvered cottonwoods and the black velvet sky with its millions of diamonds seemed to me the most beautiful things I'd ever seen. I finally decided that maybe what I'd lost in killing DiMarco was my old self, and what I was feeling was a new self coming forth. The reborn Odie O'Banion, whose real life lay ahead of him now.

After several hours, Albert said, "We should get some rest."

We pulled to the riverbank, and I woke Emmy, and we climbed up where we could see the lay of the land. A mile or so to the south, a few lights shone together, a little town. Between us and the town was nothing but open fields. We spread out the blankets, one for each of us, and lay down.

"It's dark," Emmy said. "I'm scared."

"Here." I moved my blanket so that it overlapped hers. "Take my hand."

She did, tight at first, but in a little while I could feel her fingers relax and then she was asleep. I heard Mose's deep breathing and knew he was out as well. But I could feel Albert awake on the blanket next to me.

142

"We're free," I whispered. "We're finally free."

"You think so?"

"Don't you?"

"From now on, we have to be more careful than ever. They'll be looking for us everywhere."

"Not Mr. Brickman. You got the goods on him."

"It's not him I'm worried about."

I understood who he meant. Aside from Di-Marco, the Black Witch had the darkest heart of anyone I'd ever known. We'd stolen Emmy from her. She would track us down if it was the last thing she did. And it wouldn't be just Albert and Mose and me who'd pay the price. If the Black Witch caught us, little Emmy's life would be worse than hell.

"I hope Miss Stratton is okay," I said.

"You need to worry about yourself."

"How did you know about her and Mr. Brickman?"

"I didn't."

"Then why'd we go crashing into their bedroom?"

"I had something else on him."

I remembered what Volz had said in the study: *Don't forget the moonshine, Clyde.* Then I thought about all the times Albert and Volz had been gone together, and how some deeper alliance seemed to have been formed, one that left me out.

"You were in business with Brickman," I said. "Bootlegging?"

"Don't sound so surprised. It's our family business."

"But Mr. Brickman?"

"That guy's nothing but con, Odie. I'll bet bootlegging just scratches the surface."

In the morning, Albert took one dollar from the stack of money he'd snatched from the Brickmans' safe and went into the little town whose lights we'd seen the night before. While he was gone, I opened the pillowcase, pulled out the two thick stacks of bills, and counted the cash.

I sat back and looked at Mose. "Two hundred and forty-nine dollars."

Mose signed, *We could buy a car.*

Emmy wisely suggested, "How about new shoes for you?"

Emmy wore new, sturdy oxfords that the Brickmans had bought for her. I looked down at the old ones I wore. At Lincoln School, we were given one pair of shoes every year. Because they were cheaply made to begin with and because we wore them all the time, the soles developed holes well before the year was over. Most of us slipped pieces of cardboard inside to keep out the elements as best we could.

"New shoes, new clothes, a whole new life," I said, feeling richer than I'd ever imagined.

I put the money back and took out one of the stacks of letters tied with twine. I undid the knot and began looking at the envelopes. They were all addressed to the Superintendent of Lincoln Indian Training School. The return addresses were from all over Minnesota and the Plains and beyond. I opened one at random and began reading.

Dear School Superintendent,

Our son Randolph Owl Flies is a student at your school. It is very hard for us to travel there to see Randolph. We would like him to have a present at Christmas. Please use the dollar we have sent to buy him something special. Tell him we will try to see him when the snow has melted and we can travel the road again. Sincerely, Lois and Arthur Owl Flies.

I knew Randy Owl Flies, and I also knew he never got anything at Christmas, ever.

I opened and read another letter, this from a family in Eagle Butte, South Dakota. Like the other, the writing had been done in a careful, respectful hand, and asked the superintendent for permission for their daughter Louise LeDuc to leave Lincoln School and come home for the funeral of her grandmother. Five dollars had been included for bus fare.

I remembered when Louise's grandmother died. She cried for a week. But she never went home.

Letter after letter read much the same, requests of one kind or another with a small amount of money included. I looked at the pillowcase and wondered if every dollar in there had come with some hope attached, a hope that had probably gone unrealized. I could see that the letters had all come from families of kids who, like Albert and Mose and me, never went home for the summer and who'd probably never be able to report the theft of the money.

Then I came to a letter from the Red Sleeve family, mailed from Chadron, Nebraska.

Dear Superintendent,

Billy Red Sleeve is our only son. He is needed on our farm. Things are bad. His mother cry hard when they took him. She still cries. We do not know who to ask for this. So we ask you. We can send money so he can ride a bus home. Please tell us what to do. Regards, Alvin Red Sleeve.

I lowered the letter and felt that great emptiness still inside me. I wondered if anyone would ever find Billy's body and tell his parents what had become of him. Or would they go on forever watching the bare horizon of the South Dakota plains for a small figure walking alone toward home? The pillowcase lay open, and I could see the gun that Mr. Brickman had threatened us with. I wanted to hold it in my hand and kill Vincent

DiMarco all over again.

Albert came back with a burlap sack that held a loaf of bread, a jar of peanut butter, a jar of apple butter, and four oranges, which were rare treats. I hadn't tasted an orange since I'd been delivered to Lincoln School, but the ones Albert brought turned out to be dry and rather tasteless. I'd put everything back in the pillowcase and had decided to keep to myself what I knew. At least about Billy and where the spent dollar had probably come from. I knew Albert and his code of ethics. I was afraid that if he realized its source, he wouldn't touch the money, now twice stolen, or let any of the rest of us.

"Did you hear anything about us?" I asked.

"Nothing," Albert said. "But it's still early. Word probably hasn't had time to spread yet."

We ate on the blankets. Mose signed to Albert, *Lots of money in the bag.*

"Won't last forever," he said.

Emmy said, "We can buy some clothes."

Albert looked at what we wore, the uniforms of Lincoln School — dark blue shirts and dark blue pants and our worn-through shoes. "That's not a bad idea, Emmy," he said.

Then I was sure I wouldn't tell him about the money, at least until after we were wearing new things.

When we'd finished eating, Emmy said, "I want to brush my teeth."

"We'll figure out how to take care of that later," Albert told her.

Mose tapped my brother's shoulder and signed, *Farmer.* He nodded toward the field that bordered the cottonwoods where we'd slept. A man walked between the green rows of young corn, bending occasionally to check the quality of his crop. A black dog trotted at his side. They were halfway across the field, a couple of hundred yards from us, coming our way.

"Pack up," Albert said. "We're leaving."

We gathered the food and put it back in the burlap bag and folded the blankets, but before we could descend the bank to the river, the black dog spotted us, or maybe caught our scent, and began to bark up a storm.

"Down," Albert said, and we lay on the ground.

The farmer looked our way and spoke to the dog, who bounded toward us, then ran back, then toward us again.

"Crawl," Albert said.

We crawled down the bank, and once we were under its cover, quickly threw everything into the canoe and cast off. Albert and Mose paddled like crazy, and I craned my neck, looking back at the trees that had sheltered us the night before, watching for the farmer and the dog to appear.

"Do you think he spotted us?" I asked.

"I don't know," Albert said. "But we're not sticking around to find out. Keep paddling, Mose."

We camped that night where a big cottonwood had fallen, half blocking the river. The water swept among the branches with a sound like fast wind. We were in sight of another little town, and before dark, Albert took one more dollar and went to buy us something to eat. He came back with food, the evening edition of *The Minneapolis Star,* and a troubled look on his face.

"Everybody knows," he said and showed us the headline: HEINOUS KIDNAPPING! Beneath it was a photograph of Emmy, and next to that a photo of the water tower and the final inscription I'd left painted across it in black. Then Albert read the article to us.

The story reported that Martin Greene, head boys' counselor at the Lincoln Indian Training School, had discovered Clyde Brickman, the school's assistant superintendent, tied up in his study. Brickman claimed that he'd been attacked by three unknown assailants wearing masks. They'd surprised him in his bed and had demanded that he open the safe. When he refused, they'd beat him. (There was a small photograph of Brickman, showing a dark bruise around his right eye.) When he still refused, they'd grabbed Emmaline Frost and threatened to harm her. Brickman had finally opened the safe. The assailants had cleaned out the contents, tied Brickman up, but kept the girl, swearing, in Brickman's words, "To do something terrible to her if anyone tried to follow them."

The article quoted Fremont County Sheriff Bob Warford, a red-faced, heavyset man we'd seen often in the company of the Brickmans. He was usually involved in the hunt for runaways, and he sometimes took older girls in for questioning. When they came back, it was clear they'd been roughed up, maybe worse. It was also clear they were scared to death and never talked about what had happened to them while in the sheriff's keeping.

"We're going to catch these criminals quick," Warford told the newspaper. "This won't be another Lindbergh case."

At Lincoln School, we hadn't kept up much with news of the outside world, but we all knew about the Lindbergh kidnapping and the failed ransom. Like everyone else in America, we'd grieved when we heard that they'd found the little baby with his head bashed in. And we knew about the massive manhunt still going on for the kidnappers.

"Masks?" I said. "We didn't wear any masks. Brickman knew exactly who we were. Why didn't he say so?"

"I don't know," Albert said. "Doesn't matter. This whole county's going to be crawling with cops."

"But you didn't kidnap me," Emmy said. "I

150

wanted to go."

"Won't make any difference."

"I don't want to go back," Emmy said, and I could see that she was about to cry.

Mose signed, *We won't let them take you. Promise.*

"Who tied up Mr. Brickman?" I asked.

"Had to be Miss Stratton," Albert said.

"Not a word about her in the paper. Or Volz," I said, which made me feel better. At least maybe they'd be safe.

"It does say one of the school staff is unaccounted for," Albert said, scanning further down the page. "Vincent DiMarco. Authorities are looking for him, though he's not a suspect in the kidnapping."

The sun had set and the light was leaving us. The river was silver-gray, the color of hard steel. The trees that overhung it were black against the faded blue sky. The air was still, like a held breath.

Albert picked up a stick and flung it at the river, and it was caught immediately in the branches of the fallen cottonwood. "Doesn't matter that we're just unknown assailants. Emmy's picture is going to be slapped all over front pages everywhere. As soon as anyone spots her, we're dead."

Emmy said, "I'm sorry," and started to cry. Mose put his arm around her. I could feel a darkness descending on us that had nothing to do with the night, and a great fire of

151

resistance flared inside me.

"Listen," I said. "That picture of Emmy in the newspaper was taken before the tornado. Her hair's long and curly. But with it cut so short now, she's halfway to looking like a boy. So we keep her dressed in those overalls and try to make sure nobody sees her up close. Heck, she'll just look like our little brother or something."

Albert didn't say anything right away. I could tell Mose was running it through his head. Emmy, though, brightened immediately.

"I don't mind being a boy," she said. "I can do anything a boy can do."

Mose shrugged and signed, *Why not?*

Albert gave a slow nod. "Might work. Maybe if we get a cap with a big bill to help hide her face." He looked at me and offered a grudging smile. "Just might work."

My brother had brought cheese from town and a big hunk of bologna. He sliced them up with his Boy Scout knife and we put them on the leftover bread and that was our supper. After we'd eaten, we laid our blankets on the wild grass of the riverbank and Emmy said, "Will you play something on your harmonica, Odie?"

"No music," Albert said sharply. When he saw the disappointment on Emmy's face, he softened and said, "Someone might hear. We can't risk it."

"How about a story?" I said.

"Yes, a story," Emmy said, happy again.

Mose signed, *Make it a good one, Odie.*

All day, while we'd made our way down the Gilead River, a story had been coming together in my head. I didn't know where it came from, but letting all the pieces fall into place had helped the time pass. So I told it.

There was once a little orphan girl whose name was Emmy.

"Like me," Emmy said.

"Just like you," I said.

She went to live with her aunt and uncle, two very mean people.

"Were they Mr. and Mrs. Brickman?" Emmy said.

"As it so happens, Emmy, that was exactly their name."

The little girl was terribly unhappy in the home of the mean Brickmans, I went on. *One day, as she was exploring the great, dark house, she came to a door in a high tower that had always been locked before, but someone had forgotten to lock it that day. Inside, Emmy found a comfortable little room filled with shelves of books and toys and a nice soft sofa and a little reading lamp. In one corner stood a tall, old mirror in a carved wooden frame. Emmy decided it was the nicest room in the whole house, far from the awful Brickmans. She pulled one of the books from the shelf, a book called Re-*

becca of Sunnybrook Farm.

"We had that book," Emmy said to me. "Mama read it to me."

"What a coincidence," I said and continued the story.

Emmy settled down in the sofa to read, but she hadn't been there long when she heard a small voice call, "Hello." Which was odd, because Emmy was the only one in the room. "Hello," the voice called again. Emmy looked at the big mirror in the corner and saw a little girl sitting on the sofa, just as she was. But it was not her reflection. It was a different little girl. Emmy stood up, and the girl in the mirror stood up. Emmy walked to the mirror and the girl walked to the mirror.

"Who are you?" Emmy said.

"Priscilla," the girl said. "I'm the ghost in the mirror."

"A ghost? A real ghost?"

"Not exactly," Priscilla said. "It's hard to explain."

"My name is Emmy."

"I know," Priscilla said. "I've been hoping you would come. It's been so long since I had a visit from anyone who could see me."

"Mrs. Brickman can't see you?" Emmy said.

"Only nice people can see me and hear me."

"How did you get in there?" Emmy asked.

"Put your hand to the mirror and I'll tell you," Priscilla said.

But as soon as she touched the glass, Emmy

found herself inside the mirror, and Priscilla outside. Priscilla clapped her hands together and danced with joy.

"I'm free!" she said. "I've been trapped in that mirror for oh so long, but now I'm free!"

"What happened?" Emmy cried.

"It's the curse of the mirror. I was trapped there by the little girl who was inside before me. And now I'm you and you're me and you're trapped in there. I'm sorry, Emmy. I truly am. But I've wanted so much to be free again."

Suddenly Mrs. Brickman stepped into the room. She looked sternly at the girl who'd just traded places with Emmy and said meanly, "What's all this shouting about? What are you doing here, Emmy?"

"She's not Emmy," little Emmy cried from the mirror. "I'm Emmy."

But Mrs. Brickman couldn't see her or hear her, because Mrs. Brickman was not at all nice.

"Come along, Emmy," Mrs. Brickman said. "I'm going to show you just what happens to little girls who go where they're not supposed to."

She took Priscilla by the ear and pulled her from the room.

Emmy tried to get out of the mirror, but it was no use. So she settled down with the book she'd been reading on the other side, determined to make the best of things. And you know what? She found that she was really quite happy there all by herself in that comfortable little room on the other side of the mirror.

Then one day not long afterward, Priscilla burst into the tower room and ran to the mirror.

"Oh, Emmy!" she cried. "Please let me back in the mirror. Mrs. Brickman is such a witch. I can't stand her. Please, please let me back in."

"I understand," Emmy told her. "It was awful being me with Mrs. Brickman. But I quite like it here, so I think I'll stay until a different family moves into this house, a nice family with a nice little girl. Then maybe I'll come out."

Priscilla turned sadly away and little Emmy settled down to read from a new book she'd selected from the shelves. It was called *Alice Through the Looking Glass.*

Albert eyed me and gave a nod of approval. "*Alice Through the Looking Glass.* Nice touch, Odie."

The stars seemed especially bright that night, and Emmy slept without needing her hand held. Mose and Albert, who'd paddled most of the day, fell asleep quickly. Me, my head was so full of dreaming I could barely contain it all. Seeing that photograph of the water tower and what I'd painted there, my words big as life on the front page of *The Minneapolis Star,* made me feel like some kind of celebrity. Not exactly like Babe Ruth, because everybody knew his name. But more than just an orphan nobody. I began to imagine all the wonderful possibilities that might lie ahead of us. Maybe we should change our names, I thought. Just in case. Maybe I'd call myself Buck, after Buck Jones the cowboy star. As I lay listening to the river slip through the branches of the fallen cotton-wood, I began to hope, really hope, that, like the Emmy in the story, we were finally on the safe side of the mirror.

I was wakened by a small hand on my chest. I opened my eyes, and Emmy stood in the moonlight, staring down at me, looking dazed.

"What is it, Emmy?" I whispered.

She held out her hand, and in it were two five-dollar bills from the stash in the pil-lowcase. "Put these in your shoe."

She spoke distantly, as if in a trance, and I figured she was sleepwalking. Some of the kids at Lincoln School had been sleepwalk-ers, and Volz had always cautioned us not to wake them. So I took the bills.

"In your shoe," she said.

I put them in my shoe.

"Don't say anything to anyone, not Albert, not Mose."

"What do I do with them?" I asked.

"When the time comes, you'll know."

She returned to her blanket, lay down, and from her steady breathing I understood that she was sleeping soundly once again.

I puzzled over this sleepwalking episode,

wondering if I should warn Albert and Mose. But there was something in her manner and such a serious note in her little voice that I decided to keep the whole thing to myself.

CHAPTER THIRTEEN

"What are you going to say?"

"What do you mean?"

"You have fifteen dollars in your pocket, Albert. How are you going to explain that?"

"Why do I have to explain it?"

Albert was smart, way smarter than me, but he could be pretty dense sometimes when it came to other people. We were walking into the little town where he'd bought the newspaper the night before, intending to purchase new shoes and some food for the day. We'd left Mose and Emmy to watch the canoe.

"Fifteen dollars, Albert. That's a lot of money for a couple of kids like us just to be carrying around. People are going to wonder. They might even ask. What are you going to tell them?"

"I'll tell them we earned it."

"How?"

"I don't know. Working."

"For who?"

"Look, Odie. Let me handle this. We'll be fine."

"You get us thrown into jail, I'll kill you."

"That won't happen."

"Better not."

The town was called Westerville, and like most of the towns we'd seen, it had several big grain elevators looming at the side of the railroad tracks. I could see four church spires rising up above the trees. There was no sign of a courthouse tower, like the one in Lincoln, so I figured we were still in Fremont County.

It was early enough in the day that not a lot of commerce seemed to be taking place, although the stores were open. There was a bakery, and the smell from it made my mouth water. There was a hardware store, an IGA grocery store, a drugstore, a stationery and book shop. On one side of the street was a little restaurant called the Buttercup Café. Next to it stood the Westerville Police Department, with one police cruiser parked out front, and I felt my stomach tighten. We came at last to a broad display window full of goods. Painted across the glass in fancy lettering were the words KRENN'S MERCANTILE. We stood at the window, staring at the items behind it, which included an assortment of shoes.

"This looks like the place," Albert said.

I started inside, but Albert hesitated.

"What's wrong?" I asked.

"Nothing. Just . . ." He let it drop, took a deep breath, and said, "Okay."

There was a department store in Lincoln, a place called Sorenson's, which I'd been in only once. It had so many different things for sale — furniture and clothing and appliances — that I'd thought a palace couldn't have held more kingly treasures. Krenn's Mercantile, though not as large or well appointed, displayed a dazzling array of offerings. Albert and I walked between rows of shelves that held shirts and pants and underthings, fabrics and linens. We passed a counter with cosmetics, where the air was filled with a floral scent.

We turned in to another aisle, one full of hardware, and almost ran smack into a tall, lean man dressed in bib overalls and wearing a seed cap. His back was to us, but I could see that he held an alarm clock in his hands and seemed to be scrutinizing it as carefully as he might a diamond. He turned toward us suddenly. One eye was covered with a black patch, like a pirate, and the look he gave us with his good eye was mean enough to scare off a wild pig.

The store clerk who was attending to him said, "I'll see to you boys in a minute. Just look around."

I gladly left the clerk with the one-eyed pig scarer, and we finally came to where the shoes were on display, boxes and boxes of them, with samples sitting atop. Albert walked to a box with BUSTER BROWN printed on the side. As he picked up the sample shoe, a pleasant voice behind us said, "Can I help you?"

The woman smiling at us reminded me a little of Miss Stratton — tall, slender, blond, with a plain face. Her eyes seemed a little odd, one of them not quite tracking along with the other. But they were kind eyes, and her smile was genuine and lovely.

"Uh . . ." Albert said. "We . . . uh . . ."

"Yes?" she encouraged him.

Albert looked at the floor and tried again. "W-we . . . uh . . . w-we . . . uh . . ."

It hit me. Whatever the story Albert had intended to tell her, he couldn't do it. I didn't think it was because he lacked courage. Hell, he'd faced down Clyde Brickman. If it wasn't fear, the only explanation I could think of was that he simply couldn't bring himself to lie to this nice woman.

"My brother's got a speech defect, ma'am," I leapt in. "He stutters. Terrible embarrassing to him. He's not stupid or anything, he just has trouble talking."

"I'm sorry," she said.

"See, it's this way," I said. "Our pa sent us to buy new shoes."

Her face lit with a desire to help. "Well, we can certainly take care of that. I see you're looking at our Buster Browns. They're very good shoes." She glanced down, saw our cheap, worn footwear, and without losing her smile said, "But maybe you'd rather see something a little less expensive."

There were some boots on a stack of boxes that had caught my eye. "What about those?"

Another voice boomed in, "Pershing boots, son, made by Red Wing. For my money, the best boot ever made. Helped our doughboys win the Great War."

The man who'd been waiting on the one-eyed wild pig scarer joined us.

"Manufactured right here in Minnesota. Fine workmanship. Last you forever."

"Lloyd," the woman said, "I don't think the boys would be interested in those boots."

Her eyes went again to the paper-thin leather on our feet, and the man caught her drift.

"But we also have a fine assortment of other shoes to choose from," he said heartily. "What did you boys have in mind?"

"How much are the Red Wings?" I asked.

"Five dollars and seventy cents a pair. Sounds expensive, I know, but worth every penny."

"We got fifteen dollars," I said. "But we also got to buy groceries for the week."

"Fifteen dollars?" The man's surprise was obvious, but I'd anticipated that. "Where'd you boys get fifteen dollars?"

"Their father gave it to them, Lloyd. Like

163

the young man says, to buy shoes and groceries for the week."

"You're brothers?"

"Yes, sir," I said.

"How come you don't look nothing alike?"

"Lloyd, you look nothing like your brother. Aren't you always saying you're the handsome one?"

The man looked us over good. "Are those uniforms of some kind you're wearing?"

"No, sir," I said. "Some church ladies in Worthington gave us these clothes. Maybe they got them from a school or something, I don't know. But they're lots better than what we had before."

"Who's your father?"

"Clyde Stratton," I said, grabbing at the first two names that came together in my mind.

"Don't know him," the man said.

"We just got to town. Pa's got him some work over at the grain elevators."

"They're hiring? This time of year?"

"They hired him for repairs. Pa, he's good with his hands."

"If he got a job these days, he's one of the lucky ones."

"It's good," I said, then put a dejected look on my face. "But we don't know how long it'll last."

"What about your mother?" the woman asked.

"Don't got a ma no more, ma'am. She died."

"I'm sorry to hear that, son."

"Been on the move since. And these old shoes of ours, they're plumb wore through." I took one off — not the shoe in which I'd put the five-dollar bills the night before — and showed her the hole.

She looked at the man. "Hoover shoes," she said. She pulled out the piece of cardboard I'd put inside to cover the holes. "Hoover leather, Lloyd." She looked at me with wonderful compassion.

"Your brother's just a kid, but he does all the talking," the man said to Albert. "What's wrong? You don't have a tongue?"

"Lloyd," the woman snapped. "The boy stutters."

I took my shoe back and looked at it like it was something dead. "Pa emptied his wallet and told us to buy new ones, best we could with what we got. And we only got fifteen dollars."

"And w-w-we still got to b-b-buy groceries." The words stumbled painfully out of Albert's mouth.

"For the whole week," I added.

"The Buster Browns are two seventy-five a pair," the man said. "You'll have plenty left for groceries and then some."

"I'd rather have the Red Wings," I said with such longing that even I felt sorry for me.

Albert shot me a killing look, and I knew he was afraid I was pushing it too far.

"Lloyd," the woman said sharply.

The man rolled his eyes. "Tell you what, boys. I'll give you the Red Wings for five dollars even. I make no profit on them."

Albert opened his mouth, and I knew he was about to accept, but I cut him off. "If you could see your way clear to give us three pairs for fifteen dollars, we could take Pa some new boots, too."

"You wouldn't have anything left for food," the woman said.

"We're pretty good at scrounging, ma'am. My brother here, he's real good at catching fish in that river outside of town. Me, I got a slingshot and can put out a squirrel's eye at thirty feet. And there's lots of wild greens to gather, if you know what you're looking for. But shoes? That we can't do for ourselves. And one more thing. I know it don't mean much to you folks, but today's our pa's birthday. We ain't never had the wherewithal to buy him nothing, but if we could bring him a new pair of those Pershing boots, I expect it'd be the best present we could ever give him."

I swear I saw the woman's eyes get wet with tears. "Lloyd, if you don't sell these boys the boots, you'll be sleeping on the porch swing for a month."

We walked out of town carrying three boxes

166

of new Red Wings, plus three pair of new socks, and a little sewing kit the woman had thrown in so that we could mend the holes in our old socks. When we were well beyond the last house of town, Albert said, "Lies come from you sweet as honey, don't they?"

I was pleased with what I thought was a compliment, and I said, "A gift."

"Or a curse. That woman has a good heart, Odie. She was nice to us, and all you did was con her."

Which stung. But I soldiered on. "Imagine how she feels right now," I said. "She just helped out three needy people, and that's God's truth, Albert."

"How's she going to feel when she realizes there's no Clyde Stratton working at the grain elevators?"

"Big help you were," I shot back. "Uh . . . uh . . . uh. You sounded like you were choking on your tongue."

Albert stopped and turned to me, his face sad and serious. "Listen, Odie, things have happened to you, bad things, and I know I should have done a better job of protecting you. But I don't want you to turn out like . . . like . . ."

"Like Clyde Brickman? Like DiMarco? You think that's who I am? The hell with you."

I walked away from him as fast as I could. Not only because I was angry but because I

167

didn't want him to see how much he'd hurt me.

"Wait up, Odie," Albert called.

I stopped, but not because of Albert. The sound of a police siren brought me around. Albert turned, too, and we both watched a cop car speeding toward us down the gravel road out of Westerville, kicking up a cloud of dust that would have done a herd of wild horses proud.

"Oh, crap," I said.

"Take it easy, Odie. Just stay cool."

The morning sun glinted off the windshield, blinding me to the policeman at the wheel. I stood petrified. I could look the Black Witch in the eye and hold my own against her husband, but there was something about a guy with a uniform and badge and gun that made my guts turn to jelly.

"Wave," Albert said as the cop approached. "And smile."

I lifted my hand. My arm felt like lead.

The cop car sped by so fast I wasn't even able get a good look at the driver. It shot down the road, across the bridge over the Gilead River, and kept on going.

We walked to the bridge and lingered, just to make sure the cop wasn't coming back and that no one else was around and watching us. Then we slipped into the trees along the river and made our way to where we'd left the canoe. When we got there, Albert and I looked at each other with complete astonishment.

Mose and Emmy were gone, and the canoe with them.

CHAPTER FOURTEEN

Nothing, not even the worst of what DiMarco had ever threatened, frightened me as much as finding Mose and Emmy gone.

"Where are they, Albert?"

"I don't know." He stood on the bank, looking upriver, then down. "Something must have scared them."

"Or somebody took them."

"And the canoe, too? I don't think so. They're on the river."

"Which way did they go?"

Albert studied the ground where we'd laid our blankets the night before. He walked around tree trunks, and I had no idea what he was doing.

"Here," he finally said, kneeling in some wild grass.

Two sticks had been laid on the ground in a way that formed a V pointing toward the east. It was a trail sign technique that Mr. Seifert had taught us in Boy Scouts.

"They're downriver," Albert said.

We followed the Gilead, working our way among the trees and brush, carrying the boxes of Red Wing boots. We'd gone half a mile when I heard Emmy call to us. We found her and Mose pulled up where a small creek fed into the river.

"What happened?" I asked.

Mose signed, *Kids fishing.*

Emmy said, "They were walking on the other side of the river, but they didn't see us. Mose thought we should leave."

We slipped into our new socks and boots. I put my back to the others and quickly transferred the five-dollar bills from my old shoe to my right boot. When I stood up, I thought I was wearing the clouds that angels walked on. I'd never felt anything so comfortable.

We hit the river again and spent the rest of the morning putting more distance between us and Lincoln School. I watched Emmy in front of me dragging her fingers in a bored way through the water, and I had a thought. I took the sewing kit the nice woman had given me, which included a little cutting tool, and snipped three black buttons from my shirt, which I sewed in a triangular configuration to the sole of one of my old socks. From the pillowcase, I took a piece of red ribbon that had bound up some documents, cut from it an oval, which I sewed to the sock heel. I stuffed my other old sock inside the one I'd been working on, all the way up to the toe. In the end, I had a puppet — two button eyes, a button nose, and a little red ribbon mouth. It was a bit on the soiled side, but not bad, all things considered.

I put the sock puppet on my hand. "Emmy," I said in what I thought was an appropriately high-pitched, puppetlike voice.

She swiveled toward me, and when she saw my little creation, a look of delight lit her face. I handed it to her, and she slipped it onto her hand and gave it her own special voice, a croaking thing not unlike a frog. She named the puppet Puff, because of its puffy, sock-stuffed head, and all that day she and Puff carried on a conversation between themselves and with the rest of us, and the time passed quickly.

In the early afternoon, we saw a church spire and a water tower above some trees along the railroad tracks a quarter mile south of the Gilead. Albert took money from the pillowcase and went to buy us food for lunch and dinner and maybe even breakfast for the next day.

Emmy sat in the wild grass at the edge of a plowed field pretending Puff was a hungry lion stalking Mose and me.

Offhand, I asked, "Emmy, do you remember last night?"

"What about it?" she said in a distracted way, adjusting Puff on her hand.

"Do you remember talking to me in the

middle of the night?"

"No." She growled and thrust Puff toward Mose, who shrank back in appropriate terror.

"You don't remember giving me something?"

"Unh-uh." She shook her head and turned her attention fully to attacking Mose. I decided for the moment not to pursue the question further.

We'd passed a farmhouse not far back, and I'd seen laundry hanging on a line in the backyard. I took three dollars from the pillowcase, told Mose and Emmy I'd be right back, and headed upriver.

Near the farmhouse, I crouched among the trees along the riverbank. There was an old barn, badly in need of paint. The bared places on the walls were gray and the wood looked soft and rotting. The structure leaned a bit, like a tired old man. The farmhouse was small and in not much better shape than the barn. There was a chicken coop with a bunch of hens and chicks inside, pecking at the ground and sometimes at one another. The clothesline behind the house held overalls and undershorts and shirts, some big and some not so big, the clothing of a man and his son, perhaps. That's what had caught my eye when we passed on the river.

I watched for a while and saw no sign of life and finally walked carefully into the yard. The shirts were old, patched and mended many times. I carefully unpinned two of the larger and one that was smaller. As I pulled the last from the line, it revealed a little girl standing before me, as if she'd materialized as part of a magic trick. She was not much older than Emmy, with blond pigtails and big blue eyes. She didn't look much better fed than the kids at Lincoln School. She wore a small sack dress and her feet were bare.

"Hello," I said.

"Those are my pa's shirts," she said. "And Henry's."

"Henry is your brother?" I asked.

She nodded.

"Where are they?"

"Working for Mr. McAdams."

"Does he live around here?"

"Has a big farm other side of Crawford. Pa used to farm here, but the bank took our land away."

"Where's your mom?"

"Works in town. Irons and cleans for Mrs. Drover."

"What's your name?"

"Abigail. What's yours?"

"Buck," I said.

"You stealing those?" she asked.

"Not at all, Abigail. I'm buying them."

I pulled out the dollars I'd taken from the pillowcase and used a clothespin to hang them on the line, which was too high for Abigail to reach.

"Are you rich?" she asked.

"Just lucky. It's been very nice meeting you, Abigail, but I have to go now."

"Back to the railroad tracks?"

"Maybe. Why?"

"Cuz that's where everybody comes from looking for food or work or a place to sleep for the night. Ma says it's important we do what we can. They never have money, though."

"That's right," I said. "Back to the railroad tracks. See if I can catch me a train to Sioux Falls."

"Trains don't stop in Crawford."

"Maybe I'll have to hike to the next town where they do stop."

"Lincoln," she said.

"Then Lincoln it is. Goodbye, Abigail."

I walked away, but not back to the river. I strolled up the dirt lane in front of the house to the place where it joined the county road, then to the other side, where the railroad tracks lay. I stood on the bed of broken rock, smelling the creosote from the ties, and stared back at the farmhouse. It was old and worn, like the shirts I'd taken, but I could understand how inviting it might seem to someone who had even less than Abigail's family and was walking the rails in search of a kind and restful place to come to.

I headed toward town for a while, then cut back across the next field to the river. Albert

175

had returned, and he let me have it with both barrels.

"Where the hell were you?"

"Fetching replacements for our Lincoln uniforms," I said and proudly held up the shirts.

"Where'd you get those?"

"Farmhouse upriver."

"Stole them?" There was such anger in his face, I thought he might hit me.

"I'm no thief. I paid for them."

He glanced at the pillowcase. "How much?"

"A dollar apiece."

Mose's eyebrows shot up and he signed, *For those rags?*

"Who'd you pay?" Albert demanded.

I decided it was best not to mention Abigail, so I said, "I pinned the money to the clothesline."

"Of all the stupid notions," Albert began.

"At least if people spot us now, we won't look like fugitives from Lincoln School."

"Three dollars," Albert said and looked ready to wring my neck.

"I could tell those folks needed the money."

"I don't care about the money. I'm worried they'll report us."

"Then the cops will just think we're riding the rails to somewhere."

"Yeah? And why is that?"

Because it's what I told Abigail, I wanted to say but said instead, "Because that's what

176

makes the most sense."

Albert shook his head in disgust. "Let's get going. We need to put distance between us and those three dollars."

Albert and Mose bent hard to their paddles, and I sat in the middle with Emmy, brooding. It seemed to me that no matter what I did, it wasn't good enough for Albert. Well, fine, I thought, the hell with him. I drilled the back of his head with my eyes, imagining a dozen scenarios in which he was the one who screwed up royally and I had to save him and he finally realized how lucky he was to have me for his brother.

Near evening, clouds began to mount in the west, and we could see lightning along the horizon. Emmy watched the threatening sky with fear-filled eyes.

"We need to find someplace to sleep inside tonight," I finally said to Albert.

Mose splashed his paddle lightly on the water to get our attention. He pointed toward the south side of the river and signed, *Orchard.*

Beyond the trees lining the Gilead lay a familiar sight — the boughs of apple trees, just as they'd been in the little orchard on the Frosts' farm. They were dark green in the waning light and welcoming.

"Maybe we can sleep there," I said.

"Let's see." Albert guided us to the riverbank. "You two wait here," he said and signaled for Mose to follow him.

When we were alone, Emmy looked at the apple trees with longing. "I miss Mama."

"I know."

"Do you ever miss your mama, Odie?"

"Sometimes," I said. "But it's been a long time since we lost her."

She reached inside her overalls and drew out the photograph I'd saved from the farm-house rubble and studied it, then looked up at me while little tears rolled down her cheeks. "Will I always miss her, Odie? Will it always hurt?"

"I suppose you'll always miss her, Emmy," I said. "But it won't always hurt."

I could hear now the grumble of the lightning in the distance, and I could smell the rain on the wind that came before it. Albert and Mose finally returned.

"There's a farmhouse and barn and such on the other side of the orchard," Albert said. "A good-size garden with an old potting shed. The shed's small and probably leaks some, but there's no lock on the door and it'll be a roof over our heads. We could sleep there tonight and be off early in the morning before anybody in that farmhouse wakes up."

Lightning split the sky not far to the west, and the boom of thunder followed a few seconds later. I felt the first big drops of rain begin to fall. We didn't have a lot of time to think it through. We gathered our things, stowed the canoe and paddles among thick brush on the riverbank, and made a run through the orchard for the potting shed on the other side.

I saw the farmhouse, a simple black shape in the near dark with a dim light showing through one window. The barn was not especially big, not like Hector Bledsoe's back near Lincoln. Like so many of the farms we'd seen, this was a hardscrabble operation. We ducked inside the potting shed just as the sky opened and rain began to fall in sheets. The lightning was on top of us, and there was a wind with it that howled through the gaps in the old plank siding of the shed. Emmy held to me and to Mose and squeezed her body together as small as she possibly could.

It was clear the shed hadn't been used in some time. There were no tools inside and it smelled of mildew and rot. The floor was dirt, but at least it was dry, and being in the old shed was far better than being out in that wicked weather.

When the storm finally passed, the sky cleared almost immediately. The moon came out, full now, and broad bars of silver shone through the windows of the potting shed and fell across the dirt floor. Albert took out some of the food he'd bought that morning, and we ate. Finally, exhausted from the day, we lay down to sleep, without Emmy even asking for a story but with Puff on her hand, gently cradling her cheek.

My earlier resentment had passed, as it always did. Lying on my blanket beside Albert, I was happy to have him for a brother, though I had no intention of telling him so. I didn't always understand him, and I knew that, more often than not, I was a bafflement to him as well, but the heart isn't the logical organ of the body, and I loved my brother deeply and fell asleep in the warmth of his company.

In the night, Emmy had one of her fits. I heard the commotion and woke in an instant. She lay in a pool of moonlight, writhing, her jaw clenched, her eyes rolled up in her head, every muscle of her body quivering.

We'd seen this once before, Albert and Mose and me, on the Frosts' farm, a few months after the accident that had killed her father and put Emmy in a coma. Everyone thought that when she came back to consciousness, she was fine. But several weeks later, when we saw her fall in the farmyard and begin to shake as if she'd been possessed by some terrible demon, Mrs. Frost had been forced to tell us the truth. Since the accident, on rare occasions, Emmy suffered these fits that resembled epileptic seizures but, doctors had assured her, were not. In fact, they had no explanation. The fits didn't seem to harm Emmy in the least, and after she came out of them, she was just fine and remembered nothing. Mrs. Frost didn't want this information broadly known, and she had sworn us to secrecy. As far as we knew, no one at Lincoln School was aware of Emmy's condition. I thought that if the Black Witch had known, she'd never have wanted to adopt the little girl.

Albert held Emmy in his arms until the fit passed and Emmy opened her eyes. She looked dazed and said groggily, "He's not dead, Odie. He's not dead."

"Who's not dead?" I asked.

But Emmy closed her eyes immediately afterward and went back to sleep. We wrapped her in her blanket and laid her down.

Mose signed, *Bad dream.*

Which seemed the most likely explanation, and I wondered if the dream had been about DiMarco, and the bad part was that he wasn't actually dead. I didn't want to be a murderer, but even more I didn't want DiMarco back in this world.

We all returned to our sleep.

At dawn the next morning, a gruff voice woke us: "Trespassers."

I sat up instantly, and so did Albert and Mose. Little Emmy didn't seem to have heard.

"Goddamn trespassers. Come out of there, boys."

The man was tall, awkwardly built, and held a shotgun in his hands. His face was like a diamond, a hard thing cut at sharp angles. He had a black patch over one eye. The other eye glared at us, and I recognized him from the mercantile in Westerville the day before, the man who'd bought an alarm clock.

Albert and Mose and I stood, but Emmy woke more slowly, probably the result of her fit in the night. She sat up and rubbed her eyes. When he saw her, the pig scarer stared as if he were seeing a ghost.

"I'll be damned," he said.

CHAPTER FIFTEEN

The wild pig scarer took the pillowcase that held everything of value to us.

"Barn," he said and waved his shotgun barrel toward the beat-up structure.

Who argues with a shotgun? We filed out of the shed and walked ahead of him, keeping together. I held one of little Emmy's hands, Mose the other. Albert took the lead, and like lambs to slaughter, we followed him into the dark of the barn.

The only piece of machinery inside was an old black Ford flatbed, the same kind of truck Emmy's folks had owned and the tornado had thrown on its back. The place smelled of hay, although there were just a few bales in evidence. A whole array of orchard tools hung along the front wall, and hand tools hung from a pegboard above a workbench. In one corner, wooden pallets stood stacked higher than a man was tall. There was what looked like the remains of a large cider press against the back wall, broken into pieces as if someone, in a fit of anger, had taken a sledgehammer to it. The man pointed us toward a corner of the barn that was squared off by an inside construction, a room that, from the reins and harnesses still hanging there, I figured was an old tack room.

We marched in one by one. Once we were inside the tack room, the man grabbed Emmy and pulled her away from us. Mose lurched toward her, trying to bring her back, but the man swung the barrel of his shotgun and caught Mose full across the left cheek, and he went down hard. I started for Emmy, too, but Albert yanked me back by my shirt collar.

"Won't hurt her," the man said. "Unless you try to get away."

He closed the door, and we heard a lock bolt slapped into place. Then we only heard Emmy crying as he took her off somewhere.

Albert went down on his knees to see to Mose, who wasn't moving. My brother leaned close and tilted his head to listen.

"Still breathing," he said.

"What's he going to do with Emmy?" I was ready to rip those walls apart and go out and do whatever was necessary to get Emmy back.

"Call the sheriff, I imagine," Albert said. He sat his butt down beside Mose, and I don't think I'd ever seen him more dejected.

Mose made a sound and rolled his head, and his eyes slowly opened. He blinked, then understanding came back, and he sat up, looking around wildly.

Where's Emmy? he signed, his fingers flying.

"That one-eyed pig scarer took her," I said.

"Pig scarer?" Albert said.

I didn't bother to explain. "We've got to get her back and get ourselves out of here."

Albert looked the little tack room over top to bottom. There was no window, and although the construction was old and ill-kempt, the boards that surrounded us appeared solid.

"Got an idea, Odie?" He wasn't really asking. He was just trying to show me how dumb I was.

I tried kicking at the walls with my new Red Wings. I shook loose some dust, but that was all. Mose stood up, lowered his shoulder, ran himself against the door and just bounced off. He rubbed his arm, then gingerly felt the side of his face, which was already swelling from the blow of that shotgun barrel.

"So we're just going to sit here and let them take us back to Lincoln School?" I said.

"Even if we got out, would you leave Emmy?" The quiet of Albert's voice and the soundness of his reason only fed my anger.

"If we got out, we could jump him. You, me, Mose, we could take him."

"And that shotgun of his?"

"We can't just do nothing."

"At the moment, Odie, we're plumb out of options." Albert picked up a loose hay straw from the dirt of the tack room floor and threw it. It went nowhere.

We'd been sitting silent for a long time, our backs to the tack room wall, when we heard the bolt drawn back, and the door opened. The one-eyed pig scarer stood there with his shotgun still at the ready.

"Out," he said and stepped away.

We got up and left the tack room. I was watching for an opening, that moment when I could throw myself on him and wrestle him to the ground. Or at least lead the charge that Albert and Mose would follow and together we would overpower him. But he stood well back, and with that shotgun leveled on us, there was no way we were going to get to him before he blew us apart. I was sure a man that mean-looking wouldn't hesitate to pull the trigger.

"You," he said to Mose, "grab one of them scythes. You grab that ladder," he said to Albert. "And you, boy, grab them loppers and that pruning saw."

We did as he'd instructed, and he waved us outside.

"Where's Emmy?" I asked.

"Emmaline's just fine. You want her to stay that way, do what I say."

He marched us out to the edge of the orchard, which looked poorly tended. The grass between the trees had grown high. The limbs were wild, tangled messes. Young apples hung like little green bells along the branches. I'd worked the Frosts' orchard for a couple of years, and I could see that, left unpruned, those branches would eventually snap under the weight of all that fruit. I knew, too, that careful pruning would improve the quality of what the trees produced.

"You," he said to Mose, "start down at that end with your scythe and cut all the wild grass between the trees. Work your way through the orchard row by row. If you run, I'll beat the living daylights out of these two and your precious Emmaline. Understand?"

Mose nodded. He gave us a helpless look and walked away.

"You," he said to Albert, "set the ladder up, then take them loppers from the boy." When Albert had done as he'd asked, the pig scarer said, "Cut where I tell you. You, boy, you gather up everything that drops to the ground and haul it over there back of the barn, next to that pile of junk. See it?"

I saw the junk pile and nodded. And we began.

Tree by tree, Albert pruned the wild branches. He worked first on the ground, then set up the ladder, which I held secure for him. Periodically, I gathered the fallen branches and piled them behind the barn. Because of the Frosts, this was work we knew.

But helping in the orchard that had belonged to Emmy's parents had never really felt like labor, not like working for the wild pig scarer. For one thing, the Frosts had never held a firearm trained on us. The pig scarer kept that shotgun in the crook of his arm as he directed Albert, and his one good eye seemed plenty able to track all the activity going on in the orchard.

The sun mounted in the sky. It was a humid day and sweat dripped off me in rivers. After a couple of hours, I finally said, "We won't do you any good if we die of thirst."

The man considered this. "There's a pump between the house and chicken coop. Should be a wooden bucket there. Bring it back full. And, boy, the little girl will pay the price for any stupid thing you might be thinking of doing."

I found the pump and drank my fill, listening to the chickens cackling behind the mesh of the coop. I filled the bucket, then studied the farmhouse. It was two stories, but the upper floor was small, perhaps only an attic. There couldn't have been many places to hide Emmy inside. I thought about slipping in and finding her. Then what? Emmy and I might get away, but that would leave Albert and Mose, and God only knew what that one-eyed bastard might do to them.

I carried the wooden bucket back to the orchard, and the man let Albert drink from it. Then he had me take the bucket to Mose.

Just like the Frosts' place, Mose signed after he'd drunk all he wanted.

"Except we didn't mind working there," I said.

Mose wiped the sweat from his brow. *Will he turn us in?* he signed.

"I'm betting not until he's got all the work out of us he needs."

Mose looked down the lines of orchard rows. *Long time,* he signed.

We got no lunch and we worked until the sun was low in the sky. Even Bledsoe had been kinder. When the pig scarer marched us back to the barn, the mounding of pruned branches was immense, nearly as big as the pile of junk beside it. I flopped down on the dirt floor of the tack room and every muscle in my body hurt.

Without a word, the man locked us in.

"Hungry people make bad laborers," Albert called after him.

The dirt from the floor clung to every sweaty part of me. "This is worse than the hayfields."

Mose signed, *Worried about Emmy. All right, you think?*

"He was beating up on us all day," I said. "He didn't have time to hurt Emmy."

Mose stood up and walked along each wall, testing every board. *We're getting out of here,* he signed. *Don't know how, but we're getting out.*

"And we'll take Emmy with us," I said.

We go nowhere without Emmy, his hands vowed.

There were little gaps in the wallboards of the tack room, and the late evening light filtered through. Mose's resolve to free us was like an elixir, and I felt better. I pulled out my harmonica, figuring if we couldn't eat, at least we could give ourselves a little comfort.

I began to play one of my favorites, "Old Joe Clark." It was a rousing tune, and Mose clapped his hands in time. After that I played a little ragtime number and was just launching into "Sweet Betsy from Pike" when the door was unbolted and opened, and there stood Emmy. She held a big bowl in her arms. I smelled roasted potatoes, and my mouth watered so fast and hard it hurt. The wild pig scarer stood behind her with his ever-present shotgun.

"Grub," he said and nudged Emmy forward.

After not having eaten all day, even if what was in that bowl was no better than pig slop, I was ready to gorge myself. Albert and Mose and I dug into the meal with our dirty fingers. The potatoes were surprisingly tasty, with bits of salt pork and onions laced in. The pig scarer had Emmy give us a milk bottle filled with water to wash it down. He dragged one of the hay bales and set it just outside the entrance of the tack room and sat with Emmy beside him. While he watched us eat, he took a pint-size bottle of clear liquid from a pocket of his overalls and drank from it. I was pretty sure it wasn't water.

When we'd finished every bit of the potatoes, Emmy took the bowl back and the man had her sit beside him again. It was going toward dark, and the pig scarer took a kerosene lantern from where it hung on the barn wall, lit the wick, and put the lantern on the dirt floor beside the hay bale.

"Who was blowing that mouth organ?" he asked.

"Me," I said.

"Know 'Red River Valley'?"

"Sure."

"Play it."

I did, and in the gloom of the barn, lit with just the little lantern glow, the haunting notes of that old ballad seemed like a heavy blanket of sorrow laid over us all. A great sadness came off the pig scarer. It was in his one good eye as he stared at the tack room wall, seeing something there that my own two eyes could not. It was also in the way he mindlessly drank the clear liquid from the bottle.

When I finished, he said, "Play it again."

This time I watched him even more carefully, and I could see the alcohol was hitting him hard. I thought I'd play that song until he finished the bottle and then jump him. The shotgun lay on his lap, but the reflexes of a man deep into drink were unreliable. Maybe because I was thinking this, I didn't play the tune with the same feeling I'd given it the first time, because the pig scarer suddenly cried, "Stop!" He put the cork in the bottle and stood up to leave.

"Are you going make us sleep on a dirt floor?" Albert asked.

The pig scarer considered this. I could see he wasn't standing so steadily, and I thought about taking a run at him. Albert must have guessed my intention, because he put a restraining hand on my arm.

"Maybe we could have that hay bale to spread?" my brother said.

The pig scarer gave a nod to Mose, who got up and hauled the bale into the tack room. Then the man shut and bolted the door, leaving us in the dark.

"Night, Emmy," I called.

"Night," she called back.

We broke the bale, spread it out, and lay down. With the close four walls and the dirt floor overlaid with a thin mat of straw and a locked door to keep us in, this felt oddly familiar, as if I was back in the quiet room. I didn't close my eyes right away. Not because I wasn't tired. I was thinking.

The wild pig scarer had been deeply affected by the song I'd played. Whenever someone asked for a particular song, it was generally because the tune had special meaning for them. Sad numbers seemed to be especially meaningful. Something had happened to the pig scarer, something that hurt him. But it had also made him mad enough to cut off a second airing of the tune. There were still a lot of things about life I didn't know then, but I knew this: when a man hurt really bad, it was usually because of a woman.

CHAPTER SIXTEEN

That night, Mose wept.

I woke to the pitiful sound of his sobs and sat up. The tack room was streaked with moonlight slipping between the warped slats. I saw that Albert was awake, too, sitting with his back to the barn wall.

At Lincoln School, kids often cried in the night. Sometimes it was because of a bad dream. Sometimes they were wide awake and just wept their hearts out over some private sorrow. So many came to the school already beset by demons. For others, the horrible things done to them after they arrived were enough to give them nightmares for life. Mose was the biggest, strongest, most physically capable kid I knew, and also the most agreeable. He never complained about anything, and no trial seemed too great for him. But sometimes at night, he wept those bitter, soul-wrenching tears, and wasn't even aware that he was doing it. We had tried on occasion to wake him out of whatever horrible vision was twisting him up, but when he opened his eyes, the weeping stopped immediately and he seemed to have no idea what he'd been dreaming. Whenever we'd just let the crying continue, he'd claimed to have no recollection of it in the morning.

Everything that's been done to us we carry forever. Most of us do our damnedest to hold on to the good and forget the rest. But somewhere in the vault of our hearts, in a place our brains can't or won't touch, the worst is stored, and the only sure key to it is in our dreams.

Wake him? I signed to Albert.

He shook his head.

I wondered about Emmy. Was she crying her eyes out now? Because of the things I'd seen firsthand at the school, and because of the stories I'd heard from kids who'd come from other schools, stories of unimaginable violation, I understood the terrible things an adult could do to a helpless child. What kind of man was the wild pig scarer? If I'd believed in a just God, a compassionate God, I might have prayed. But I believed in a different God now, the Tornado God, and I knew he was deaf to the cries of the suffering. So I listened for a long time to Mose's sobs, which nearly broke my heart. And I thought about Emmy's fit the night before and her situation now, and ours. All the bright hope I'd had only two days earlier as we set out on the

Gilead for a new land and new lives seemed to have turned to dust.

We started work in the morning without food, carrying on with the same labor we'd begun the day before. Mose swung the scythe, cutting back the orchard grass. Albert pruned, following the pig scarer's directions, and I gathered the cuttings and mounded them behind the barn. I saw that the great trash pile already there included, among other things, an enormous number of clear, empty pint bottles. The pig scarer was a man who liked his liquor. I figured that went a long way in explaining the neglect of the orchard and the farm in general.

Midmorning the honking of an automobile horn came from the direction of the farm-house.

"You boys keep working," the pig scarer said. "Try anything, little Emmaline pays the price. Understand?"

"Yes, sir," Albert said.

The pig scarer took off through the orchard. I let him get ahead, then dropped the cut branches I'd been gathering and started to follow.

"Where are you going?" Albert said.

"Just to see what's up."

"Get back here," he snapped.

But I didn't pay him any mind. I slipped tree by tree toward the farmhouse, keeping to the shadows under the great spread of the branches. I stopped where I could see a police car parked between the barn and the farm-house. A man in a khaki uniform stood with his back to the orchard and to the pig scarer, who was crossing the yard in front of the chicken coop. The chickens began to cackle noisily, and the cop turned. He was big, Nordic looking, with a face burned by the summer sun.

"Ah, there you are, Jack. Where you been?" he said in greeting.

"Pruning in my orchard."

"With that shotgun?"

"Coyotes," the pig scarer said. "What do you want?"

"Just alerting folks. You heard about the kidnapped girl?"

"Read about it in the paper. Saw her picture. Cute little thing. Reminded me a lot of Sophie."

"Our roadblocks haven't turned up shit. We're thinking the hooligans that snatched her might be on foot and still in the area. Some folks over toward Lamberton reported that somebody took shirts from a clothesline yesterday."

"Stole 'em?"

The cop shook his head. "Left money, which is what got us to suspecting it might be one of the men we're looking for. Some of the money they stole when they did the kid-napping."

"Got a description?"

"Naw, only a little girl was home at the time, and she couldn't tell us much. Considering she was all alone, I figure she was lucky. A lot luckier than little Emmaline Frost. We figure the guys who took her might be making a run along the railroad tracks. And listen, Jack, they're armed and dangerous. If we spot them, Sheriff Warford's orders are to shoot first, ask questions later. So I'd keep that shotgun handy for a while if I was you."

"Is that all?"

"You see anything, you let us know."

The pig scarer gave a nod.

The cop studied the farmhouse, the barn, the chicken coop. "Any word from Aggie and Sophie?"

"I expect you got other people to notify."

"All right then." The cop got back into his car and drove away along the lane between the apple trees.

I quickly returned to the orchard, where Albert had climbed down from the ladder.

"Who was honking?" he asked.

"A cop. Came to warn Jack about us."

"Jack? Is that his name?" He looked in the direction of the farmhouse and barn. "He didn't say anything to the cop?"

"Nothing. That's good, right?"

Albert shrugged. "Who knows?"

"That cop said the sheriff's orders are to shoot us first and ask questions later. Jeez, everybody's gunning for us."

"Did you see Emmy?"

"No."

"Here he comes." Albert remounted the ladder.

All morning I mulled over the why of the pig scarer's silence about us and figured his plan was probably to use us until the work was done and then turn us in. Maybe there'd even be a reward by that time. The whole while, I kept asking myself, *Who are Aggie and Sophie?*

We labored all that day, with only water from the bucket. The sun was low in the sky when the pig scarer finally called a halt and marched us back to the tack room. We lay down exhausted and hungry and miserable, and I was sure now that the pig scarer's plan was not to turn us in to the authorities but to work us to death.

"Albert," I said. "How much did you and Volz and Brickman charge for a pint of moonshine?"

He was lying on our thin bedding of hay, and he rolled his head wearily toward me. "What difference does it make?"

"How much?"

"When he was on his own, Herman sold it for seventy-five cents a pint. Brickman was going to sell all the new batches for a dollar. What are you thinking about, Odie?"

"Nothing," I said, because my plan wasn't

fully formed yet.

An hour later, the tack room door was unbolted and opened, and the pig scarer stood there with Emmy at his side. She no longer had on the overalls she'd been wearing when we hightailed it from Lincoln School. Now she wore a pretty green dress.

I signed quickly to her, *You okay?*

She nodded but couldn't sign back because of the big bowl she held in both hands.

"Set their food on the floor, girl," the pig scarer said.

When she put the bowl down, I saw that it was filled with scrambled eggs mixed with the same kind of chopped up and roasted potatoes we'd eaten the night before. Emmy reached into a pocket of her dress, brought out three spoons, and handed one to each of us. We dug in right away.

"You going to feed her?" I asked around a mouthful of food.

"She's ate."

"Nice dress," I said.

The pig scarer glared at me as if what I'd offered was the worst insult in the world, and I was afraid for a moment that he'd clip me across the face with the barrel of the shotgun in the same way he had Mose.

"He only meant she looks happy," Albert said.

Which made the pig scarer relax. He took a pint bottle from the back pocket of his overalls and sipped. While he did this, the hand with his trigger finger was momentarily occupied.

Mose signed, *Jump him?*

But we were too busy eating, and the pig scarer recorked the bottle and said, "What's all that hand stuff?"

"He can't talk," I said.

"What? Dumb?"

Which was a term I hated. I knew its meaning, but it always sounded like an insult.

"Somebody cut out his tongue," I said.

"Who?"

"He doesn't know. It happened when he was little."

Then the pig scarer surprised me. He said, "Anyone'd do that to a child should be horsewhipped and hung."

When we finished the eggs and potatoes, Emmy took the bowl and our spoons, and as he had the night before, the pig scarer set a hay bale in front of the tack room door, lit a lantern, and ordered, "Play that mouth organ, boy."

" 'Red River Valley'?"

"Something fast," he said.

I played "Camptown Races," just about as snappy a tune as anyone could ask for. I followed that with a couple of more old standards. While I played, the pig scarer took frequent pulls off his pint bottle, and soon he was tapping his foot in time to the rhythm.

201

And there it was again, the magic of music. This was a man who'd shown us nothing but harshness, had not smiled in all the time we'd been with him, but the music had found a way to slip beneath all that hard, bitter armor and touch something softer and more human inside him.

When I finished that last song, the pig scarer assessed his pint bottle, which was nearly empty, and slapped the cork back in the neck. I could tell he was ready to bring the evening to an end.

"How much did you pay for that moonshine?" I asked.

His one good eye studied me with suspicion.

"Seventy-five cents? A dollar?"

"Dollar and a quarter," he finally said.

"Any good?"

"Might as well be drinking kerosene."

I tapped the spit from my harmonica and put the instrument into my shirt pocket. "I know a way to get you the best corn liquor you ever tasted," I said. "And it'll cost you practically nothing."

CHAPTER SEVENTEEN

The next morning the one-eyed pig scarer put Mose and me to work in the orchard and left in his truck with Albert. He threatened to turn us over to the sheriff if we crossed him in any way. As soon as he was gone, I dropped my rake, told Mose to keep working that scythe, and started to leave.

He grabbed my arm and signed, *What are you doing?*

"I'm going to find Emmy," I said.

He shook his head. *He'll hurt her,* he signed. *You, too.*

"I have to make sure she's all right. But you need to keep working or he'll see that you've been slacking off."

He shook his head vigorously.

"Mose, we have to know about Emmy. And if we're going to get ourselves out of this, we need to know everything we can about him, too."

What if he comes back? he signed. *Catches you?*

203

I kicked over the water bucket so that it emptied. "I'll tell him I had to fill it."

I could see he wasn't happy and probably not completely convinced, but he finally let me go.

The farmhouse door was locked, but the windows were raised and the pig scarer hadn't bothered to latch the screens, so I slipped inside easily. I'd expected the place to be a pigsty but was surprised by its neat appearance. I suspected that in the same way we'd been put to work in the orchard, Emmy had been put to work here. The large main room was situated around a big potbellied stove, the primary source of heat for the farmhouse in winter. I stood in the kitchen nook next to a table and three chairs. A divan served as a divider between the main room and a little sitting area with a couple of old, upholstered wing chairs. Between the chairs, on a table whose finish was worn almost down to the bare wood, sat what in those days was called a farm radio, powered by a battery pack. Herman Volz kept one in his carpentry shop and let us listen to music while we worked. And there'd been one in the Frosts' farmhouse, and sometimes when we'd finished our labors, Mrs. Frost had let us listen to *Death Valley Days* or *The Eveready Hour* or *The Guy Lombardo Show* with Burns and Allen.

There were two doors off the main room. I

tried the first. Inside was a bedroom, sparely furnished — an unmade bed, a chest of drawers, a washstand with a big enamel bowl and a straight razor, and hanging on the wall above that, a simple, round mirror. Atop the chest of drawers sat a photograph in a fine wood frame. It showed the pig scarer and a woman, sitting side by side on the divan in the other room. Nestled in the man's lap was a little girl with pigtails, who appeared to be about Emmy's age and who, in fact, resembled Emmy a good deal. The pig scarer and the woman looked deadly solemn, but the little girl was smiling.

I tried the door to the second room. Locked. I knelt and peered through the keyhole but couldn't see much. "Emmy?" I said quietly.

At first, I heard nothing, then a rustling, like I used to hear when Faria was scurrying across the floor of the quiet room.

"Odie?" came Emmy's voice from the other side of the door.

"Are you all right?"

"Get me out, Odie."

"Give me a minute."

A keyhole lock was one of the easiest to get around. I rummaged in the kitchen drawers and came up with a long finishing nail and a piece of stiff wire, which I bent at one end. I inserted the nail, then the bent wire, and, in a minute, had the door open. Emmy burst out and threw her arms around me. She was still wearing the dress from the night before.

"Did he hurt you?" I asked.

"No, but I don't want to be here. Can we go?"

"Not yet, Emmy. It's not safe."

"But I want to go."

"Me, too. And we will, just not yet." I knelt down so my eyes were level with hers. "Is he mean to you?"

She shook her. "He's just very sad. He cries at night, and when I hear him, it makes me want to cry, too."

I stood and walked into the room where she'd been locked up. The bed was small and neatly made. The room was stuffy, and I saw that the pig scarer had nailed the only window shut. The work looked recent, and I figured it had been done to ensure that Emmy didn't escape that way. A little chest the color of a green apple sat on the floor, and when I opened it, I found that it was half-filled with girls' clothing — dresses and whatnot — neatly folded. There was also a child's chair in one corner from which a Raggedy Ann doll stared at me with black button eyes.

"He took Puff away, Odie. He told me the doll was mine, if I wanted it," Emmy said. "But it scares me."

Outside Emmy's room was a ladder that led to the upper story.

"Stay here," I told her and began climbing.

As I'd suspected from the beginning, what I found was the attic, a long low-ceilinged space containing mostly junk. Half the room was curtained off, and when I pulled the curtain aside, I found the rudiments of a living area — bed, chest of drawers, chair, washstand and mirror, and a chamber pot. There was nothing that gave me a clue about who had lived here, but one element of the scene disturbed me greatly. The bedding had been thrown to the floor and the cover of the thin mattress had been cut to shreds so that the cotton stuffing inside spilled out like the entrails of a gutted animal.

Downstairs Emmy was holding herself, frightened. "Odie, I want to go away from here. Please, I want to go now."

"We can't, Emmy. Not right away." I made my voice silk soft, calm and soothing. "He has Albert, and he might hurt him if we leave. For sure, he'll turn us in, and the sheriff will catch us and send us back. We need to wait a little while longer." Then came the hardest part. "I have to lock you back in the room."

"No, Odie. Don't leave me. Please don't leave me."

"I have to, Emmy, just for now. But we're getting out of here, all of us together. I promise." She stared at me, her eyes little white buttons of fear. "Do you believe me?" I said.

It was hard on her, so hard it hurt me to

see, but she finally nodded.

"All right, then. But, Emmy, if he tries anything with you, anything you're afraid will hurt you, you take off running and you don't stop until you're as far from here as your legs'll carry you. I want you to promise me that."

"I don't want to go without you and Mose and Albert."

"If he tries to hurt you, promise me that you'll run. You need to promise."

"I promise," she said at the edge of tears.

"Cross your heart."

She did.

"Okay, back into your room. He'll probably let you see us again at supper."

She went, head down, and I suspected that as soon as I locked her back in, she would throw herself on the bed and soak the sheets with her tears.

Outside I picked up the water bucket and started back to the orchard. Before I'd gone a dozen steps, I heard the drone of an automobile engine approaching on the dirt lane that split the orchard. I ducked behind the chicken coop. A dusty Model A came to a stop in front of the house, and a woman got out, a straw basket in the crook of her arm. She shaded her eyes, glanced around the farmyard, and called, "Jack?" She waited a moment, then walked to the door and knocked.

"Jack?" she called again.

She turned back to the farmyard, looked everything over carefully. I could see in her a kindred spirit, because the next thing she did was reach to open the door of a house where no one was home. When the door didn't yield, she started peeking in at the windows.

I stepped from behind the chicken coop. "Can I help you?"

She was clearly startled, her face awash with guilt. "I was just . . . I . . ." Then she scowled. "Who are you?"

"Uncle Jack's nephew," I said. "Who are you?"

"Frieda Hines. A neighbor. I came for my weekly eggs."

"Uncle Jack didn't say to expect you."

"No? Well, he's forgetful sometimes these days. Especially since . . . well, you know. I didn't realize he had family here," she said, warming to my presence. She walked toward me. "But it's good he's not alone. Where is he?"

"In town. Supplies," I said.

"Nephew." She scrutinized me in the same way she had the farmyard just before she'd tried to trespass. "He never mentioned you."

"Never mentioned you either."

"What's your name?"

"Buck."

"His side of the family or hers?"

"Who do you think I take after?"

She laughed. "You're Aggie's kin, I can tell. Is she all right?"

"Fine," I said.

"We were all so worried when she took off that way, in the middle of the night. I heard she went back to Saint Paul. Is that right?"

"That's right."

"How's little Sophie? It's been almost a year."

"She's not so little," I said. "Shooting up faster'n a weed. But she's still got her pigtails."

"Of course." She tried to hide the sly look before she asked her next question. "And Rudy?"

I wasn't quite sure about that one. I'd learned a long time ago that in uncertain situations it was best to assume an attitude of secret knowledge and keep my mouth shut. So I did.

"Deserted her, didn't he? *Men.*" She practically spat the word.

"You want me to tell Uncle Jack you were here for your eggs?"

"Thank you, Buck. I can come by for them tomorrow morning, if that will work for him."

"I'm sure it will, ma'am."

"Well, you just go right on with whatever. It's been a pleasure to meet you."

She got back into her automobile and drove away, waving a hand at me as she did so.

When I returned to the orchard, Mose was

still hard at work, swinging his scythe. He looked relieved to see me and signed, *Find Emmy?*

"She's all right," I said.

Find out anything about him?

"Maybe," I said.

I took up my rake and spent the morning trying to imagine the pig scarer's sad life and wondering what had really happened to the woman and the little girl in the photograph, and thinking about someone named Rudy, and worrying over that ruined mattress.

CHAPTER EIGHTEEN

When the sun was directly overhead, the pig scarer drove up the lane and parked near the barn. He sent Albert to fetch us, and we unloaded the materials from the truck bed while he held his shotgun and directed our labor. Into the barn we carried a three-by-five sheet of copper, a two-foot length of rigid copper pipe, ten feet of copper tubing, a sack of metal brads, several pounds of cornmeal and sugar, a thermometer, and yeast.

When the last of it was unloaded, I said, "A woman came by looking for you."

The pig scarer stopped dead still. "Woman? You talked to her?"

"She said her name was Frieda Hines. She came for her eggs."

"Eggs, goddamn it." He squeezed his good eye shut in disgust at his forgetfulness. "What did you tell her, boy?"

"That I was your nephew and you were in town buying supplies."

He thought a moment. "She come all the

way out to you in the orchard?"

"I was filling the water bucket at the pump."

"You didn't say anything else? About the others maybe?"

"Not a word, I swear. She asked about Aggie and Sophie."

A look came over his face, as if a hard wind had just hit him.

"She asked about Rudy, too."

His next words came out like slivers of ice. "What did you say?"

"Didn't have to say anything. She had it all figured out on her own. Believes they're in Saint Paul. Well, Aggie and Sophie, anyway."

"And Rudy?"

"Seemed pretty clear to her that he deserted them." I gave a shrug. "Sounded good to me."

The pig scarer thought this over, then offered me a satisfied look, as if he approved of how I'd handled things.

"Aggie and Sophie. Your wife and daughter?"

He considered whether to answer, then gave a simple nod.

"She's coming back for her eggs tomorrow morning."

"I'll be ready for that biddy," he said.

Albert and Mose went to work. It was going to be a small operation, only a gallon still, so I knew it wouldn't take any time at all to put together. While they worked, I made the mash for the corn liquor. The pig scarer stood by, shotgun in hand, watching with silent interest.

After a while, I ventured, "That's a cider press in the corner."

He looked at the machinery broken into pieces against the back wall. "Was," he said with a note of regret.

"Looks like a tornado hit it. What happened?"

"You ask a lot of questions."

"I play the odds. Every once in a while, I get an answer."

I thought he almost smiled. Instead he said, "Old and just fell apart."

Like hell. Somebody had taken a sledge-hammer to that press, or my name wasn't Odie O'Banion. Revenuers did that sometimes. But maybe sometimes men who went crazy with rage did, too.

By evening, the little still was completed and the mash was fermenting. Though it would take several days before we would be ready to do the first run, the pig scarer seemed pleased. That night when he unlocked the tack room door, Emmy brought us a good meal of baked chicken and roasted carrots. After we ate, the pig scarer sat on the hay bale outside the tack room, with Emmy at his side, and said, "Can you play 'Goodbye Old Paint' on that mouth organ of yours?"

" 'Leaving Cheyenne,' you mean? Sure."

I pulled out my harmonica, but before I

put it to my mouth, the pig scarer surprised me. He lifted a fiddle from behind the hay bale and settled it beneath his chin.

"Go on," he said.

So I launched into that old cowboy tune, and the pig scarer began to bow that fiddle along with me. He was pretty good, and we sounded not half bad together. The whole time I was aware of the fact that both his hands were occupied with the instrument and not his shotgun. But he wasn't stupid. He'd positioned the hay bale far enough out that even Mose, who was the fastest of us all, probably couldn't have reached him before the shotgun was in his hands. Still, it gave me hope.

"You play a good fiddle," I said.

"Haven't had occasion for a while." He cradled the instrument gently in his hands and for a moment seemed somewhere else. "Sophie used to beg me to play at night when I put her to bed." Saying that name woke him from whatever reverie he'd been in, and he set the fiddle down.

The song had put me in mind of horses, so I asked, "What happened to the nags who used to wear these harnesses?"

"Sold 'em," he said. "Year ago. Was going to modernize, buy myself a tractor."

"Never did?"

"You see one around here anywhere, boy?"

"Nope. And I don't see any animals either,

except those chickens in that coop."

"Used to have some goats," the pig scarer said. "Mostly pets for Sophie."

There was that name again, stumbling accidentally from his lips. As soon as it was out, it seemed to turn like a boomerang and hit his heart. He sat up straight, snatched the hooch bottle from his back pocket, and took a long pull.

"What happened to the goats?" I asked.

"Ate 'em," he said.

"You ate your daughter's pets? That doesn't seem right."

"How old are you, boy?"

"Thirteen." Which wasn't true, strictly speaking. I still had a couple of months to go, but it sounded better. Older, wiser. Tougher.

"When you got a couple more decades behind you," he said, pointing a finger at me, "then you can talk to me about what's right." He stood up directly, grabbed his shotgun and fiddle, and said to Emmy, "Collect those chicken bones and them dishes. Night's over."

"He didn't mean anything by it," Albert said.

"Think I give a good goddamn about what that boy means or don't mean, Norman? Come on, girl." He hustled Emmy out and bolted the tack room door.

I lay in the dark thinking about the bitterness inside the pig scarer and the sadness that was there, too, and I figured they were probably twins joined at the hip. I thought maybe it wasn't love that consumed him but a terrible sense of loss, which was something all of us who'd taken to the Gilead knew about. I'd considered loss only from my own perspective and Albert's and Mose's and Emmy's, because our parents had been taken from us. But it worked the other way, too. Losing a child, that had to be akin to losing a good part of your heart.

Slowly, the pig scarer was becoming like Faria when I'd first met the little rat. The more I knew about him, the less frightful he was.

In the moonlight that slipped between the wall slats, I saw Mose tap Albert on the arm and spell out in sign, *Norman?*

"The old clerk at the hardware store was asking all kinds of questions," Albert explained. "Said to Jack, 'What's the boy's name?' I told him I wasn't a boy. Jack said I was no man neither. So I told the clerk my name was Norman. Neither boy nor man."

Damn, that was smart, I thought. Me, when I was pressed, all I could come up with was some stupid movie cowboy's name. Albert, he'd come up with a corker. I decided next time somebody asked me, I was going to give them a name just as slick as Norman.

By our fourth morning with the pig scarer,

we'd finished the work in the orchard, and he set us to painting the barn and tending the big garden. Except for the fact that we'd been locked in the tack room every night and fed only once a day, it hadn't been that different from the work we'd done on the Frosts' farm. We saw Emmy every evening at supper, and she seemed to be doing okay. After we ate, the pig scarer would bring out his fiddle and I would put my harmonica to my lips and we'd play tunes together. He didn't seem to me to be a bad sort. It was just that life had been pretty cruel to him. He'd been visited by his own Tornado God.

I asked him one night about that eye patch he wore.

"Lost it fighting the Kaiser," he said. "The war to end all wars. Ha!"

"You don't believe it did any good?" Albert asked.

"There are two kinds of people in the world, Norman. People who have things and people who want the things other people have. A day don't go by that there's not war somewhere in this world. A war to end all wars? That's like saying a disease to end all diseases. Only way that'll happen is when every human being on this earth is dead."

Mose signed, *Not everybody's greedy.*

Emmy translated for the pig scarer.

"Boy, I never knew anybody didn't have their own best interests at heart, and the hell with everyone else." He scrutinized each one of us with his good eye. "Be honest. Given the chance to get yourselves free of me, you'd slit my throat, wouldn't you?"

Although I'd killed a man already in order to be free, slitting the pig scarer's throat was a sickening thought. "Not me," I said.

The pig scarer drank the last of the alcohol he'd brought with him, eyed the clear, empty glass bottle, and flung it against the barn wall, where it shattered with an explosion that destroyed the fragile camaraderie the evening's music had created.

"Let me tell you something, boy. Whatever you think you're not capable of doing, the minute you think it, the moment it enters your mind, just in the imagining, it's already been done. Only a matter of time before your hands follow through."

He grabbed Emmy, yanked her to her feet, bolted the tack room door, and shut us up in the dark.

It rained all the next day, a steady drizzle, and the pig scarer had us working inside the barn, sharpening and oiling his tools, seeing to the fermenting whiskey mash, while he stayed in the house with Emmy. I took a good look at the broken-up cider press against the barn's back wall. That cider press had been the object of some great rage. I'd been thinking about what the pig scarer said the night before, about the moment when something terrible comes into your head, that it's only a matter of time before you do it. I couldn't see into his head or his heart, but whatever was there, no matter how terrible, I figured the pig scarer was capable of it. I kept thinking about Aggie and Sophie and Rudy, and wondering more and more what had really happened to them. And all along I'd been trying to figure a way to escape.

That day, while eyeing everything in the barn, I finally had a decent idea. There was a roll of stiff, heavy wire hanging on the wall among the hand tools. I used a pair of cutters, clipped off a two-foot length, and made a hook at one end.

Mose signed, *What doing?*

"You'll see. Albert, lock me in the tack room."

When I was inside and he'd set the bolt in place, I slipped the wire through a knothole in one of the warped door boards and worked it until the hook snagged the knob at the end of the bolt. I carefully drew the wire back and the bolt with it, and in less than a minute, I'd freed myself.

Albert and Mose both gave me a look of admiration.

When escape? Mose signed.

Albert said, "Not until we can free Emmy, too. Hide that wire under the hay in the tack room, Odie. And good work."

The rain seemed to have put the pig scarer

in a foul mood. Or maybe it was the discussion from the night before. Whatever, he wasn't talkative when Emmy brought us our supper, and he didn't have his fiddle with him. As soon as we'd finished eating, he ordered Emmy to gather up everything and locked us in for the night.

The rain finally let up, and the cloud cover broke. The moon was up and slid its bright yellow fingers through the cracks in the barn wall and across the tack room floor. I could hear Mose and Albert sawing z's, but my own eyes wouldn't close. I lay there thinking about the pig scarer, about the foul mood he seemed to be in, and I worried about Emmy. Finally, I slipped the wire from its hiding place under our mat of hay and crept to the door. I threaded the wire through the knothole, hooked the bolt knob, and drew it back slowly. When the bolt was clear, I edged the door open.

The hand on my shoulder made me jump. I spun and Mose stood there in moonlit stripes.

Where going?

Emmy, I signed. *Worried.*

Me, too. Coming with you.

Most farmhouses I'd visited had a dog, but not the pig scarer's place. More and more, I thought of him as a man so deep in his misery that it had become what he breathed and ate and clothed himself in. I figured he wanted

221

nothing, not even the companionship of a dog, to lessen that misery. I didn't know the why of it but expected that it had something to do with losing his wife and daughter. Or maybe just Sophie, because I hadn't heard him mention his wife's name at all. Mose and Albert and me, we were just free labor to him. But Emmy, she might mean something else, or the promise of something else, and if she didn't fulfill that promise, who knew what the pig scarer in his misery might do?

We crept to the farmhouse, our shadows tagging along behind. Through an open window I could hear the sound of music from the radio inside. I eased myself against the wall and slowly peeked over the sill. The room was lit by an oil lamp. The pig scarer sat in one of the upholstered wing chairs, drinking moonshine from a pint bottle. When we had the still up and running, we'd probably save him a fortune. He laid his head back and closed his good eye. I signaled to Mose, and we headed around to the back of the house.

The window of Emmy's room was still nailed shut, but a river of moonlight flowed through the clear pane and fell across Emmy, who was asleep in her bed.

Mose smiled and signed, *Angel*. Then he signed, *Devil,* and nodded toward the front room.

Not the Devil, I thought. But maybe a man capable of doing the Devil's work.

The door to Emmy's room opened suddenly. Silhouetted against the lamplight stood the pig scarer. I dropped to the ground and Mose did, too, and I held my breath hoping we hadn't been spotted. A few moments later, the window above us rattled. Everything in me screamed *Run!* Mose must have sensed my panic and put his hand over mine on the ground and gave his head a faint shake. We stayed that way for five minutes, frozen against the back side of the house, but nothing more happened. The window didn't shatter and the pig scarer didn't shoot us. We finally eased ourselves up and risked another peek through Emmy's window. She was still asleep in bed and was alone once again.

Back now, Mose signed, and I started to follow him to the barn.

Before we could cross the farmyard, the front door of the house opened, and the pig scarer stepped out with a lantern in his hand. He closed the door behind him and began walking, a little unsteadily, until he'd entered the orchard.

Free Emmy? Mose signed. *Get away from here?*

I shook my head and signed, *He might come back quick. We'd be in big trouble.* I glanced where the pig scarer had gone. *Follow,* I signed.

Mose shook his head and signed, *You crazy?*

223

The pig scarer was far enough away that I could whisper. "Where does a man go in the middle of the night, Mose?"

Pee, Mose signed.

"He could pee in the yard. Come on, before it's too late." And I took off.

The moon lit the scythed grass between the rows of trees with a silver luminescence. Mose and I kept to the black shadows of the apple trees. The pig scarer's lamp was easy to follow. He headed west to the end of his orchard. When Mose and I arrived at the last of the trees, we saw him fifty yards out, kneeling beneath a lone oak in a fallow area, bent so far over that his forehead touched the ground. The sound of his deep sobs was enough to make a stone weep. It's impossible to witness such open grief and not feel pity wrung from your heart. I'd heard little kids at Lincoln School cry all night long, and I'd heard Mose, too, but I couldn't recall ever hearing a man cry this way. It made me think that no matter how big we grew or how old, there was always a child in us somewhere.

Mose touched my arm and signed, *Go now.*

I'd seen what I came for, though I still didn't understand it exactly, and I nodded and we slipped back toward the barn.

CHAPTER NINETEEN

The pig scarer was in a surprisingly good mood the next morning. I wondered if the tears, like rain, had washed him clean of his misery, at least for a while. Or maybe it was because of the news Albert gave him, that the mash was ready for its first run in the still. Or it could have been something else entirely.

The stack in the woodshed was pitifully low, and Albert told the pig scarer that we would need that and more for both the firing of the still and any cooking that he hoped to do on the stove in the farmhouse. When Emmy had finished gathering eggs from the chicken house, which was one of her daily chores, he put her to work helping Albert get things ready for the first run of the still. He took a two-man saw from where it hung on the barn wall and handed it to Mose, then he pulled down an ax for himself. He pointed toward a wood cart in the corner and said to me, "Bring that, and you and the mute come with me."

He led the way, carrying his ever-present shotgun, and we walked through the orchard to the edge of the Gilead River. The whole distance the pig scarer merrily whistled "Wabash Cannonball," as if whatever labor awaited us was something to look forward to. He stopped where a great cottonwood stood, long dead but still upright, its branches dry and brittle, its trunk riddled with holes where squirrels or maybe woodpeckers nested. The tree was only a stone's throw from the brush on the riverbank in which we'd hidden the canoe, and I caught Mose's eye, and we exchanged a look of concern.

"There she is, boys. Been meaning to take her down for a while. Looks like today's the day."

The morning air was fresh and smelled of blooming wood lily and wild rose and prairie smoke, which had all taken root in the fallow between the orchard and the river. It was going to be a hot day, I could tell, and the idea of spending hours cutting down a tree and splitting it into pieces small enough to feed a stove or a still fire wasn't particularly enticing. But the beauty of the day itself and the mood of the pig scarer helped. Sweating in Hector Bledsoe's hayfields wouldn't have been half the hell it was if the man himself had been anything but a bastard. The pig scarer was downright jovial that day, and it made a difference.

Before he and Mose set to work cutting down the cottonwood, he walked around the base of the trunk, as if taking its measure. On the side that faced the river, he knelt and said, "Son of a gun." He reached down and pulled something from the ground, then held it out in his hand so that we could see.

"A toadstool?" I said.

He shook his head. "A morel, tastiest mushroom there is. Been a long while since I went hunting morels. Here," he said to me. "Take this and go see if you can find any more along the river."

It was brown, four inches long, and looked like the ratty cap some gnome might wear in a Grimms' fairy tale. It didn't look appetizing in the least, but I was a whole lot more interested in locating mushrooms than in working up a sweat on that old cottonwood.

"You find 'em," the pig scarer said, "you bring 'em back here directly." He winked at me with his one good eye. "I know what you're thinking, that you're getting out of the hard work. There'll be plenty waiting for you when you get back, I guarantee it."

I walked away. At my back I heard the saw teeth begin to bite into the cottonwood.

I went slowly among the trees on the riverbank, looking closely at the ground and all the wild things that grew there. I found several more of the odd-looking mushrooms. The river curved around the edge of the orchard, and very soon I was completely out of sight of the pig scarer and Mose. I was intent on my mission, eyes to the earth, when I looked up and realized I wasn't far from the lone oak tree where the pig scarer had knelt the night before and had wept his heart out. I glanced back to be sure I couldn't be seen and ran to the oak.

What I found was a little graveyard, a family burial plot. I'd seen them before in rural areas, where the laws that governed interment didn't reach or were ignored. Some that I'd seen had fences around them, but not this one. There were a number of wooden grave makers, upright plaques so bleached by the sun and weathered that whatever had once been written on them was now obliterated. There were also three graves with no markers whatsoever, but they were clearly outlined by wild clover. I stood there thinking that probably I was looking at the pig scarer's family, those who'd come before him and had maybe first tilled the soil. Because he was the only one at the farm, I wondered if he might be the last of them, the end of the line. I considered our one-eyed Jack, and how lonely it must feel believing that you're all alone, with no one to remember or grieve for you when you're gone. I had Albert and Mose, and now Emmy. The pig scarer seemed to have no one.

Still, those three unmarked graves gave me pause, especially coupled with the fury evident in the torn-up attic room, and I left the little cemetery full of unsettlingly dark speculation.

When I returned with my hands cupped full of morels, I found the cottonwood had been felled and Mose and the pig scarer were taking a break from their labors, sitting atop the trunk, which was prone on the ground. They had their shirts off, and their skin was glistening with sweat. The pig scarer was smiling, as if he loved the work. And, oddly, so was Mose.

"The hunter home from the hill," the pig scarer declared exuberantly, and when he saw the mushrooms, he clapped me on the back and said, "A fine haul, boy. This'll spice up our chicken dinner tonight real swell. Put them under the wood cart and get ready to sweat."

They'd already sawed several sections off the trunk, and the pig scarer put me to work lifting those sections and loading them on the cart. They were heavy and the labor was hard, and while I was at it, Mose and the pig scarer continued working the saw.

We took another break, and the pig scarer said, "You got a name?"

"Buck," I said.

"How about our mute friend?"

I looked at Mose. He spelled out in sign, *Geronimo.*

The pig scarer laughed when I told him.

"Sure it is," he said. "What tribe?"

"Sioux," I said.

"Let me show you boys something." He took a pocketknife from his overalls, cut a slender branch from the cottonwood, and showed us the cut end. "See that star in there?"

He was right. At the heart of the branch was a dark, five-pointed star.

"Your people have a story about this," he said to Mose. "They say that all the stars in the sky are actually made inside the earth. Then they seek out the roots of cottonwood trees and slip into the wood, where they wait, real patient. Inside the cottonwood, they're dull and lightless, like you see here. Then, when the great spirit of the night sky decides that more stars are needed, he shakes the branches with his wind and releases the stars. They fly up and settle in the sky, where they shine and sparkle and become the luminous creations they were always meant to be." He looked at the star in that cottonwood branch with a kind of reverence. "And we're like that, too. Dreams shook loose. You boys and me and everybody else on God's earth. Your people, Geronimo, they got a lot of wisdom in 'em."

Mose smiled as broadly as I'd ever seen.

"You didn't like the story?" the pig scarer asked me, because I wasn't smiling like Mose.

"It's fine, I guess," I said.

"You like it here, Buck?"

"It's hard work."

"Let me see your hands." He studied the calluses on my palms. "You're used to hard work."

"Doesn't mean I like it."

"Everything's hard work, Buck. You don't wrap your thinking around that, life'll kill you for sure. Me, I love this land, the work. Never was a churchgoer. God all penned up under a roof? I don't think so. Ask me, God's right here. In the dirt, the rain, the sky, the trees, the apples, the stars in the cottonwoods. In you and me, too. It's all connected and it's all God. Sure this is hard work, but it's good work because it's a part of what connects us to this land, Buck. This beautiful, tender land."

"This land spawned a tornado that killed Emmy's mother. You call that tender?"

"Tragic, that's what I call it. But don't blame the land. The land's what it's always been, and tornadoes have been a part of that from the beginning. Drought, too, and grasshoppers and hail and wildfire and everything that's ever driven folks off or killed 'em. The land is what it is. Life is what it is. God is what God is. You and me, we're what we are. None of it's perfect. Or, hell, maybe it all is and we're just not wise enough to see it."

"Those orchard trees were in pretty bad shape before we got here. You love this land so much, why'd you let them go to hell?"

"Failed 'em, Buck, plain and simple. Failed 'em. That's on me. But finding all of you in that old potting shed has proved to be a blessing, and I feel refreshed."

I wondered if this was the same man who'd nailed the window shut in Emmy's room and had shattered the liquor bottle against the barn wall and had cried his heart out under the oak tree. In a way, he was just like this land he loved, killer tornado one minute, blue sky the next. I wondered if it was the alcohol that caused the changes. Or was it just who he was and had always been, and maybe that was why Aggie had left him. If, in fact, that's what she'd done.

"Tell you what, Buck," he said. "If you need a break, cart that wood to the barn. There's a chopping block near the potting shed. You've seen it. Dump those sections, and before you come back, fill the wooden bucket at the pump with water and haul it here. I'm feeling a little parched. Think you can do that?"

"I can do it," I said.

"What do you think, Geronimo?"

Mose smiled and gave a nod.

"Don't dawdle, Buck. Work to be done. And I want a report on how things are coming along at the still, too."

I put the morels into the cart, but when I grabbed hold of the handles, I could have sworn I was lifting five hundred pounds. I threw all my weight into the effort and the cart began to roll.

I dumped the wood at the chopping block next to the shed, grabbed the morels I'd collected, and went inside the barn to check on Albert's progress with the still.

There was something in my brother that compelled him to do a job right, whatever that job was. The little still he'd built for the pig scarer — copper cooker and coils of copper tubing — was a thing of shining beauty. At the lower end of the coiled copper, which was called the worm, sat a clean, half-gallon glass milk bottle collecting the hooch as it dripped.

Emmy was with Albert. She wore a different dress that day, a little blue jumper. She knelt in front of the small, open furnace beneath the cooker, her face aglow from the flames there.

"I get to put the wood in, Odie," she said.

I asked my brother how it was going.

He nodded toward the milk bottle, which was already half-filled. "Clockwork. How's it going out there?"

I told him about the graveyard I'd found and about how Mose and I had followed the pig scarer there the night before.

"I don't know what to think, Albert. I kind of like him, but there's something scary about him, too."

Emmy said, "He's nice to me, but I wish

he'd let me stay out here with you."

"I wish he'd feed us more," I said.

"He doesn't have much food," Emmy said. "He doesn't eat any more than we do."

"He's got our money. He should spend a little of it and stock his cupboards."

"Maybe he's not spending it because it's our money," Albert said.

Which, if true, made me inclined to like the pig scarer even more. So much so that I decided I was ready to stop thinking of him as the pig scarer. From now on, he would be Jack.

I left the barn, set the morels on the doorstep of the farmhouse, and filled the wooden water bucket, but I didn't take it immediately back to where Jack and Mose were at work on the cottonwood tree. My conversation with Albert and Emmy had got me to thinking. I wondered what Jack had done with the pillowcase full of the things we'd taken from the Brickmans' safe. I set the bucket beside the front door of the farmhouse, slipped inside, and stood a moment, thinking. If I wanted to hide something from us, where would I put it?

First, I checked Jack's bedroom, which had no closet, so the only two possibilities were the chest of drawers and under the bed. Nothing. I didn't bother with Emmy's room. I opened the kitchen cupboards, looked under and in back of the furniture in the living area, and finally eyed the ladder leading up to where the shredded mattress lay with the stuffing spilled out like entrails. I had a visceral reaction to the idea of going up there again, a sick twisting of my stomach. But I wanted to find that pillowcase, so up the ladder I went.

The curtain still cut off the area that held the bed and mattress and chamber pot. I rummaged through the items stored in the other part of the attic room, which included a shipping trunk of wood and leather. I lifted the lid and found a handmade quilt, carefully folded, a wedding dress, also folded and put away with great care, a Bible, a pair of bronzed baby shoes, and other mementos from the past. Digging deeper, I came across an army uniform and with it a framed photograph. Two men in military dress stood in front of a barracks. One of them was Jack, before he'd lost his eye fighting the Kaiser. The other appeared to be the same age. They were both smiling, and Jack had his arm around the other man, in the way of friends. Along the bottom of the photograph, written in white ink, were the words *Death before dishonor. Rudy.* Which reminded me a little bit of Herman Volz's vow when we'd parted: *I defend your honor and mine to the death.*

I put everything back in the trunk, closed the lid, and finally pulled the curtain aside.

There was the mattress still on the floor

like an animal eviscerated. I looked the area over carefully but could see nothing that might hide the pillowcase and its contents. The longer I stood there looking, the greater the belief I had that something terrible had occurred here, something frightening. I stumbled back and hurried down the ladder, fleeing that cursed place. At the bottom of the ladder, I stood awhile to settle myself.

That's when my eye was caught. In one corner of the kitchen, the boards rose just a hair above the rest of the flooring. I knelt and pried up the cover of a small larder, a little hole beneath the house meant to keep food stored and cool. It contained no food, but the pillowcase was there, along with the blankets and the water bag Volz had given us. I checked the pillowcase. The letters and documents and the bound book were still inside, but the money was gone, all of it. That didn't surprise me. If I were Jack, I'd probably have snatched the cash in a heartbeat, too. But I was surprised to see Brickman's gun. I'm not sure what possessed me — maybe it was the result of having just come from that upper room full of the evidence of rampage — but I grabbed the pistol, dropped the pillowcase back into the larder, and closed the lid. I went quickly to the barn, shielding the weapon from Albert and Emmy as I entered. I put it in the tack room under the hay matting, next to the wire I'd fashioned for escape. I hurried back outside, grabbed the water bucket, put it in the wood cart, and returned to the Gilead and the felled cottonwood.

CHAPTER TWENTY

That evening began with a celebration. Jack invited us into the house and we sat at the little table, just like family. We ate roasted chicken, along with the morels I'd gathered and Jack had sliced and sautéed in butter. I swore they were the best things I'd ever tasted. There was, of course, liquor. Jack poured the clear corn whiskey from one of the half-gallon milk bottles into his glass and sipped as he ate and talked and laughed.

"Been a long time since there was laughter in this house," he said. "Norman, you've done a hell of a job with that still in the barn. Geronimo, I never saw any man work harder or better than you did today. Emmaline, I thank you for cleaning up this place and for letting sunshine back in. And, Buck?" He studied me with his one good eye. I wondered what he would say. I hadn't worked as hard as Mose or created anything like Albert's marvelous little still or given him the kind of comfort Emmy seemed to offer. "Thank you for bringing music back into my life. You and that harmonica, you've saved me."

Jack talked, talked a blue streak, talked like someone who'd been shut up in his own quiet room way too long. Despite the camaraderie, his shotgun was near at hand. After supper, we gathered the dishes and washed them while Jack drank his corn liquor, and then he said, "Buck, pull out that harmonica of yours and let's have a little hoedown in the barn."

He grabbed his fiddle and shotgun and told Emmy to bring the milk bottle, and we all moseyed across the farmyard. The sun, which was the color of a blood orange, hung nailed above the horizon, and long bars of red light came through the gaps in the old barn walls and lay on the brown dirt floor like little streams of hot lava.

"Geronimo, bring us a couple of those bales of hay and set 'em here. Buck, you take one, I'll take the other. Norman, are you and Emmaline in a mood to kick up your heels?"

My brother didn't reply, but Emmy cried, "I like to dance."

"Well then, girl, you just dance your little heart out."

We played a bunch of old folk tunes my father had taught me or that I'd learned from a songbook my mother had given me on my sixth birthday, which was not long before she died. Emmy danced joyfully, and Mose joined her, reeling himself wildly. They came to-

239

gether and then apart like spinning tops, sending dust swirling into the air. Albert stood by, and although he didn't dance, he kept time to the tunes with claps of his hands. Between numbers, Jack drank his liquor, and beads of sweat formed on his brow and more and more his eye took on a fevered look.

It was almost dark and the light was nearly gone from the barn when Jack said, "Let's play 'Red River Valley.' "

"You sure?" I said.

He glowered at me. "Just do what I say."

And there it was again. Blue sky one moment, the threat of a tornado the next.

He took a long swallow from his milk bottle, then set it in the dirt beside his hay bale. He snatched up his bow, nestled the fiddle beneath his chin, and gave me a nod.

We began to play the slowest, saddest tune of the evening. Emmy sat in the dirt of the barn floor, and Mose sat with her. Albert stood leaning against a wall. I could barely see the corners of the barn now, the light was so dim. But I could see Jack's face as he played. His eye was closed, but that didn't keep the tears from rolling down his cheek. When we finished, he was quiet for a long while, with the fiddle still beneath his chin. He finally opened his eye and stared where Emmy sat in the gloom of the barn.

"You like that one, Sophie?" he asked.

"I'm Emmaline."

Which seemed to startle him. "I know you're Emmaline, goddamn it." For a moment, I thought he might throw his fiddle at her. "Evening's over." He grabbed his shotgun, which had been leaning against his hay bale the whole while, and stood. "Pick up that bottle, girl. You boys, back in the tack room. Now!"

Emmy hurried to do as he'd asked. I put my harmonica in my pocket and started toward the tack room, then I heard the soft thud of the milk bottle and turned back. Jack and Emmy stood together, looking down where the bottle lay on its side, its contents making mud of the dirt on the barn floor.

"Goddamn it!" Jack screamed. "Goddamn it to hell, girl! Look what you done."

"I'm sorry," Emmy said. "It's dark. I can't see."

"Excuses," he said. He grabbed her arm. "We'll see about excuses."

"Let her go," Albert said.

"Shut your trap, boy."

"Let her go," Albert said again, standing straight and tall, blocking the door to the barn.

Jack did let her go, but only to take his shotgun in both hands and level the barrel on Albert. "Move aside, boy."

"Promise me you won't hurt her."

I saw Mose edging toward the workbench where the tools and such were kept. Out of his one good eye, Jack saw him, too.

"Hold it right there, Indian."

Mose stopped. But now I turned and began to walk.

"You, Buck, where you going?"

"The tack room, just like you said."

Jack gave a snort. "One of you knows what's good for him anyway."

Inside the tack room, I grabbed the gun from where I'd hidden it under the loose straw that morning, and I stood in the doorway. I didn't think Jack could see what I held in my trembling hands.

"Move," Jack ordered Albert. "Move, boy, or I swear you won't live to regret it."

"Emmy," I said. "Step away from him."

Jack turned his good eye my way, which meant he couldn't really watch Emmy, and she ran quickly to Mose, who put himself between her and the shotgun.

"Mutiny," Jack said. "I take you in. I feed you. And what do you do? You turn on me. Every one of you."

"We're leaving," Albert said.

"Like hell," Jack said.

And looking at that shotgun, I also thought, *Like hell.*

"Don't push me, boy," Jack warned. He brought the shotgun up and nestled the stock against his shoulder, and he and Albert stared at each other and there was not a sound to be heard in the whole world.

Move, Albert, I wanted to cry. Because I knew, knew absolutely, that Jack would carry through with his threat. There was something in him, some monstrous rage, and because of that mattress lying shredded in the upper room of the farmhouse, I'd already seen the evidence of what it could do.

I didn't think. I just pulled the trigger. The sound of the gunshot shattered the evening into a million pieces.

Emmy screamed, and Jack dropped in a heap to the barn floor.

Loss comes in every moment. Second by second our lives are stolen from us. What is past will never come again.

I'd killed Vincent DiMarco, which had done something to me that could not be undone. But if you asked me, even to this day, I would tell you that I've never been sorry he was dead. Jack was different. I knew it wasn't his fault, the rage inside him. I'd seen a different Jack, a Jack I liked and, who knows, given time and other circumstances, a Jack I might have been happy to call my friend. Shooting him was like shooting an animal with rabies. It had to be done. But when I pulled that trigger, I lost something of myself, something even more significant than when I'd killed DiMarco, something I think of now as a sliver of my soul. And in the moment after, I sat down hard in the dirt of the barn floor, done in by regret.

Albert bent over Jack, then looked up at Mose and said, "Right through his heart, looks like." He walked to me, but I barely felt his hand on my shoulder. "We need to go, Odie."

He helped me up and walked me outside, where Emmy and Mose were already waiting. Emmy hugged me and put her cheek against my chest.

"Your heart, Odie," she said. "It's beating like a wild bird all caged up."

I saw Mose sign to Albert, *Money?*

"Gone," I said. My voice sounded somehow separate from me, as if someone else were speaking.

I told them about the pillowcase in the larder, and Albert and Mose went together into the house to fetch it. My strength failed me again, and I had to sit down in the dimness of the farmyard. I looked at my hands, empty now, and wondered, distantly, what had become of the gun.

Albert and Mose came from the farmhouse with the pillowcase, the water bag, and the blankets Volz had given us, and also the clothing Emmy had worn when we first came there.

"Looked everywhere," Albert said. "Couldn't find the money. Maybe he's already spent it. We need to be moving."

We made our way through the orchard with

the moon on the rise, walking among the trees we'd tended, across the grass Mose had trimmed with his scythe. We'd put something of ourselves into the soil and into what grew there, even if only briefly, and I felt a kinship with it and remembered how Jack, in speaking of it, had called it tender. Although I'd done a terrible thing that night, and maybe Jack had done terrible things, too, I understood that the land was not to blame. I tried to take it a step further, to feel God there, all around me, as Jack had. But my heart wasn't in it. I felt only loss, only emptiness.

Mose and Albert pulled the canoe from its hiding place among the brush and set it on the water of the Gilead. I was still dazed, and Emmy helped me in and took the place in front of me. Mose stepped into the bow, Albert into the stern, and we glided off. I could see the course of the river before us, milk white in the moonlight. I heard the plop of something heavy hit the water near the back of the canoe. I didn't have to ask what it was Albert had thrown there.

And so we moved on, heading toward what I hoped, though more and more dimly, might be the new life I'd so desperately imagined for us.

■ ■ ■ ■

- PART THREE -
HIGH HEAVEN

■ ■ ■ ■

CHAPTER TWENTY-ONE

From the height of a certain wisdom acquired across many decades, I look down now on those four children traveling a meandering river whose end was unknown to them. Even across the distance of time, I hurt for them and pray for them still. Our former selves are never dead. We speak to them, arguing against decisions we know will bring only unhappiness, offering consolation and hope, even though they cannot hear. "Albert," I whisper, "stay clearheaded. Mose, stay strong. Emmy, hold to the truth of your visions. And, Odie, Odie, do not be afraid. I am here, waiting patiently for you on the banks of the Gilead."

Only ten days had passed since we'd fled Lincoln School, but already it felt like forever. The weather turned and we drifted under gray skies. We spoke little, hoped less. The memory of what we'd left behind us, which so far was mostly death and despair, felt like a heavy, dragging anchor, and because we couldn't find the strength on our own, the river moved us forward at a crawl.

The second night after we'd left Jack's place, we camped near enough a little town that we could hear the music of a dance. Fiddles, guitars, an accordion. I longed to haul out my harmonica and play, join in the tunes that I knew were lifting the spirits of those in the hall — American Legion? Elks? Church annex? But we'd left a dead man behind us, and for fear that we'd be discovered, Albert forbade me to play anything.

He'd gone into the town near dark and had come back with a ham bone that still had some meat on it and a bunch of potato and carrot peelings, all of which he'd found wrapped in a newspaper in a garbage can behind a café. He also returned with a rip in his shirtsleeve courtesy of a bony-looking mongrel lurking near the garbage can who was just as hungry as we were. It wasn't much of a meal, and we gave the lion's share to Emmy. Turned out we were the headlines in the newspaper that had been used as wrapping, but not, thank goodness, for what had happened at Jack's farm. As near as we could tell, that crime hadn't yet been discovered. The newspaper was the *Mankato Daily Free Press,* published in the city to the east, the direction the Gilead was taking us. This was the headline: THEFT AND KIDNAPPING! NOW MURDER?

Albert read the story to us aloud. They'd found Vincent DiMarco's body at the bottom of the cliff in the quarry. Because they'd discovered a still near the quarry, which the authorities believed DiMarco had been operating, Sheriff Warford had initially thought the man might have been drunk and stumbled off the cliff edge. But because the official autopsy had revealed no alcohol in DiMarco's blood and because DiMarco had been missing since the night of the kidnapping and robbery, the sheriff's thinking had turned toward murder. Near the end of the article was a paragraph about Billy Red Sleeve. It said that in the search of the quarry following the discovery of DiMarco's body, the body of the missing Indian boy had also been found. That was it. No further explanation. Just a dead Indian kid.

"At least his family won't be wondering now," I said.

"They blamed Volz's still on DiMarco," Albert pointed out. "That's got to be Brickman's doing, keeping his hands clean."

"And Volz out of it," I added, feeling greatly relieved.

Still no mention of us, Mose signed, indicating himself and Albert and me.

"I don't know why," Albert said, shaking his head. "But it's lucky for us." He reached into the pillowcase and brought out an old seed cap, one that I'd seen Jack wear sometimes. I figured Albert had grabbed it along with everything else. Always thinking ahead. He adjusted the strap in back and handed it to Emmy.

"Wear that from now on," he said.

"Why?" she asked.

"Jack recognized you from the newspaper picture. Somebody else will, too. Keep that bill pulled down low to hide your face whenever other folks are around."

That night, little Emmy lay in Mose's arms and cried and cried, and when we asked her why, she couldn't say exactly, except that she felt all alone. I thought I understood, because I still remembered my first few weeks at Lincoln School, when it seemed like Albert and I had lost everything. I cried a lot then, mostly at night, like so many of the other kids. We were afraid, sure, but that was only part of it. We were also grieving, but that, too, was only part of it. There is a deeper hurt than anything sustained by the body, and it's the wounding of the soul. It's the feeling that you've been abandoned by everyone, even God. It's the most alone you'll ever be. A wounded body heals itself, but there is a scar. Watching Emmy weep in Mose's strong arms, I thought the same must be true for a soul. There was a thick scar on my heart now, but the wound to Emmy's heart was still so recent that it hadn't begun to heal. I watched as Mose signed on her palm again and again, *Not alone. Not alone.*

We camped the next night in a hollow, a place where no lights were visible to us and we believed we were hidden from the eyes of others. Albert decided we could risk a fire. We gathered branches that had fallen from the cottonwoods and other trees along the riverbank, and Albert, who'd taken to heart every lesson he'd learned from the Boy Scout manual, put the branches artfully together and struck a flame. There is something about a fire on a dark night, a fire shared with others, that pulls the gloom right out of you. We sat around the cheery little blaze with the branches popping as they burned and the flames dancing, and although we hadn't eaten that day, I could feel our spirits rise along with the smoke that drifted toward the stars. It felt like forever since any of us had laughed or even smiled, and it was good to see on the faces of the others a look not necessarily of joy but certainly of release and comfort.

"Play a song for us, Odie," Emmy said.

I glanced at Albert, and he nodded.

For the first time since we'd left Jack dead in the barn, I pulled out my harmonica and began to play. I chose "The Yellow Rose of Texas," because it was lively and everyone knew the words. Albert and Emmy sang along, and Mose did a graceful ballet with his fingers.

I said, "This one's for Mose," and I played

"Take Me Out to the Ball Game." He smiled big and, when the song was done, signed, *Miss the smell of a leather glove.*

"There's baseball in your future yet," Albert said.

Emmy clapped her hands together. "You'll be a famous ballplayer someday, Mose. I can see it."

Mose shook his head and signed, *Just happy to be free.*

Emmy said, "Will you play 'Shenandoah,' Odie?"

I wanted to keep the music light, but I knew the song was special to her because it had been special to her mother. So I put the harmonica to my lips and blew that sad, beautiful tune. We were quiet afterward, staring into the fire, lost in our thoughts.

"Know what I want?" Emmy said suddenly. She looked from Mose to Albert to me. "I want to sit with you around a fire like this every night until I die."

Mose grinned and signed, *Burn up all the wood in the world.*

"And just think about that smoke, Emmy," Albert said, laughing. "It would cloud up the whole sky."

A voice came to us from beyond the firelight. "Indians believe the smoke carries their prayers to heaven."

The man materialized out of the dark, big

and powerful, shoulders like those of a buffalo, with hair like a buffalo's winter hide flowing over them. He wore an old black cowboy hat, a snap-button shirt, dirty Levi's, and scuffed, pointed-toe boots. He looked as if he'd just walked away from a cattle drive, except for the fact that he was clearly Indian. He stood at the edge of the firelight, a burlap bag slung over his shoulder, his eyes unreadable.

"Heard the music. Mind if I join you?"

Emmy scooted against Mose, who put his arm around her. Albert stood up in a challenging way and stared the man down. I glanced around, looking for something to use as a weapon, and finally settled on a big cottonwood limb that was just within reach, if it came to that.

"Don't know if you're hungry," the man said. "But I got these to cook up, if you'll let me use your fire." He reached into his burlap bag and pulled out two catfish wrapped in newspaper. "Be glad to share 'em."

It sounded like a friendly offer, but having just escaped Jack's captivity, I wasn't at all eager to welcome a stranger into the warm glow of our fire. On the other hand, we'd had almost nothing to eat for the last two days. I'd thought many times about the two five-dollar bills that lined the inside of my right boot and using it to buy food, but Emmy, on the night she'd come to me and had spoken trancelike, had said I'd know when the time was right to pull them out, and I didn't feel that yet. So the idea of a meal of hot, tasty catfish was tantalizing.

Albert finally gave a nod.

The Indian plucked two straight, sturdy sticks from the bundle we'd put together to feed our fire. He took the catfish, which he'd already cleaned and scaled, threaded a stick down the mouth of each, and jammed the sticks into the ground, so that the fish were angled over the flames and the coals. Then he sat down on the far side of the fire.

"Young to be out on your own," he said. "But then, I been on my own since I was thirteen."

"Are you a cowboy?" I asked.

"Was. Been running cattle for a man in South Dakota. Nobody's paying for cows right now, so I got let go. Decided to come back home."

"Where's home?" I asked.

He opened his arms. "Here."

"Right here?" I tapped the ground.

"Yep. And back that way and down that way, too." He pointed both directions along the Gilead. "This was all my land and the land of my fellow Sioux. We don't have papers saying so. But we never sold it. It just got took."

He eyed Mose with particular interest and spoke to him in a language I didn't understand. From the look on Mose's face, it was clear he didn't understand either. But Emmy answered, "Yes."

The Indian's eyes grew big and he smiled. He spoke again in that odd language, and Emmy replied in kind.

The Indian saw us boys gawking. He pointed to Mose. "I asked your friend there if he was Sioux. Then I asked the little girl how it is she understands my language. She told me she's got Sioux blood in her."

"I didn't know you could speak Sioux," I said to Emmy.

"Daddy taught me. But nobody would let me use it at Lincoln School. You remember that rule, Odie."

I did. I remembered, too, the strappings and the nights in the quiet room meted out to those children who forgot it.

With the ice fully broken, I asked the Indian a question that had troubled me since he first appeared. "Where's your pole?"

"Pole?"

"Fishing pole." I nodded toward the catfish roasting over the fire.

"Didn't catch them with no pole and hook. I noodled 'em."

"Noodled?"

"You know." He wiggled his fingers. "Dumb catfish, they think these are worms. When they bite, I just grab 'em."

It sounded dangerous, and I couldn't help

257

thinking of Herman Volz and his four and a half fingers. But the Indian had a full set of digits on each hand.

Emmy still sat close to Mose, though not under the protection of his arm anymore. Since they'd conversed in Sioux, her fear of the Indian seemed to have vanished. She spoke to him again in that language and he answered.

"She asked me what my name is," he translated for us. "I told her it's Hawk Flies at Night. But most folks call me Forrest."

"Why?" I asked.

"That's the name on my white man's birth certificate."

"You have two names?"

"More'n that. So what names do you all go by?"

"Emmy," Emmy said immediately.

Albert and I both gave her a sharp look, but it was too late to undo any damage her naïve truthfulness might have done.

"Buck," I said.

"Norman," Albert said.

"And what about you?" he asked Mose.

Mose signed his name.

"Mute?" the Indian asked.

"Somebody cut out his tongue," Emmy said. "When he was real little. His name's Mose."

The Indian tipped back his cowboy hat and shook his head. "There's no end to the cruelty in this world, and no matter how far down you reach, no bottom. But you got one thing going for you, Mose. You're Sioux. There's good, noble blood running through your veins. Don't let anyone ever tell you different."

Forrest had salt and pepper in his burlap bag, and he seasoned the catfish when they were done cooking. With a pocketknife, he cut off pieces and gave some to each of us, cautioning us to watch for bones. We ate like there was no tomorrow, and Forrest seemed to take pleasure in that. In the end, I realized he'd eaten only a little himself, giving most of the meat to us.

"Mind playing that mouth organ some more, Buck?" he said.

I took out my harmonica and launched into "Buffalo Gals," maybe because Forrest had from the very first reminded me of that great beast of the plains. Then I played "Comin' Round the Mountain," and the others, including Forrest, joined in. We were laughing, having ourselves a high time. I was considering what my third number might be when Forrest reached into his burlap bag and brought out a mason jar filled with clear liquid. He unscrewed the lid and took a slug. Then he set the jar down on the ground beside him.

Hooch. It had never bothered me much before, but after our encounter with Jack, its sudden appearance was disconcerting. I could see a wariness come into the faces of the others as well.

"How about 'Leaving Cheyenne'?" Forrest said. "Knew a cowpoke out of Oklahoma could play that on his guitar and sing it so it broke your heart."

I put my harmonica to my lips, and Forrest put the mason jar to his.

He didn't get drunk, didn't turn mean, not the way Jack did. Mostly, he got more talkative. Finally, he dropped the bomb on us.

"You boys got a price on your heads, you know that? Five hundred dollars."

He gauged our reactions, and whatever the look was on our faces, it seemed to amuse him. He laughed and reached into his burlap sack. I tensed and saw that Albert and Mose had both gone rigid, ready to launch themselves.

What Forrest brought out was that day's issue of *The Minneapolis Star*. He handed it across the fire to Albert, and we looked over his shoulder. Emmy's kidnapping had made the front page again, with another photograph of her. This time it was a story of the reward the Brickmans were offering for any information about the men who'd taken her. The information was to come directly to Thelma or Clyde Brickman, no questions asked.

"Yeah, I know who you are. But don't worry. See this?" Forrest pointed toward the shaggy hair sticking out from under his cowboy hat. "When I was a child, there was a bounty on this, too, just cuz I was Sioux. I got to admit, when I read the stories, I was afraid for Emmaline there, just like everybody else. But I can see she's in no danger. Newspapers," he said with disgust. "Anything to sell a few copies." He took another pull off the contents of the mason jar. "Got to hand it to you. You've sure made monkeys out of a lot of cops."

"Billy the Kid," I said.

"What's that?" Forrest said.

"We're just like Billy the Kid. Desperadoes."

"Desperadoes," Forrest agreed and toasted us.

Albert, who'd turned quiet and dark, said it was late; we needed sleep. Forrest screwed the lid back on the mason jar and returned the hooch to the burlap bag. He took out a rolled blanket and spread it on the far side of the fire. It wasn't long before I could hear the deep, sonorous breathing of the Indian, mixed with an occasional snore.

Mose and Emmy bedded down together on a blanket, Mose with his arm over the little girl. I'd laid myself down beside Albert. I was bone tired but feeling pretty good. The tasty catfish. The music. And the fame. Just like Billy the Kid.

Before I went to sleep I glanced at my brother. Albert lay very still, his eyes wide open, staring up at the waning moon like a man long dead.

CHAPTER TWENTY-TWO

The touch on my arm woke me.

At Lincoln School, because we all knew about DiMarco's proclivities where children were concerned, we slept lightly, and an unexpected touch in the night was an alarm. My eyes shot open and I tried to rise, but I found myself pinned to the ground. When I opened my mouth, a hand clamped itself there to stifle my scream.

In the dim moonlight above me, I saw Albert and Mose. Albert had a finger to his lips, warning me to be quiet. When it was clear that I was fully awake, Mose let me go. Albert signaled for me to get up. He grabbed the blanket I'd been sleeping on and signed, *Follow us.* Mose handed me my boots.

Red coals still glowed among the ashes of the fire, and on the far side, the Indian still lay breathing deeply. We crept past him down to the river, where the canoe was already in the water and Emmy was waiting. Albert folded the blanket we'd slept on and put it with the other in the center of the canoe. The pillowcase and canvas water bag were there, too. Mose held the canoe while the rest of us got in, then he stepped into the stern, shoved us off, and we arrowed down the Gilead.

I didn't know the why of it. As Mose and Albert dipped the paddles, I tried to figure what it was that had motivated my brother to sneak us off that way. I liked Forrest. He'd been decent and had seemed not that different from us, a man drifting before the wind of circumstance. Was it the hooch? Was Albert afraid of a repeat of Jack?

I waited until we were well away from our night's camp to risk speaking.

"What are we doing, Albert?" I kept my voice low.

"Putting distance between us and Hawk Flies at Night."

"Why?"

"He was going to turn us in."

"How do you know?"

"That mason jar full of bootlegged liquor."

"What about it?"

"It was square."

"So?"

"You ever seen a square mason jar?"

It wasn't something I'd thought much about, but I did now. "I guess not."

"Me neither, until Brickman strong-armed me and Herman Volz into cooking mash for him. He bought special square mason jars to put the hooch in. Said they packed better if they were square."

"Forrest got his booze from Brickman?"

"That's what I'm saying."

"And he was going to turn us in for the reward?"

"What do you think? Would you throw away five hundred dollars?"

Emmy curled herself up and went to sleep. Mose and Albert paddled through the night. Occasionally in the distance, I could see an isolated glimmer, maybe the yard light of a farmhouse. I figured Albert was right. Five hundred dollars was a lot of money, but I'd have given every cent of it to be safe in one of those houses. To be in a place I called home.

In the late afternoon, we stopped. We'd put a lot of distance between us and Forrest. Mose and Albert were beat. We sat on a little hill above the river, where a great, solitary sycamore provided shade. The hill rose out of prairie and afforded a view of the whole area. The railroad bed had veered away from the river. There were no farmhouses near, no barns, no fences, nothing tainted by a clumsy human hand. For as far as the eye could see there was only high grass and wildflowers, bending like dancers to some tune they heard in the wind, and above us a stately canopy of white sycamore branches and green leaves.

Beautiful, Mose signed languidly. *Let's stay*

265

here awhile.

"How about forever?" I said.

"We could build a house," Emmy said. "We could live in it together."

Mose signed, *Albert could build it. Albert can build anything.*

"We're not staying here," Albert said. "We're going to Saint Louis."

I remembered Saint Louis, but only barely. We'd visited there once after my mother died, but we never went back.

Mose signed, *What's in Saint Louis?*

"Home," Albert said. "Maybe."

He reached into the pillowcase and brought out one of the stacks of letters that he'd thrown in with everything else. They were still bound with twine, but not tied with the simple shoestring knot that Brickman had used. It was a slippery eight loop, a complicated knot, which could be easily loosened or tightened without untying, one we'd learned in Boy Scouts. I didn't know when he'd done it, but Albert had gone through the letters. He loosened the knot, slipped out the top letter, and handed it to me. It was addressed to Superintendent, Lincoln Indian Training School.

"Read it," Albert said.

I pulled the letter from its envelope.

Dear Sir or Madam,
I have recently become aware that there

266

are two boys in your care at the Lincoln Indian Training School whose surname is O'Banion. The older is Albert, who has attained his fourteenth birthday. The other boy generally goes by Odie and is four years younger than his brother. I haven't the means to care for these boys, but I would like from time to time to send some money. These amounts should be used to supply the boys with whatever they need, items for which the school is not responsible but that may make their time in your care a little easier.

For reasons of my own, I don't want the boys to know the source of this money. Enclosed you will find $20.

God bless you for the good work you are doing on behalf of all the children in your care.

The letter wasn't signed. I read it again, then stared at Albert. "Aunt Julia?"

He nodded. "Aunt Julia."

"The Brickmans told us she was dead."

"Look at the postmark."

There was no return address, but I studied the printing of the faded red cancellation stamp. I made out SAINT LOUIS and a date. "She sent it two years ago."

"A long time after the Brickmans told us she died."

I reached eagerly for the stack of letters.

267

"Are there others?"

"Just that one."

"What happened to them? She said she'd send money from time to time."

"I don't know," Albert said. "But this one's enough for me. I wasn't sure where we were going when we started out. Now I know."

Mose signed, *Home for all of us?*

Albert said, "We're family, aren't we?"

We decided to stay the night on the hill, that little island of peace rising out of an ocean of prairie, safe under the wide-spread boughs of the sycamore.

I'd begun to have trouble sleeping. It had started after I shot Jack. Sometimes I couldn't go to sleep, or if I did, I woke from nightmares set in the prison that had been Jack's barn. In those terrible dreams, he would open his one good eye and stare up at me accusingly from the dirt of the barn floor. I would try to tell him I was sorry, so very sorry, but it was as if my mouth was wired shut, and in my struggle to sleep, I woke myself.

That night I hadn't been able to fall asleep. I lay staring up at the sycamore branches, which formed a kind of roof above us, my stomach empty, complaining, and I kept thinking, *Home.* Which was something I'd never known, not really. Before Lincoln School, we'd lived on the road, and before that in the upstairs of a house that belonged to an old woman with many cats and that I recalled only in small, disconnected pieces. Lincoln School had housed me, but it wasn't home. I tried not to get excited about Saint Louis and Aunt Julia, but that was like asking a starving kid not to salivate at the smell of hot food.

I left the others sleeping and stepped away from the sycamore tree. What I saw then was a thing of such beauty that I have never, across the eight decades of my life, forgotten it. The meadow that rolled away from the hill was alive with fireflies. For as far as I could see, the land was lit by millions of tiny, luminescing lanterns. They winked on and off and drifted in random currents, a sea of stars, an earthbound Milky Way. I have been to the top of the Eiffel Tower at night and gazed across the City of Light, but all that man-made brilliance didn't hold a candle to the miracle I witnessed on a June night along the bank of the Gilead River when I was a boy.

I felt a hand slipped into my own, and I looked down to see Emmy standing with me. Even in the dark, I could see the shine of her eyes. "I want to come back here someday, Odie."

"We will," I promised.

We stood together for a long while, hand in hand, in the midst of that miracle, and although my stomach was empty, my heart was full.

Next morning, after we loaded the canoe, my brother looked to the west and gave a low whistle.

"Red sky at morning," he said.

All along the western horizon, the sky looked like a strip of inflamed skin. Mose and Albert paddled like crazy to try to stay ahead of the weather, but they hadn't eaten since the catfish Forrest had shared nearly two days earlier, and they tired quickly. Although the clouds moved sluggishly, by late afternoon they'd overtaken us. A wind rose at our backs, and just before the storm hit, we reached the confluence of the Gilead and the much larger Minnesota River. Rain fell heavily, but we kept going, looking for a good place to pull up against the riverbank. Finally, we spotted a long spit of sand covered with bulrushes. We drew up and unloaded the canoe. Mose and Albert tipped it against a tree on the bank and hung one of the blankets as cover, and we gathered, wet and tired, under its protection.

The Minnesota was a broad river with a much faster current than the Gilead. We watched huge tree limbs carried swiftly past, only to be caught in places where the water eddied in angry, brown swirls. Wet and tired and hungry and intimidated by the fast water,

I began to wonder about the advisability of Albert's plan to follow rivers all the way to Saint Louis.

The rain continued to fall and our spirits continued to plummet. I could see weariness on the others' faces, and I felt it myself right down to my bones. Not even the promise of home could lift me up.

Night descended, and the rain finally ceased, and from somewhere out in the darkness came music and the most beautiful voice I'd ever heard.

CHAPTER TWENTY-THREE

What is it? Mose signed.

"Got me," Albert said.

"An angel." The look on Emmy's face told me she believed it.

"Whoever it is, she's got a swell voice," I said. "And just listen to that trumpet."

"Gabriel's horn," Emmy said.

"I don't know about that, but he sure knows his stuff." I looked to Albert. "We should check it out, don't you think?"

"Not all of us."

"I'm not staying here," I said.

"I want to go, too," Emmy said.

Mose signed, *All for one and one for all.*

Albert spent a moment weighing things. "All right," he said, giving in. "But we need to be careful. There's five hundred dollars on our heads. Even an angel would be tempted."

We left the sandy spit, climbed the steep riverbank, and made our way through a thin line of trees. On the other side was a railroad bed and tracks, then a broad meadow, and beyond the meadow, a town. The sky was still overcast, and the reflection of the town lights made the low clouds look like smoke above a raging fire. In the center of the meadow stood a huge tent surrounded by smaller ones. The large tent was brightly illuminated from inside, and shadows moved across the canvas walls. A number of automobiles had been parked in the meadow.

"A circus?" I said.

"You ever hear of a circus band playing religious music?" Albert said. "That's a revival."

"What's a revival?" Emmy said.

"Let's go see." I started forward.

Albert grabbed my arm. "Too risky."

A gentle wind blew out of the west. Our clothes were damp and the breeze was chilling. Emmy held herself and shivered.

Mose signed, *Emmy's cold and wet. The tent is shelter.*

"She's all over the papers," Albert said. "Someone might recognize her. Hawk Flies at Night did."

I sniffed at the air. "Do you smell that?"

"Food," Emmy said.

"Good food," I said. "I swear it's coming from that big tent."

Mose signed eagerly, *Do they feed people at revivals?*

"I don't know," Albert said.

273

"Please, Albert." Emmy looked up at him with pleading eyes. "I'm freezing. And I'm so hungry."

Emmy had put on the seed cap Albert gave her. "Pull that bill down real low," I told her. She did, and I said, "There, Albert. Can't hardly see her face at all."

My brother relented. "Let Mose and me go first. If everything's okay, we'll give the high sign."

As we crossed the meadow, music broke out again from inside the big tent, a hymn I recognized from the services the Brickmans had held in the gymnasium at Lincoln School, "Lord of All Hopefulness." That beautiful angel's voice rose above the others and above the instruments as well. It was a voice that spoke to a deep human longing, probably in those already inside the tent, but also in me. Emmy and I waited near the entrance, while Albert and Mose checked things out. The music stopped, and I heard a woman begin to speak. Mose appeared and signaled us to come ahead.

Inside, the tent was lit by electric lamps hung from the support poles. Benches had been placed in rows with an aisle up the middle that ran to a raised platform, where a piano stood and behind it folding chairs on which sat several musicians with their instruments. Above the platform hung a banner that proclaimed, SWORD OF GIDEON HEAL-

ING CRUSADE. A woman held center stage. Her hair was a long, sleek tumble the color of fox fur, and she wore a flowing white robe whose long hem trailed behind her as she moved. The tent was little more than half-filled, mostly older men and women dressed in clothing not much better than the things Emmy and Albert and Mose and I wore. There were a few kids scattered here and there, enough so that we didn't stand out. Albert and Mose were sitting together on a bench on the left side of the center aisle. Emmy and I took a bench on the opposite side. The air was warm inside the tent, but Emmy nestled against me and I could feel her shivering. The good smell of food — chicken soup, I'd decided — was powerful, but I couldn't see any sign of it.

". . . and so we are all afraid," the woman in the white robe was saying. "Afraid of hunger, afraid of loss, afraid of what today holds and afraid that tomorrow will be no better, or maybe even worse. In these dark days, we're terrified that we'll lose our jobs, our homes, that our families will be torn apart. We're reluctant to answer the knock at the door because maybe it's the Devil waiting there with a foreclosure notice in his hand. We drop to our knees and pray to God for deliverance from all this misery. We look toward heaven, hoping for a sign that things will get better."

She stood in the center of the stage, under the bright light, her long hair like a flow of glowing embers, her robe pure snow, her eyes so clear that even from the back of the tent they were like fresh, green willow leaves. She spread her arms wide, and the fabric of her robe opened as if she'd suddenly sprouted wings. A man stepped onto the stage and handed her a wooden cross that was nearly as tall as she. She took it in her hands and lifted it high, and the lights of the tent dimmed until the only one still shining was at her back. Across all those benches and the people there, she and that cross cast a long shadow.

"The sign has already been given to us," she cried in a voice lovely as a nightingale's. "It came as a promise drenched in blood, spoken in agony and in love. 'Father, forgive them.' " She raised the cross higher and intoned, " 'Father, forgive them.' " She lowered the cross, and her voice dropped with it, and she said gently, liltingly, " 'Father, forgive them.' Brothers and sisters, God so loved the world that he gave his precious only son to save us. This is not a God who would ever turn his back on you. In your darkest hour, even when Satan is knocking at your door, God is beside you. Even when you believe you are steeped so deeply in sin that you must be lost to him, God is with you, and he forgives your sins. He asks only that you believe in him with all your heart and all your mind and all your soul."

She smiled wondrously, and Emmy drew away from me and leaned toward her as if sucked in by some powerful, unseen wind.

A man near the front stood and cried out, "Sister Eve, we need a sign. Please, give us a sign, now, tonight."

"I can't give you a sign, brother. That comes from God alone."

"Through you, Sister Eve, I know. I've seen it. Heal my son, Sister. Please, heal my son." The man reached down and drew up a kid who looked no older than I. The boy was hunched, his spine so crooked it bent him nearly double, and he could barely look up. "My boy Cyrus was born with the Devil on his back. He's been this way his whole life. I heard you take the Devil out of people, Sister Eve. I'm begging you, drive the Devil out of my boy."

A look of deep compassion washed over the woman's face. She handed the cross back to the man who'd brought it to her and opened her arms toward the crook-backed boy.

"Bring him to me."

It was painful to watch the kid make his way up the steps of the platform. His father helped, and when they were both before Sister Eve, the boy stood, but still so terribly bent that it was clearly painful to lift his eyes to her. She knelt down and put her face level with his.

"Cyrus, do you believe in God?"

"Yes, ma'am," I heard him utter. "I do."

"Do you believe that God loves you?"

"I do, ma'am. I do."

"And do you believe that God can heal you?"

"I want to, ma'am." I could hear the choking in his voice, and although his back was to me and I couldn't see his face, I was pretty sure he was pouring out a flood of tears.

"Believe, Cyrus. Believe with all your heart and soul." Sister Eve reached out, placed her hands on his misshapen back, and the snow-white folds of her robe fell across his shoulders. She raised her eyes toward the canvas tent roof. "In the name of God whose divine breath fills us with life, in the name of God who shapes our hearts on the anvil of his love, in the name of God by whose boundless grace the halt and the lame are healed, I ask that this boy's affliction be taken from him. Take out of his body, take out of his bone, take out of his whole being every last unclean thing and let this child walk upright again. In the sweet name of our Lord, let him be whole."

And son of a gun, that crippled boy began to draw himself up. It was like watching a leaf unfurl. I could have sworn I heard the cracking of every vertebra as his spine straightened. He stood fully erect, and the lights came back up, and he turned toward all of us sitting on the benches, and I saw that I had been right. A waterfall of tears ran down his cheeks. His father was crying, too, and embraced him.

"Thank the Lord, and God bless you, Sister Eve," the grateful man cried.

"Praise the Lord," someone shouted from the benches, and others took up the cry.

Maybe there was supposed to be more healing, I didn't know. Maybe they were going to pass an offering plate or something. But if this was so, it didn't happen. What did happen was this. As the man and boy sat themselves back down, a voice from behind us hollered, "Bullshit!"

All heads turned toward the tent entrance, where four young men stood together, grinning like rattlers and unsteady on their feet. One of them held a pint bottle of what I was pretty sure was bootlegged liquor. He'd been the one to call out, and he called out again, "Bullshit, you phony bitch."

The other three laughed and handed the bottle around.

The man who still held Sister Eve's cross set it down and stepped up next to her on the stage. He was a burly guy with a nose and face that made me think he might have once boxed heavyweight. Sister Eve raised a hand to keep him at a distance, then she addressed the rowdy group in back.

"Do you have any idea what brought you to me tonight?" She spoke gently, as if coaxing a frightened animal.

"Yeah, I heard about your dog and pony show, this healing crap. Wanted to see it for myself. Sister, let me tell you, I've seen better shows on a burlesque stage." He hooted, grabbed the bottle, and took a pull.

"You're here because your soul needs tending," she said.

"I got something you can tend, Sister, but it sure as hell ain't my soul." He made a lewd gesture with his hips and gave a drunken whoop.

"Get out," someone shouted. "We don't need you busting in here, you drunken ass."

A general murmur of agreement arose.

"It's all right." Sister Eve raised her arms to quell the rising tide of anger. "Come unto me, all ye that labor and are heavy laden, and I will give you rest. Take my yoke upon you and learn of me; for I am meek and lowly in heart, and ye shall find rest unto your souls."

"I'd rather find rest unto those big boobs, Sister." That got a good laugh from his cohorts.

Sister Eve left the stage and walked slowly down the aisle, the long hem of her robe trailing behind. Everyone turned as she passed and watched mesmerized as she approached the group of drunken men at the back. She stood before them like a white lamb before dark, hungry beasts. "Take my hand." She held it out to the rude young man.

He seemed startled, then a wary look came into his eyes.

"Take my hand, and I will refresh you."

He stared at her open palm and didn't move.

Sister Eve smiled gently. "Are you afraid?"

That got him. He reached out and roughly grasped her hand.

Sister Eve closed her eyes for a moment, as if praying. When she opened them again, the look she gave him was warm with understanding. "How old were you when she died?"

Now the young man looked stunned, as if she'd smacked him between the eyes with a pipe wrench. "When who died?"

"Your mother. You were very young, weren't you?"

He jerked his hand from hers. "Leave my mother out of this."

"She died in a fire."

"I said leave her out of this."

"You watched her burn."

"Goddamn you!" He raised his fist as if to strike her.

"You believe it was your fault."

"No," he shouted and waved that fist in the air. "No," he said again, but with less force this time.

"You've carried this burden too long. I can take it from you, if you'll let me."

281

"Get away from me, bitch."

"Let go of this burden and you will be refreshed. You will feel whole again, I promise."

He let his arm drop and stared at her, eyes huge and, I thought, pleading. "I . . . I can't."

"Because you believe you are too full of sin. So are we all. Yet we are all forgiven. We just need to believe it. Take my hand and believe."

He bowed his head and stared at the ground, as if he couldn't bring himself to look into her eyes.

"Take my hand," she said, so quietly I could barely hear.

Like a thing long dead, his arm rose ever so slowly. He placed his hand again in Sister Eve's palm and fell to his knees before her. He began to weep, deep sobs that racked his body. She knelt and took him into her arms.

"Do you believe?" she said in the most comforting voice I'd ever heard.

"I believe, Sister."

"Then let your soul be at rest."

She held him awhile longer, and finally stood and brought him up with her. "Go now in peace, my brother."

He couldn't speak. He simply nodded and turned, and he eyed the three young men who'd come with him in a way that made them step back. They retreated from the tent and he followed.

Sister Eve opened her arms to us all. "The

table has been prepared. Let us thank the Lord and share in his bounty."

A flap at the side of the tent was drawn back, revealing a long table on which sat a couple of big, steaming pots, and the smell of chicken soup wafted in, the aroma of heaven.

CHAPTER TWENTY-FOUR

That night, I lay on my blanket, once again unable to sleep. I could hear the soft rustle of the Minnesota River only yards away, sweeping through the bulrushes along the edge of the sand spit. We were near enough to the town — whose name I didn't know yet — that occasionally I heard the undercarriage of a truck rattling like metal bones as it bounced along the streets. Along the river, the tree frogs sang a natural, lulling melody that did nothing to make me drowsy.

I knew the reason I couldn't sleep. It was because I understood the young drunk at the healing crusade. He believed his heart was so full of badness that it could never be cleansed. I was a murderer twice over. If ever a soul was damned, it was mine.

Then I heard the voice of the angel, so soft I wasn't sure it was actually there. I got up, climbed the riverbank, and made my way through the trees and across the railroad tracks. I stood at the edge of the meadow, where I could see the huge tent. Behind it was the town, a few lights still shining here and there among the hills. Most of the automobiles were gone, the meadow nearly deserted. A soft glow lit the tent canvas, not at all the brilliant blast from the host of electric lamps that we'd seen earlier. Maybe from just one or two. The music wasn't the great flourish it had been but was quiet now. There was only the piano, and the horn, and that heavenly voice.

I crossed the meadow. The flap that covered the tent entrance wasn't closed all the way, and I found that if I knelt, I could see inside.

They were gathered around the piano on the platform: the trumpet player, the piano player, and Sister Eve. A single light shone above them. Sister Eve no longer wore a white robe but was dressed in a western shirt with snap buttons. Her blue jeans were rolled up at the ankles, and I could see that on her feet were honest-to-God cowboy boots. They were playing a song I'd heard on the radio at Cora Frost's house, "Ten Cents a Dance," a sad melody about a woman paid to dance with men but desperate for someone to take her away from all that. The trumpet notes were long, mournful sighs, and the beat the piano player laid down was a funeral dirge, and Sister Eve sang as if her soul was dying, and oh, did that sound speak to me.

When the song ended, they all laughed, and

the trumpet player said, "Evie, baby, you oughta be on Broadway." He was tall, with slicked black hair, and a pencil-thin mustache across the pale white skin above his upper lip.

Sister Eve pulled a cigarette from a small, silver case, and the trumpet player lifted a lighter and offered her a flame. She blew a flourish of smoke and said, "Too busy doing the Lord's work, brother." She took up a glass that sat near her on the piano and sipped from it.

"What next?" the piano player asked. He was as slender as a sipping straw, his skin the color of dark molasses, and he wore a black fedora tipped at a jaunty angle.

Sister Eve drew on the cigarette, then her lips formed a little O, and she puffed out two perfect smoke rings. "Gershwin really sends me. I've always been a sucker for 'Embraceable You.' "

Which was a song I knew, though I didn't know who'd written it. I felt the weight of my harmonica in the pocket of my shirt, and my lips twitched with eagerness. As the piano player laid down the first few bars, I moved out into the dark of the meadow, sat down, pulled out my mouth organ, and played right along with them. Oh, it was sweet, like being fed after a long hunger, but it filled me in a different way than the free soup and bread earlier that night had. Into every note, I blew out that longing deep inside me. The song was about love, but for me it was about wanting something else. Maybe home. Maybe safety. Maybe certainty. It felt good, in the way I'd sometimes imagined what prayer might feel like if you really believed and poured your heart into it.

The notes ended, and I sat in the warm glow that had come from being a part of the music. The tent flap lifted. Silhouetted against the light from inside stood Sister Eve, motionless, staring into the night.

Morning dawned bright and warm, but we all slept late. When Albert finally rolled out of his blanket, he said, "We need to get on the river, make some distance. I'm still worried about Hawk Flies at Night. But first I'm going to see if I can scrounge some food to take with us."

"Couldn't we stay just one more day?" Emmy said. "The soup last night was so good. And I'd like to see the town, Albert."

"One town is pretty much like every other." His words came out harsh, although I didn't think he meant them that way. It was just that Albert, once he had a thing set in his mind and thought it was for the best, became a big boulder rolling downhill, and God help you if you got in his way. But he saw Emmy's hurt look, and he knelt so that his face was level with hers. "I don't want us to get caught, Emmy. Do you?"

"No." Her mouth turned down and her lower lip trembled, just a little.

"You're not going to cry, are you?"

"Probly," she said.

Albert gave an exaggerated sigh and rolled his eyes. "Okay. You can go into town, for just a little while, then we leave, all right?"

"Oh, yes," she said, and her whole demeanor changed in a flash.

Emmy's emotions had always been up front and true, but it was clear to me that she'd played Albert. I didn't know if this was a good thing, but I figured, given our circumstances, it was probably inevitable. You can't hang out with outlaws and not become a bit of one yourself.

"I've got a lot of scrounging to do, and I don't know where that might take me. I might have to fight off another hungry dog, so it's best if you don't go with me. And you can't go by yourself." He looked at Mose and me and made a quick decision. "You go with her, Odie. Make sure she keeps her seed cap pulled down low. If someone from the crusade last night spots you, it won't seem strange the two of you being together. Anybody asks, you're two brothers, got it?"

I grinned at Emmy. "I always wanted a little brother."

Mose signed, *What about me?*

"Somebody needs to stay with the canoe,"

Albert said. "Besides, you're Indian and mute. If anybody tries to talk to you, you'll get noticed, and we need to stay invisible."

I could tell this galled Mose, but he grudgingly accepted Albert's logic.

"I'll go first," my brother said. "You guys wait a little while, then follow."

Albert headed up the riverbank and through the trees and was gone.

Mose sat down, picked up a rock, and threw it at the river.

"Mad?" I asked him.

Hate being Indian, he signed.

I handed Emmy her seed cap, took her hand, and we climbed the riverbank.

We quickly learned the place was called New Bremen. The center of town was built around a square where a big courthouse stood. We strolled the sidewalks, standing in the shade of green awnings, staring into store windows. I was nervous, exposing ourselves this way, but we walked slowly and no one seemed to notice us and Emmy was delighted. We passed a Rexall drugstore, and next to it was a confectionery.

"I wish we could take Mose some licorice," Emmy said, eyeing the sweets inside. We all knew licorice was Mose's favorite.

We sat on a bench next to the little sweet shop and watched automobiles roll past on the square, people going in and out of the stores. New Bremen was much larger than

Lincoln, the streets and sidewalks much busier. A group of boys carrying baseball gloves and bats jostled their way across the square and disappeared behind the court-house, heading toward a ball field somewhere.

"We could live here," Emmy said.

"Nice town," I admitted. "But Saint Louis is where we're going."

"Is it nice?"

The truth was that we were heading toward a big city I barely remembered, looking for a woman I hardly knew and whose address was a mystery. But it was a chance for family, the only chance we had, and it was far better than anything we'd left behind.

"It's real nice," I said.

The drugstore door opened and two people came out, laughing. Right away, I recognized Sister Eve. Instead of her cowgirl outfit or the white robe, she wore a green dress with gold frill along the collar and a fashionable gold hat, the kind I'd seen in magazines. Her shoes matched her hat and had little straps around the ankles. The trumpet player was with her. He wore a white suit and a white panama hat. As he stepped out onto the sidewalk, he slipped a couple of fat cigars into the pocket of his suit coat.

They turned in our direction, and Sister Eve's gaze fell on us. She smiled immediately.

"Well, hello there. I saw you two last night. Did you enjoy the soup?"

"Yes, ma'am," I said. "It was good."

"And you?" She bent to Emmy.

"Uh-huh," Emmy said.

I wanted to nudge Emmy, remind her to pull the bill of her seed cap low, but she lifted her face to Sister Eve, beaming.

The woman's eyes, as green as two spring leaves, shifted from Emmy to me and back to Emmy. "You're alone here?"

"Yes, ma'am," I said.

"And you were alone last night. Where's your mother?"

"Dead," I said for both us.

"And your father?"

"Same," I said.

"Oh, dear."

She sat beside us on the bench. The trumpet player looked put out, folded his arms, and leaned against the drugstore window.

"What's your name?"

"Buck," I said. "Like Buck Jones."

"The cowboy," she said with a smile. "And you?" she said to Emmy.

I tried to answer, but Emmy beat me to the punch and told the truth. "Emmy."

"Emmett," I said quickly. "But we call him Emmy. He's my brother."

"Who takes care of you?"

"We take of ourselves," I said.

"Just the two of you?"

"Just the two of us."

She reached toward me, plucked the har-

291

monica from my shirt pocket, and eyed me knowingly. "You play a nice tune. I heard you in the meadow last night." She put the mouth organ back, then gazed long and deep into Emmy's face. "Give me your hand, dear." She took Emmy's little hand into her own and closed her eyes. When her lids opened again, she gazed at Emmy as if she'd known her forever. "You've lost a great deal, but I can see that you've been given something extraordinary in return. I want you to come back for the crusade tonight. I'll have something special for you." She focused on me, as if I were the responsible one. "Will you promise me?"

There was no breeze, but it felt to me as if there were one, blowing fresh off Sister Eve. In her white robe the night before, with her long fox-fur hair, she'd seemed more beautiful than an angel. Now I saw that her cheeks were freckled every bit as much as Albert's, and down the left side of her face, just in front of her ear, ran an ugly scar, which her long hair partially hid. She held me with her eyes. I couldn't look away. Not just because they were wonderfully clear and their look gave me a feel as refreshing as mint. Gazing into them, it seemed as if I was looking into water so deep I knew it could drown me in an instant but so seductive I wanted to leap right in.

"I promise," I heard myself say.

The trumpet player looked at his watch. "Evie, baby, we gotta run."

"Candy first, Sid," she said. "What would you like?"

"Lemon drops," Emmy said immediately.

"Buck?"

I thought about Mose and said, "Licorice, please."

Sister Eve looked up at Sid, who rolled his eyes, but nonetheless went into the confectionery and came out with the candy.

"I'll see you tonight, Buck," Sister Eve said. She gave Emmy a knowing smile. "And you be a good . . . boy." She stood and walked away arm in arm with the trumpet player.

As soon as they left, I turned to Emmy and said as sternly as I could, "You can't just go around telling everyone your real name."

"It'll be okay," she said, as if she knew something I didn't. "We can trust her."

I watched Sister Eve walking casually away. I didn't know why exactly, but I believed Emmy was right.

CHAPTER TWENTY-FIVE

"No," Albert said. "Absolutely not."

"I promised her," I argued.

"Big deal. We're leaving. Now."

When we'd returned to the river, Albert and Mose had already packed everything in the canoe. Mose was still brooding a little about not being able to go into town, but the licorice perked him up some. It was near noon, and he sat eating his black candy in the shade of a tree on the riverbank, while Albert and I battled it out. Emmy, my little ally, stood beside me.

"One more night, Albert. What harm can it do? And Sister Eve said she'd have something special for us."

"Yeah, handcuffs."

"She's not like that. I could tell."

"What if you're wrong?"

"He's not wrong, Albert," Emmy said. "Sister Eve is nice. She wouldn't rat on us."

Mose laughed and signed, *Rat on us? You sound like a gangster, Emmy.*

"We're leaving and that's all there is to it." Albert turned toward the canoe.

"Who died and made you God?" I shouted at his back.

He swung around. "You want to stay? Fine. Stay. The rest of us are leaving."

Mose didn't move from the shade, and Emmy edged even closer to my side.

"How about we take a vote?" I said.

"Vote?" As if it were a cussword.

"We live in a democracy, don't we? Let's take a vote. Majority wins. How many want to stay? Raise your hand."

I lifted mine, and Emmy's shot up, too. Albert scowled at Mose, who didn't seem in any hurry to cast his ballot. Lazily, he raised a hand.

"Fine," Albert said. "I'll visit you all in the penitentiary."

He stomped toward the canoe and made as if to get in. It was all for show. I knew my brother and knew that he would never desert us. He stood beside the broad, brown flow of the Minnesota River and shook his head.

"Mark my words. We'll live to regret this."

It was dusk when we headed up from the river to the crusade tent. There seemed to be a lot more automobiles parked in the meadow than there'd been the night before. Most of the benches in the tent were already filled, the result, I figured, of word getting out about the boy whose crooked spine had been straightened by Sister Eve's healing touch. In the front row sat the young man who'd been such a beast the evening before and then had been tamed by Sister Eve. Albert and Mose sat behind me and Emmy, who had her seed cap on. The night was hot and humid. Seated next to me was a bear of a man, huge and disheveled. Judging from the way he smelled, he must have just come from mucking out his barn. He was with a woman who leaned heavily against him, her eyes closed. Sleeping, I figured. But I didn't think she'd be sleeping once Sister Eve took the stage.

Out of the blue, Emmy whispered to me, "Do you have your harmonica?"

"Right here." I lifted it from my shirt pocket.

"Do you know how to play 'Beautiful Dreamer'?"

"Sure," I said. "Why?"

Before she could answer, the musicians filed in and took their places on the raised platform. The trumpet player stood up and cried, "Praise the Lord, brothers and sisters! Praise the Lord!"

Sister Eve swept into the tent from the opening where the soup had been served, wearing her white robe, her hair falling around her shoulders in auburn rivulets. She came to the center of the platform and spread her arms so that once again she seemed to have wings.

"Jesus said, 'If anyone is thirsty, let him come to me and drink.' My brothers and sisters, let us gather at the river and drink from the living water of the Holy Spirit and be refreshed."

Immediately, the musicians behind her began to play and Sister Eve broke into song, her beautiful voice lifting up the words, "Shall we gather at the river, where bright angel feet have trod . . ."

I knew the old gospel tune. It had been one the Brickmans used a lot, and I found myself belting out the words along with Sister Eve, pouring my heart into them as if I believed they were absolutely true.

She danced across the stage that night, speaking hope to all the people with their rumps settled on those hard benches, her hair tumbling across her face, where, from the heat inside the tent and the intensity of her evangelistic fervor, her own living water poured down in streams of sweat. She sang and exhorted and, in the end, opened her arms wide and invited anyone who needed the healing touch of God to come forward.

A man on crutches hobbled up, followed by a woman without any obvious affliction. At the touch of Sister Eve's hands, the man on crutches threw them away. He practically danced off that platform. The woman without anything visibly wrong tried to tell Sister Eve about her stutter. It was excruciating listening to her as she battled to get her words out. Sister Eve took the woman's head and squeezed it with the viselike grip of her two palms. She begged in the name of the Holy Spirit for this woman to speak clearly, as God intended. When Sister Eve lifted her hands, the woman tried for a moment to form words and finally said, as clear as you like, "Thank you, Sister." Then she looked stunned, like a cow hit with a sledgehammer. "God be praised," she cried. "God bless you, Sister Eve. God bless you." When she left the platform, she was pouring out tears as if her eyes were rain clouds.

The man who sat next to me, huge and hulking and foul-smelling, stood. In one hand, he held a shotgun. With his other, he pulled up the woman who'd been leaning against him, fast asleep. He hooked his arm around her, stepped into the aisle that ran between the benches, and hauled her forward, her feet dragging along the ground.

I realized then that the woman hadn't been asleep. And the foul smell had not been from mucking out a barn.

At the platform steps, the man stopped and gawked up at Sister Eve. If she was surprised by the scene in front of her, she showed no sign of it.

"What is it you're seeking, brother?" she asked.

"My wife. She don't talk to me no more. I

heard you fix people."

"What's your name?"

"Willis."

"And what's your wife's name?"

"Sarah."

"The name of a godly woman in the Bible. Sit with me, Brother Willis. Both of you."

She settled herself on the top step, the folds of her robe tumbling down below her in a cascade of white. The shaggy bear named Willis sat down, holding the body of his wife upright between him and Sister Eve. He propped the shotgun against the steps within easy reach. Sister Eve took the dead woman's hand, held it between her own, and closed her eyes for a long while. When she finally opened them, she said, "Life is hard, isn't it, Brother Willis?"

"You can say that again. It ain't easy on the farm these days. Price of corn ain't been good for a long time."

"You don't sleep," she said.

"I lie awake nights worrying. Bank's sent us letters. Why I keep my shotgun with me, in case they try to jump me. They ain't taking my farm."

"And Sarah, she's been sitting up with you night after night, trying to give you comfort."

"She's the only thing keeps me going. But she don't talk to me no more. She lost her voice. Why we come here. I heard you heal folks."

"I don't heal them, Willis. It's God who heals. I'm just the lightning rod."

"You pray over her. You make her talk to me again."

"Do you believe in God, Willis?"

"As much as the next man."

"And what about Sarah?"

"Always reading her Bible. Says it gives her comfort."

"And in turn she gives you comfort."

He gave his wife a look that seemed full of longing. "Just the sound of her voice is enough."

"But she doesn't speak to you anymore."

He bent his head and stared at the ground. "Struck dumb, I figured. Maybe because of some awful sin."

"Her sin, or yours?"

He didn't reply. She leaned toward him, her voice barely above whisper. But it was so quiet in that tent we could've heard a fly buzzing up there around Sister Eve.

"Tell me about the sin, Willis."

He breathed heavily through his nostrils, a sound like a wild animal might make. He cleared his throat, a deep, unsettling rumble. "She . . ." he began. He shook his head, as if trying to make his thoughts fall into place. "She said she was leaving me. Going back to her people. I got mad, real mad. We said harsh words."

"You hit her," Sister Eve said softly. "And

that's when she stopped talking to you."

"I told her I was sorry. I got down on my knees and begged her to forgive me, to say something to me, anything."

"She can't speak to you anymore, Brother Willis. You know that. Not in this life. But she's waiting for you in a wonderful place where there is no worry. Where there's no pain. Where what you're given can never be taken from you. A place where there's only love." She reached across the dead woman. "Take my hand, Brother Willis."

He stared at it as if sorely tempted. I was sure that in the same way she'd tamed the beast in the young man the night before, she'd gentled this man's deeply troubled spirit. But he surprised me. Surprised us all. Surprised even Sister Eve.

"No," he bellowed and leapt to his feet. He grabbed his shotgun, rammed the butt against his shoulder, and aimed the barrel at Sister Eve's nose. "You fix her, goddamn it. You make her talk to me again, or so help me, I'll blow your head right off."

I've seen fear a thousand times in my life. Although it has many faces, it often has no voice. Sister Eve stared into the barrel of that shotgun, and I could see that her fear was so great she couldn't speak. Without her words, I figured there was no way she would be able to work the miracle that homicidal bear of a man wanted, or any other miracle.

"Play, Odie," Emmy whispered to me. "Play 'Beautiful Dreamer.' "

It made no sense, but then nothing made sense as I waited for the blast of that shotgun to obliterate Sister Eve's face. Like everyone else in the tent, I was certain we were about to witness carnage. And once begun, there was no guarantee the killing would stop with Sister Eve. My lips were dry, my throat made of sandpaper. I could barely breathe. I had no idea if I could blow a tune at all. But I drew the mouth organ from my shirt pocket and put my lips to it. Emmy placed her small hand on my leg. She looked up at me and smiled, as if she believed in me absolutely.

I began to play. Although the music I blew was soft, in the silence of that tent and to my own ears, it seemed deafening. Faces turned toward me, the face of Willis right along with them. I was sure his shotgun barrel would swing my way. I played a full measure, my heart kicking wildly in my chest. I was about to stop, thinking it was time to end this craziness, when a voice from heaven joined me in the song. Sister Eve.

Beautiful dreamer, wake unto me.
Starlight and dewdrops are waiting for
    thee.
Sounds of the rude world heard in the day,
Lulled by the moonlight have all passed
    away.

The look of rage that had twisted the huge man's face began to soften. The shotgun barrel drooped in his hands. I played on and Sister Eve lifted her ethereal voice and sang like a comforting angel.

Beautiful dreamer, queen of my song,
List while I woo thee with soft melody.
Gone are the cares of life's busy throng.
Beautiful dreamer, awake unto me.
Beautiful dreamer, awake unto me.

With tears in his eyes, the great beast fell to his knees, laid his head in his dead wife's lap, and wept his heart out. The shotgun lay fallen on the ground, and the young man whose beast had been tamed the night before jumped from the bench where he sat and snatched it up.

Sweat dripped from my face and I felt a little faint. I lowered my harmonica and glanced down at Emmy.

"You never played better, Odie," she said.

CHAPTER TWENTY-SIX

"His wife's favorite song," Sister Eve said. " 'Beautiful Dreamer.' It may have been the only thing that could reach all the way down to his heart. How did you know that, Buck?"

We sat in the private dining room of the best hotel in New Bremen, a place called the Morrow House, a whole roasted chicken on the table, along with mashed potatoes and gravy and asparagus. Despite the swank surroundings, I'd insisted that Emmy keep her seed cap on. She and I were stuffing the food down like there was no tomorrow. Sister Eve and the trumpet player sat with us. They ate more slowly and sipped "grape juice," which I knew was really red wine, with their meal. Sister Eve had changed out of her white robe and wore a blue dress. The trumpet player wore a gray suit with wide lapels and a diamond stickpin through his red tie.

"I didn't," I told Sister Eve. "Emmy said I should play it."

"Did he now?" She studied Emmy curiously. "Where do you two orphans stay?"

"We've got a little camp down on the river."

"Do you live in the camp? I mean permanently?"

"Not exactly. We're on our way to Saint Louis."

"What's in Saint Louis?"

"I have family there. We have family there," I corrected.

"It's a long way to Saint Louis."

"I guess so," I said. "But Emmy and me, we'll make it."

Sister Eve lifted her glass and considered her wine. "We're going to Saint Louis. Not directly. We hit Des Moines and Lawrence, Kansas, first." She took a sip of her wine and said casually, "You could come with us."

The trumpet player looked like he was going to choke on his chicken. "Would cause us a boatload of trouble, Evie."

"How's that?" Sister Eve asked.

"Might be construed as kidnapping." He dabbed his napkin delicately at his thin mustache.

"Kidnapping? The whole country is full of children who've been abandoned, Sid. Believe me, I know a thing or two about that." She turned back to me. "We could deliver you to your family's doorstep."

"Now, wait a minute," the trumpet player said.

"Sid." She gave him a look that shut him

up good.

I glanced at Emmy, whose face beneath her seed cap gave me no clue about her own inclination, one way or the other. I liked the idea of the soft life, but the decision wasn't mine alone.

"We need to think it over," I said.

"That's fine."

I wasn't drinking anything alcoholic, but the smile Sister Eve offered me was absolutely intoxicating.

When we got to the river that night, Albert and Mose were sitting by the fire.

"Did you eat?" Albert asked.

"Like kings," Emmy said with delight.

"How was the soup?" I asked.

We hadn't talked to them since we split up before entering the big tent. Willis and his shotgun had pretty much brought the meeting to a close. A deputy who'd been in attendance had tapped a couple of other men from the benches, and they'd hauled the man-bear away, still sobbing. Others had carted the body of his wife to the bed of a pickup truck and set off for the morgue. Sister Eve had invited everyone to the table for soup and bread, then she'd found me and Emmy.

Mose patted his belly and signed, *Best I ever ate.*

Emmy sat down beside the fire and blurted, "Sister Eve wants us to stay with her."

Albert said, "We're going to Saint Louis."

"She's going to Saint Louis, too," I said. "Des Moines, then Kansas, then Saint Louis."

"She draws a crowd. The last thing we need is a crowd. Sooner or later, somebody's going to spot Emmy."

"We could be careful."

"Careful is what we're doing. There's no way we're going to hook up with a revival tent show."

"It's a healing crusade," I insisted.

"Call it what you will, we're steering clear."

If I hadn't known in my heart he was right, I might have insisted we put it to a vote. Emmy seemed not to care one way or the other and looked ready to nod off.

"It was a nice dream," I said, mostly to myself.

After we all lay down, I stayed awake, staring up at a night sky dusted with stars. I listened to the song of frogs in the bulrushes and thought about the musicians who backed up Sister Eve, and I imagined what it might be like to play my harmonica in their company. The few times I'd had the opportunity — with Miss Stratton and with Jack — it had been magic in a way, like one heart calling out and another answering.

"Let it go, Odie," Albert said quietly.

"She was nice. Maybe we would have been happy."

307

"She's working a con."

"How do you figure?"

"Those people who get healed, they're shills."

"Not that grizzly bear tonight."

"Did you see any healing with him? If you hadn't saved her, she wouldn't have a head."

I turned, trying to see my brother's face. I wondered what dreams he had. My dream was to be a musician maybe, or a storyteller, because people got paid for doing this, and these were things I loved. What did Albert love? What called to him from his own heart? I was surprised that I had no idea.

"Anything looks too good to be true, Odie, you can bet it's a con," he said, sounding a little sad. "You look close enough at this Sister Eve, you're going to find there's something about her that stinks to high heaven." Albert rolled over and put his back to me.

I woke the next morning to an astonishing sight: Sister Eve on the sand spit, sitting beside the fire with Albert and Mose. She was dressed again like a cowgirl and seemed to fit right in with that rugged outdoor scene. The fire crackled, and Albert and Sister Eve talked in low voices. When Mose joined in, signing, Albert interpreted for her. I sat up, scooted off the blanket, and walked barefooted to the powwow.

Sister Eve smiled at me. "Good morning, Buck. Or should I say Odie?"

"What are you doing here?"

"I thought I might come to say goodbye. Then I met these two hooligans."

Albert and Mose, who seemed comfortable as you please in her company, grinned at that playful characterization. I couldn't help thinking of the young man whose inner beast Sister Eve had tamed. It seemed that she'd worked the same magic on my two companions.

"I've convinced your brother and Mose that, rather than trying to make your way to Saint Louis on the rivers, it would be much safer for you to travel there with me." She lifted a white sack. "Would you like one?"

Inside were donuts. Big, perfect, glazed, drool-inducing donuts.

"Sit down," she said.

I settled myself on the sand and ate a donut. I couldn't remember ever tasting something so good, so soft, so sweet.

"Here's the deal," she said, opening her hands in both explanation and invitation. "I've hired Mose and your brother to help with the work of the crusade, at least until we get you to Saint Louis. I'll put them up with the others who do that for me. You and Emmy will stay with me at the Morrow House. We'll tell everyone that you're my nephew and Emmy is my niece. I've got a couple straw hats with big, wide brims I'll give her. Much nicer than the seed cap, but they'll still do a good job of hiding her face."

"You know who she is? How?"

"Not important. What's important is that we keep you safe and get you where you want to go. I can do that."

"Like the trumpet player said, it could get you into trouble."

"Sid's a worrier. I've danced around trouble all my life."

I glanced at Albert. "It's really okay with you?"

Albert shrugged. "She convinced me."

I looked at Mose, who grinned and signed, *Donuts every day.*

"What do you say, Odie?" Her face was serious, her voice deeply inviting. "Are you on board?"

I'd gobbled the last of my donut and was ready to swallow anything Sister Eve told me. "Heck, yes."

"Do you want to wake up Emmy and ask her?"

Emmy lay curled on a blanket, still sound asleep. I shook her gently. She rolled onto her back and opened her eyes, just a whisper.

"You awake, Emmy?"

She made a sound, not much, but enough that I knew she could understand.

"It looks like we're going to stay with Sister Eve for a while."

She blinked up at me sleepily.

"I knew that," she said, rolled over, and went back to sleep.

CHAPTER TWENTY-SEVEN

I hadn't taken a shower since the day we left Lincoln School. Standing under a steady stream of clean hot water was like heaven. Sister Eve bought us new clothing and had our old things washed, and we settled into the life of a traveling Christian healing show.

Emmy and I were given a bedroom in the suite of rooms Sister Eve rented at the Morrow House. To keep folks from suspecting a connection with us, Albert and Mose waited another day at our camp on the river. When they joined the troupe, they were given cots in the tent the men shared. The women of the crusade occupied another tent. Everyone had at least one work assignment, but most juggled several jobs.

Mose was put in the kitchen tent, helping prepare the meals that followed each crusade service and also the meals that fed everyone who traveled with Sister Eve — there were nearly a dozen of them. The cook was a big man, bald as an ice cube, with a tattoo of a bare-breasted mermaid on his right forearm. He called himself Dimitri, although like everyone else who traveled with Sister Eve, that probably wasn't his real name. He spoke with a thick Greek accent, and Mose loved him. Dimitri, who seemed to have no trouble interpreting the simple signs Mose used to communicate, swore he was the best laborer he'd ever seen.

Albert worked with the roustabouts, most of whom were also crusade musicians. In no time at all, his mechanical knack and ability to jerry-rig a solution to any problem won their admiration. They took to calling him Professor because he had a general knowledge of just about everything.

Whisker, the piano player, took me under his wing. He was thin, his arms and legs like soda straws, his skin the color of molasses. He was old, or what seemed old to me then, maybe fifty, and his eyes looked tired. He taught me about music in a way that Miss Stratton never had time for. I knew how to read sheet music, but I'd never been a part of a larger body of musicians. Whisker worked with me on timing and listening to the other instruments and feeling what he called the "noble bubble," by which he meant that moment when all the notes of each musician slid effortlessly around and among one another so that a piece of music became such a beautiful sound that it captured the spirits of both player and listener and carried them effortlessly upward.

"Like in a bubble," I said.

"Zactly," he said and grinned, showing tobacco-stained teeth. He sipped from the glass that always sat atop his piano, filled with two fingers of bootlegged whiskey that never seemed to diminish in volume no matter how long he nursed it. "Doesn't always happen, Buck, but when it does, feels like God's lifting you up in the palm of his hand."

His real name was Gregory but everybody called him Whisker, including himself. "My mama used to say I was so thin I could hide behind a cat's whisker. Kinda stuck." The other musicians were friendly and welcoming, but I could tell that Sid, the trumpet player, wasn't fond of me in the least. I thought it was simply because of the danger in which he believed our presence had placed the crusade, but Whisker clued me in to another possibility.

"He's jealous."

We were having lunch at one of the long tables where, at night, we ladled out soup and handed out bread.

"Jealous of me? Why?"

"You got something natural in you, something special that comes out through that mouth organ of yours, something that can't be taught or learned. Maybe it'll make a musician out of you, maybe something else.

Who knows? But it's there. Also, Sister Eve likes you a lot. You're her nephew, her family. Puts you one up on Sid. Man, that cat hates it when Sister Eve pays too much attention to anyone else."

I didn't know much of Whisker's history; nobody talked a lot about their past, so we fit in pretty easily. He did tell me he came from Texas sharecroppers, and growing up he'd wanted nothing more than to escape the cotton fields of the panhandle.

"Hard work on hard ground flat as a griddle cake," he said. "Done nothing in my whole life rough as picking cotton."

I asked about his family and he said he hadn't seen them in more than twenty years.

"Do you miss them?"

"Got a new family," he said and opened his arms to the crusade tent.

The crusades began at dusk, and within a couple of days, I was among the musicians on the platform. Sister Eve held forth on the Lord and we backed her up with music that lifted the soul. The hopeful raised their voices in familiar gospel tunes. At the end, the lights went down except for one that shone directly on Sister Eve, and the blind and the crippled and the broken came and knelt at her feet, begging for her healing touch. They did not go away disappointed. Even if the blind eyes weren't given sight, if the twisted leg didn't right itself, through her very countenance, it seemed, Sister Eve gave them hope.

"They eat it up like molasses on oatmeal," I overheard Sid tell one of the other musicians. "Doesn't matter they walk away still crippled. They leave with a light shining in their hearts, and it makes all the difference to those poor devils. They crack open their wallets and the money pours down like rain."

That should have put me on the alert. But I figured it cost a lot to feed the people who came to the tent meetings. Times were tough, and for many, the soup and bread dinner was probably the only real meal they'd had that day. What paid for the food was the generosity of those who didn't stick around for the meal, those who had some money and whose hearts and consciences were touched by Sister Eve.

My favorite times were when, long after the crusade service was over and the hungry had been fed, Sister Eve and Sid gathered around Whisker at the piano, and they let me join them, and we made the kind of music a church choir would never touch. Sister Eve was crazy about songs out of Tin Pan Alley, written in what Whisker explained to me was the thirty-two-bar form — four sections, each eight bars in length. A lot of Irving Berlin tunes were thirty-two-bar, he explained. They weren't difficult to play and were full of schmaltz, and Sister Eve knew how to wring out every ounce of feeling. She'd sip bootlegged whiskey — they all would — and smoke a cigarette and wrap her throat around the velvet of a song in a way that made you want to cry. Little Emmy was usually dead asleep by then, laid out on a blanket in the back of the tent. When the night finally came to a close, Sid would carry her to his car and drive us back to the hotel and lay her in bed, then say good night to Sister Eve at the door to her suite.

"Like this all the way to Saint Louis?" I heard him ask one night, his voice full of longing.

"All the way, Sid," she said. " 'Night, honey."

Sid wasn't the only one under her spell. Everyone who traveled with her loved Sister Eve. They were a misfit bunch, castoffs, down-and-outers. But in the same way she gave hope to the halt and the lame, Sister Eve buoyed the spirits of us all. I thought about the kids at Lincoln School, who, in so many ways, were just like Sister Eve's people, lost and broken. I thought that if only she had been in charge instead of Thelma Brickman, the Black Witch, life there could have been so different.

Sister Eve told me that the crusade was scheduled to stay two weeks in New Bremen. On our fourth night, when everyone had filed out of the tent to head to their homes or to the long table for soup and bread, Sister Eve sat down on the steps of the platform. I sat beside her.

"I'd kill for a cigarette and a shot of booze right now, Odie." She bumped me playfully with her white-robed hip.

"These people think you're perfect. They better not catch you drinking and smoking."

She laughed and put her arm around my shoulder. "Only God is perfect, Odie. To the rest of us, he gave all kinds of wrinkles and cracks." She lifted her hair from her cheek, showing me the long scar there. "If we were perfect, the light he shines on us would just bounce right off. But the wrinkles, they catch the light. And the cracks, that's how the light gets inside us. When I pray, Odie, I never pray for perfection. I pray for forgiveness, because it's the one prayer I know will always be answered."

I saw Albert all the time but didn't worry about people connecting us. We didn't look much alike. I figured that was because Albert, with his red hair, took after our father's side of the family, and I took after our mother's. I often sat with him at a long table when Mose and the other folks who worked the kitchen served us meals.

"How is it, living up there at the Ritz?" he kidded me one day at lunch.

"You know, Albert, I've been thinking. What if we don't find Aunt Julia in Saint Louis? I mean, we don't even know where to begin looking."

"We'll cross that bridge when we come to it."

"But what if?"

"You've got something on your mind?"

"Well, I've been thinking. Maybe we could just stay with Sister Eve."

Albert was chewing on a bologna sandwich. He looked toward the big tent, then beyond it across the meadow where the river ran and where he'd hidden our canoe.

"It's too good to last, Odie," he said.

"Why?"

"When has it ever been easy for us?"

"That doesn't mean it can't be."

"Look, it's when you relax that you get hit in the face. Don't get too comfortable. And look out for Sid. That guy's got it in for you."

"Sister Eve can handle him."

"Sister Eve can't watch him all the time. Mark my words, Odie, he's a snake."

Sid and Sister Eve spent a part of every day in the hotel going over what she called the books. In addition to his trumpet playing, Sid acted as her business manager, paying the bills, making sure the groundwork was laid in the towns ahead, seeing to publicity. He must have been good at it, especially the publicity part, because people showed up at the crusade who'd come from long distances, as far away as the Twin Cities. Even Whisker, who had no special affection for Sid, gave him credit.

"When I first hooked up with Sister Eve down in Texas, she wasn't much of a show. Did her praying and her healing, like she does now, but when Sid came along everything changed. That white robe makes her look like an angel? That was Sid's doing. Those lights, a full backup of musicians, even the soup and bread, that's all pure Sid."

"How'd he become a part of the family?" I used that word because that's how I'd begun to think of the crusade folks.

"Same way all us lost souls did. Sister Eve just found him. He was part of a carny show in Wichita when we put on a crusade there couple of years ago. He was blowing his horn and doing a snake act. That cat fell for her the way everybody does."

"Where did she come from?"

"You don't know? She's supposed to be your aunt." He laughed. "I always knew you were like the rest of us. She found you lost, tapped you, and you just followed her. Don't worry, Buck. Your secret's safe with me." He shook his head. "Got no idea where she comes from. With that fondness she's got for cowboy boots, I figure she must've come out of the West somewhere. That and the fact the snakes don't seem to bother her."

"Snakes?"

"Oh, right. You ain't seen Sid and her handle the snakes yet. Now that's something, let me tell you."

"What do they do with them?"

"Use them to make folks understand that Satan can be handled if you got God on your side. It's quite a show. They don't do it much up North, but in the South, man, those crackers eat it up."

"Can I see them?"

"Don't suppose it'd do any harm."

Within the crusade's tent village was a small tent just back of the kitchen where Sister Eve prepared herself for the service each evening. Whisker lifted the flap over the opening and beckoned me to enter. Inside was a dressing table with a mirror, and in front of it a padded bench. Next to the vanity stood a rack where a number of white robes hung, along with other clothing. There was a big traveling trunk and scattered around it lay several pairs of shoes, mostly the plain, white flats that Sister Eve wore during the meetings, but also a couple of pairs of cowboy boots. On a low, narrow table near the back wall of the tent sat three glass enclosures, what I would learn were called terrariums, a word that was new to me. There was some vegetation in each terrarium and also a big rock or two for the snakes to slither around and, I supposed, hide behind.

"What kind are they?"

"Them two snakes look exactly like corals." He nodded toward the glass cage where a couple small, black-yellow-and-red-banded snakes slithered over one another. "You know about coral snakes?"

I told him I didn't.

"Terrible poisonous. And that one there we call Mamba. Watch." He tapped the glass of the middle terrarium, and the snake inside, which was dark gray and three feet long, rose up, spread the skin around its neck and head, and looked prepared to strike at him. Whisker laughed. "Just like a cobra."

"But it isn't?"

"They just look dangerous but they ain't. They's just snakes that people mistake for the poison ones. But this one" — and he nodded toward the largest of the terrariums — "this one is different. He's the real thing. We call him Lucifer."

"Lucifer?"

He leaned toward the glass and the snake coiled and lifted itself to strike. "This here's a bona fide rattlesnake. When Lucifer shakes his tail, let me tell you, little brother, it makes my bones shiver."

"Sister Eve handles all the snakes?"

"The coral-looking snakes and Mamba. Only Sid handles Lucifer. Him and that snake been together a long time, I guess. Was part of the carny act he was doing when Sister Eve found him."

"They never get bit?"

"Sometimes. But the corals and Mamba,

their bite don't do nothing. And Sid, he always milks out the venom before he handles Lucifer."

The snake was coiled, so it was hard to tell its length, but its body was as thick as my wrist. It looked right at me, forked tongue darting in and out, as if trying to taste me.

"What does he eat?"

"We drop mice in there mostly. He swallows those critters whole. Sometimes little rats, too, if we catch them running around the kitchen tent."

I thought of Faria in the quiet room back at Lincoln School. I imagined him being gobbled up whole by that big rattler, and it made me hate the snake.

"You don't be trying to handle these snakes," Whisker cautioned. "Only Sister Eve and Sid do that."

"Don't worry," I said, backing away from Lucifer. "I'm never touching those things."

Chapter Twenty-Eight

The crusade was family. They worked together, trusted one another, found pleasure in each other's company. Before Albert and Mose were taken on, there'd been six men and four women. Until Emmy showed up, there'd been no children, and everyone in the crusade took her under their wing like mother ducks. Although she was often in the company of Sister Eve, even when she was alone, Emmy moved freely about the little tent village, helping where she could, but mostly bringing delight. She wore the wide-brimmed straw hats Sister Eve had given her all the time so that she could tip the brim low to hide her face whenever someone from the outside world came around. I'm sure everyone in the crusade knew that she wasn't really kin to Sister Eve, but I don't think they knew her true identity, or if they did, they didn't care.

Some of the men were pretty rough-looking. Dimitri, with his bald head and huge chest and tattoos. Torch, one of the musicians, whose hair looked like something coughed up by a cat. Tsuboi, a kid about Albert's age whose face, the whole right side of it anyway, was a mutilation of scar tissue. Whisker told me it had happened when he was thrown from a train he was trying to snag for a ride. Though no children traveled with the crusade, not all the women were childless. Cypress, an exotic-looking woman with long hair the color of a river at night, had three children who'd been taken from her because of drink. She didn't drink anymore, at least not that I ever saw, and when Emmy was around her, her face lit up as if a warm fire was burning in her heart. What few belongings each of them had were kept under their cots, where anyone could have stolen something. No one did.

In a way, they weren't that different from the kids at Lincoln School, who'd been thrown together with almost nothing. But Lincoln School had been overseen by the likes of DiMarco and the Black Witch and her lizard-on-two-legs husband, and fear had been what we'd all shared the most. With the crusade, the spirit of Sister Eve ran through everything, and that made all the difference.

There was routine to the days, and seldom idle time. Whatever work needed doing was accomplished in the morning — potatoes peeled, canvas mended, the big tent and the

325

whole area around the village cleaned of every bit of litter. A couple of men took one of the trucks and went to neighboring towns, posting notices of the crusade. When our work was finished, Sister Eve often sent us out to help in the community. I learned that she'd preceded the crusade to New Bremen and had visited local ministers and the Catholic priest and had asked about parishioners in particular need of assistance. There weren't many farmers who could afford to pay hired help, and wherever possible, Sister Eve offered her people, men and women alike, whose labor was free. From almost the day we joined the crusade, Mose and Albert and I went out to help. Our first day we mended fences, the next day repaired a barn roof. A couple of days later, I helped Albert fix the engine on a tractor the farmer swore would never run again. We cut jimsonweed from a cornfield, and the next day bucked hay, just as I'd done for Hector Bledsoe, but it was different this time because we were helping folks desperately in need so the labor didn't feel onerous. I thought how different it might have been at Lincoln School if the reason we were helping out Bledsoe had simply been that he was a man in need and not that he and the Brickmans got wealthy from our labor.

Every morning, after he and Sister Eve had gone over the books, Sid disappeared for a couple of hours, God knew where. Every afternoon, Sister Eve took a powder as well, and it was a while before I discovered the why of her vanishing.

At the end of a week, while Mose was at work in the kitchen tent and Emmy with him, and Albert was trying to repair the gas generator that powered the electric lights for the revivals every night, and we hadn't been promised out to help some farmer in need, I found myself with rare free time on my hands. I decided I would get to know New Bremen a little better.

I came to a park with a ball field where a group of neighborhood kids had thrown together a pickup game. They called to one another and joked, and their lives seemed to be all about play and the comfort of easy friendship. I descended a steep hill to the flats along the river, where grain elevators rose like castle keeps at the edge of the railroad tracks. A steepled, white church also stood near the tracks, and on the dirt streets around it were more houses, smaller and cheaper-looking than those built among the hills above. Through the opened church door came the moan of an organ as someone practiced hymns for the upcoming Sunday service. I followed the tracks to a wooden trestle, which crossed the Minnesota River. I sat on the crossties, staring down into the opaque, cider-colored water below, and tried to imagine what it might have been like if I'd been born to the quiet life in New Bremen.

Which turned out to be a thing I couldn't do. Not because imagination failed me, but because I was afraid to dream in that way. In my whole life, I could recall no dream ever coming true.

I walked from the trestle along the riverbank, following a path the locals had worn, maybe kids coming down to enjoy all the adventure that a river offered. On the far side were fields of young corn, nearly knee-high and verdant green, and beyond them rose hills that carried the sky on their shoulders. On that lazy summer afternoon, alone with the river and the lovely valley it had carved, I felt a deep desire to belong there, to belong anywhere.

Without realizing it, I had walked all the way to the place just below the meadow where we'd landed the canoe the first night I'd heard the voice of an angel call to me from the revival tent. To my great surprise, Sister Eve was there, sitting cross-legged on the sandy spit where she'd talked us all into joining the crusade. She was alone, her head bowed, and it was clear to me that she was deep in prayer. I didn't want to interrupt her reverie, so I turned and began up the riverbank as quietly as I could.

"Odie," she called to me softly.

"Sorry," I said. "I didn't mean to intrude."

"No intrusion. Join me." She patted the sand at her side.

"This is where you come?" I said. "Every afternoon?"

"Wherever we take the crusade, I try to find somewhere set off a bit so I can be by myself. It's not always a place as lovely as this."

"So you can pray?"

"So I can refresh myself." She spread her arms wide as if to embrace the river. "And so I can open my heart to the beauty of this whole divine creation. If that sounds like prayer to you, then call it prayer."

It was painfully clear that she felt something I didn't, something wondrous and fulfilling in that place where I possessed only a deep longing. She lifted her face to the sun, and her hair fell away from her cheek, exposing the long scar that ran there.

"This reminds me a little of the Niobrara," she said.

"What's that?"

"A river in Nebraska, where I grew up."

"Can I ask you something?"

"Anything."

I knew it was rude, but curiosity was eating me alive. "That scar."

Which didn't seem to surprise her in the least, and I wondered if it was a question she got asked a lot.

"Remember I told you God gives us all cracks so that his light has a way to get inside us? This scar, Odie, that's my crack. It was given to me the day of my baptism."

"I thought you just got dunked in water for that."

"In my case it was a horse trough."

I figured this had to be a good story, and I wanted to hear it, but before I could ask, someone called from the riverbank above us, "Sister Eve. Come quick. It's Emmy."

They'd laid her on a cot in the women's tent, and much of the crusade had gathered around her. Albert hovered over her, and Mose knelt at her side holding her little hand. Emmy's eyes were closed, her face drained of color. I went down on my knees beside my brother.

"What happened?"

"Another of her fits."

"What is it?" Sister Eve asked.

"We don't know exactly," I said. "She hit her head on a fence post a while back. She's been like this ever since. She usually comes out of it."

Her eyes fluttered open and she stared up at me, dazed.

"He's okay," she mumbled. "He's okay."

"Who, Emmy?"

She gripped my hand with a sudden, unexpected fierceness. "Don't worry, Odie," she said. "We beat the devil."

Then she let go, closed her eyes, breathed

deeply, and was asleep.

"Let's get her to the hotel," Sister Eve said.

Everyone cleared away. Mose carried Emmy out to the automobile that Sid usually drove, a shiny red DeSoto. He laid her on the backseat, and Sister Eve covered her with a blanket that had been folded there. I sat with her and cradled her head on my lap. Mose and Albert sat up front with Sister Eve, and she drove us to the Morrow House. Upstairs, Mose laid Emmy gently on the bed, then he and Albert headed back to the crusade village. Sister Eve sat with Emmy, holding her hand, and asked me to leave and to close the door behind me. I stood at the window of the parlor room, where we usually ate breakfast, and stared outside at the town square. I watched people going about their business in a normal fashion. And I knew that would never be me.

The door to the hallway opened and Sid came in. He eyed me in a way that reminded me of how Lucifer, the rattlesnake, had looked at me.

"Heard about the little girl."

"Her name is Emmy," I said.

"I told Evie you kids would be nothing but trouble."

"Everyone is trouble, Sid, you included." Sister Eve came from Emmy's room, leaving the door open behind her.

"How is she?" I asked.

"Fine, Odie. Awake now. She's asking for you."

Emmy was sitting up, her back propped against a couple of pillows. She smiled at me.

I sat on the bed. "You okay?"

She nodded. "Sister Eve told me what happened."

I hadn't closed the door completely, and I could hear raised, angry voices from the other room. I'd never heard Sister Eve and Sid argue before. It scared me, in large part because they were arguing about us — Emmy and me and Albert and Mose. I'd figured from the start that our time with Sister Eve would become like every other good thing I'd ever had. Gone.

Sid said, "When we leave this burg, those kids go their own merry way."

"I say what we do and don't do, Sid."

"You want to keep me in this show, you cut those kids loose."

"If you want to leave, Sid, I won't stop you."

"Listen, Evie, you remember how it was before you met me? You were a two-bit sideshow act. I made you Sister Eve."

"God made me Sister Eve."

"Was it God got you an offer of a weekly radio broadcast in Saint Louis?"

"What?"

"I got a telegram from Corman. If you want to go national, he's offering a big auditorium in Saint Louie. They'll broadcast straight from there to millions of Americans every Sunday."

"Millions?"

"Millions, baby. You'll go national."

"When?"

"We do Des Moines but cancel the Kansas stop and head straight to Saint Louis."

The other room was quiet. I looked at Emmy and she looked at me.

"That's where the kids are going, Sid. We're taking them with us. When we get there, I'll help them find their family, and then they'll be out of your hair. Deal?"

Another long quiet. "Deal," Sid finally said.

I'd been told lies all my life, and I knew one when I heard it.

CHAPTER TWENTY-NINE

Lucifer studied me. I studied Lucifer. He had me at an advantage because he never blinked. The other snakes generally seemed lethargic and docile in the glass cages, but Lucifer was always ready to strike. He repulsed and fascinated me at the same time.

After Whisker showed me the rattlesnake, I'd begun sneaking into Sister Eve's tent, just to look at that sinuous reptile and to make certain that he was still imprisoned behind that glass. Lucifer had slithered his way into my dreams at night, sometimes chasing me, sometimes springing up to strike at me with terrifying suddenness. Sometimes he and the murdered one-eyed Jack leapt at me from the dark of a nightmare together, and I'd wake and couldn't go back to sleep. Emmy would assure me dreamily, "Everything's okay, Odie."

But she was wrong, and I knew it.

All that might have been good in my life had been destroyed by the Tornado God.

Though I recalled my early years only vaguely, I remembered them with a sense of happiness. Then the Tornado God had taken my mother. After that, despite being on the road constantly, my father and Albert and I had found ways to be a family and to be happy. Then the Tornado God had lodged three bullets in my father's back. The Lincoln Indian Training School might not have been such a bad place, all things considered, but I knew in my heart that the Tornado God had put the Brickmans in charge just to make it hell. For a brief moment, I'd hoped that my life might be saved by Cora Frost, but the Tornado God had snatched her away, too.

So I didn't trust that everything would be okay. The Tornado God was watching, always watching, and I was sure he had something diabolical and destructive up his sleeve. This time, however, I thought I was a step ahead. I knew the source of the ill wind that was sure to blow in. It would come from Sid.

We all have secrets. With them, we're like squirrels with nuts. We hide them away, and bitter though they may be, we feed on them. If you're careful, you can follow a squirrel to his cache. The same was true for Sid, I thought. So I became his shadow.

In the morning, he would breakfast with Sister Eve and Emmy and me, then drive off in the red DeSoto and be gone until noon. What he did in that time was something he kept secret.

I asked Whisker about it, and he shrugged and said, "Always goes off like that somewhere. Never thought to ask where. His business."

I meant to make it mine.

We'd been with the Sword of Gideon Healing Crusade — Whisker told me Sid had given it that name because it sounded "kinda manly and holy and promising and comforting all in one big appetizing helping" — for well over a week when, on a morning we were all free of chores, a bunch of the men, young and old, put together a baseball game in the meadow near the tents. Whisker joined in, and I was surprised to see that even with his spindly arms, he swung a pretty mean bat. They put me in the outfield because they figured I couldn't do much damage there, which was all right by me.

There was some argument in the beginning over which side would get Mose. By then, everyone in the show had seen the grace in Mose's every movement. He was a young lion, sinuous and powerful, an otter in his easygoing playfulness. Everyone liked Mose and everyone wanted him on their team. Albert was another matter. My brother could be dark and brooding sometimes, and although he worked magic with engines and such and could jerry-rig any kind of contraption, he claimed a disinterest in athletics. I figured sitting on the bench at Lincoln School had soured him on the risks associated with taking part in organized sports. He declined at first to be a part of the game that day. But the sides were uneven without him, and cajoled mostly by Mose, he finally gave in. Like me, he was exiled to the outfield.

Our side was up to bat when I noticed Sid watching the game. He was usually gone in the mornings, so this was unusual. But his red DeSoto was parked near the tents, and I figured that at some point he'd take off on his mysterious business. The game was going hot and heavy, and Mose came to the plate. The women who helped with the crusade looked on and cheered, and Mose gave them a big grin in reply. Then he pointed toward left field, indicating that was where he intended to hit the pitch, and he signed, *Home run.* Just like Babe Ruth and Lou Gehrig, I thought.

Dimitri, the big Greek cook, was pitching for the other side. He had arms like rhino thighs and hurled the ball so fast and hard that Tsuboi, who was catching, gave a little cry each time it hit the thin pocket of his old glove. Dimitri threw twice, and Mose let both pitches fly by without a swing. On the third pitch, Mose split the air with his bat, and the crack of it against the horsehide was like a gunshot and the ball went sailing, a diminishing white dot in the blue sky above left field.

Sid, like everyone else, was mesmerized — by the hit itself, by the endless flight of the ball, and by the sight of Mose running the bases with all the power and grace of a colt in the Kentucky Derby. This was my chance.

I slipped away and slid into the red De-Soto, onto the floor in back, drew the folded blanket off the seat, and lay it over me. It was stifling hot, but I didn't have to wait long before I heard Sid open the driver's side door. He settled himself behind the wheel and we took off. He drove, I reckoned, for more than half an hour before pulling to a stop. He killed the engine and got out. As soon as his door closed, I sat up and peeked through the window. We were in a city, parked alongside a curb in front of a line of buildings, storefronts and offices. The nearest city I knew of was Mankato. I watched Sid stroll down the sidewalk, a brown leather satchel in his hand. He paused, set the satchel down, lit a cigarette, then continued on.

I left the DeSoto and followed at a safe distance. He disappeared around a corner. I ran up and carefully peered around the building. He'd stopped halfway down the block in front of a café, where he took a final drag off his cigarette, tossed what was left onto the street, and went inside. I crept to the café window.

Inside, Sid sat in a booth talking to some people. At first, I couldn't see them because

Sid's body blocked my view. He pointed south, as if giving directions of some kind. He opened his satchel, took out an envelope, and handed it over. He stood up, said a few more words, then turned to leave. That's when I saw who was in the booth, and I knew that Albert had spoken the truth. Sister Eve was too good to be true.

Back in New Bremen, Sid parked in front of the Morrow House, grabbed his satchel, and went inside. I slid from the back and followed after him. He went directly to Sister Eve's suite. I waited a few minutes, then went in myself. They sat at the table where Sister Eve usually had breakfast delivered. She looked up and, when she saw me, seemed relieved.

"There you are, Odie. We thought we'd lost you."

"I was just bumming around town," I said.

She studied me closely. "Are you all right?"

I wasn't. I was so full of anger I wanted to spit. I wanted to explode at her, at them both. But I kept the lid on.

"I'm fine," I said. "But I think I'd like to lie down for a while."

I went to the bedroom I shared with Emmy and shut the door, but not all the way. I left it open a crack and stood beside it, listening.

"I told them to meet us in Des Moines," Sid said, keeping his voice low.

"We don't have to do this, Sid."

"You've listened to me this far, Evie. And haven't I got you places?"

"All right," she said, giving in, but not happily.

"And here are the papers to sign for Corman."

I peeked through the crack and saw him pull a document from his satchel, which he laid before Sister Eve.

"Should I read this?"

"Just sign, baby. Everything will be set in Saint Louis when we arrive."

After she'd done as he'd asked, he took the papers, put them back in his satchel, and set it on the floor next to his chair. There was a knock at the door to the suite.

"Come in," Sister Eve called.

The door opened and I heard Whisker's voice. "Got some trouble down at the tent, Sid."

"What is it?"

"Cops looking for somebody. Say they have a warrant."

"For who?"

"Guy name of Pappas. I think it might be Dimitri."

"I'm coming."

"I'm going with you," Sister Eve said.

I was still peeking through the crack in the door, and I saw her get up and start toward the room where I stood. I hurried to the bed and lay down. She tapped lightly.

"Yeah?" I answered, trying to sound a little groggy.

She nudged the door open. "Sid and I are going down to the tent, Odie. I'd like you to stay here until we come back, all right? Don't go out until we return, promise?"

"Sure," I said. "What's going on?"

"Nothing to worry about. Just stay here."

I heard them leave, and as soon as they were gone, I crept from the bedroom. Sid's leather satchel still sat on the floor next to the chair where he'd put it. I grabbed the satchel, set it on the table, and opened it. It was stuffed with papers and documents, with handbills for the show, and with envelopes like the one I'd seen him give the people in the café in Mankato. I opened one of the envelopes and found that it held three ten-dollar bills. Each of the other envelopes, five in all, held varying amounts — two more with thirty, two with fifty, and one with a hundred — all in the same ten-dollar denomination. In a side pocket of the satchel, I found a small, silver-plated revolver. In another pocket was a large brown snap case. I released the snap and lifted the lid. Inside lay a syringe and several vials of clear liquid.

When Albert and I had traveled with our father as he made his rounds delivering bootlegged liquor, we'd routinely visited a man who ran a speakeasy in Cape Girardeau. On our last visit, my father had trouble rousing him, pounding at the door for a long time before the man finally opened up. He looked disheveled and disoriented and stood swaying in the doorway. In one hand he held a syringe, in the other a vial of clear liquid. When my father saw this, he hustled me and Albert back to our truck and drove away immediately. When I asked him what was wrong with the man and why we hadn't completed the delivery, my father said angrily, "I don't service dope fiends."

Dope, I thought, looking at the snap case in my hand. Sid was a dope fiend. Which didn't surprise me in the least.

I thought about taking one or even all of the envelopes. But I could hear Albert's voice in my head, giving me hell for stealing. So I left the money. But I did take the snap case with its syringe and vials of dope. I could at least deprive Sid of that illicit pleasure.

I left the hotel and went down to the meadow where the Sword of Gideon Healing Crusade had set up shop. I saw Sid's red De-Soto next to a couple of police cruisers parked near the big tent, and I kept well away, lurking among the cottonwoods along the railroad tracks above the river. After a while, I saw the cops troop out, Dimitri in handcuffs between two of them. Sister Eve and Sid followed behind. Dimitri went into the back of one of the patrol cars, and Sid and Sister Eve spent a moment talking with the officers, then the cops pulled away. Sid returned to the big tent immediately, but Sister Eve stood alone for a while, staring in the direction Dimitri had been taken. She looked like a shepherdess who'd lost a lamb to the wolves. Then she followed where Sid had gone and disappeared into the tent.

I thought about tracking down Albert and Mose and Emmy and telling them what I'd seen in Mankato, telling them that we had to leave, leave now. Instead, I stomped my way down to the sand spit where we'd camped and where I'd first heard Sister Eve's beautiful, siren voice calling and where she'd shared with me a little of the history of her scar. Everything about the day was oppressive — the heat, the humidity, the sense of betrayal, of another dream dying. In a copse of birch trees across the river, crows had gathered in a rookery, and their constant calling fell on my ears like harsh taunting, and in them, too, I heard the echo of Albert's words warning me: *One by one.*

I hated Sister Eve. I'd believed her. About God, about her healing, about the beautiful life that might be ahead of us with the crusade, about everything. Now I could see that she was a fake and none of it was true. How stupid could I be? How many times did my heart have to be broken before I wised up? I sat in the shade of a cottonwood and watched the brown water sweep past, and before I knew it, I was crying. They were hot, angry tears, and I was ashamed to be shedding them so openly and glad that I was alone.

But I wasn't alone for long.

"Odie!"

I heard Emmy's cry and looked up to see her and Albert and Mose making their way down the riverbank, coming from the direction of the meadow and the tent village. Emmy ran toward me and threw her arms around me as if I'd been lost to her forever.

"Oh, Odie, I was so afraid."

I saw that she was crying, too.

"I'm okay," I told her, trying to wipe away my tears before Albert and Mose saw them.

"Where were you?" Albert demanded as he approached. "You just disappeared from the ball game. We've been looking for you everywhere."

"We have to leave," I told him without prelude. "We have to get out of here."

Mose signed, *Why?*

My voice was so choked with anger that I could barely speak, and I signed back, *Because I hate Sister Eve.*

They all stared at me as if I'd suddenly grown antlers or a third eye.

"But we love Sister Eve," Emmy said.

"You didn't see what I saw."

"What did you see?" Albert asked.

"Remember when you told me that something about Sister Eve stunk to high heaven? I know what that is now."

I told them how I'd sneaked into the back of Sid's automobile when he'd driven to Mankato and how I'd followed him to the café. I told them how I'd watched him give an envelope full of money to someone. And I told them how, when he stepped away from the booth where they sat, I saw who they were. I paused a moment to gather myself.

Who was it? Mose signed desperately.

"You remember the man with the hunched-over boy in the first tent show we saw? That boy who was bent over so bad he could barely walk? And when Sister Eve touched him, his spine just straightened right up? They were both there. And the woman who stuttered and we couldn't understand what she was saying? She was there. And the cripple guy who threw away his crutches? Yeah, he was there, too. All of them being paid off for the show they put on. Or maybe being paid for the next one, because when Sister Eve gets to Des Moines, they'll be there, too."

They stared at me, all of them as speechless as Mose.

"Don't you get it?" I screamed at them. "She's a fake. Everything about her is a lie."

"No, Odie," Emmy said. "She's an angel."

"Some angel," I said bitterly, and tears rolled down my cheeks again and I didn't bother trying to stop them.

Mose signed, *What about the man with the dead wife?*

"She didn't heal the dead wife, did she? And if Emmy hadn't told me to play my harmonica, Sister Eve wouldn't have a face now, would she? Tell me who saved who that night."

"She's healed so many people, Odie," Emmy argued. "They can't all be fakes."

"I saw a lot of envelopes with money in them. I think whenever Sid disappears in the morning, he goes to pay off the people who've put on a show for Sister Eve."

What about Whisker? Mose signed. *Tsuboi? Everybody else? She helps them.*

"Or just uses them," I said. "Until they get hauled away like Dimitri."

"We should ask Whisker," Emmy said. "He wouldn't lie."

"How would you know? You're just a kid." I said it harshly, and as soon as the words were out of my mouth and I saw how they struck Emmy, I regretted them.

Albert hadn't spoken in a while. Now he said, "Whisker's your friend, Odie. Would you know if he was lying?"

I said, "I'm thinking he won't lie if I ask him straight."

"Then ask him straight," Albert said.

"All right, I will. But one thing first." From my shirt pocket, I pulled the snap case.

What's that? Mose signed.

"Sid's a dope fiend." I opened the case and showed them the syringe and vials.

"Doesn't surprise me," Albert said. "Get rid of it, Odie."

"That's exactly what I was going to do."

I snapped the case closed and threw it as far as I could. When it hit the river, it disappeared with barely a splash.

"Let's go get some answers," Albert said.

CHAPTER THIRTY

At the tent, we were told that Sister Eve and Sid had gone to the police station to try to spring Dimitri, who, we learned, was wanted on suspicion of selling bootlegged liquor, which to Albert and me was really no crime at all. We found Whisker alone on the platform inside the big tent, his thin, fast fingers doing a little skip across the piano keyboard. When he played during a crusade service, his head was bare, but most other times, he wore a little black fedora at a jaunty tilt. As we mounted the platform, his dark blue lips curved in a warm smile.

"Hey, Buck. We were worried. You kinda disappeared."

"Just had to get away and do some thinking, Whisker."

His fingers stopped tickling the ivories and the skin around his eyes crinkled seriously as he studied me. "Whatever you were thinking, it looks like it didn't sit with you all that well."

"I've got a question to ask you, Whisker. I

need the truth."

He sat back on the piano bench, and his eyes went from me to Albert, to Mose, and finally to Emmy. It was hot in the tent, and a little sheen of sweat formed a glistening mustache above his upper lip. "Knowing the truth ain't always what it's cracked up to be, Odie."

"Will you tell me the truth or not?"

"If I know it."

"Sister Eve, does she really heal?"

"Now what kind of question is that?"

"Just answer it."

"Odie, I seen more miracles inside this tent than I can recall."

"Real miracles or fake? Fake like that boy with the bent-up spine and the woman with the twisted tongue."

"Ahhh," he said with a nod. "So, you think you know the truth about those folks, do you?"

"I saw Sid paying them off."

"Them's Sid's people all right."

"What about all the others?"

Whisker put his fingers on the keys again and softly began to play a tune, which I recognized from the radio: "Little White Lies." He bent his head as he played, but after a few bars, peered up from under the brim of his fedora. "Sister Eve's the one you need to be talking to."

"She's a liar."

"She's a lot of things, Odie," he said, continuing to play. "A liar ain't one of them."

"She claimed to heal those people, Sid's people, and that was a lie."

"When you're a kid, Odie, things seem cut-and-dried, but it ain't that way. Talk to Sister Eve. I guarantee she won't lie."

"Whisker —" I tried again, but he cut me off.

"Like I told you, talk to Sister Eve."

We went to her tent to wait for her return. I'd been inside many times when no one was around, but it was a first for the others. Their eyes went big when they saw the snakes in the terrariums on the low, narrow table, but I explained to them that only Lucifer was really dangerous, the others were fake. "More lies," I said.

We didn't have to wait long before I heard Sister Eve outside, talking to some of the women who cooked with Dimitri. She assured them that Sid was taking care of things and Dimitri would be rejoining us soon, then she came into her tent. When she saw the looks on our faces, she smiled reassuringly.

"Don't worry about Dimitri. Sid's taken care of things."

"This isn't about Dimitri," I said.

She looked at me closely, then at the others. "What's wrong?"

"You're a liar." As soon as I said it, tears welled up in my eyes, because it felt to me as if I was killing something, something beautiful, but I tried to tell myself that you can't kill a thing that never was.

"A liar?" She absorbed the accusation, nodded, and sat on the padded bench before her dressing table. "Give me your hand, Odie."

Like iron, I stood unmoved and unmoving.

"Don't be afraid," she said. "Just give me your hand. What harm can it do?"

From outside came the sound of preparations in the cooking tent, the clank of pots and pans as the kitchen crew began to put together the meal that would be served to those who came to the crusade that evening. I heard Dimitri's voice giving orders, and I knew that Sid had found a way to spring him. In the big tent, a couple of other musicians had joined Whisker, and they began practicing one of the hymns that would be sung that night, "Be Thou My Vision." Still, I didn't move.

I felt Emmy's touch on my arm. "Go on, Odie."

Sister Eve held her hand motionless in the air before me, and finally I reached out and took it. She closed her eyes, and after a long moment, said, "I see." She smiled, let go of my hand, and patted the bench at her side. "Sit, Odie."

"I don't want to sit with you," I said.

"I understand. So, you followed Sid and you think you know the truth."

"I saw him with those phonies. You didn't really heal them."

"I've never claimed to heal anyone, Odie. I've always said it's God who heals, not me."

"Heals through you, then. But that's not the way it is. Nobody's healed. You're a fake and they're fakes."

"You're upset, Odie," she said.

"Fake!" I screamed at her. "As fake as this cobra."

I turned from her and went to the low table where the terrariums sat and without thinking reached into the glass enclosure that held the harmless snake Whisker had told me they called Mamba. I brought it out writhing in the grip of my hand, and I stepped toward Sister Eve and thrust it at her, as if in evidence. Sister Eve reacted not at all. It was Emmy who screamed. She danced away from me and backed right into the narrow table where all the terrariums sat. She tumbled, and the table went over with her, and I heard the shatter of glass. In the next instant came the awful rattle of Lucifer.

I stood paralyzed, but Albert was a blur of motion. He leapt the tipped-over table, grabbed up Emmy, and held her out to Mose, who snatched her away in his arms. Just before he came back over the table to safety, I heard him give a little cry of pain.

Sister Eve was up, and she knelt where Emmy now stood. She put her hands on Emmy's shoulders and looked her over quickly. "Did he bite you?"

"Unh-uh." Emmy shook her head while tears streamed down her cheeks.

"Thank God for that," Sister Eve said.

Then a voice spoke, the kind of voice a stone might have if it could speak. Albert said, "It got me."

The bite was high on his right calf, two marks bleeding red below the cuff of the pant leg he lifted to show us. Lucifer, unseen, continued his rattling on the far side of the tipped-over table. Mose, in one powerful motion and with a startling crack, snapped off one of the table legs, and I watched him bring it down again and again behind the barrier of the tabletop until the rattling ceased.

Emmy's scream brought in some of the crusade folks, Dimitri and Sid among them. Sid took in the broken table, the shattered terrariums, and finally Albert's bared calf.

"Was it Lucifer?"

Albert nodded.

"Christ," Sid said.

"What do we do?" I pleaded.

"Don't panic. I've got antivenom. He should be fine. Keep him calm and immobile, Evie. I'll be right back."

"Where are you going?" Sister Eve asked.

"To the hotel. I keep the antivenom in my satchel. I'll only be a few minutes."

My legs suddenly threatened to give out under me. "A brown satchel?"

"Yeah, brown."

"A snap case with a syringe and some vials?"

"Yes." He shot me a stern look. "Why?"

I could barely say the words. "It's not there."

"What? Where is it?"

"In the river."

"The river?"

"I threw it in. I thought it was dope."

"Good God, Odie." He grabbed my shoulders, and I thought he was going to crush me with his bare hands. Instead he shoved me away and whispered, "Oh, Christ."

"What do we do, Sid?" Sister Eve said, so calmly she might have been asking, "What shall we have for dinner?"

"We get him to a doctor. Now."

Sid drove, Emmy and Mose up front beside him. I sat in back with Albert and Sister Eve. I could feel my brother's body shaking, and I didn't know if it was because of the poison or because he was as scared as I was.

"I'm sorry, Albert," I kept saying. "I'm so sorry." I wanted to beg him, *Please don't die,* but I was afraid to say the word *die.* I didn't even want to think it. Yet there it was, a big balloon inside my head, crowding out all other thinking. Soundlessly, I screamed, *Don't die, don't die, don't die!*

The doctor's office was just off the central square in New Bremen, a two-story red-brick house with a white picket fence and a sign hung out front: ROY P. PFEIFFER, M.D. & JULIUS PFEIFFER, M.D. We piled out, and Albert hobbled inside surrounded by us all. There was a little waiting area off the foyer, where a mother in a flowered housedress sat with her small child. A bell over the door tinkled as we entered the house, and a moment later a woman appeared, smiling. She was young and wore pants, which wasn't the way a lot of women dressed back then, especially in small towns. When she saw our large entourage and the frantic looks on our faces, she lost her smile and said, "Who's the patient?"

"He is," I said, taking Albert's hand.

She glanced at his rolled-up pant leg and her brow furrowed. "What's the trouble?"

"Snakebite," Sid said. "A rattlesnake."

That clearly surprised her, but she composed herself quickly. "Bring him in here."

She led us to a room with an examining table, on which she had Albert lie down. "I'll be right back," she said and disappeared.

There was a cabinet full of little bottles and beneath it a stainless-steel table with several drawers. There was a sink, a standing metal lamp with a big metal shade, a wooden writing desk with a chair, a few small pastoral paintings on the wall, and a window that overlooked a rose garden in the backyard. The window was up and the scent from the roses wafted in, overpowering the vague smell of medication. I'd never been in a doctor's office before. At the Lincoln Indian Training School, there'd been what they called an infirmary, which was nothing more than a room with four beds where children with some communicable disease like chicken pox or mumps or measles were sent to be isolated while their contagion ran its course. It was also the place where, while Albert and Mose and I were there, a couple of children were sent to die. The examining room in Dr. Pfeiffer's home seemed much more encouraging.

The woman returned quickly with a man of perhaps sixty. He wore a white shirt with the sleeves rolled to his elbows and a red bow tie with little white polka dots. His glasses had thick lenses, so that his eyes loomed huge and blue behind them. His gray hair was ruffled, as if from a strong wind.

"I'm Dr. Pfeiffer," he said, addressing Sid. "Is this your son?"

"No. Just a —" Sid fumbled for the right word.

"He's with me," Sister Eve said. "One of my young workers from the Sword of Gideon Healing Crusade."

The doctor's gray eyebrows lifted in a way that made me understand exactly what he thought of Sister Eve and her healing crusade. But he said, "A rattlesnake bite. You're sure."

"Quite sure," Sister Eve said.

"On your calf, son?" the doctor said, finally giving his attention to Albert.

"Yes, sir."

Albert turned his leg so that the doctor could see the two bleeding wounds. Although it hadn't been long since Lucifer had plunged his fangs into my brother, the skin around the wounded area was already black and swollen, with poison-looking tendrils climbing upward toward his knee and down toward his ankle.

"He needs antivenom," Sid said.

"Antivenom," the doctor said in a dead echo. "Mr. — ?"

"Calloway. Sid Calloway."

"Mr. Calloway, we haven't had a rattlesnake bite in Sioux County in decades. The rattlesnakes, if there ever were any here, were driven out a long time ago. So far as I know, there isn't any antivenom anywhere in these parts. You're sure it was a rattlesnake?"

"Believe me, it was a rattlesnake. And how do you know there's no antivenom?"

"Because a rattlesnake bite around here would be news, and I'd know if someone had proper treatment for it. But I'll have Sammy make some phone calls." He turned to the young woman in pants. "Try the De Coster Surgical Hospital in Mankato. See if they can

357

offer any help." He turned back to examining Albert's leg. "Maybe we can get some of that poison out," he finally said.

He went to the stainless-steel table, opened the top drawer, and pulled out a scalpel. From the cabinet, he drew down one of the bottles of medication and held the scalpel above the sink while he poured the contents of the bottle over the blade. He took a white towel from a stack sitting on the table, folded it in half, and returned to Albert.

"Roll onto your stomach, son." When my brother had done so, the doctor said, "This is going hurt some, okay?"

"Okay," Albert said.

Dr. Pfeiffer slid the folded towel under Albert's leg, then made two incisions that formed a V between the fang marks, and blood ran freely down the skin of my brother's calf. Pfeiffer went back to the table and from another drawer took out what looked like a syringe without a needle and a small glass bulb with a rubber tube attached. He plugged the syringe device into the end of the tube, set the glass bulb firmly over the incisions he'd made, and began pumping the syringe, which sucked the air from inside the little glass bulb, creating a vacuum. The bulb filled with blood and, we hoped, snake venom, and when the doctor pulled it loose, the dark red mixture gushed down onto the folded towel. The doctor repeated the procedure three times, and in the end, the towel was a soaking, bloody mess.

On completion of the last procedure, as Pfeiffer was treating the wounded area with iodine — which made Albert grit his teeth and groan — the young woman returned. "They've got nothing. But they suggested I call the Winona General Hospital. There are still rattlers in the bluff country and they treat snakebites from time to time. So I called and explained our situation. They're sending someone in a car with antivenom."

"Winona," Dr. Pfeiffer said, in a tone that didn't sound promising. "That'll take four or five hours. Did they have any suggestions what to do in the meantime?"

"Try suctioning out the poison and keep him calm."

"That's it?" He studied Albert's black, swelling calf, and his eyes behind those thick lenses were huge blue pools of doubt. He taped gauze over the wounds and said, "Get him into the observation room, Sammy, and make him comfortable. I want to talk to Winona General myself."

Sid and Mose supported my brother, who could barely walk now, and followed the woman with pants and a man's name down a short hallway to a room with a bed, where Albert lay down. Despite the summer heat, he was shaking something awful, and Sammy put a light blanket over him.

A few minutes later, Pfeiffer appeared at the doorway and said to Sister Eve, "May I speak with you?"

They stepped into the hallway, and I went and stood near the door so that I could hear what was said.

"The physician at Winona General has advised me that if the poison makes its way to his heart and lungs, the chances of saving him aren't good, and even if we do, there's a good chance of permanent damage to his internal organs. They suggested that if we want to be certain of saving the boy, we need to consider amputating that leg before it's too late."

"When is too late?"

"I don't really know. But if I take the leg and it helps, then maybe we've saved him. If I take the leg and he dies, what have we lost?"

"Can't we wait for the antivenom?"

"According to Winona General, in four or five hours, that boy could be dead."

I thought about what life would be like for Albert if he had only one leg. I remembered seeing a man in Joplin once, when I was on the road with Albert and my father. The man wore an old army uniform. He had only one leg and was supporting himself with a crutch. As we passed, he held out a hat to us and said, "Lost my leg fighting for America in the Great War. Could you help me out?" My father gave him the change in his pocket, and we walked on. In my mind's eye, all I could see was Albert on a street corner somewhere, holding out his hat for the charity of spare change.

I stepped into the hallway and said, "No."

Pfeiffer scowled at me.

"His brother," Sister Eve explained. "Odie, it may be the only chance we have to save his life."

"He wouldn't want a life with one leg," I said and fought back tears. "He'd rather be dead. Wouldn't you?"

Pfeiffer looked to Sister Eve. "The boy has no parents to make this decision?"

"We're orphans," I said.

"We should ask Albert what he wants," Sister Eve suggested.

"I'm not sure the boy's in any condition to make that kind of decision," Pfeiffer replied.

"Why don't we see?"

She returned to Albert's bedside and knelt as if she were about to pray. She took Albert's hand in hers. "Listen to me, Albert."

He rolled his head on the pillow so that he could see her face.

"The doctor thinks he might be able to save your life if he amputates your leg."

Albert was slow to respond, but he finally said, "I'll die if he doesn't?"

"That's a possibility."

"But he's not sure?"

Sister Eve lifted her eyes to Pfeiffer, who

gave a shrug.

"He's not sure."

"I want my leg," Albert said, his voice trembling.

"All right." Sister Eve leaned and kissed Albert on the forehead. She stood up and turned to Pfeiffer. "You heard."

Pfeiffer said, "I have other patients to see to, but I'll continue to check in. Keep him as calm and comfortable as you can. I'll come if you need me." He and Sammy left, and the rest of us were alone with Albert and the poison that was climbing toward my brother's heart.

CHAPTER THIRTY-ONE

Through the long afternoon of that hot day in the summer of 1932, while we waited for the arrival of the antivenom we hoped would save my brother's life, the creep of time was pure torture.

Albert grew worse as the hours passed. The black inched up his leg, which ballooned in a frightening swell of flesh. Sweat streamed from every pore in his body, soaking his clothes and the bedding beneath him, and because of the pain, he groaned miserably and constantly. Near sunset, he began to labor in his breathing as well.

Another doctor had arrived, Pfeiffer's son, Julius, returning from home visits. Pfeiffer called him Julie. Sammy, it turned out, was his wife. If I hadn't been so eaten up with worry over Albert, I'd have found it amusing that the man was called by a woman's name and the woman by a man's. But it was clear they were devoted to each other, and it was clear as well that the young Dr. Pfeiffer had no better idea what to do about Albert's snakebite than his father did. He suggested wrapping Albert's leg in ice in an attempt to reduce the swelling, which he and Sammy did together, but it seemed not to help at all. Albert was in such misery that the young doctor finally suggested morphine for the pain, which worked to a degree but left Albert groggy.

There were three chairs in the small room where Albert lay dying. As my brother grew worse, the two Dr. Pfeiffers and Sammy took turns sitting in one of them, and the rest of us — all except Sid, who'd gone back to the tent village to post notices of cancellation for that night — sat in the other chairs in shifts. The room felt stifling despite the open window, and the scent of the roses from the backyard garden did nothing to dull the hovering sense of doom. To this day, I cannot smell a rose without thinking immediately of that deathwatch in New Bremen. When we weren't with Albert, we sat in the waiting area alongside the other patients who came seeking treatment. A woman with a boy whose cough was a persistent bark. A man with a great goiter ballooning from the side of his neck. A young mother and father, hardly more than teenagers, with a baby not far removed from newborn. A man with his wife, who had a dish towel full of ice pressed against her eye because, he explained gruffly to Sammy, she was "stupid in the kitchen." Sister Eve was sitting with me when the man said this, and her comment to him was "When you kick your dog, do you also blame him for the bruise?"

I had to get out of that house, and as the man glared at Sister Eve, I stood and left through the front door. On the porch, a swing hung from chains, and I sat there. The sun was low in the west, floating on a sea of dark clouds gathering along the horizon.

Sister Eve came and sat beside me on the swing. She pushed gently with her feet, and the swing rocked easily back and forth, and she said, "You haven't asked me, Odie."

"Asked you what?"

"To heal Albert."

"Because you're a fake." Hours before, I would have thrown that accusation at her like a rock, but the fire of my anger was long dead, and all that remained was ash.

"Because of what you saw with Sid and the others?"

"I suppose I knew all along. Albert warned me that I'd find out something about you stinks to high heaven. You can't heal people."

"I told you before, Odie, that I've never claimed to heal people. I've always said God does the healing."

"But nobody's really healed." Although I'd thought my anger had died away, I felt an ember still burning.

"Those people you saw with Sid, they were healed of exactly the afflictions they claimed. Just not in that particular moment. Jed and his son Mickey, the Lord healed them in Cairo, Illinois. Lois had her stutter taken away in Springfield, Missouri. Gooch — he's the man with the crutches — the strength returned to his legs in Ada, Oklahoma. There are others you haven't seen."

"I don't understand."

"In the crusade service, you saw a re-creation of what actually happened for them. It was Sid's idea. He believes we need to, as he puts it, 'prime the pump,' when we first arrive in a new town. To a degree, he's probably right."

It was true that since the first night I'd sat in the big tent and seen what purported to be healing, attendance had swelled. Every bench inside was packed every night now, and people were forced to stand along the edges. There'd been more healings, and at the end of a service when Sister Eve invited the crowd to eat soup and bread together, even those who'd experienced no healing themselves left with an undeniable glow on their faces.

"Sometimes, Odie," Sister Eve went on, "in order for people to reach up and embrace their most profound belief in God, they need to stand on the shoulders of others. That's what Jed and Mickey and Lois and Gooch do. Their experiences are the shoulders for others to climb on. And, Odie, it works. People come forward and I take their hands and I can feel how powerful their faith is, and that's what heals them. Not me. Their faith in a great, divine power."

She used the toes of her shoes to keep the swing rocking, and I felt myself being lulled by the motion and by the hypnotic flow of her voice.

"Jed, Mickey, Lois, Gooch, these are also people who have no work, no home, no way to provide for themselves. Traveling with the crusade ensures their livelihood. But that's no excuse, I suppose, for the fact that what they do for me now is, in fact, a fraud. I've argued with Sid over this, and I've always given in. Maybe it's time to stop."

"You take their hands," I said, remembering how she'd taken mine, "and you see things?"

"That's it in a nutshell, Odie. I can see where they've been and where they are now. I can see what they've lost and what they seek. I can see the holes so many believe their souls have dropped into, and sometimes that helps me lift them back up to a place of faith."

"How?" I eyed the scar half-hidden by the long sweep of her fox-colored hair. "Something to do with your baptism?"

"In a way." She ran her finger down the length of the scar. "My father gave me this,

367

when I was fifteen. We lived on a farm, or what passed for a farm in the sandhills of Nebraska, crops scratched from soil never meant to grow corn. He was a bitter, disappointed man with the Devil always at his back. One day, that Devil stepped in front of him. He beat my mother, and when I tried to intervene, he beat me, broke a jug of corn liquor across the side of my face, knocked me unconscious. When I woke up, I found myself lying in our half-filled horse trough, my mother dead on the ground beside it. My father I found hanging from a rope he'd thrown over a beam in our barn. I walked away from that, a long walk, Odie, but I discovered that what my father had done changed me forever, gave me something unique, this ability to see into the minds and lives of others. He took from me, yes, but without having any idea of what he was doing, he also gave."

"And you can really heal?"

"How many times do I need to tell you it's not me? It's faith that heals. Sometimes when I see into a person's heart, I understand that their faith will never be strong enough, and what I try to give them is a measure of peace, maybe insight to help them on their way."

"Like the man who killed his wife?"

"Yes, Odie, like him."

I stopped the swing and turned to her eagerly. "If Albert believes, really believes, can you heal him?"

She smiled beautifully. "Not me."

"God then."

"Do you believe in God?"

"I want to. I really want to. If you heal Albert — if God heals Albert — I will, I swear. I'll believe everything."

"Do you know what a leper is?"

I did and nodded.

"And do you know the story of the ten lepers healed by Jesus?"

I knew a few things from the Bible. The stories of Christmas and Easter and the Good Samaritan and such, the big selling points. The ten lepers was a new one to me.

"Jesus is on the road one day when ten lepers call out and beg him to heal them. Jesus takes pity and does as they've asked. Only one thanks Jesus for the miracle. And to that man, Jesus explains, 'Your faith has made you well.' You see? Jesus takes no credit. It's the man's faith that has healed him. I believe Albert can be healed, but only if his faith is strong enough. And I can't give him that."

"But maybe I can," I said, jumping from the swing. "I'll make him believe."

I headed quickly to the room where Albert lay. The young Dr. Pfeiffer stood at his bedside, checking Albert's pulse. I ignored the doctor, knelt, leaned to my brother, and said, "Albert, can you hear me?"

His eyes had been closed, but they opened

now, just a crack.

"Listen to me, this is important. Sister Eve can heal, she can. She's not a fraud. She's the real deal, I swear to you. All you have to do is believe, Albert. Believe in God. Believe with all your heart. That's it. Tell her that you believe, Albert. Please, please tell her that you believe." Tears fell onto the sweat-drenched pillowcase, a river of my tears. I'd taken Albert's hand in mine, and I squeezed it desperately. "You don't have to die. Just tell her you believe."

Sister Eve knelt on the far side of the bed and gently held Albert's other hand. He turned the slits of his tired eyes to her. She spoke softly, as if coaxing a skittish animal to come and be fed. "It's the truth, Albert. You can be healed. The belief is in you, the belief in a loving God. I can see that your mother put it there a long time ago. It's still in your heart, Albert. Look down deep inside and you'll see that God is there, waiting with his healing light, his healing touch, his healing love. Believe in him, Albert. Believe in him with all your heart and all your mind and all your soul, and you will be healed."

Albert stared at her with his dulled eyes and made no response.

"Say it, Albert," I pleaded. "Tell her you believe."

"Let go of all the darkness, Albert," Sister Eve cooed. "It's easier than you think. It will be like letting go of a great weight. It will be as if you have wings, I promise."

"Just say it, Albert. For God's sake, just tell her you believe."

My brother's lower lip twitched. His mouth opened and one word escaped in a long, exhausted sigh: "Liar."

"No," I cried. "It's not a lie, Albert. She's not a fake. Just believe, goddamn it."

But he closed his eyes again, turned his face from her, and said not another word.

"Heal him, Sister Eve," I begged, wiping my eyes with my fist. "You can do it."

She ignored my plea and whispered to my brother, "There's nothing to fear. The journey ahead of you will take you to a place of peace."

I knew what she was doing. She'd looked into my brother's heart and understood that his faith would never be strong enough for healing, and now she was offering him the only thing she could, which was comfort. She knew he was going to die.

"Don't let him go," I cried to her.

"It's in God's hands, Odie." Her eyes were soft green pillows of kindness. "In God's alone."

But as I knelt at my brother's bedside, all I could think about was the shepherd eating his flock one by one.

Near dark, the storm that had been building

on the horizon overtook New Bremen. It threw lightning bolt after lightning bolt at the town and poured down rain in a way the earth had not seen since Noah. I saw rivers of rainwater fill the streets and Dr. Pfeiffer eye his pocket watch hopelessly, and I knew the antivenom would never arrive in time.

Because I was the one responsible for Albert's snakebite, the one who'd brought Death calling, and because I was a wretched coward as well, I couldn't stand to watch my brother die. So I ran.

CHAPTER THIRTY-TWO

By the time I reached the Minnesota River, I was soaked to the bone. When I'd fled the home of the physicians, I'd had no direction in mind, no destination, no plan. I simply couldn't remain where Albert lay pale and lifeless on the bed. Emmy had called out to me, but I hadn't turned back or even slowed down. I'd run, trying to escape the pain that ripped me apart but that no matter how fast my legs moved I could not outrun. When I reached the river, which flowed black and fast in the early dark brought on by the storm, it blocked my way and I could go no farther. I sat down on the wet sand and wept. After I'd cried every tear I could, I lifted my head to a sky still tormented by lightning and cursed, "You bastard." I didn't have to say his name. He knew.

By the time Sister Eve found me, the storm had passed, the worst of it anyway. Rain still fell, and Sister Eve, like me, was drenched. Her hair clung to her face in wet strands, and water dripped from her eyebrows and nose and chin. She sat beside me and said nothing until I finally spoke.

"You should have healed him."

"I couldn't, Odie."

"He was right about you. You're a liar."

"I've never told you anything but the truth. Did I tell you I would heal your brother?" She looked up at the sky, which was like heaven weeping down on her face. "I knew the moment I took his hand that I couldn't heal him."

A train approached on the tracks above the river, and the weight and rumble of the passing cars made the sand below me tremble, and the sound of the engine horn as it retreated was the sad wail of a beast in torment.

When the evening fell quiet again, Sister Eve said, "You believe you've lost everything. I understand that. I understand the darkness you're in. But even in the darkest night, God offers a light. Will you take my hand and come with me? There's something you need to see."

I had no strength to resist. I stood, put my hand in hers, and like a zombie, let myself be led. We walked through the soggy meadow, empty of vehicles except for the trucks of the Sword of Gideon Healing Crusade, past the tent village, where I could hear Whisker playing an extra-sad rendition of "Am I Blue?"

We climbed the hill to New Bremen, crossed the empty square, and finally came to the house where I'd fled from death. I stopped, pulled away from her, and stood in the rain, unmoving.

"I can't go in there."

"I understand, Odie. But you need to."

I wasn't ready to look upon Albert a last time. I wasn't ready to say goodbye.

"I can't."

She held out her hand, and rain gathered in her palm. "Trust me."

She led me into the house, down the hallway to the small room. Emmy and Mose were inside, and Sid, and the young Dr. Pfeiffer, who stood at the side of Albert's deathbed, blocking my view of my brother's pale, lifeless face. The doctor heard us enter and turned and stepped away.

There was Albert, just as he'd been when I ran away, his head on the pillow, his eyes closed. Sister Eve let go of my hand, and I thought I was probably supposed to go to my brother and . . . and what? How do you say goodbye when your heart is telling you how horribly wrong that would be? How do you let go when everything inside you is screaming to hold on?

I never did figure that one out. Because in the next moment, Albert's eyes opened, he turned his head to me, and he said, "Hey, Odie."

■ ■ ■ ■

Mose signed to me, *Doctor kept saying he couldn't understand what was keeping Albert alive. Should have been dead. Said it was a miracle. Only explanation.*

It was late in the evening by then, the storm long past, the rain ended, Dr. Pfeiffer and Dr. Pfeiffer and Sammy all abed, Sid back in his room at the hotel, and only Mose and Emmy and Sister Eve and me left to watch over Albert. The car from Winona General Hospital had arrived only moments after I'd fled, and the antivenom had been administered. His leg was still black, but not like it had been before. Some muscle tissue had been destroyed, which would cause him to limp slightly for the rest of his life. He was still weak and his breathing was a little raspy, but he wasn't dead. He was just sleeping now, long and deep.

Sammy had brought out cots for the rest of us. Emmy and Sister Eve slept in the room with Albert. Mose and I were put in the waiting area, where a candle burned on a table near us so that I could see Mose signing.

"A miracle," I said quietly. "Do you believe in God?"

I could see him rolling the question around in his head. *I don't know about the God in the Bible,* he signed. *But I know you and Albert*

376

and Emmy, and now Sister Eve. And I think about Herman Volz and Emmy's mother. I know love. So if it's true, like Sister Eve says, that God is love, then I guess I believe.

Mose went to sleep, but I watched the candle burn down, and finally I got up and went out onto the porch and sat in the swing. The town was dark and quiet. The sky had dressed itself in black and was sequined with stars. The clock on the courthouse struck once. The front door opened, and Sister Eve stepped out and sat with me on the swing.

"The doctor said Albert should have died. He said it was a miracle that he didn't. You took my brother's hand and saw that his faith wasn't strong enough to save him. Did you see that a miracle would happen?"

"I can't see what's up ahead, only what's in your heart at the moment. So I see where you've been and where you want to go. I can see what you want on your journey, but I can't see if it will come to you."

"What did Albert want?"

"What he's always wanted. To protect you. In his heart, he thought he'd failed."

"He didn't." I could feel the roll of tears down my cheeks, but they were tears of gratitude for a brother like Albert. I wiped them away and said, "What about Mose? Have you held his hand?"

"Of course."

"And what does he want?"

"To know who he is."

I thought about an Indian kid found in a ditch beside his dead mother, his tongue cut out, and no idea where he'd come from.

"And Emmy?"

"Emmy doesn't know what she wants yet, but she will."

"You've seen that?"

"I told you, I can't see the future. I just know Emmy and I know God."

Each time we rocked, one of the chains that held the porch swing gave a tired little groan. I finally mustered the courage to ask my next question.

"What about me? What do I want?"

"You're the easiest of all, Odie. The only thing you've ever wanted is home."

We swung gently back and forth in the comfort of each other's company, and I thought, in the long night after Albert should have died but didn't, that with Sister Eve and the Sword of Gideon Healing Crusade, maybe I'd finally found what I was looking for.

CHAPTER THIRTY-THREE

Albert spent the whole of the next day at the Pfeiffers' clinic with one of us constantly at his side. Mostly this was me, but occasionally Mose and Emmy took a turn. He was alone only once, for an hour or so in the afternoon when I left him napping and popped out to the confectionery on the town square with a quarter that Sammy, who had no children, had given me out of kindness. I bought lemon drops for Emmy and licorice for Mose and Tootsie Rolls for me and Albert, all in celebration of the miracle of my brother's life. That night, I stayed with him on a cot in his room but got little sleep. Albert tossed and turned and called out feebly from the depth of some nightmare. I spent most of those dark hours beating myself up for having thrown Sid's brown snap case with the antivenom into the river. I was glad when dawn finally came.

Late that morning, the Pfeiffers gave their blessing to move Albert to the tent village. Sid and Sister Eve came at noon to pick him up and pay the bill. Mose and Emmy were along. We helped Albert into the red DeSoto and drove to the meadow.

The crusade had originally been scheduled to stay for two weeks, but Sister Eve and Sid had decided that evening would be the final service before they packed up and headed to their next stop. Sid was excited. He wanted to use my brother in that last service, parade him for all to see, a kid who should have died but had been saved by Sister Eve. She absolutely forbade it. Sid gave in rather easily, and I figured that was the end of it. I couldn't have been more wrong.

In the late afternoon, Whisker bought that day's edition of the *Mankato Daily Free Press,* and Albert was big news. He wasn't the lead story, which was all about something called the Bonus Army, a massing of veterans in Washington, D.C., who were demanding delivery of some promised government relief. His picture was on page 2, along with an account of the snakebite that should have killed him but didn't. The article intimated that it was a miracle for which Sister Eve was responsible. It showed Albert lying peacefully asleep in the little room with Dr. Roy Pfeiffer standing at his bedside. The only bright spot in all this was that in the caption under the photograph it said that the boy's name was being withheld for reasons of privacy.

I had never seen Sister Eve really angry

before, but she exploded at Sid. They were alone in the tent that was her dressing room. The broken terrariums had been cleared away, the harmless snakes long ago slithered off to freedom. There is no privacy in a tent, and we heard every word of the argument.

"I swear, Evie, I don't know anything about this."

"Don't lie to me. This screams Sid Calloway."

"All right, all right. I called a reporter in Mankato and told him that what his readers needed right now was a little shot of hope. He interviewed Pfeiffer, both of them actually, and confirmed the story. He wanted to interview the kid, too, but I wouldn't let him."

I figured all this had occurred while I was out at the confectionery buying candy, and I kicked myself for ever having left my brother's side.

"No, you just let him take that young man's photograph so he could splash it all over southern Minnesota. My God, Sid, what were you thinking?"

"What was I thinking? That a miracle like this is exactly what we need going into Saint Louis. Evie, you'll be bigger than Aimee McPherson."

"That's not what I want, Sid, not what I ever wanted."

"No? You should have seen your eyes when I told you about Corman and broadcasting out of Saint Louis. Like big diamonds, they were, all glittery at the promise."

"The promise of reaching more people, Sid. Not for me. For them. Don't you understand? This has never been about me."

"Look, Evie, before me you were playing the two-bit circuit. But no more. You're going to Saint Louis, where you'll reach millions of people, just like you've always wanted, and you're going because of me, because I understand what it takes to get these rubes' attention."

"Rubes? Is that how you think of the people who come here every night looking for something hopeful? Sid, the world is in great darkness, and for whatever reason, God gave me a light and made me a beacon. It's sacred what I do."

For a long while, there was nothing from the other side of the canvas but silence.

"I guess I made a mistake, Evie," Sid finally admitted. "I'm sorry."

"It's not me you need to apologize to. It's those kids, whose whole future you've jeopardized. Go on," we heard her say. "I hope they can forgive you."

I had never cottoned to Sid. From the get-go, everything about him felt too slick. When he found Emmy and me in the big tent standing at the side of the cot where Albert lay, he ran his fingers over the thin black line of his mustache and stared at the meadow grass trampled nearly dead by the feet of all those who'd come looking for hope or a miracle.

"Okay," he finally said, "I may have made a mistake."

"You really stepped in it," I said. "Thanks a lot."

"My whole focus is on building Eve's following, kid. Don't you want that for her? She's got a gift."

"And you're not doing half bad mooching off her," I pointed out.

"Listen, you —"

Whisker, who was up on the platform sitting at the piano, cut him off. "Don't deny it, Sid. Boy's right. We all ride on Sister Eve's coattails."

"You stay out of this, Whisker," Sid snapped. "What I'm trying to say is that I'm sorry if I've caused you any trouble. Although nothing seems to have come of it yet."

"Key word, *yet,*" I threw at him.

"Well, I just wanted to say I'm sorry."

His apology had the dull ring of a cracked bell, but I didn't see any point in needling him further. He turned and left the tent, and as soon as he was gone, I said, "We have to be ready to go."

"Tired," Albert said. "Just want to lie here."

"Somebody's going to see that picture of you," I told him. "Sooner or later it's going to bring the Black Witch down on us."

Albert stared up at the tent ceiling and said

weakly, "Maybe not."

He looked so beat I wasn't sure he could even stand up. But it was more than just a physical debility. The snakebite hadn't killed him, but the venom had deadened his spirit. Albert had been the engine driving us, pushing us forward, always forward. The dull eyes and monotone voice came not from my brother but from the shell that seemed to be all that was left of him.

"We're leaving and that's that," I said. "I'm going to tell Mose."

He was working with Dimitri, and when I gave him the word, he just nodded. He turned to the big Greek and made a sign, not one that we'd ever taught him, but something he and Dimitri must have created between them. The Greek said, "You're the best damn worker I ever saw." He held out his hand for Mose to shake. "I wish you well, son."

When we returned, Sister Eve was sitting on the grass at the side of Albert's cot, holding my brother's hand. She looked up and smiled.

"Sid has his faults, but he's not a bad man at heart. He's got some connections with the law in town here, and he's gone off to see what he can do to make sure you're safe until we leave tomorrow. I want you to stay with me."

"It's kidnapping, Sister Eve," I argued. "Can Sid get around that?"

Give him a chance? Mose signed.

I shook his head. "Too risky. Emmy back with the Brickmans. You and Albert and me in jail. We need to leave."

I looked to Albert, who'd always been the shoulder I leaned on, but he just closed his eyes.

"Get our stuff together," I told Mose, using the commanding voice I'd heard from my brother so often. "We need to be off."

Sister Eve looked terribly unhappy but gave no more objection. "Whisker, go to my hotel room and gather up the children's clothing. Put it all in my suitcase and bring it back here." After Whisker had gone, she said, "Mose, get whatever things you and Albert brought. I'll ask Dimitri to put together some food for you to take when you leave. Hurry now."

A couple of hours later, we were standing together in the big tent, ready to depart. Mose was supporting Albert, pretty much bearing all his weight. The first cars were arriving for the evening service, and Sister Eve and Whisker walked us out the back way. Behind the tents, we said goodbye. Whisker shook my hand, his long, reedy fingers warm and reluctant to let go. "Sure going to miss you, son. You keep playing that mouth organ, you hear me. You got the music in you."

Sister Eve knelt before Emmy and said, "You have something amazing and beautiful in you. You'll realize that someday. I would love to be there when you do." To Mose, she said, "I've never known anyone stronger here." She touched his chest over his heart, and then she hugged him. To Albert, she said, "You'll recover, and when you do, I know you'll guide them all well." She kissed his cheek. Finally, she handed me a small paper bag and said, "I've put some cotton balls, antiseptic, gauze, and such in there. You have to keep your brother's wounds clean. I've also put a few other useful items in." Then she leaned to me and whispered into my ear, "This is important. It's up to you to make sure that Emmy is safe. Promise me." And I did. Then she said, "Remember this. It's an old saying but a true one. Home is where your heart is."

She kissed my cheek, too, and we were preparing to leave when I saw something that made all my hope sink. Among the cars arriving in the field was an all-too familiar silver Franklin Club Sedan, and right behind it came a Fremont County sheriff's cruiser.

"The Black Witch," I said, and my heart began to race.

"Go," Sister Eve said. "I'll take care of them."

We hurried off, although Albert, in his weakened condition, kept us from going as fast as I would have liked. We crossed the meadow and the railroad tracks and entered the trees on the bank above the river. Mose and Albert and Emmy made their way down to the water's edge, then Mose headed toward the bulrushes where he and Albert had hidden our canoe. I stayed among the trees, watching as Clyde Brickman, that snake with legs, got out, went to the passenger's side, and opened the door. The sight of Thelma Brickman, thin and dressed all in black so that she looked like a burned matchstick, was ice water on my soul. A heavyset, red-faced man emerged from the cruiser, and I recognized Sheriff Bob Warford, who'd terrorized so many runaways from Lincoln School. The Brickmans and Warford started toward the big tent, and Sister Eve came out to greet them.

I didn't stay to see anything further. I hopped down the bank to the river, where Mose had the canoe already on the water. He'd put in the canvas water bag, the blankets, the pillowcase with the letters and other documents we'd taken from the Brickmans' safe. He'd tossed in the suitcase with the clothing Sister Eve had purchased for Emmy and me, as well as the basket of food Dimitri had thrown together for us. Albert was in no condition to paddle, so he sat in the middle with Emmy on the blankets, holding the food basket in his lap. I sat in the bow, Mose pushed us into the current and took the stern, and we paddled as hard as we could away from the place where I hoped Sister Eve was somehow misdirecting the Black Witch and her toady husband.

The river curled around the eastern edge of New Bremen. We passed the flats where houses stood near grain elevators and the white steeple of the little church rose above the treetops. We slid under the railroad trestle where I'd sat before I stumbled onto Sister Eve praying upriver. We left the town behind. The current, coupled with our own efforts, took us between fields where young corn and soybeans rose out of the turned earth. The sun had fallen below a long, undulating ridge that edged the fertile floodplain. We moved inside the broad blue shadow of those hills, and for a long time no one spoke. Partly, I suppose, this was because Mose and I were putting all our effort into making distance, and I was breathing too hard for words. But I believe our silence was also because, once again, we were grieving loss. It was a feeling that should have been familiar to us by then, but does anyone ever get used to having their heart broken?

About the time dusk began to slide into true dark, we came to a wooded island, and I called back to Mose, "We need to stop for the night."

Mose used his paddle to rudder us toward a small stretch of sand beach at the tip of the island. I leapt out and pulled the canoe ashore and helped Emmy and my brother disembark. Mose came last, bringing the blankets and the basket of food. Flooding over the years had laid up a wall of driftwood along the upper edge of the sand, which the sun had bleached white, so that the whole construction resembled a jumble of great bones. In the lee of that wall, I stretched out a blanket for Albert, who lay down immediately. Emmy put out the other blankets, and Mose opened the food basket. Inside were ham sandwiches and apples and a small container of lemonade, which we consumed but barely tasted. We sat in the gloom of approaching dark and were quiet, depressingly so. I felt the weight of sadness on us all and knew I had to do something, so I gathered driftwood and built a fire. Albert made a feeble attempt at objecting — "Dangerous" he said — but he was in no shape to argue. As the stars gathered above us one by one, and the glow from the flames pressed outward to keep the utter dark at bay, I played some lively tunes on my harmonica, which seemed to brighten us up a bit, then I put my mouth organ away and said to the others, "Let me tell you a story."

CHAPTER THIRTY-FOUR

A woman lived in a clearing in a forest of trees so tall and thick they blotted out the sun. It was always dark among the trees, dark as night, and over the years the woman's eyes had grown used to seeing things that other people could not. She saw the shadows of dreams, the ghosts of hope. Nothing was hidden from her.

The land beyond the forest was full of hunger and pestilence.

"What's pestilence, Odie?" Emmy asked, her blue eyes wide in the firelight.

"It's terrible sickness of all kinds."

"Is this a sad story, Odie?"

"Wait and see."

One day four travelers came to the clearing in the forest, where the woman lived in a little hut. They called themselves the Vagabonds.

"What's a vagabond?" Emmy asked.

"A wanderer. Someone who has no home."

"Like us?"

"Exactly like us."

One was a mighty giant, one a wizard, one a

fairy princess, and one an imp. The woman gave them shelter and food, and when she asked for news from the outside world, they told her how awful things were beyond the forest. They told her how the giant had once thrown a boulder that had felled a great dragon, how the wizard had devised magical machines, how the fairy princess had charmed fierce beasts, and how the imp was always getting the other three into trouble.

"Sounds familiar," Albert said from where he lay.

The Vagabonds told the woman they were tired of wandering and asked if they could stay with her, but she looked into them, all the way down to their souls, and knew the true reason for their wandering. They were in search of their hearts' desires, which were different for each of them, and she knew they would never find what they were looking for if they stayed in the safety of her forest.

Instead, she sent them on an odyssey.

"What's an odyssey?"

"A long journey, Emmy, filled with adventure."

On the far side of the forest was a castle where a witch lived.

"The Black Witch?" Emmy asked.

"As a matter of fact, all she wore was black."

"I hate her," Emmy said.

"With good reason," I said.

The Black Witch kept children locked in a dungeon. She had cast a spell that caused her to look beautiful in the eyes of adults, and whenever hunger or disease made orphans of the children, they were sent to the castle to be put in the witch's care. Once inside those stone walls, there was no escape. What the adults didn't know was that the witch lived by eating the hearts of the children. Even though she'd eaten lots of hearts, she was still as thin and black as a licorice stick, and her hunger was never satisfied. In the dungeon where she'd locked them away, there was no sunlight except what could make its way through a little crack high up between the stones. For a while every day, the smallest ray of sunshine would enter the dungeon and the children would put out their hands and feel how warm it was. Which was good, except for one thing. It gave them hope, and hope made their hearts grow big, which was exactly what the witch wanted. Hearts fat with hope that would feed her gigantic appetite.

The forest woman told the Vagabonds that they were meant to destroy the witch. So they set off together to seek her out and, although they didn't know it, to fulfill their hearts' desires. Before they left, she gave the imp a vial filled with a magical mist and told the imp that when everything looked darkest, he should open the vial and release its contents into the air.

Because of her black magic, the witch knew the Vagabonds were coming, and she sent an army of snakes to attack them. Some of the snakes were poisonous, rattlesnakes and cobras and such, whose bites could kill, and some were boa constrictors and pythons, who wrapped their bodies around their prey and squeezed them until their eyes popped out.

Long before they reached the castle, the Vagabonds spied the witch's army. The giant, who traveled with a club as big as an oak tree, went first, swinging his mighty club and killing snakes right and left. The wizard cast a spell so the snakes' poison couldn't hurt the Vagabonds. The fairy princess used her wings to fly above them and sprinkle the snakes with fairy dust that turned many of them to harmless worms. But the snakes kept coming, so many that they threatened to overwhelm the Vagabonds, and things looked pretty bad.

That's when the imp remembered the vial the forest woman had given him, and he pulled out the stopper and released the mist into the air. The little cloud grew huge and gray and blinding to the snakes, and they couldn't see the four Vagabonds, who slipped away and left them far behind. Blind and confused, the snakes began fighting among themselves, killing one another until the whole army had destroyed itself.

"And that's the end of that adventure," I said.

"But what about the Black Witch, Odie?" Emmy said. "Do they ever kill her?"

I tapped the end of her nose with my finger and said, "Their odyssey isn't over, and that's another story."

It had grown late. The fire was dying and the sliver of a new moon had risen over the island. Emmy lay wrapped in her blanket, safe between Mose and me. Albert, still weak from his ordeal, lay at my other side, his eyes already closed. After a while, I heard deep, sonorous breathing from them all. I was still plagued with the insomnia that had beset me after I killed Jack, and after a while, I stood quietly and walked across the sand, a soft stretch of pale gray under the stars and the slender moon. The river was broad and still and black in its sweep around the island. In the distance beyond the trees that edged the riverbank, a gathering of lights marked a small village. I imagined the people in the houses there, safe in their slumbering, happy in the comfort of the love they shared as families, as friends. I'd envied them once, but no longer. Like one of the Vagabonds, I had no idea where I was headed, but it didn't matter. Because I knew exactly where my heart was.

■ ■ ■ ■

- PART FOUR -
THE ODYSSEY

■ ■ ■ ■

CHAPTER THIRTY-FIVE

We stayed on that island in the middle of the Minnesota River for two full days while Albert continued to recover his strength. The wall of jumbled driftwood, much of which was whole tree trunks that had been carried on the raging river's back during floods, offered us both shelter and a blind behind which to hide from prying eyes, although in the time we were there, I saw not a single soul along the riverbanks. I made Emmy another sock puppet to replace Puff, which Jack had taken from her. For this one, I fashioned bunny ears and took one of the cotton balls from the medical supplies Sister Eve had given me to tend Albert's wounds and tied it with thread as a little tail. I diluted some iodine with a little water, put a small drop below the button eyes as a pinkish nose, and on either side made three whiskers with black thread. When I presented it to her, she was delighted and promptly named the puppet Peter Rabbit.

When she'd handed me the paper bag of medical supplies, Sister Eve had told me she'd put in a few other useful items. They turned out to be five ten-dollar bills. I thought maybe it was one of the envelopes I'd seen in Sid's satchel. It wasn't nearly the size of the windfall we'd found in the Brickmans' safe, but it was still a lot of money in those days. The second morning on the island, I took one of the tens, and Mose and I crossed the river channel in the canoe. I made my way to the nearby village, whose lights I'd seen in the night, and found a small market, where I filled the water bag and bought food supplies. When I saw that they sold night crawlers as bait, I bought some of those, too, along with a roll of fishing line and a package of hooks. I also picked up the most recent issue of the *Mankato Daily Free Press* because Emmy was part of a front-page story about the Federal Kidnapping Act — or the Lindbergh Law, as it was to become popularly known — which Congress had just recently approved and which made the taking of Emmy a federal crime, a capital one. We could get the chair.

When I gave him the newspaper, Albert read it to himself, so as not to alarm Emmy. Mose and I were already well aware of our precarious situation. The one element that offered a measure of relief was that Sister Eve and the Sword of Gideon Healing Crusade weren't mentioned. According to the article, there was still no news at all concerning the fate of Emmaline Frost, the kidnapped girl. Thelma Brickman had been interviewed about the impact of the Lindbergh Law on her own heartbreaking situation. She was eloquent in expressing her fear for the safety of her sweet little girl, and God alone knew what horrors those deviants might be subjecting her to. "Whoever they are," the article quoted her, "these criminals must be the Devil's own disciples, and they deserve the swift and merciless punishment this new law dictates."

Albert said, "I think our camp needs some livening up, Emmy. Could you gather some wildflowers for us?"

She looked delighted at the prospect and scampered off.

"I don't understand it," I said, when she'd gone. "The Brickmans know we took Emmy. Why don't they just say that?"

"Because it could get messy for them," Albert said. "I think they want to conduct their business with us as privately as possible."

"How? Ambush us and kill us?" I'd said it in dark jest, but I could see from the look on his face that Albert wasn't kidding.

"Something I haven't told you," he said. "Bring me the pillowcase."

I retrieved it from the canoe and handed it to my brother. He reached inside, drew out a small book bound in black leather, which he opened. Page after page was filled with names, dates, money amounts.

"A ledger," Albert said. "Payoffs of some kind. Sheriff Warford's name is in there. The Lincoln police chief, too. And the mayor."

"Payoffs for what?"

"I don't know. Maybe the bootlegging. Maybe other things." My brother closed the book, looking as drawn as he had when the snake venom was climbing toward his heart. "Bet there's lots of folks in that county who think it would be best if we all just disappeared and this ledger never came back to haunt them."

"Shoot first, ask questions later," I said, recalling what the cop had told one-eyed Jack. "But we're not in Fremont County anymore. Maybe we should just turn ourselves in to the police around here and tell them everything we know. Show them all those letters in the pillowcase and that ledger book and tell them how Emmy doesn't want to be the Black Witch's daughter at all."

"And how you killed two men?"

It wasn't an accusation, just a cold reminder of the reality of our situation.

He killed to protect himself and us, Mose signed.

"Couple it with kidnapping, and who's going to believe us? Jail for us all at the very least," Albert said in that dead voice he'd been using since the snakebite. He glanced down at the headline. "Maybe worse."

We fed that newspaper to the fire.

I had earthworms and fishing line, and I rummaged around in the driftwood until I found three straight sticks that would serve as poles. While Albert lay in the shade of a huge ash tree whose branches overhung the driftwood wall, Mose and Emmy and I stood on the sand at the river's edge. I'd attached a dry little twig to each line as a bobber. Emmy, who'd grown up on a farm, had no compunction about skewering an earthworm with her hook, and she had her line in the water even before Mose and I did. We fished through the afternoon without a nibble.

Finally Mose put down his pole and signed, *I'm going to noodle.*

Which, I recalled, was how Forrest, the Indian we'd encountered before New Bremen, had said he'd caught the catfish he'd shared with us.

Mose wiggled his fingers like worms to give us an image of what he was planning. Then he followed the edge of the island until he came to a place where a great cottonwood had been undercut by the river and the arcing lacework of the exposed roots formed little caves that were half-filled with river water. Mose scooted out along one of the thick roots, laid himself down, reached his hand into the water among the roots, and held it there. I couldn't see his fingers, but I suspected they were wriggly and delectable-looking to a fat catfish.

Emmy watched and whispered in a frightened voice, "Will they eat his fingers?"

"I guess they'll try," I said, and the image of Herman Volz and his hand with only four and half digits filled my mind. I didn't know about catfish, but I hoped their teeth were a lot more forgiving than those of a band saw.

Mose was nothing if not patient. He lay on that thick root long after Emmy's attention had drifted, and mine, too, and we left him to his noodling and went into the woods that covered the island. The trees were thick with vines, and the ground under the broad reach of the boughs was covered with brush. Emmy and I made our way slowly. I told her we were exploring the island because we were vagabonds on an adventure.

"To kill the witch?" Emmy said.

"And all the other monsters who threaten children," I proclaimed.

I grabbed a vine and pulled it loose from the trunk where it had hung, and I tried to swing, in the way Johnny Weissmuller had done in *Tarzan the Ape Man*, which was one of the few movies I'd been allowed to see in the theater in Lincoln. The vine broke under my weight. I came crashing down and landed in the middle of a clump of sumac, square on my butt. I sat for a moment, a little stunned, and heard Emmy calling my name with concern. Then I turned and looked down and screamed.

The mouth of a skeleton next to me hung open in a ghastly smile of greeting.

Chapter Thirty-Six

Mose came running. A minute later, Albert was there, too, but looking weak and winded. They stood beside Emmy and me — I'd leapt away from that macabre grin as fast as I could — and we all gaped at our only companion on the island. It was a full skeleton, completely intact, head to bony toes. Tendrils of vegetation grew up between its ribs and vined out the empty eye sockets. Like the driftwood piled on the tip of the island, the bones were bleached to a ghostly white. For a long while, we simply stared.

Finally Mose signed, *Who?*

Albert said, "No telling."

"It's not very big," I noted.

"About your size," Albert agreed.

A kid, Mose signed.

"What do you suppose it's doing here?" I asked.

"Just like the driftwood, maybe," Albert said. "The river dropped it here."

I crept near the skeleton again, less afraid

now, and knelt and examined our companion more carefully. "Look." I pointed to the side of its skull, to an indentation surrounded by a spiderwebbing of cracks. "I'm no cop, but I'd bet somebody whacked this kid on the head."

Murder, Mose signed.

"I wouldn't jump to any conclusions," Albert said.

I spotted something lying at the feet of the skeleton and picked it up. Dark brown and brittle, it almost fell apart in my hand, but we could all see what it was.

"A moccasin," Emmy said.

"An Indian kid," I said. And I thought about Billy Red Sleeve. "What do we do?"

"Nothing," Albert said.

I looked at him, the shell of him anyway. He might have been just too exhausted to care, still recovering from his ordeal with the snakebite, but I thought it went deeper. In New Bremen, he'd had one foot in the grave. Death had looked him in the eye, and I think he was still afraid.

Nothing? Mose signed, and I could see a rare fury rising in him.

"Whatever happened was a long time ago," Albert said in a tired voice. "Who knows? Maybe a hundred years ago. There's nothing anyone can do about it now."

I couldn't get out of my head the image of Billy Red Sleeve, lying so long forgotten in the quarry where DiMarco had thrown his little body. "We can't just leave it."

"What do you suggest?" Albert's words were stone cold now. "That we alert the authorities? What a good idea that would be."

We bury him, Mose signed.

"I'm not going to handle those bones," Albert said.

Mose, who was almost never confrontational, faced my brother and signed angrily, *He was an Indian kid, like me. If I'd died in that ditch with my mother, I would have wanted a decent burial. So we give him a decent burial. I'll handle the bones.*

Mose and I used sticks scrounged from the driftwood wall to dig a hole in the soft dirt. Three feet down, water began to seep through the soil, and we stopped. Mose carried the skeleton in pieces and set the bones in the little grave, arranged, more or less, as we'd found them, so that what was left of the Indian child appeared to be lying in repose.

Before we covered the bones with dirt, Mose signed, *Say something, Odie.*

My first thought was, Why me? But it was obvious that Albert wasn't interested, and this was what Mose wanted.

"This kid," I began, "was just like us. He loved the sun on his face, the dew on the morning grass, the song of birds in the trees. He loved to skip stones on the river. At night he liked to lie on the sand and stare up at the stars and dream. Just like us. He had people who loved him. But one day he went away and never came back, and they were heartbroken. They vowed not to speak his name again until the day he returned. That day never came. But every night his mother stood on the riverbank and called his name, and if you listen close at night, you can still hear the wind over the river whisper that name so he will never be forgotten."

"What name, Odie?" Emmy asked.

"Listen to the wind tonight," I said.

Mose bent over the grave and signed, *I will never forget you.* And he began to cover the bones with dirt.

Mose, it turned out, had been successful in his noodling, and he brought to our little camp two fat catfish for dinner. He cleaned them with Albert's Scout knife and, just as we'd seen Forrest do nearly two weeks before, threaded them on sticks thrust into the sand and tilted over the fire to cook. We ate the fish with bread I'd bought at the village market, and we split a Hershey's bar for dessert.

After dark, we sat around the fire, staring into the flames, each of us lost in our own thoughts. I was brooding about Albert, who was only a ghost of himself. But because of the skeleton we'd buried, I was also thinking about my father, who'd been laid in a pauper's grave in the cemetery in Lincoln. As far as I knew, there'd been no service for him. They just threw him into the hole and covered him up.

I'd seen his grave twice. The first time was a perfunctory visit in the company of Mr. Brickman not long after Albert and I landed at the Lincoln Indian Training School. He showed us the grave, then stood away to give us a few minutes alone, and finally whisked us back to the school. I hadn't reacted much during that visit, nor had Albert. We just stood staring down at the little marker planted in the earth like an isolated paving stone. I didn't cry, or even feel like crying under Brickman's impatient gaze.

The second time was on my twelfth birthday. I'd pretty much forgotten what my mother looked like by then, and my father's face had begun to fade as well. I wanted desperately not to forget him, so I slipped away from the school and returned to the cemetery. I had some trouble finding his marker because the pauper's grave hadn't been well cared for, and weeds had grown up and obscured the stone. I knelt and cleared away the wild growth and read the name on the marker, which was all there was, a name, and spent an hour remembering everything I could about him.

He'd been a man who liked music and liked to laugh. I remembered that whenever he bent to hug me, his cheek against mine was rough with stubble. He'd read us stories when we went to bed at night and his voice had changed and become the voices of different characters. I think now that under other circumstances he might have been an actor. What he'd been was a bootlegger, and after my mother died, he'd been a runner for other, more powerful bootleggers. He'd been raised in the hills of the Ozarks, where making corn liquor was a time-honored tradition, and he hadn't been ashamed of how he earned his living. He'd brought us from Missouri up to Minnesota on a liquor run, and we'd camped along the Gilead River just outside Lincoln. That night, Albert and I had stayed by the river while my father drove his Model T pickup into town to make his delivery. He never returned. The sheriff's people came for us, and that's when we learned the truth of his death. He'd been shot in the back and left for dead. They never explained a motive, never identified a suspect. My father was just a crook and had met a crook's end. And Albert and I were the sons of a crook, and our sentence was life under the Black Witch's thumb. Why two white boys in a school for Indian kids? Thelma Brickman had always explained it this way: "We offered to take you in because the state school for orphans is already full. You should be grateful that you're not begging on the streets." But Cora Frost had told us that the Brickmans got a monthly check from the state for our care.

Although my mother was a vague shade in my past, I still remembered my father, and Albert remembered him, too, and we knew where we'd come from, and that we had family in Saint Louis, an aunt who'd tried to send us money, to take care of us in the only way she could. Emmy remembered both of her parents and even had a photograph to help keep them fresh in her mind. But when I looked at Mose, who was deep in serious thought as he gazed into the flames, I realized he probably remembered no one. And I thought of what Sister Eve had said when she told me about what each of us was seeking and that Mose was looking for who he was.

We lay down early that night. Emmy and Albert went right to sleep, but I lay awake. Mose couldn't sleep either, and after a while, he got up and walked past the low flames still flickering among the coals of the fire and went to the river's edge and sat alone. I let him be for a spell, then rolled out of my blanket and joined him.

I didn't want to disturb the others, so I signed, *What are you doing?*

After a long while, he finally signed, *Listening.*

The water, as it ran against the sand, murmured, and from the woods behind us came the song of tree frogs, and every once in a while the fire popped. A soft wind blew across the river valley, but all I heard from it was a rustling among the trees on the island.

I have a name, Mose signed.

Moses, I signed back.

He shook his head. *Sioux name,* he signed, then spelled out A-M-D-A-C-H-A.

How do you know?

Sister Eve. Held my hand and told me.

What does it mean?

Broken to Pieces. Named after a great-uncle. A warrior.

I listened to the shivering of the trees in the night wind and remembered the story Jack had told us about the stars inside cotton-woods and how the spirit of the night sky shook the trees to set them loose. The spirit must have wanted stars that night, because the sky was aglitter with a million pinpoints of light.

Should I call you Broken to Pieces now?

Before he could answer, we heard a commotion behind us, and Albert cried out, "It's Emmy."

He held her as she spasmed in his arms. Mose and I sat with him, and we each took one of her hands, and Emmy's pain was ours, too. These spells never went on long, but they racked her whole small body, and it was torture watching.

When the episode had passed and she'd

411

gone limp, her eyes opened and she said, "They're dead. They're all dead."

"Who, Emmy?"

"I couldn't help them," she said. "I tried but I couldn't. It was already done."

"Is she talking about the Indian kid?" I asked.

"More than one," Albert noted. "She said they're all dead."

I looked down at Emmy, whose eyes were open but glazed. "Are there more dead kids on this island, Emmy?"

"I tried. There's nothing I could do."

"Tried what?" Albert asked.

She didn't answer, just closed her eyes and fell into a deep sleep. We wrapped her in her blanket and sat with her as the last of the flames from our little fire died out, leaving only the dull glow of red coals.

"They're all dead," I said, repeating Emmy's words. "What did she mean?"

Albert stirred the fire with a stick. "What she says in her fits always sounds like nonsense."

Maybe isn't, Mose signed. He turned and peered at the dark stand of trees that covered the island and hid God knew what.

"This place is giving me the creeps," I said. "I think we should leave."

Mose nodded and signed, *First thing in the morning.*

What little sleep I got that night was restless, and although I didn't remember them exactly, my dreams were full of menace. When the sky began to show signs of morning, Mose and I got up, and in the cool blue of first light, packed our things and loaded the canoe. Albert tried to help but wasn't much use. Emmy was sunk in such a profound slumber that she didn't stir as Mose lifted her and laid her gently in the canoe. Albert sat in the middle, the position he'd occupied before his snakebite, and I took the bow. Mose shoved us off the island and stepped into the stern, and we lifted our paddles.

Although we didn't know it yet, the current of the Minnesota River was sweeping us toward revelations that would open our eyes to a darkness even greater than the Black Witch.

CHAPTER THIRTY-SEVEN

There were no railroad tracks shadowing this stretch of river and, for a significant distance, no towns, and along the banks only thick stands of trees, so no prying eyes to discover us. We made good distance that first morning. Emmy had awakened in the peach light of dawn with, as usual, no recollection of her spell the night before. She seemed refreshed and full of smiles, and both her spirits and her lively conversations with Peter Rabbit buoyed me and even seemed to lift Albert's spirits. Mose, of course, was silent, but something came from him that told me he was still in that dark place he'd gone after our discovery of the Indian kid's skeleton.

Near noon, we pulled up to the bank where a little brook emptied into the silty brown river, and we ate the last of the food I'd bought at the village market.

"How long do you reckon we've been gone from Lincoln School?" I asked Albert.

He was slow answering. "A month, give or

take a day or two."

"How long before we reach the Missis-sippi?"

"Days," he said with a heavy sigh.

"And how long after that before we reach Saint Louis?"

"Weeks. Months. I don't know."

"Months? That's forever."

"Would you rather be working Bledsoe's hayfields?"

"I'd rather be eating at the Morrow House and sleeping in one of their soft beds."

Emmy sighed, but not sadly, a kind of pixie sound. "I'd rather be a princess riding on the back of a swan."

"And eating nothing but ice cream," I added.

She held up her sock puppet. "With choco-late sauce," Peter Rabbit said in a little rabbit voice.

"What about you, Mose?" I asked.

He'd put his back to the rest of us and was chucking stones at the river, flinging them hard so that they hit the water with little explosions. He didn't respond.

"Come on," I said. "What would you rather be doing?"

He turned toward me, and what I saw in his face scared me. He signed, *Tracking down my mother's killer.*

Which brought an end to the game.

We stayed on the river until late afternoon

and made camp on a little strip of beach at the base of a rock bluff. I tried my hand at fishing again, and this time had some success, pulling in a big something that definitely wasn't a catfish. I made a spit over our fire that night, and skewered and roasted the fish. Its firm white flesh came easily off the bone and tasted far better than any catfish I'd ever eaten. I didn't understand until much later that I'd landed a walleye, a prized catch in Minnesota.

As night came on, we could see a glow in the east as if from a fire. I'd observed the same sort of phenomenon once when we camped with our father south of Omaha and the distant city had lit up the night sky.

"Mankato?" I asked Albert.

"That's my guess," he said.

"We're not very far. We'll be there in the morning."

Albert shook his head. "We'll stay here until tomorrow afternoon, then we'll pass through at dusk. Less chance of being spotted."

That was the kind of plan the old Albert would have put forward, and I found it encouraging. Except that it meant we'd have to wait in the company of Mose, whose foul mood, the first I'd ever seen him in, weighed on us all. I thought maybe my harmonica would help, so I hauled it out and played some lively tunes that I knew were among Mose's favorites, but the hard shell he'd put around himself didn't crack, and even when Emmy danced a little jig that was cute as hell, Mose showed no emotion at all. In its way, his brooding was as alarming as one of Emmy's fits.

The next morning found us all in bad spirits. When I'd cleaned the walleye, I'd left the mess of its innards on the sand at the river's edge, and a storm of blackflies descended, attacking not only the fish leavings but us as well. Albert swore at me and I swore back, and Emmy broke into tears, which brought out the protective side of Mose and he signed at Albert and me so vehemently I thought he'd break his hands.

"I'm not sitting around here all day with you," I snapped at Albert.

"Fine," he shot back. "Why don't you swim to Saint Louis?"

I took off, storming along the bluff, then through a copse of birch trees, heading away from the river. In the night, I'd heard the sound of freight cars clattering over rails to the south, and also the far-off howl of an engine horn. I made my way to the tracks, which were less than a quarter of a mile distant, and followed them toward the city whose glow we'd seen in the night. The whole way I cursed my brother and the bad luck that had made us desert Sister Eve, and I railed at the weeks or months or, who knew, even years before we'd reach Saint Louis, if we ever did. I knew cops everywhere were looking for Emmy, and if they caught us our gooses were cooked but good. I thought maybe I wouldn't go back to the others. Maybe I was better off on my own.

I walked for a couple of hours and finally reached Mankato, where both the river and the railroad took a dramatic turn toward the north. The city, with a population of thousands, lay along both sides of the river's curl. Warehouses and industrial buildings stood in big blocks at the river's edge. A long, high, tree-lined bluff rose behind the city, and along the flat at the base of the bluff lay the downtown business district, where I'd once dogged Sid and had spied on him as he met and paid the people who traveled with the crusade and had been "healed" time and again. I made my way into that busy center of commerce. Automobiles zipped down the streets, and after the long quiet of my canoe journey, their beep and rattle felt like an assault. The midday was humid, the air stifling, and the unpleasant odor of hot tar hung over everything.

I'd been to cities before — Saint Louis, Omaha, Kansas City — but that had been so long ago that I had no real recollection of them. The time I'd spent in Mankato following Sid had been so brief that I didn't have a clear sense of the place. After years in Lincoln, which was a small town, and our time in New Bremen, which was only slightly larger, I felt I was standing in an alien, unwelcoming land. And I was alone. That's what hit me most. I was all alone. In my anger at Albert, this was what I'd wanted, but when I understood the reality of it, my heart sank, and I longed to be with my family again.

I'd just made my decision to hightail it back to our camp, when I heard a commotion up one of the streets and curiosity got the better of me. I followed the sound of raised voices, turned a corner, and found myself at the edge of a crowd gathered in front of the local armory. Cops prowled the perimeter, and I'd have turned away immediately but for the promise that came with the smell of hot soup and, even better, the yeasty aroma of fresh-baked bread. I couldn't see the food because of the wall of bodies in front of me. I could, however, see a man standing on the steps of the armory, well above the heads of the crowd, and he was shouting through a megaphone.

"Hey, you fellas," he hollered, "how many of you slogged through French mud or sat hip deep in stinking trench water or threw yourselves down on Gerry barbed wire?"

His question was answered with encouraging shouts and cheers.

"And how many of you saw your comrades-in-arms slaughtered before your very eyes?"

This didn't get such an agreeable response,

but it sent an audible ripple through the crowd.

"And what did they promise those of us who were lucky enough to come back? They promised us bonuses for our service, compensation for the horrors we witnessed or were a part of. But they told us we'd have to wait for our money. Well, we can't wait. We don't have jobs now, do we?"

There was a resounding chorus of "No!", which made sense given the state of the clothing most of the crowd wore.

"And we have no roofs over our heads, and we don't have food to feed ourselves or our families, do we?"

This really got to the crowd, and they raised their fisted hands and shouted, "No!"

"We need that money now. Today. Not years down the road. Hell, we'll all have starved to death by then! Are you with me?"

Judging from the roar of approval the crowd delivered, they were.

That's when the cops swept in. They came out of the side streets and the alleys carrying truncheons and shoving their way among the crowd, dividing them into islands of confusion, sending them running every which way.

"You, Mr. Cop, did you fight in France?" the man with the megaphone called out.

But I guessed not, because the policeman he'd addressed simply whacked him on the head with his billy club and I saw him tumble.

Chaos engulfed the scene, and I found myself buffeted by fleeing bodies and thrown against a brick wall. I crawled into the safety of an alcove that was the entrance to a printing shop, where I cowered until the street had emptied, and a man poked his head out the door of the shop and snapped, "Get on, boy. Don't be loitering here."

I quickly headed back to the railroad tracks and followed them out of the city, eager to return to the place where I'd left my brother and Emmy and Mose, wanting more than anything to be in the safety of my family again, surrounded by the comfort of our love. Sure, we sometimes got angry and yelled at one another, but we never swung billy clubs.

By the time I found where I'd joined the tracks that morning, it was late afternoon and the shadows were long across the land. I made my way down to the river, to the rock bluff where we'd stayed the night, my heart singing at the prospect of rejoining the others.

But when I reached the strip of beach where we'd camped, I was still alone. Everyone had gone.

CHAPTER THIRTY-EIGHT

I spent my twenty-fourth birthday hunkered down inside the shell of a burned-out café in Brest, France, with German bullets cutting the air around me. I was scared but, honestly, not nearly as frightened as I'd been when I was twelve years old standing on that empty beach on the bank of the Minnesota River, thinking I'd lost the only family I had.

The remains of the fire still smoldered, and the sand still held the impressions of our bodies where we'd slept in the night, but the beach was empty. My first thought was that Albert had been so angry he'd convinced the others to abandon me. But he was my brother, and we'd been at each other's throats before. He wouldn't just desert me, no matter how far I'd pushed him. I looked for a sign, a trail marker of some kind like the one Mose had left earlier on the Gilead. I found nothing like that, but I did discover something disturbing — large footprints in the wet sand at the river's edge, larger even than Mose would have left. And then I looked carefully at all the footprints. Emmy's were small and easy to spot. Albert and Mose wore Red Wing boots of the same size, and their prints, though larger, were exactly like those my boots made. But there were other shoe prints, man-size, and the paw prints of dogs. Someone had been there, several someones. Something had happened, and Albert and Mose and Emmy had been forced to flee.

But flee where?

I looked at the river, the brown current pushing east toward Mankato, and I figured there was only one way for them to go.

The rest of the afternoon I followed the course of the river all the way back to the outskirts of Mankato with no sign of my family. It was dusk by then. I was tired and hungry and discouraged. I'd convinced myself that my brother and Mose and Emmy hadn't fled the beach but had instead been caught. The Black Witch had worked some kind of dark magic and had tracked them down. I'd been gone when the capture had taken place, but that didn't mean I was lucky. It meant that I was absolutely alone.

I came to a trestle that crossed another river, a tributary to the Minnesota. A couple of hundred yards north, I could see the place where the rivers met. I sat on the crossties and dangled my feet and tried to make sense of my situation. Albert and Mose were probably already behind bars, and I considered simply giving myself up. What could they do to me? Did they put twelve-year-olds in the electric chair? If that's where Albert was going, then maybe that's where I was going, too. We would meet our end together.

I'd crawled deep into a hole of misery when I heard something that made my heart sing a little. From among the trees downstream came the reedy voice of a harmonica. I knew the tune, "Arkansas Traveler." I took my own instrument from my shirt pocket and began to play a counterpoint to the melody. The other voice paused, as if surprised, then picked up the tune and we played together to the end. I climbed down from the trestle and headed toward the trees from which the music had come.

At the place where the two rivers met stood a community of temporary shelters. The little structures had been built of materials you might have found in a city dump — cardboard, sheet metal, corrugated siding, scrap lumber, wooden crates. There were lean-tos of driftwood covered with tarps. Here and there, a tent had been pitched, but mostly it was a village predicated on desperate necessity, given shape and substance by the discards of those who were better off. Fires burned in cut-down barrels or in the open, and I could smell food cooking.

The voice of the harmonica kept calling. I

wove along pathways between the shelters, where folks looked up from their fires or peered at me from the entryways of their hovels.

I came at last to what looked like a big tepee, a cone of long branches covered with canvas. It stood in the high grass that edged the big river. Near the tepee sat an old pickup truck whose bed was jammed with furniture and whatnot. In front of the tepee door was a stone fire ring with a nice blaze going at its center, and a big black cook pot hung over the flames. Three adults sat on low crates around the fire, one of them a squat, balding man with sun-darkened skin and a harmonica to his lips. Their faces turned toward me, and the man lowered his mouth organ. They stared, not with hostility but as if with an expectation of what they knew would come next.

"I play, too," I said feebly and showed him my harmonica.

"That was you a while ago?" he asked.

"Uh-huh."

A woman sat next to him. I judged them to be about the same age, the age my parents would have been, but her face seemed far more careworn than his. Her hair hung about her shoulders in limp blond strings badly in need of washing. She wore a flour sack dress, old but of a colorful pattern, with ballerinas and butterflies. Her feet were shod in beat-to-hell work boots, and as far as I could tell, she wore no socks.

But the one who commanded my attention was a woman of great age, a loose construct of folds and wrinkles out of which two dark eyes studied me intently. She wore a shawl over an old dress that came to her ankles, and the stem of a corncob pipe was lodged in the corner of her mouth.

"Are you alone?" she asked in a voice surprisingly gentle.

"Yes, ma'am," I said.

"Folks?"

"Don't have any."

"Orphan?" the younger, careworn woman said.

"Yes, ma'am."

"Are you with somebody here?" the old woman asked.

"No, ma'am. Just came in on the railroad tracks up there."

"Awfully young to be a hobo," the other woman said.

"Lots of young ones on their own these days, Sarah," the old woman said. "Hard times for us all. Have you eaten, son?"

"I ate a bit this morning."

"You're welcome to join us. Soup's almost ready."

"Mother Beal," the man said.

"We can spare the boy some soup, Powell," the old woman said. All the wrinkles on the lower part of her face formed themselves into a smile. "And then maybe he can pay us back with some music."

What I would come to learn in time was that Powell Schofield; his wife, Sarah; and his mother-in-law, Alice Beal, had lost their farm in Scott County, Kansas, and had set out for Chicago, where Mother Beal had family and Schofield hoped to find work. Their truck engine had begun to act up and they had no money for repairs — no money for anything, even gas — and they'd been in the thrown-together village, which they told me was called Hooverville, for more than a week. There were Hoovervilles everywhere, another thing I learned later. Like many of the men in the encampment, Schofield had heard there was work to be had in the canneries in the area, a report that had turned out to be terribly untrue. Now they were stuck.

Mrs. Schofield stirred the soup in the black pot and said, "Powell, will you round up Maybeth and the children? Tell them supper's ready. And tell Captain Gray he's welcome to join us if he brings his own spoon and bowl."

The man stood. He wasn't big but was powerful-looking, his chest and arms muscled from the work of a farmer. He trudged off among the makeshift abodes, heading toward the sound of kids playing, which I'd heard on my arrival.

Mother Beal eyed me carefully. "Buck Jones, eh?"

Because that's what I'd told them when they asked my name. I was growing rather fond of it.

"Like the cowboy movie star?"

"Yes, ma'am."

"Uh-huh," she said and looked me up and down. "Those clothes are awfully nice, and if I'm not mistaken, those boots are Red Wing, not far from new. A suspicious mind might think you're a runaway."

Which I was, sort of, though more of an escapee.

"No family to run away from," I said. "My father died four years ago, my mother a couple of years before that."

"No other family?"

"An aunt in Saint Louis. That's where we're going. I'm going," I corrected.

"Saint Louis is a long way," she said.

"Weeks and weeks," I agreed.

"And just you and no other resources?"

"Just me."

Mrs. Schofield tasted the soup and added a pinch of something from a little bag she took out of her dress pocket. "That sounds aw-fully . . ." She paused with her hand over the steaming cauldron. "Brave," she finally said.

Mother Beal laughed. "Plumb crazy is what I was thinking. But look where seventy years

428

of judicious living has got me." She took the pipe from her mouth and swung the stem in a long arc that encompassed all the flimsy shelters of Hooverville. "And look at them. Most folks here had no idea this was just around the corner. So much is beyond anyone's control." She smiled at me. "So, Buck, I'm the last person to tell you whatever you got in mind is crazy. All I'm going to say is God be with you."

Mr. Schofield returned with three children in tow, one of them a girl no older than I. She wore a boy's shirt and a boy's dungarees, patched in several places, and her feet were bare. She smiled shyly at me and went immediately to work helping her mother with the final meal preparations. This was Maybeth Schofield, and despite the boy's clothing, I thought she was the prettiest girl I'd ever seen. The other two were twins, eight years old, Lester and Lydia. Some distance behind them trailed a tall figure, limping his way toward the fire. When he came from the shadow of the trees and fully into the evening light, I realized I'd seen him before. He'd been the man with the megaphone exhorting the other veterans in the crowd to rise up and demand the bonuses that had been promised them for their military service. A dark bruise spread across the side of his face, and I remembered watching the cop clobber him with a billy club. But that didn't explain

429

his limp.

"Lost it in the Argonne," he said, tapping his right pant leg, which produced a wooden sound.

We were eating by then, and that's when I learned much of the history of the Schofields and Captain Bob Gray. Maybeth sat with the twins on the other side of the fire. Her hair was the color of her mother's, the soft gold of the alfalfa after it had sun-dried in Bledsoe's fields, but softer looking and cleaner than her mother's. Whenever I caught her looking at me, she would quickly look away. For a reason I couldn't have explained then, that simple, demure gesture captured my heart.

"The rain didn't come the way it was supposed to," Mr. Schofield said. He'd finished his soup — a tasty concoction of chicken broth and vegetables — and threw a stick angrily on the fire. "Last two years, the corn just didn't come up. Had nothing to feed my livestock. They was all skin and bones. Bank told me to go to hell when I asked for more credit. Then they took the farm. The bastards."

"There was a little more to it than that," Mother Beal said.

"Yeah, well, that was the crux." He stood abruptly. "I got things to see to." And he strode off into the dark under the trees.

Mother Beal watched him go. "Drought, he says."

"Mama," Mrs. Schofield cautioned her.

"I'm just saying there were farmers around us who found a way."

Captain Gray — that's what he preferred to be called — was on a mission of his own making, attempting to recruit men to travel with him to Washington, D.C., to join the thousands of other veterans gathering there to demand payment of the promised bonuses.

"There are plenty of us here in Minnesota desperate for that money. It's no handout we're asking for. It's what was promised. A government should keep its promises."

"I don't know why a government would behave any differently from the people who comprise it," Mother Beal said around the stem of her pipe. "When it comes to money, people often behave in ungracious and ungrateful ways."

After the meal was finished, Mother Beal said, "Children, help us clean up. Buck, you promised us a tune on that mouth organ of yours."

"You play the harmonica?" Captain Gray asked. "Got me a squeeze box back at my shack. Mind if I play along?"

"That'd be all right," I said. "Can I help clean up?" I asked Sarah Schofield.

"Obliged, Buck, but we can handle this. You figure what you're going to play."

I watched Maybeth help her mother. She gave instructions to the littler ones with a maternal patience, and she moved with a cat-like grace, and for some reason I couldn't name, her bare feet, slender and brown from the sun and from the dirt, seemed especially beautiful. I tried to think of a song that might impress her. I wanted something lovely and lyrical, but also a little sad and lonely, because that's what I'd been feeling, and I wanted her to understand. I finally settled on "Shenandoah."

When Captain Gray returned, he brought not only his concertina but also a large scrap of white wood on which HOOVERVILLE had been painted in large black letters. That word had been crossed out with red paint and below it was now the word HOPERSVILLE.

"This sign's been hanging on the tree next to my shack for way too long," Captain Gray said. "I thought it was time we called this place something brighter. What do you think, Mother Beal?"

"I think it's perfect, Captain Gray," she replied.

We played some tunes together. My reper-toire was broader than his, but we knew a few of the same melodies, and as we played, folks came away from their own little places and gathered around the fire. And a kind of miracle happened, or what I thought of then as a miracle. One man brought out a sack of ginger cookies and passed them around to the children who were there. Someone else offered up a jug of cider. Apple slices appeared and some cheese and bread. And while Captain Gray and I played, and a few of the folks who knew the tunes sang along, the people in the gathering, none of whom had much, found a way to feed one another.

Mrs. Schofield finally said, "It's late and the children need to be abed."

"One more," I said. "Something special."

"All right. But just one."

I played "Shenandoah," just as I'd planned. At the end, I looked across the fire at Maybeth Schofield. Her eyes were two blue pearls wet, as if with dew, and when she smiled at me, my heart cracked wide open.

Chapter Thirty-Nine

Before Lydia and Lester were put to bed inside the Schofields' tepee, Mother Beal brought out a Bible, an old edition, bound in fine leather of a mahogany color and with pages edged in gold.

"Can you read, Buck?"

"Yes, ma'am."

"Would you care to read a passage to end our day? It's what we do in our family. Despite what must seem like desperate circumstances, we don't believe the Lord has deserted us."

I'd begun my journey on the Gilead with a profound belief in God, but a different kind of God, one that rained terror. I hadn't let go of my fear that such a god was out there, dark and powerful and waiting, a shepherd who ate his flock. But Sister Eve had given me a different image to consider, and when Mother Beal handed me the Bible, I didn't feel at all like a fraud when I read from it. I chose the Twenty-third Psalm because it was the passage most familiar to me.

After I'd finished, Mother Beal said, "Mighty appropriate, Buck, given our current situation. Good night, children."

Mrs. Schofield ushered her two younger ones into the tepee. Before I returned the Bible to Mother Beal, I saw pages in the very front with names and dates handwritten.

"Our family tree," the old woman explained. She scooted her crate next to the one on which I sat and drew a finger down each page, elucidating her lineage, from the first name and date — Ezra Hornsby, September 21, 1804 — to the most recent names — Lester and Lydia Scofield, May 18, 1924. Among the things I learned was an explanation for the tepee. Her father, Simon Hornsby, had been an Episcopal missionary among the Sioux in the Dakota Territory, which was where she'd been raised and had learned the beauty and utility of that simple construct.

I stared at those pages, which were a solid map of family, and I was envious. These people knew who they were, where they'd come from, and understood the larger fabric into which their lives had been woven. Me, I felt like I was dangling out there, a thread all alone.

Mother Beal laid the Bible on her lap. "Where do you intend to pass the night?"

I'd been so caught up in the flow of the evening that I hadn't thought about it at all.

"I guess maybe I'll bed down in the tall grass somewhere."

"Maybeth, go get a blanket and give it to Buck."

"No, ma'am, I couldn't," I said.

"You can and you will. Maybeth?"

The girl went into the tepee and returned with a folded wool blanket. Before she could give it to me, her father stumbled into the firelight and sat down heavily on a crate. His eyes were dazed in a way I recognized, and the smell of whiskey was on him strong.

Mother Beal said, "And what did you use to buy it?"

"What?" he said in a terrible attempt at innocence.

She stared him down and he lowered his eyes.

"My mouth organ. A trade."

Mrs. Schofield came from the tepee and saw her husband bent contritely at the fire. I thought she'd light into him, but she drew him into her arms. He laid his head on her shoulder, as a child might with his mother, and closed his eyes. She gave Mother Beal a look I couldn't, at that age, interpret but I have since come to think of as profound maternal compassion, a strength emanating from a deep well of endurance that, across my life, I've come understand was not particular to Sarah Schofield. I've witnessed it in other women who have suffered much without losing their hope or their gift for embracing with forgiveness those who are broken.

"Let's go to bed, sweetheart," she said, and led him inside the tepee.

"Maybeth, why don't you help Buck find a soft spot for the night?" Mother Beal said. "I'll wait here for you. Don't be long."

We walked out of the firelight but not far because there was only a quarter moon in the sky and the night was rather dark. The high grass of the riverbank gave way to sand, and I found a spot a few dozen yards from the Schofields' encampment and laid the blanket out on the beach. The stars were legion, and the Milky Way was a soft, blurry arc across the heavens.

"I'll stay a bit, if you like," Maybeth offered. "It's kind of scary out here."

"I'm not afraid."

"I didn't think so," she said.

We sat on the blanket, and Maybeth crossed her legs and rubbed the patch that covered one knee.

"I had a nice dress," she said. "Blue. But I gave it away."

"Why?"

"Janie Baldwin needed it more. She was picking strawberries from a garden in town, stealing them, really, and a dog attacked her. Tore her dress almost completely off her. The Baldwins, well, they're worse off than we are."

"Your family's nice."

She looked back toward the glow of the fire. "I worry about Papa."

I thought of my own father and how he'd made his living supplying the whiskey for men like Powell Schofield. I wasn't sure what do with that.

"There's my star," she said, pointing toward the upper glimmer in the cup of the Big Dipper.

"Your star? You own it?"

"I claimed it. There are more stars in the sky than people on earth, so there are plenty to go around. I claimed that one because if you follow the line that connects it with the one below, you'll find the North Star. It helps me know where I'm going. What star is yours?"

"The one below," I said. "The one that connects and helps show the way."

We gazed at our stars until Maybeth said, "I better go back."

"Thank you for the blanket."

I thought she would leave then, but she stayed a moment longer. "How old are you?"

"Thirteen," I said. It was almost true.

"Me, too. Do you know *Romeo and Juliet*? Shakespeare?"

Because of Cora Frost, I knew about the playwright. I vaguely knew the story line, two people who were in love and it didn't turn out particularly well for them.

"Juliet was thirteen and Romeo wasn't

much older," she said. "People married young back then, I guess."

Watching her across the fire earlier that evening, I'd thought about kissing Maybeth Schofield and had tried to imagine how that might feel.

"Good night, good night. Parting is such sweet sorrow that I shall say good night till it be morrow."

In the quiet after she spoke, I stared at the river, a ghostly, starlit flow before me, and thought again what it would be like to kiss Maybeth Schofield.

"Buck?"

I turned my face to hers, and she leaned to me and pressed her lips against mine for the briefest of moments. Then she stood and ran back to her family's camp.

I lay that night staring up at the two stars that would forever be connected in my thinking, filled with a fire that was completely new to me and whose burn was not pain but infinite pleasure. "Maybeth," I said aloud, and there seemed such a sweetness on my tongue.

Then I thought about Albert and Mose and Emmy, and once again I was afraid, terrified that maybe I'd lost them forever. It wasn't just fear that stabbed at me, but guilt as well because, for a little while, in the company of the Schofields, I'd forgotten them. What kind of brother was I?

■ ■ ■ ■

Morning came early in the newly dubbed
Hopersville. When I rolled over in my blanket,
I could smell the cook fires already burning.
I sat up, looked at the river, a broad reflec-
tion of a rose-colored sky, and I knew what I
had to do that day.

Mrs. Schofield had her own cook fire going. A black pot half-filled with water hung
over the flames, and a sooted coffeepot had
been set among the embers at the fire's edge.
No one else seemed to be up yet, and Mrs.
Schofield sat alone with a steaming blue
enamel cup in her hand. She smiled at me.

"Are you always an early riser, Buck?"

"When I have things to do," I said.

"Do you drink coffee?"

I didn't, but I was almost thirteen, old
enough to marry, at least in the old days, and
I figured I must be old enough for coffee,
too.

"Yes, ma'am," I said.

"Grab yourself a cup from that red crate in
the back of the truck."

The tailgate was down and on it sat the red
crate, which contained cups and plates and
flatware, and pots and pans. The rest of the
pickup bed was jammed full of everything
the Schofields had brought with them from
Kansas. I took one of the cups from the crate,

440

and Mrs. Schofield filled it from the blackened coffeepot. The brew was bitter and not at all to my liking, but I smiled as if it were ambrosia and thanked her.

"So you have a plan, Buck?"

"There are some friends I have to find."

"Around here?"

"Maybe," I said. "I hope."

"Where are you going to look?"

I'd thought about that much of the night. If the cops had somehow apprehended my family, they were near enough to Mankato that I thought that's where they might have been taken for processing. I intended to visit the police department and find out for sure. Beyond that, I didn't have much of a plan.

"Around," I said.

"Big place, that. Might they be here in Hopersville?"

"I doubt it, ma'am. If they'd heard me playing my harmonica, they'd have come running."

Mother Beal emerged from the tepee, her long gray hair all mussed from a night's sleep. So early in the morning, she looked like an old tree bent and battered by a storm. She straightened her back and it was like firecrackers popping. When she saw me, she smiled.

"Sleep well?"

"Yes, ma'am. Thanks again for the blanket."

"It's what people do, Buck. Help one

441

another. My, my, that coffee smells wonderful."

Maybeth was up next. She must have brushed her hair before she came out because it was long and soft and didn't look at all slept on.

The sun had just risen. The light of the new day broke through the trees and I saw Maybeth drenched in gold and my heart leapt.

"What can I do, Mama?" she asked.

"We'll need oatmeal and molasses," Mrs. Schofield said.

Maybeth headed toward the truck and Mother Beal said, "She might need some help, Buck."

We stood at the dropped tailgate, and Maybeth said, "I dreamed about you last night. Did you dream about me?"

"Yes." It wasn't exactly a lie because, although I hadn't actually dreamed about her, I'd certainly thought about her a good deal and had imagined more kisses.

"That box," she said, pointing. "Could you pull it out here?"

It was corrugated cardboard, filled with canned goods and jarred preserves of all kinds, none of it store bought.

"You made this stuff?" I asked.

"Mostly Mama and Mother Beal, but I helped. Most of it came from our garden in Kansas."

She drew out a jar of amber-colored liquid,

the molasses.

"And that box." She pointed toward another, and when I pulled it onto the tailgate, she took out a round box of Quaker Oats.

The twins had risen by then, but it was a while before Mr. Schofield made his appearance. By then Mother Beal had said grace and we were eating. Without a word, Mr. Schofield sat beside his wife and she ladled out hot cereal for him.

"Buck," he said, "I wonder if I could have your help today."

"Whatever for?" Mother Beal asked.

"I'm going to give a shot to fixing that truck engine."

I saw Mrs. Schofield and Mother Beal exchange a look, but they said nothing.

"I don't know a lot about engines," I said.

"Me neither, Buck, but if I don't get her running we'll never make it to Chicago."

I thought about Albert, who could probably have worked magic on the broken engine, and that made me think about the mission I'd set for myself that day, one I was afraid might be hopeless.

"Powell," Mother Beal said, "maybe Buck has other plans."

"No, ma'am," I said. "I can help."

But it was a doomed effort from the beginning. After a couple of hours that served only to set the man to using language that would have done a sailor proud, he gave up. Engine parts lay scattered on the ground, and I thought that if ever there'd been a shot at fixing the truck, it was gone now. Mr. Schofield looked at the result of our labor, shook his head, and said, "I need a drink."

Without a word to his family, he walked away under the trees.

"Maybeth," Mrs. Schofield said.

"I understand, Mama." Maybeth moved to follow him.

"May I help?" I offered.

Mrs. Schofield gave a nod.

We set off together, and in a bit Maybeth took my hand, and although there was still my family to be found, I didn't feel alone anymore.

CHAPTER FORTY

Hopersville was alive with activity. The hovels may have been makeshift, but the lives they housed were real and vital. Though a lot of the residents in that town of shacks were single men, there were a number of families in the encampment, and the sound of the children's laughter was little different from the sound that might have been heard in a more settled place.

Maybeth and I followed her father at a distance. He skirted a rocky, tree-covered hill that rose above Hopersville and followed the railroad tracks into Mankato. It was clear he knew exactly where he was going. We didn't talk, but I felt a profound sense of sadness from Maybeth as she watched the hunched figure of her father. At a dirt road that intersected the tracks, he turned right and, a hundred yards farther on, disappeared into the kind of place I knew well. A lot of people would have called it a speakeasy, but my father had always referred to these places as

445

blind pigs, don't ask me why. Albert and I had accompanied him into dozens as he'd made his deliveries of bootlegged liquor. If Mr. Schofield was the man I was beginning to understand him to be, I figured he wouldn't come out for a long while.

Maybeth stood in the morning sun and stared at the shabby wayside. "I don't understand."

"My father said that in some men it's a kind of sickness," I told her. "They crave the drink."

"That's the real reason we lost the farm," she said. "He blames the weather. He blames the banks. He blames everything and everyone but himself."

Her words were angry now, the sadness flown.

"He'll be a while," I said. "I've got business in town. Want to come?"

In Mankato, I found a newsstand and checked the morning paper. I figured if the authorities had nabbed my family, it would have made headlines. But there was nothing. Which didn't necessarily ease my worry. I asked about the sheriff's office and was directed to the county courthouse, an imposing structure with a tall clock tower atop which stood an immense statue representing Justice, a blindfolded lady holding a set of scales.

Maybeth had been patient as I'd gone

about my business and she'd asked no questions. But now she said, "What are we doing here?"

At the edge of the walk that led up to the courthouse steps was a stone bench. We sat down, and I looked deeply into her eyes. "Can I trust you?"

Her answer was to lean to me and plant a kiss on my lips, a long one this time.

I told her my real name and all that had happened in the last few weeks, everything except for the killings. How do you tell the girl you love that you're a cold-blooded murderer?

"You think they're in there?"

"If the police picked them up, then maybe."

"Are you just going to walk right in and ask?"

"I'm not sure."

"They'll be looking for you, won't they?"

"My name hasn't been in any of the papers, so maybe not."

"Just by asking, you might give yourself away."

She was probably right, and I sat there staring at all that chiseled stone with no idea how to get at the answers inside.

"I could ask," she said.

And I wanted to kiss her again. So I did.

"It might be dangerous. You could get into big trouble."

"I want to help." She stood up and smiled

down at me. "Don't worry, I'll be back."

She walked to the courthouse and up the steps, and that huge hall of justice swallowed her whole.

I waited a long time, nearly half an hour according to the clock in the courthouse tower. I was sure something had happened to her, she'd asked the wrong question of the wrong people, and now, like my family, she was a prisoner. And it was my fault. I stared at that stone fortress and could think of no good reason to keep myself free. I stood and marched up the sidewalk, up the steps, and was just reaching for the door when Maybeth came back into the light.

She took my arm and we returned to the stone bench.

"I talked to a woman who works for the police, but she's not police herself," Maybeth said in a conspiratorial tone. "She types and stuff. There's something big going on. A manhunt she called it. But that's all I could get out of her. Nothing about your family." The fear in her face mirrored my own. "Are you the manhunt?"

Manhunt, I thought, and jumped to the conclusion that my worst fear had been realized. They'd grabbed Albert and Mose and Emmy, and now they were looking for me.

"I guess so."

"What are you going to do?"

"I can't just leave my family in there. I have

to get them out."

"How?"

"I don't know. I have to think. Let's walk."

We made our way along the streets of Mankato, I don't know for how long, Maybeth silent beside me. I beat my brain trying to think how I could spring my family, but I always came back to the fact that I was nobody and had nothing.

"I should go back," Maybeth finally said. "Mama and Mother Beal will be worried. Come on, Odie."

"Buck," I said. "My name is Buck now."

At the harshness in my voice, she stepped away. But instead of leaving, she took my hand. "When you don't have anything else to believe in, that's when you need to believe in miracles."

I looked at her patched pants, her scuffed shoes with their worn-down heels and twine in place of laces, her thin shirt faded nearly white from the sun. I thought about the farm they'd lost in Kansas and her father right now in a blind pig, probably drinking away what little they still possessed. The Schofields had lost everything, and yet Maybeth still believed in miracles.

She tugged gently on my hand. "Come with me. We can figure this out together."

Where else did I have to go? So I turned with her, and we headed back.

Before we got to Hopersville, however, we

449

came across a monument to a legion of the dead. In a small grassy area, set behind the rails of an iron fence, stood a huge slab of granite, smoothed and shaped like the headstone for a grave. Into its face had been chiseled

HERE
WERE HANGED
38
SIOUX INDIANS
DEC. 26TH 1862

"Oh my God," Maybeth said. "That's awful. What happened?"

"I don't know."

I stared at that gray memorial to some great human cataclysm, and what it brought to mind was Emmy. I thought about what she'd said when she came out of her last fit and before she'd slipped back into a healing sleep. She'd said, "They're dead. They're all dead." It seemed a stretch, but I couldn't help wondering, had this been what she'd seen? And if so, how had she known?

Which got me to thinking again about Albert and Mose, and especially about little Emmy. It seemed to me in that terrible moment, standing before such a solid and solemn reminder of tragedy, that all I ever did was let people down. I'd killed Jack. I'd got Albert snakebit. I'd promised Sister Eve that I'd watch out for Emmy, keep her safe, but she was probably already back in the greedy hands of the Black Witch, and Albert and Mose were rotting in jail, and there wasn't a damn thing I could do about any of it.

"Come on," Maybeth said and took my hand.

When we returned, we found a tub of hot water near the fire and Mrs. Schofield hanging wet laundry on a line strung between two trees. Like everyone else in Hopersville, the Schofields drew their water from a pump in a large park on the far side of the tree-covered hill, hauling it a long distance for their cooking and washing. Maybeth told me that sometimes fetching the water could be a harrowing experience because the townspeople hated Hopersville and if you encountered them in the park, they threw insults and sometimes even rocks. Just the thought of anyone being cruel that way to Maybeth made me angry.

It was well after noon by then. Mother Beal was sitting on a crate, knitting. The twins were playing marbles around a circle Lester had drawn in the dirt. When they saw Maybeth, they cried out for her to play.

"In a while," she put them off. "We followed Papa —" she began in explanation to Mother Beal.

"He's back," the old woman said with a sigh of exasperation. She nodded toward the tepee, from which came a loud snoring. "He used your mother's pearl brooch this time."

"I haven't worn that brooch in years," Maybeth's mother said from the clothesline.

"He could have traded it for gas money, Sarah."

"Enough to get us where? Not all the way to Chicago."

Mother Beal's eyes went to the truck, much of whose engine lay disemboweled on the ground. "We may never get there now."

"He tried, Mama," Mrs. Schofield said.

Mother Beal's face was hard, but her voice was not when she said, "I've got some bread and cheese, if you two kids are hungry."

Just then, Captain Gray came limping into the Schofields' camp. "Police are sweeping through Hopersville, looking for someone."

"Who?" Mother Beal asked.

"I don't know. But they're tearing everything apart. Best not get in their way."

Now I could hear the barks of dogs, lots of them, and distant shouts.

Mr. Schofield stumbled from the tepee, trying to buckle his belt, his eyes a little unfocused as if still in a drunken haze. "What's going on?"

"Police," Mother Beal said. "Searching for someone."

"Go, Buck," Maybeth said. "Run."

Everyone stared at me, surprise and suspicion on their faces. I heard the dogs coming toward us, but I just stood there, undecided.

"Go!" Maybeth gave me a shove. "I'll find you."

Without any idea of what it was all about, Mother Beal said, "Go on, son. And God be with you."

I took off at a run along the bank of the Minnesota River. A hundred yards away, I dove behind a thick growth of sumac and lay where I could see what went on in Hopersville. Officers with dogs on leashes moved swiftly through the encampment, rousting men from the shanties, barking at them harshly, a sound little different from the dogs'. If a man objected, a billy club was the response he got. I felt terrible and guilty because I knew I was the cause of all that disruption in a place where lives were already brutally disrupted. I watched three cops with a dog approach the Schofields, and I hoped that because there were children present the family might be spared the worst. But when Captain Gray stepped between the officers and the family, he was shoved to the ground and a snarling dog went at him. Mrs. Schofield cried out and tried to help, but she went down under a blow from a billy club. Her husband, who still hadn't succeeded in securing his belt, stepped toward the cop as if to defend his wife, but his pants fell down and he tripped himself and tumbled over Mrs. Schofield. Maybeth rushed to help her parents and was rewarded with a cop's boot to her ribs. Mother Beal pulled the twins to her bosom and shielded them with her old body.

I couldn't take it, couldn't just stand by and not try to help those good people who'd opened their hearts to me and their home, such as it was. I was blind with a rage far greater than any fear, and I stood up to run to their aid. I had no idea what I would do, but I wasn't going to let this travesty continue.

Before I could take a step, a powerful hand grabbed my shoulder from behind, and a low voice growled, "Got you."

The hand spun me around. And I stared into the face of Hawk Flies at Night.

CHAPTER FORTY-ONE

I tried to pull away, but the Indian held me in a vicious grip.

"Let me go, you bastard." I kicked at him.

"Easy, little man," he said. "Keep your voice down. They're waiting for you."

"Who?" I tried another kick.

"Amdacha."

"Who?"

"Broken to Pieces. You call him Mose. Him and your brother and the little girl."

That made me go still. "Where?"

"Across the river. Quick, before those bullies spot us."

"I can't leave them." I looked desperately toward the Schofields' encampment, where the altercation was continuing, and Maybeth lay on the ground next to her mother and father, holding her side where she'd been kicked, and the twins were screaming bloody murder, and old Mother Beal was up and giving those boys in khaki a good what-for with her tongue.

"You can't help them," the Indian said. "If they're smart enough to build a tepee, I'm guessing they're smart enough to get through this. But if the law lays its hands on you, Buck, you'll never see the light of day again."

One of the cops had gone into the tepee, and he came out now and shouted something above the cacophony. The cop with the dog pulled the canine off Captain Gray, and the law moved on. In our direction. The Indian and I crept low behind the cover of the sumac, and together began to run. We didn't stop until we reached a bridge that spanned the river.

We found them in a dense copse of poplars a quarter of a mile downriver from Hopersville. The canoe had been carried into the trees and laid on its side. From the river and from the far bank, it would have been nearly impossible to spot the camp — unless a fire attracted someone's eye, but there was no sign of a fire having been lit. The blankets lay together in the soft undergrowth, and I could see that this was where the others had passed the night.

When the Indian and I appeared, they came scrambling. Albert and Emmy, anyway. Mose only looked up from where he'd been sitting, which was apart from the others, and stared at me as if I were simply a stranger, someone who meant nothing to him. Emmy hugged me and she was crying from happiness. Even

Albert, who was normally about as emotional as a pipe wrench, smiled huge and embraced me.

"Where'd you find him, Forrest?" my brother said.

"Across the river, like we thought," the Indian replied.

"I went back to our camp yesterday and you were gone," I said.

"We heard dogs and men coming," Albert said. "We had to leave."

"We couldn't even make a trail sign to let you know," Emmy said. "We had to get out of there so fast."

"We heard dogs again a while ago," Albert said. "In that shantytown across the river. What happened?"

"The cops came looking for me, tearing everything apart."

"Not looking for you," Forrest said. He'd made himself comfortable on a blanket on the ground.

"Who?" I asked.

"There's a state hospital for the criminally insane downriver a few miles. Two days ago, some crazy man escaped. Pretty dangerous, they say."

"How do you know this?" I asked.

"On the other side of the river, I kept my ear to the ground. But if they'd caught you instead, Mr. Kidnapper, that would still have been a fine feather in their caps."

"And bad for us," Emmy said and gave me another hug.

Mose was chewing on a long blade of wild grass, looking darkly ruminative.

"What's up with him?" I asked Albert.

"He's been like that since we found the skeleton."

"He won't even talk to us anymore," Emmy said.

"Don't be hard on him," Forrest said. "There's something he needs to do. Now that Buck isn't a missing person anymore, I think it's time he did it."

"What?" I asked.

But Forrest wouldn't say. He got up, walked to Mose, sat down, and spoke to him quietly for a long time. Mose listened and, when Forrest had said his piece, gave a single nod.

Forrest came back to where the rest of us were sitting. "We may be gone a while."

"You want us along?" Albert asked.

"This is for Amdacha and me. You all just stay put until we return."

Forrest started out of the trees, and Mose followed, not even bothering to glance our way. He was clearly deep into something troubling and personal, and I hoped that his normal affability was still with him somewhere.

When they'd gone, I said, "How'd you hook up with Forrest? Aren't you afraid he's going to turn us in?"

"He was waiting for us, Odie," Emmy said. "When we came here on the river, he signaled us. Albert didn't want to pull up, but Mose made it clear we were going to. Hawk Flies at Night said he was watching for us."

"Just waiting here?"

Albert said, "He read about me and the snakebite, and he didn't have anywhere he had to be. It was Mose he was really worried about."

"Why Mose?"

"I guess because Mose is Sioux, like him."

"We thought we heard you playing your harmonica last night," Emmy said. "But it was dark, and Forrest said we should wait until morning, and he would go looking for you. That way, we wouldn't get caught. He's nice, Odie."

"What happened to you?" Albert asked.

I told them everything, except about Maybeth and me and the kisses. That was a gem of a memory all my own. After that, the day passed with excruciating slowness, mostly because, now that I was safe, all I could think about was Maybeth and the Schofields, and I was concerned about their safety. Finally, I couldn't take it anymore.

"I have to go back," I told Albert. "I have to make sure the Schofields are okay."

"We're not getting separated again."

"I'll come back, I swear, Albert."

"No." He tried for that voice of authority

he'd always wielded, but the old iron-willed Albert was still missing.

"I'm going." I stood up.

Albert stood up, too, but slowly. "You're not."

"Don't fight," Emmy said. "If he has to go, Albert, he should go. It's not like last time, when he stomped off mad. This is important."

Albert looked too tired to fight. But he said rather meanly, "If you don't come back, we're not looking for you."

"I'll be back before dark."

I returned to Hopersville, and as I walked through the shantytown, I saw the destruction the police had left in their wake. Lean-tos had been knocked down, cardboard enclosures torn apart, the thin boards of piano-crate abodes splintered. Corrugated tin had been pulled off the sides of shacks, and doors torn from makeshift hinges. I figured the authorities had used the search as an excuse to try to shatter the spirit of the community and maybe disperse its unwanted inhabitants. When I reached the Schofields' tepee, I found that it had been shoved down and lay like something dead on the ground. But folks were gathered around the little encampment, faces I recognized from the night before, when we'd shared food and music, and were at work pulling the tarps free of the long poles as Mother Beal gave directions for the re-raising of the structure.

Maybeth came running. She threw her arms around me and clung to me as if I'd been lost forever. "Oh, Buck, I was so afraid for you."

I stepped back and put my hand gently on her side, where she'd been kicked. "Are you all right?"

"A little sore, but I don't care. You're safe. That's all that matters."

"How's your mother?"

Mrs. Schofield sat with the twins near the disemboweled pickup truck. She had her arms around them and was speaking in a low, soothing voice.

"She said those billy clubs weren't any worse than the hailstones in Kansas. She's tough, my mom."

The same couldn't be said for her father, who was nowhere in sight. I didn't ask, figuring I had a pretty good idea of what had become of him. Sooner or later, he'd return from his visit to the blind pig, and by then, the hard work would be done.

Mother Beal smiled at me when I joined in the effort to raise the tepee. "Wondered if you would be back. Good to see you, Buck."

When it was up again, Mother Beal told everyone there, "I'm making stew and biscuits for supper. You're all invited."

"I can't stay," I told Maybeth.

"Why not?"

"I found them. My family. I have to get back."

"Does that mean you'll be moving on?"

"Not yet. I won't go without saying good-bye, I promise."

"Goodbye." On her lips, it was like the toll of a soft, sad bell. "I don't like that word."

I didn't either, and as I walked through the long shadows of late afternoon, I tried not to imagine the moment when it would have to be said.

Forrest had returned to camp, but he'd come alone.

"Where's Mose?" I asked.

"Your friend has work to do," Forrest said.

"Will he come back?"

"Maybe. When he's ready."

He'd brought food — bread and cheese and apples and a big hunk of bologna, and he'd refilled the water bag.

"How'd he get the food?" I asked Albert quietly.

"I gave him some of the money Sister Eve gave us."

I stared wide-eyed at my brother. "You trusted him with our money?"

"Not much choice," Albert said. "You were gone. I couldn't leave Emmy alone. And he brought back the change, every last penny."

Something was happening to us. When we'd begun our journey, Albert was distrustful to a fault, more likely to be crowned the king of

England than put his faith in a man we barely knew. Mose, the most easygoing kid I'd ever known, had turned his back on us. Me, I was desperately in love. We'd been on the rivers only a month and already we were in places I couldn't have begun to imagine at the Lincoln Indian Trading School.

CHAPTER FORTY-TWO

Mose didn't come back the next day. Albert and Emmy and I were worried, but Forrest assured us he was all right. I wasn't so certain. Even if he wasn't in any danger, I'd never seen him in such a dark place. In the late morning, I returned to the Schofields' camp, looking for Maybeth. She wasn't there, her mother told me as she hung wet laundry, but would be along shortly. The twins were playing down by the big river, and Mr. Schofield was nowhere to be seen, but I could guess where he'd gone. Mother Beal invited me to sit with her while she smoked her corncob pipe.

"You look a little down in the mouth, Buck," she observed. "Not usually the way a young man looks when he's in love."

"I'm not in love."

She smiled around the stem of her pipe. "If you say. So, what's the burr under your saddle?"

I told her about Mose, though I didn't tell

our whole, sordid history.

"I lived a long time among the Sioux," Mother Beal said. "A people beset by all kinds of travail, but I found them to be good and kind and strong. That was especially true when they held to the practice of their old ways."

She drew on her pipe and thought a bit.

"In the old days," she continued, "when a Sioux boy was eleven or twelve, he would go out alone to seek a vision. They called it *hanblecheyapi*, which means, I believe, crying for a dream. It was a way of connecting with the spirit of the Creator, which they call Wakan Tanka. When I was a girl and the prairie grass was higher than a man's head, I used to go way out and sit with it all around me so that I couldn't see anything but the blue sky above, and I'd close my eyes and try to feel Wakan Tanka and wait for a dream to come."

"Did it?"

"I often felt a deep peace. Maybe that's what God is, and Wakan Tanka, in the end, and maybe that's what the search for a vision is all about. It seems to me, Buck, that if you can find peace in your heart, God's not far away. This friend of yours, it sounds like his life hasn't been an easy one. It's possible what he's looking for is peace in his heart, and maybe he needs to be alone to find it."

Maybeth came into camp from the direction of the river. She wore a different shirt

465

than I'd seen her wear before and different pants, not so patched up. Her hair was brushed, her face clean and tanned and smiling. And most notable, she didn't smell of woodsmoke. In Hopersville, where everyone cooked over a campfire, clothing always gave off the heavy scent of burned wood and char. Because of our fires as we traveled the river, Albert and Mose and Emmy and I smelled the same way. Whenever the scent was all around you, you didn't notice. But Maybeth smelled of Ivory soap, and it was like perfume.

"Hello, Buck," she said, as if finding me there was a complete but delightful surprise.

"Buck's lost a friend," Mother Beal said. "I believe he could use some comfort."

"Walk with me," Maybeth offered.

We strolled through Hopersville, where folks were still putting things back together from the destruction of the day before, and although there was all kind of chaos around us, I barely noticed. We climbed a trail up the wooded hill above the shanty town and found a flat rock in the cooling shade of a tree with a view of the beautiful Minnesota River valley, and Maybeth held my hand, and we kissed.

Romeo never felt a deeper love for Juliet than the one I felt for Maybeth Schofield. On that summer day in 1932, with the police across southern Minnesota still beating the

466

bushes for Emmy and those of us who'd snatched her, and with the Schofields stranded far short of the new life they'd hoped for themselves in Chicago, and all around us the desperation brought on by a great Depression, I saw only Maybeth and she saw only me.

When we finally strolled back into the Schofields' camp, Maybeth's father had returned, unsteady on his feet, but with his head beneath the hood of the old pickup. He was mumbling, swearing under his breath, while Mother Beal looked on with impatience, and Mrs. Schofield offered periodic encouragement.

"Can you give him a hand, Buck?" she pleaded. "I'm afraid he might hurt himself."

"I'm not sure I can help, ma'am. But I know someone who works miracles with engines."

"Do you? Can you bring him here?"

"I'll ask, but it'll be up to him."

"Oh do, Buck. Please."

"I'll try to be back this afternoon," I said.

I left Maybeth with her family and returned to our camp. Forrest was gone, but Albert and Emmy were playing Go Fish with an old deck of cards, one of the things Albert had thrown into the pillowcase along with everything from the Brickmans' safe. I explained the Schofields' situation and asked for his help. But I could tell immediately from the stone look he gave me that it was going to be an uphill battle.

"Too risky," he said, putting down the cards he held.

"We can't go on afraid forever," I said.

"It's not forever. It's just until we get to Saint Louis."

"If we ever do."

"You think it's a mistake, trying to find Aunt Julia?"

That wasn't the mistake. The mistake had been falling in love with Maybeth Schofield, which had changed everything.

"I just think we can't hide forever. And I think these people really need our help. Your help."

Emmy began to gather up the cards. "You have to help them, Albert," she said, as if she were the adult and he the child.

"Why?"

"Because you know it's the right thing to do."

Albert looked to heaven and rolled his eyes. He shook his head, as if it were hopeless, then he finally gave a nod. "Okay, but just me. You two stay here. Less chance we'll be spotted."

"Thank you, Albert," I said, thinking that my brother wasn't such a bad egg, and thinking that Emmy was wise beyond her years, and thinking how grateful Maybeth would be. Thinking that most of all.

Albert limped off, his leg still paining him,

and was gone all afternoon. So was Forrest. And God only knew where Mose had disappeared to. I began to worry. What if none of them came back? What if Emmy and I were alone? And that's when I remembered the words Mose had signed again and again into Emmy's palm when trying to comfort her near the outset of our journey: *Not alone.*

He was right. We weren't alone. We had each other, Emmy and me, and now we had the Schofields. Maybe Chicago would be a better place than Saint Louis. Better mostly because Maybeth and I would be together. And I thought that might be just fine with me.

"I miss Mose," Emmy said.

I did, too. Not the Mose who was dark and moody, but the Mose who'd always had a ready smile and, although he couldn't really sing, had always seemed as if there'd been a song in his heart. Then we'd found the skeleton of the dead Indian kid and everything had changed.

Emmy began building a little house of twigs, and I asked her, "Do you remember saying to me that they're all dead?"

"Who?"

"When you had your last fit, you said, 'They're dead. They're all dead.' Do you remember that?"

"Unh-uh. It's always like a fog." She knocked down the twig house and, sounding bored, said, "Tell me a story, Odie."

The sun was well to the west, the shadows among the poplars growing long, birds settling in the branches as if preparing for the night.

"It begins this way," I said.

The four Vagabonds had traveled far since their battle with the witch's snake army, and they were tired and decided to make camp beside a river. In the distance rose the towers of a castle.

"The castle of the witch?" Emmy asked. "Where the children are trapped in the dungeon?"

"No, this a different castle. Just listen."

The Vagabonds weren't sure about the castle, and with good reason. The whole land was under the shadow of the Black Witch, and the Vagabonds knew it was dangerous to trust anyone. They drew straws to see who would approach the castle to take its measure. The imp drew the short straw. He bid goodbye to his companions and made his way alone up the river, where the castle rose on the far side. He came to a bridge long ago abandoned and overgrown with vines. When he crossed, he found the road on the other side in bad shape. The land all around was a jungle that grew right up against the walls of the castle. The castle gate was wide open and there weren't any guards, and the imp cautiously entered.

Inside, he found people walking like the dead, no life in their eyes, their bodies thin as Popsicle sticks. They were starving, but there was more to their horrible situation than hunger. The Black Witch had stolen their souls. They were living but they had no life. The imp tried to speak to them, but it was like talking to the stone of the castle walls. They didn't have the will, or maybe even the strength, to speak. They walked in a terrible silence, and because they didn't have the gumption to leave the castle, they went round and round in useless circles.

The imp had a magic harmonica, given him long ago by the great imp who was his father.

"Just like your harmonica," Emmy said.

"Not like mine," I said. "A magic harmonica."

"It's like magic when you play, Odie."

"Hush," I said. "Let me finish the story."

He drew out his harmonica, wanting to bring a song of hope to that dreary place. As he played, a beautiful voice joined him, singing from the tallest castle tower. It seemed magic, in the same way his harmonica was. He followed the sound up a long, winding staircase and came at last to a room, where he found the loveliest princess imaginable.

"What was her name?"

"Maybeth," I said. "Maybeth Schofield."

"Maybeth Schofield? That's not a princess's name. It should be something like — like

Esmeralda. That's a princess's name."

"Who's telling this story?"

"All right. Maybeth Schofield." But she made a face as if she'd just tasted liver.

He asked the princess what had happened, and she told him about the spell the Black Witch had cast over the people. In the same way she ate children's hearts, the Black Witch had taken the souls from all those in the castle to feed on them.

"But not yours?" he said.

"She left mine in order to torture me. Watching my people grow thin and weak and hopeless hurts me," she told the imp. "But when I heard the music from your harmonica, it made me want to sing. When I looked out the window, I saw a change in my people. I saw life returning to their faces. I saw fire in their eyes again. I think if you keep playing and I keep singing, we might save them."

And that's what they did. He played his magic harmonica and she sang in her beautiful voice, which came from her deep love for her people, and slowly everyone in the castle, everyone who'd lost their souls, woke up, and new souls grew in them and they were whole and happy again.

"Did the imp marry the princess? And did they live happily ever after? And what about the other Vagabonds?"

Before I could answer her questions, Albert

472

came into camp, his hands black with oil and grease.

"Did you fix the truck?" I asked.

"Yeah, but what good is a truck with an empty gas tank? They're still going nowhere."

He took a soap bar from the pillowcase and headed down to the river to wash up. While he was there, Forrest returned, but without Mose.

"Where is he?" Emmy asked.

"Your guess is as good as mine," the Indian said with a careless shrug.

"You don't know?"

"If a man needs to be alone, he finds the best place for that by himself. I haven't seen him since yesterday."

"You don't care," I said.

"I don't worry," he replied. Then he smiled a little. "You were gone awhile, too, Buck. But here you are. Have faith in your friend."

We had a cold evening meal and settled down without a fire. It was early July, and the night was hot. I lay on my blanket, unable to sleep, thinking about Mose, who seemed lost to us in more ways than one. And thinking about Maybeth and the plight of her family. And wondering how the story of the princess and the imp might end.

In the night, I got up, took the flashlight and the last of the money Sister Eve had given us, and left camp while the others slept.

CHAPTER FORTY-THREE

The coals from the Schofields' campfire still glowed red. Although I'd thought everyone might be in bed, Mr. Schofield sat near the dying fire, hunched over, looking like a man who'd lost his soul.

"Hey there, Buck."

"Evening, Mr. Schofield. Is Maybeth around?"

"Gone to bed a while ago. Sound asleep, I imagine."

I had no real plan, but of all the folks I might encounter, Mr. Schofield was the last I wanted to talk to, so I stood there awkwardly. He stared up at me, waiting for me to leave, I reckoned, or to give a good reason for staying.

"Have yourself a seat, Buck," he finally said.

He threw a couple of sticks onto the coals, and flames leapt up immediately. A fire is a welcoming proposition on its own and, coupled with Mr. Schofield's sad but sincere invitation, was impossible to turn down. I sat on one of the overturned crates.

"Couldn't sleep?" he said.

"No, sir."

"Me, neither. I want to thank you for sending your brother over to fix my truck. He's a wizard, that one."

"The smartest guy I know."

"Where are you two headed?"

"Saint Louis."

"What's in Saint Louis?"

"An aunt."

"Family, huh? That's important." His eyes shot toward the tepee. "Most important thing in the world. Believe me, Buck, if you have family, you can lose everything and still count yourself a rich man."

We sat for a while in a silence that was uncomfortable to me but didn't seem to bother Mr. Schofield. He simply gazed into the fire, lost in his thoughts.

"They figure it was the drink," he said out of nowhere. "But it wasn't."

"Beg your pardon?"

"Why we lost the farm. It wasn't the drink. You ever farmed, Buck?"

"No, sir, not really."

"Hardest life there is. Everything's out of your hands. Got no control over the rain or the sun or the heat or the cold or the grasshoppers or the wilt or root rot or smut or blight. You pray to God for what you need — rain in dry spells, blue skies when the fields are flooded. You pray the frost won't come too late in the spring or too early in the fall. You pray hail won't break every young cornstalk. You pray and pray and pray. And when your prayers aren't answered, and let me tell you, Buck, they seldom are, you got nothing left but to scream at God and maybe turn to drink for a little comfort."

"Tornado God," I said.

"What's that?"

"God is a tornado."

"That he is."

"That's what I used to believe," I said.

"Still worth believing, Buck. I swear I don't know another God."

"The one who gave you Maybeth. And Mrs. Schofield. And Lester and Lydia. And Mother Beal, too, though she's kinda rough on you. You just said a man can lose everything and still think of himself as rich."

"I did now, didn't I?" He gave a little laugh. "And you know what else? There's you and your brother. You've brought a little sunshine to us Schofields, and I want you to know I'm grateful."

He clapped me on the back, in the way of a true comrade.

"It's nice having another man around to talk to, Buck. That's a rare pleasure for me. I live in a henhouse."

When I'd left the others sleeping on the far side of the river, I didn't have a clear idea of what I was going to do when I got to the Schofields' camp. I'd hoped Maybeth might still be awake, but now that I was sitting with her father and we were talking like two men, I made a decision.

"Mr. Schofield, do you have any idea how you're going to get everyone to Chicago?"

He slumped again. "Just the thought of that makes me want to have a drink."

"I have something for you, sir."

I reached into my pocket, drew out the money I'd taken from the pillowcase, and held the bills toward Maybeth's father. His eyes grew as big and alive as two coals from the fire.

"What the hell?"

"It's just over forty dollars. I want you to have it, to get your family to Chicago."

"Where did you get forty dollars?"

"I didn't steal it," I said. "I swear."

"I can't take your money, Buck."

"Please, sir. You and your family need it more than I do."

"I don't know what to say."

"Say you'll take it. And promise that you'll use it, all of it, to get to Chicago."

He looked up from the proffered money and swore solemnly, "I promise."

He took the bills and slid them into his pocket. In the gleam of the firelight, a tear crawled down his cheek and then another. It was hard watching a grown man cry, and I looked away into the dark of Hopersville, where other campfires burned, and around them sat souls who were still lost, and I thought that giving Mr. Schofield that money had felt so good, so intoxicating, that if I'd had enough, I would have done my best to save them all.

"Where've you been?" Albert sat up. In the beam of the flashlight, his eyes were squinty and accusing.

"Nowhere." The lie didn't sit well on my conscience, so I eased down next to my brother. "I gave away our money."

"What?"

"I gave away our money."

"All of it?"

"All of it."

"To who?"

"Mr. Schofield. He needs it to get his family to Chicago."

"And we need it to get to Saint Louis."

"We'll get to Saint Louis."

"Do you ever think before you do something stupid?"

"Sister Eve gave it to us hoping it would do some good. I did the same thing."

My brother drew his knees up and hugged them and shook his head hopelessly. "He'll just drink it up, Odie. Mark my words. Good money after bad. Hell, I got no idea how we're going to make it to Saint Louis now."

I didn't sleep much that night, as usual. I worried that maybe Albert was right and that all I'd done was make the Schofields' situation worse. I thought about Maybeth, and I ached inside, love and concern braided into a rope of thorns around my heart.

Forrest rolled out of his blanket at first light, built a little fire, and threw together oatmeal in a big tin can, which, according to its label, once held peaches. The others were still sleeping, but I got up and joined him at the fire.

"Quite a bet you made last night," he said, stirring the oatmeal. "Forty dollars' worth."

"You heard?"

"Quiet night," he said. "Good ears."

"What do you mean 'bet'?"

"That a leopard'll change its spots. Drink's a tough devil to face down. I seen it lay lots of good men low. But, Buck, here's the thing. If you never make that kind of bet, you'll never see the good that might come from it."

"You think it wasn't a bad idea?"

"Like your brother said, could turn out you're throwing good money after bad. But me, I admire your leap of faith."

Albert, when he woke, kept giving me the evil eye and ate his oatmeal behind a wall of silence. I could have told him about the two five-dollar bills, which I'd hidden in my boot weeks ago and were still there, but I thought, The hell with him.

When I'd finished my breakfast, I stood up. "I'm going to see the Schofields. Want me to empty my pockets?" I said to my brother. "Make sure I didn't steal anything else?"

I could see he was trying to compose himself. "We still have a long way to go. I'm just doing my best to keep us all safe."

Which I understood, and although I was damned if I would tell him so at that moment, I was grateful for it.

CHAPTER FORTY-FOUR

Hopersville was slowly coming to life. As I strolled through the little makeshift village, folks were starting cook fires, men smoking their first cigarettes of the day, everyone stretching out their kinks and wiping sleep from their eyes. A few who knew me now, by sight if not by name, gave me amiable greetings.

When I reached the Schofields' tepee, Mother Beal was sitting on an overturned crate, stirring something in the big cook pot that hung above the fire.

"Cream of Wheat, Buck," she said when she saw me. "You're welcome to join us."

"I already ate," I said. "But thanks."

Mrs. Schofield came from the tepee, ushering the twins ahead of her. The kids made straight for the river, which looked like molten gold now in the slant of the rising sun. Their mother came to the fireside, and although she smiled at me, the gesture was cursory.

"Any sign of them?" she asked Mother Beal.

"Not yet."

"Maybeth?" I asked.

"Went to fetch her father," Mother Beal said.

"Where is he?" I asked, a dark fear taking shape on my horizon.

The women didn't reply, but the looks on their faces nailed the sad truth to my understanding. Good money after bad.

"God only knows what he took to pay for his drink," Mother Beal said. "He's already sold off everything dear."

"Maybe we're wrong, Mama," Mrs. Schofield said.

This was a plea rather than a statement, and it broke my heart to know the part I'd played in this recent and bitterly disappointing undoing of her husband.

Mother Beal made no reply but simply went on stirring the pot of hot cereal.

"Here she comes," Mrs. Schofield said.

That Maybeth was alone was telling enough, but her whole demeanor — her head down, her shoulders slumped, her walk slow — was also a clear broadcast of failure.

"I couldn't find him, Mama," she said when she reached us. "I looked everywhere."

I thought about her going alone into that blind pig and other places like it, searching in vain for her father, and every bit of the goodness I'd felt in giving that man our money drained right out of me. I considered confessing my part in visiting this misery on them, but I didn't have the courage.

"He'll come when he's drunk up all of whatever he took for collateral," Mother Beal said. "In the meantime, this Cream of Wheat is hot and ready to be eaten. Maybeth, will you call the twins?"

We sat in a glum silence while they ate their meal. Even the usually raucous twins seemed to feel the weight of their family's despair and said not a word. I worked at trying to grasp the spirit of hopefulness that was one of the gifts of my time with Sister Eve. Instead, I found myself dwelling on thoughts about the skeleton of the Indian kid we'd buried on the island in the river, and about Mose, who'd sunk himself into a place beyond our reach and then had disappeared, about all that money I'd given away in a moment of stupid generosity, and finally about the fact that I was still a fugitive from justice and only one step away from spending my entire life behind bars. When darkness comes over your soul, it doesn't come in light shades; it descends with all the black of a moonless night. In the faces of the women around that cook fire, what I saw was the vacant look of abandonment, and I knew it was all my fault.

"I'll find him," I said, thinking this might be a way to atone, but also thinking that it would be a way to escape the despair of that little gathering.

"I'll go, too," Maybeth offered.

We rose and set off together.

"He doesn't usually start his drinking until later," Maybeth said as we walked. "It's this whole situation, being stuck here with no idea how to get unstuck. He's really a good man, Buck."

I wished I believed that were so, but I knew the truth of the situation. I'd given her father the wherewithal to change his family's dire circumstances, and all he'd done was head off on a tear. Good money after bad. I hated it when Albert was right.

"I don't know if I've ever felt so low," she said. "It kills me to see Mama and Mother Beal working so hard to hold us all together. And then Papa goes and does something like this."

I held Maybeth's hand. Even though her face was clouded with worry, she was still the most beautiful thing I'd ever seen, and her ache was mine. My conscience was screaming at me to confess, but my heart was cowering at the prospect of falling out of her good graces. I wanted to help but had no idea what to do at that juncture. So I did what came naturally to me. I hauled out my mouth organ and began to play a tune, the liveliest that came to mind, Gershwin's "I Got Rhythm."

A few bars in, Maybeth began to sing, and I was amazed that she knew the words.

She was smiling now, singing how you wouldn't find old man trouble around her door, and her face seemed more beautiful than ever. Then her eyes rounded wide, and I caught what she'd just heard — the sound of her father singing along in a drunken tenor. His voice came from a short distance away, somewhere in Hopersville. I kept playing, and Mr. Schofield sang right along, and we followed the sound of his warble to where he sat on an upended water bucket, his back against the raggedy wall of Captain Gray's mostly cardboard shanty, keeping company with the captain himself. He gave us a broad smile and opened his arms in welcome.

"Will you look at this, Captain? My two favorite young people, glowing like angels in the morning sun."

"Papa," Maybeth said, her voice severe. "I've been looking for you everywhere."

"Not everywhere apparently," he said, beaming. "For here I am, love."

"Drunk," she said and cast a cold eye that included the captain.

Mr. Schofield raised his hand in a solemn pledge. "I haven't touched a drop today. If I'm drunk, it's only with happiness. And there's the cause." He poked his finger at me.

Despite his protestation, he sure seemed stewed. But close as I was to him, I caught no smell of booze. I did catch the smell of gasoline, however.

"Our deliverer, Maybeth child. And the fruit of his generosity." Her father reached down and touched a red, spouted, five-gallon gas can with SKELLY printed on the side. "This is our ticket out of Hopersville. Next stop, Chicago."

Maybeth looked rightly confused. "You haven't been drinking?"

"As I said, not even a taste. I went off this morning in search of a gas station. And then a store, where I bought a little gift for everyone, you included."

He reached down to a brown paper bag, stuffed full, and what he drew out made Maybeth gasp with surprise and pleasure: a blue dress.

"It's almost exactly like the one I gave Janie Baldwin," she cried and, taking the dress, held it to herself as if appraising in a mirror how it might look on her. I was thinking that it might look pretty wonderful.

"Buck, I hope you don't mind me using a little of your gift to gift a few others," Mr. Schofield said.

"It's your money now," I told him.

"Well, then I don't guess you'll mind that I gave Captain Gray here a little gift, too. Enough money for a bus ticket to D.C. so he can join that Bonus Army gathering there."

I didn't know what a bus ticket to Washington, D.C., might cost. I just hoped there was enough left to get the Schofields to Chicago.

Mr. Schofield laughed. "I can see from your face you're worried that I've blown the whole wad. Rest easy, Buck. I've done my calculations and there's still plenty to see us all the way to Chi-Town."

Captain Gray reached out to shake my hand. "And as for me, from the bottom of my heart and the core of my wooden leg, I thank you, Buck."

Maybeth eyed me with amazement. "You have money?"

"Not anymore," I said. "I gave it all to your father."

I thought she was going to scold me for trusting cash to a man who knew the environs of a blind pig intimately. Instead, she leaned to me and, in front of her father and Captain Gray and anyone else who might have been watching, kissed me. Full on the lips. A long time.

"All right, all right," Mr. Schofield said, lifting himself from the overturned water bucket and grabbing up his gas can. "Come along, Maybeth. We've got us some packing to do."

He headed away toward the Schofields' tepee, and Maybeth turned to follow.

And that's when the reality of what I'd done hit me. Maybeth would be leaving. Maybeth would be gone.

CHAPTER FORTY-FIVE

Gone. Gone. Gone.

The word, like a death knell, rang in my head as I walked with the Schofields back toward their tepee. Maybeth held the blue dress in one hand and my hand in the other, and her step was light. My own feet were chunks of lead and my heart was ready to break.

Gone. So final. A headstone of a word. The ending.

Mrs. Schofield rose from where she sat beside the fire, and Mother Beal turned a wary eye on us as we approached. When she saw the gas can, Mrs. Schofield looked with disbelief at her husband.

"Is that . . . ?" she ventured.

"Enough gas to get us to a station where we can fill the tank," he said.

"How . . . ?"

"It was Buck here. His doing. His generous heart."

Mother Beal's brow wrinkled as she studied

me. "You bought gas?"

"That and more," Mr. Schofield said.

He reached into the paper bag, drew out a scarf in a colorful floral print, and gave it to his wife. "That'll keep the wind off you on our way to Chicago, Sarah."

Mrs. Schofield draped the scarf over her hair, tied it beneath her chin, and tilted her head. "How do I look?"

"Like the angel you are," her husband said and gave her a peck on the cheek.

"Where are the twins?" Mr. Schofield asked.

"Playing by the river," his wife replied.

"Well, I've got a box of crayons and a Little Orphan Annie coloring book for them." He glanced at his mother-in-law. "And I have something for you, too, Mother Beal."

From the paper bag, he brought a small roll of bills bound with a rubber band. He held it out to the old woman. "I'm a man of many weaknesses. This is what's left of the money Buck has generously shared. I'd be obliged if you would take it and act as overseer of our finances until we arrive in Chicago."

She reached up and solemnly accepted his offering. "I thank you, Powell." Then she looked at me. "I'm not going to ask where a young man with no obvious resources comes up with enough money to save a family not even his own. I'm going to believe that you

489

came by it honestly, and I'm going to simply say thank you and praise the Lord."

Then she surprised me. She stood up, stepped toward me around the fire, and gave me a great, soul-embracing hug, burying my face in her bosom.

"Well," she said, releasing me and scanning the encampment. "We'd best get started."

Word spread quickly, and folks showed up to give the Schofields a hand. Maybeth fairly danced through the preparations to depart, and although I could understand her eagerness to be on the road to Chicago, I was hurt that she didn't seem at all to grasp what that meant for me, for us. The tarps and blankets were removed from the tepee, but the decision was made to leave the skeleton of the structure intact in case someone else might want to take up residence there.

When all was nearly in readiness, Maybeth smiled broadly at me and said, "You can ride with me and the twins in back."

Which caught me by complete surprise. "You think I'm going with you?"

"Aren't you? I thought that was why you got us the gas, so we could all go to Chicago together."

"They're your family, Maybeth. Mine is somewhere else."

"No, Buck. You have to come. What about us?"

"I can't go. I want to, but I can't."

"Bring your family, too."

"And what? Toss out some furniture to fit us all in? And don't forget, we're wanted criminals. I won't risk getting all of you in trouble. I'm going to Saint Louis."

A pearl rolled down her cheek, one small tear. "I don't want to go then. I want to stay with you."

"Your folks wouldn't let you. It would break their hearts. And they need you, you know that. Besides, there's no room in our canoe."

"Oh, Buck."

She threw her arms around me and we stood near the empty tepee, which was nothing but sticks now, the dark bones of a creature whose substance had vanished.

The Schofields were fitting the last of their belongings in the truck bed. "Maybeth," Mr. Schofield called.

"Leave them be, Powell," Mother Beal said.

Maybeth took my hand and we strolled to where we could both see the river flowing out of one distance and into another, a byway that was both my past and my future. The air was scented from the morning cook fires, but a breeze came off the water, cool against our faces and smelling faintly of all the silt carried by the Minnesota, which would deliver it to the Mississippi, where it would be taken all the way to the sea. Maybeth faced me and kissed me and leaned her head on my shoulder and murmured, "You'll write me letters and I'll write you and we won't lose each other."

"And send them where?"

"My aunt's name is Minnie Hornsby. She lives in Cicero. It's right outside Chicago."

"Where will your letters to me go?"

"General delivery, Saint Louis."

I didn't think it would work, but if it made her feel better, that was fine.

We walked to the truck. The twins were already in back, nestled among everything the Schofields had left to them. Mr. Schofield was behind the wheel, his wife beside him. Mother Beal stood at the opened passenger door. I helped Maybeth into the truck bed, and she settled onto a suitcase that had been laid flat with a pillow on top.

Mother Beal put her arm gently around my shoulders. "Buck, the heart is a rubber ball. No matter how hard it's crushed, it bounces back. And remember this: 147 Stout Street."

"What's that?"

"My sister Minnie's address in Cicero. You take care of yourself, you hear?"

"Yes, ma'am. I'll try."

She lifted herself into the cab, and Mr. Schofield started the engine. Albert had done well, and the motor fairly hummed. As the truck pulled away, those who by circumstance had first been neighbors and then friends waved goodbye, and I stood among them, the rubber ball of my heart crushed flat. Mr.

Schofield drove slowly until he reached the dusty track that led into Mankato, and the last I saw of Maybeth, she held one hand high and, with the other, wiped her eyes.

CHAPTER FORTY-SIX

Nothing is ever everything, but the loss of a true love feels that way. All-consuming. The blackest hole. The emptiest place in the universe. Maybeth was gone and it felt as if my life was over.

If you have never been in love, if, especially, you have never been young and in love, you might not understand the misery of parting or what I felt as I stood next to the bones of the Schofields' tepee, beside the ashes of their dead fire, while the folks of Hopersville drifted back to their own lives.

Captain Gray clasped my shoulder, said, "They'll be fine now, Buck. And thanks, again, son, for all you've done," and he joined the stream of bodies draining away.

I was completely alone. I stood for a few minutes where, only a short time before, there'd been life, song, laughter, the smell of hot food, the warm blanket of family, and Maybeth. Now there was nothing. An everything, all-consuming nothing.

I walked, and where my feet took me, to this day I cannot say. It was past noon when I found myself at the camp among the poplars, where I'd left Albert and Emmy and Forrest. To my surprise, Mose was with them.

But he was not the old Mose. The old Mose had been a feather on the wind, and no matter where circumstance blew him, his heart remained light and his spirit somehow dancing. From the Mose who now sat by himself, well away from the others, came a threatening dark, and the eyes that watched my return were tortured.

"Hungry?" Forrest said. He seemed to take no notice of the storm cloud that was Mose. He tossed me an apple and a hunk of cheese from our dwindling supply. "Norman, pass Buck that water bag so he can wet his whistle, too."

I sat beside Emmy, and her look said it all, her little face pinched with concern. She glanced at me, gave the slightest nod in Mose's direction, and lifted her shoulders in a faint shrug of incomprehension. Albert pretended to busy himself with some kind of metal pot that came in two pieces and had a swivel handle.

"What's that?" I asked him.

"Military mess kit. Bought it yesterday — when we still had money — in a mercantile in North Mankato so we wouldn't have to cook with old tin cans anymore." He fit the two metal pieces together, swung the handle over them, screwed it in place, and held it up for me to admire.

"Big deal," I said.

"At least when I used our money, it was for us."

"What a big heart you have, Grandma."

"The better to take care of us all," he said.

"I can take care of myself."

"Fine. And what about Emmy?"

"I'm all right," she said.

"Because you have us," Albert said.

He was mad at me, but in his anger, he'd lashed out at Emmy and her face went sad.

A rock hit the ground between Albert and me, thrown with such force that it bounced away into the trees. We looked up to see Mose on his feet, staring daggers at us, his whole body tensed as if he were preparing to fight us both.

You are so small, he signed. *Your spirits so selfish.*

I looked to Forrest, but he seemed not surprised in the least by this sudden outburst.

All you see is what's in front of your eyes. All you care about is yourselves.

I could have argued that I'd just helped a whole family or pointed out that we were doing our best to keep Emmy safe or reminded him that because we'd helped her there was a price on our heads and we were only one step away from prison or worse. But there were other rocks at his feet, and I wasn't all that sure he wouldn't be inclined to throw another, maybe this one right at me, and he'd already brought down a man that way. This was a Mose I didn't know; I had no idea what he was or wasn't capable of.

"What is it you see now, Mose?" Emmy asked, not out of fear, I could tell, but from a deep concern.

History, he signed. *I see who I am.*

I wanted to ask him who that was, but I was honestly too afraid. It was Emmy who ventured, "Tell us."

Mose considered this, his face still a mask of anger. Then he relaxed, stood tall, and signed, *Follow me.*

We trooped after him, all of us except Forrest, who simply watched us go. I felt a conspiracy between him and Mose, though to what end I had no idea. At that moment, because I didn't know this new Mose, and a good deal of Forrest was still a significant mystery, I found myself wary of what we might be walking into. I could sense the same from Albert, who kept glancing at me and Emmy over his shoulder in a watchful way.

Since we'd stumbled upon the skeleton on the island, nothing had been the same. I wondered if we were cursed. I'd read of such things in stories, people disturbing the dead and paying a terrible price. Or maybe because of his Sioux heritage, Mose had been possessed by a vengeful spirit. Whatever the truth, I wanted to go back. Back to the river. Back in time. Back to that place beneath the sycamore tree on the Gilead, where the fireflies had been like a million stars, and beside me, Emmy had held my hand, and for the briefest of moments, I'd felt completely free and deeply happy.

"They're all dead," Emmy said.

Which brought Mose to a halt. He turned slowly and nailed her with his dark eyes. Then he signed, *Thirty-eight.* He looked at me and Albert, as if we ought to understand, but saw clearly that we didn't and turned and continued walking.

Mose led us to a place I'd been before with Maybeth, a small patch of grass enclosed by the rails of an iron fence and, rising from the center, a granite slab like a headstone. Mose stood unmoving before the slab, as if he, too, were cut from granite, and gazed at the words chiseled there:

HERE
WERE HANGED
38
SIOUX INDIANS
DEC. 26TH 1862

"All dead," I said, repeating the words Emmy had spoken, not only minutes before but also days before, when she'd come out of her fit on the island.

"Is this where you've been all the time?" Albert asked.

Mose shook his head and signed, *Alone, thinking. And at the library.*

"Library?" I said. "What for?"

Learning who I am.

Emmy said, "Who are you?"

Mose, he signed. *And not Mose.* Then he spelled out *A-m-d-a-c-h-a. Broken to Pieces.*

"Did Forrest bring you here?" I asked.

Mose nodded.

"Did he tell you about the hanged Sioux?"

Some. I learned the whole story on my own, at the library.

"What is the whole story?" Albert said.

Mose signed, *Sit.*

I won't give you the full, sad, eloquently signed account that Mose delivered, but here's what he told us in a nutshell.

By the late summer of 1862, most of the land on which the Sioux in southern Minnesota had lived for generations had been stolen from them by treaties poorly explained or blatantly ignored. Because of the greed of the white men who'd been appointed as Indian agents, the allotments of money and supplies that had been promised to the Sioux hadn't materialized. Starving women and children finally begged one of the agents for food.

Do you know what the agent told them?
Mose signed. He dropped his hands, and because of the tortured look on his face, I wasn't sure he was going to continue. *He told them to eat grass,* he finally went on.

Ill-fed and ill-clothed, angry and desperate, some of the Sioux of southern Minnesota went to war. The conflict lasted only a few weeks but with hundreds dead on both sides. The soldiers rounded up almost all the Indians in that part of the state, even those who'd had nothing to do with the war, and put them into concentration camps. In the winter that followed, deaths from disease rose into the hundreds. Those who survived were dispersed among reservations and settlements as far away as Montana.

Nearly four hundred Sioux men were put on trial for their part, real or conjectured, in the bloody conflict. The trials were a sham. None of the Sioux were allowed legal representation. They had no chance to defend themselves against the charges, a great many of which were false. Some hearings lasted only minutes. In the end, more than three hundred were condemned to be executed. President Abraham Lincoln commuted the sentences of all but thirty-nine, who'd been found guilty of the most egregious acts. On December 26, 1862 — *the day after Christmas,* Mose signed, and his bitterness was obvious — thirty-eight of those condemned men were marched to a scaffold ingeniously constructed in the shape of a square to execute them all at the same moment.

Their hands had been tied behind their backs and hoods had been placed over their heads, Mose signed. *They couldn't see one another, so they shouted out their names in order to let the others know they were all there, all together in body and in spirit. They were condemned but not broken. Amdacha was one of these men.*

Mose lifted his face, tearstained, to the sky and for a moment could not go on.

Then: *An enormous crowd of white people had gathered to watch. At the appointed hour, with one stroke from an ax blade, all thirty-eight men dropped to their deaths. And that crowd, that crowd of eager white spectators, cheered.*

As Mose told the story, tears coursed down my cheeks, too. All this — this gross inhumanity, this unconscionable miscarriage of justice — had taken place in the area where I'd spent the last four years of my life, yet not once, in any lesson taught at the Lincoln Indian Training School, had I learned of it. To this day, I can't tell you if I wept for those wronged people or for Mose, whose pain I could feel powerfully, or if I wept because of the guilt that weighed so heavily on my heart. I'd come from different people than Mose. My skin was the same color as that of the people who'd cheered when Amdacha died, the same color as those who'd done horrible things to a whole tribal nation, and I felt the taint of their crimes in my blood.

A cop car approached and slowed down.

"We should go," Albert said quietly, eyeing the patrol car as it passed.

He started away, and Emmy and I came after him. But Mose lingered, his head bowed as he watered the grass around that headstone with his tears.

CHAPTER FORTY-SEVEN

At dusk, I headed back to Hopersville. Among the trees, charcoal-colored in the dim of approaching night, fires burned, little oases of light, islands of welcome. I was thinking about the Schofields, about how, from the moment they'd laid eyes on a kid who was no kin to them, they'd taken me in, showed me kindness, generosity. Love. I wanted to hold on to that, and the only way I could think of was to return to their camp. In a way, like going home.

As I came along the river, a figure rushed to greet me in the near dark. My heart leapt at the hope that it would, by some miracle, be Maybeth. But after a moment, the man's limp told me exactly who it was.

"Buck," Captain Gray said, a little out of breath. "I figured you might wander back. You need to leave. Right now."

"Why?"

"Some people came looking for you today. One of them was a cop, a county sheriff."

"Warford? Big red-faced man?"

"That was him."

Sheriff Shoot First And Ask Questions Later, I thought to myself.

"What did the others look like?" I asked.

"There was another man — tall, slender, black hair, dark eyes."

"Clyde Brickman. And was the other one a woman?"

"Yes, his wife, I believe. You know them?"

"Yeah, and they're all bad news."

"They said they'd heard about a kid with a harmonica staying in camp. Wanted information. About him and a little girl he might be with."

"What did you tell them?"

"Nothing. But they were offering money, and desperate as we all are, I'm sure they had some takers. You need to make yourself scarce."

"Thanks," I said. Then I said, "When you get to D.C., give 'em hell."

"That I will," Captain Gray said with a solemn nod.

I quickly returned to camp. In the time we'd been on the outskirts of Mankato, because we'd seen no one anywhere near our little copse of poplars, we'd grown a bit careless, and I found that Albert had built a fire. He had the pans from his military mess kit over the flames, and I smelled hamburger frying.

"Put out the fire," I said.

He looked up, the features of his face all drawn taut, ready to argue. "Why?"

"The Brickmans are here and Sheriff Warford's with them."

Emmy had been sitting cross-legged watching Albert cook. I heard her catch her breath. Mose was on the far side of the fire, where, whenever he was in our company, he'd been keeping himself separate from the rest of us. He'd been hunched over, staring thoughtfully into the flames, but at the mention of Brickman and Warford, he sat upright, rigid.

Forrest said calmly, "I believe I hear the river calling you again."

Albert doused the flames and we ate our hamburgers very rare on white bread and in sullen silence. I don't know about the others, but I'd begun to hope that maybe we had outrun the Brickmans or at least had outlasted their anger, and they'd returned to Lincoln School, content to resume their reign of terror over all those we'd left behind. Now, in the dark around the dead campfire, I was afraid that we would never be free of them, that there was nowhere we could run that they wouldn't follow.

"First light, we're on the river," Albert said. "We'll be out of here before anybody's stirring." Then he said something that hit me like a rock. "Will you come, Mose?"

I couldn't see Mose's face clearly in the

dark, but I could see his hands as he lifted them and signed, *Don't know.*

I didn't sleep much that night. It wasn't just my usual insomnia. It was the world I knew breaking apart. I got up and walked to the river's edge, sat on a big rock, and stared up at the two connected stars, Maybeth's and mine, which would always point north. That's where the river would take us next. The moon hadn't risen yet and the river was a dark flow, and although I'd once thought of it as a current that carried with it the promise of freedom, now it seemed to offer only disappointment.

Then I had a thought so black that I could taste its bitterness: Why had we ever left Lincoln School? It was a hard life, sure, but it was also, in its way, predictable. The police weren't after us there. The Brickmans were demons, but I knew how to deal with them. Albert and Mose were almost finished with their schooling and would be free to do as they chose, and as for me, I could manage the years I had left. Here, on the river, there was no certainty except that the Brickmans and the police would hound us until we were caught. I was sure a night in the quiet room would seem like a picnic compared to what awaited us after that.

In the rat gray light before dawn, we rose and quietly loaded our canoe. Mose helped, though he gave no indication whether he'd continue with us. I was worried about his answer, so I didn't ask. It was Emmy who finally broached the subject.

"Please come, Amdacha," she said, using his Sioux name. "We're family."

Mose looked at her a long time, then a long time at the river. Finally he signed, *Until I know you're safe.*

I understood that it was only for Emmy he was agreeing to come, not Albert or me. Family? Dead as the hope with which we'd begun our journey.

"What are you going to do, Forrest?" Albert asked as we prepared to shove off.

"I'm not sure yet."

"You could come with us," Emmy offered.

Forrest gave her a grateful smile but shook his head. "No room for me in that canoe of yours. Besides, this is my home. I've got family here. Time I visited them." He looked to Albert. "You're on your way to Saint Louis, but you'll have to visit another saint first. Saint Paul. I know folks there, good folks, who'll be happy to help you."

He took a scrap of paper and a stubby pencil from his shirt pocket, scribbled something, and gave it to my brother. He shook Albert's hand, then mine, then tousled Emmy's hair.

He turned to Mose, Amdacha now, and put

his hand on his shoulder. *"Wakan Tanka kici un."*

Emmy whispered to me, "May the Creator bless you."

Amdacha held the stern while Albert climbed into the bow and Emmy and I took our place in the center of the canoe. Amdacha stepped in, lifted his paddle, and Forrest shoved us into the current.

CHAPTER FORTY-EIGHT

It had been a month since we'd fled Lincoln School, and I was tired of the running. All that morning, I sat in the canoe and brooded in silence. The others were quiet, too, even Emmy and Peter Rabbit. There was nothing about the landscape to lift our spirits. All along the river lay the evidence of cataclysm. Debris, dry and rotting, hung in the low branches of the trees on either side, and wherever the river curved, driftwood lay piled against the high banks. The bleached limbs of whole, submerged cottonwoods that had been ripped from the valley floor long ago and become anchored on sandbars rose up midstream like the bones of dinosaurs. Maybe it was the effect of all this evidence of destruction that kept us silent, or maybe the others, like me, simply felt as misplaced and hopeless as those uprooted trees.

Around noon, we pulled to a sandy beach shaded by the branches of a great elm. We ate some lunch from our dwindling stock of food.

"Look," Emmy said, pointing toward a cottonwood across the river whose trunk was split ten feet above the ground. A mattress, stained and decomposing, lay caught in the fork of the divide. "How did it get up there?"

"A flood," Albert said.

"That big?"

"This river was born in flood, Emmy," Albert said. "Ten thousand years ago there was a lake in the north, larger than any lake that exists anywhere today. It was called Agassiz. One day, the earth and rubble wall that held it back broke, and all the water came rushing out, a gigantic flood that was called the River Warren. It carved a valley miles wide across Minnesota all the way to the Mississippi. This river we're on is all that's left of that great flood of water."

My brother was always showing off what he knew from his reading. Even though I found it pretty interesting, I wasn't about to tell him so.

"Will it flood while we're on it?"

"It might, if it rains enough."

Please don't let it rain, I thought to myself.

But Emmy's eyes grew huge with wonder. "I would like to see that."

Mose — I was still trying to get used to thinking of him as Amdacha — sat apart from us, not far but enough that it felt like a

510

separation.

"Odie, you never told me if the imp and the princess got married." When Emmy saw my look of incomprehension, she said, "The imp and princess in your story. Did they get married?"

While I considered my reply, a long piece of driftwood came into view, got caught in an eddy, and began to spin.

I hadn't told any of them about Maybeth and me, not a word. When Albert had gone to help Mr. Schofield fix his broken truck, I'd let on that it was just a family I'd come to know, a family in need. I wasn't sure why I'd kept my true relationship with the Schofields a secret or my deep feelings for their daughter. I tried to tell myself it was because I wanted Maybeth — even if it was just the memory of Maybeth — all to myself, unsullied by the need to explain anything, protected from the jabs Albert might take at this first love of mine.

But as I watched that piece of driftwood going round and round, I finally accepted the truth, which was that I'd already sensed the cracks threatening to divide Albert and Emmy and Mose and me, and I was afraid that we were falling apart. In that terrible moment, I couldn't help wondering, much to my own dismay, if I'd chosen to stay with the wrong family.

"The imp and princess didn't get married,"

I finally said to Emmy. "The princess stayed to help her people and the imp went his own way."

"Oh," she said, her face sad.

"Love doesn't always work out," I told her and threw a rock at the river.

We canoed until dusk, when we reached the outskirts of a town.

Albert said, "Forrest gave me a general idea of the river. That must be Le Sueur ahead. Let's pull in for the night."

We made camp in a little cove. As we settled in for the evening, we heard what sounded like gunshots coming from the town.

"Who's shooting?" Emmy asked.

"And who are they shooting at?" I added.

Albert cocked his head and listened, then a smile came to his lips. "Not gunshots. Fire-crackers. Today's the Fourth of July."

Although at the Lincoln School we were never allowed fireworks, every year on Independence Day, we were paraded into town, where we joined other citizens gathered near Ulysses S. Grant Park to watch the Jaycees shoot off their skyrockets and artillery shells and booming mortars. I think now how unfitting it was to force children who had no freedom, whose freedom had, in fact, been ripped from their people decades before, to take part in this observance. But the truth was we all loved these mesmerizing displays of aerial splendor, and after the lights had gone out in our dormitories, we whispered among ourselves, replaying the best moments and recalling especially the magnificence of the finale.

The fireworks in Le Sueur began not long after dusk. The park must not have been far from the river, because the explosions in the sky and the sound of their reports came very close together, the booms shaking the air around us.

"Oh, look," Emmy cried when a huge chrysanthemum of magenta sparks blossomed amid a shower of gold. In her excitement, she grabbed Amdacha's hand. I saw him flinch, then relax and, to my great amazement and relief, smile, the first smile I'd seen on his lips in what seemed like forever.

"Play something, Odie," Emmy begged when the night grew quiet again.

My heart was beginning to feel light but not particularly patriotic, so I put my Hohner harmonica to my lips and blew the notes for "Down by the Riverside," a song Emmy's mother had taught me and whose tune and lyrics always lifted my spirits.

Emmy picked up on it right away, throwing her little heart into singing, "Gonna lay down my sleepy head, down by the riverside . . ."

Albert joined in a few bars later, "Ain't gonna study war no more, ain't gonna study war no more . . ."

At the third stanza, Amdacha began to sign the words.

We risked a fire that night and sat together, talking quietly around the flames, as we had on many nights since we'd taken to the rivers. It began to feel to me as if what had been broken was coming together again, but I knew it would never be exactly the same. With every turn of the river, we were changing, becoming different people, and for the first time I understood that the journey we were on wasn't just about getting to Saint Louis.

Emmy lay her head against my shoulder and nodded off. I put her on her blanket, but she woke for a moment and held to me, so I lay down to keep her company.

Albert and Amdacha stayed at the dying fire, their faces dimly lit by the last of the flames.

"I'm sorry," Albert said.

What for? Amdacha signed.

"I knew my mother and father. I know where I came from." He'd been staring into the coals of the fire, but now he looked up. "I never thought how hard that must be for you."

What's most important is who I am now.

Albert picked up a stick and stirred the coals, so that a few more flames sprang to life. "I was scared you wouldn't come with us."

I'll go back. Someday.

"Because you're Amdacha now?"

Broken to Pieces, I thought.

Amdacha lifted his eyes to the night sky, thought about this for a moment, gave his shoulders a faint shrug and signed, *Ah, hell, you can still call me Mose.*

■ ■ ■ ■

- PART FIVE -
THE FLATS

■ ■ ■ ■

CHAPTER FORTY-NINE

It was another two days before Saint Paul came into sight. Our first real glimpse of what lay ahead was the imposing stone of Fort Snelling, whose gray ramparts dominated the bluff above the confluence of the Minnesota and the Mississippi Rivers.

As we passed beneath the great fortress, Mose stared up, his eyes filled with hatred. *That's where the soldiers who killed my people came from,* he signed. He looked at the river bottoms, scanning the trees and shadows as if searching for something. *They built a stockade here and shoved nearly two thousand women and children and old men into it. Hundreds died in the winter that followed.*

For Mose, everything that had occurred since we'd left New Bremen had torn open his soul. Across the days on the river as we canoed toward Saint Paul, I'd watched him struggle with the terrible pain of that rending, and at night, I'd listened as he cried out unintelligibly in his sleep. So I thought I understood his rage when we passed beneath those stone walls, which were a symbol of all that had been cut out of his life.

We entered the Mississippi at sunset, the surface broad and mirror smooth, the river bluffs aflame with the last light of day. Albert guided us to the riverbank for the night. We emptied the canoe, lifted it from the water, settled ourselves among the trees, and began gathering driftwood to build a fire, which was only for the comfort of the light it would give because we had no food left to cook. We'd had nothing to eat for more than a day. I'd considered the five-dollar bills in my boot, using them to buy food, but Emmy had told me that I'd know when the time was right, and I just didn't feel it yet.

We'd encountered towboats pushing loads on the Minnesota, but the first two we saw on the mighty Mississippi were twice as long, ten barges in one tow and eight in the other. The waves from their passing battered the shoreline, and I thought how easily our canoe might be swamped if we found ourselves caught in the wake of one of those flotillas.

When we'd begun our journey, the moon had been nearing fullness, and that night it was full again. I lay under the trees on the river bottoms and stared up at the man in the moon, whose face, through the branches, was cracked and broken. I couldn't sleep. We were finally on the Mississippi River, which would take us to Saint Louis. But how far that was, how many more full moons ahead of us, I had no idea.

I heard Mose rise and watched him slip away. I thought he was just getting up to relieve himself, but when he didn't return for a long time, I became worried. I tugged my boots on, left my blanket, and followed where he'd gone, deeper into the bottomlands. I found him in a small clearing, sitting with his legs crossed, his face lifted to the night sky, cast in white from the moonglow. He was chanting in a low voice, no words because he lacked a tongue, but it was clear to me that he knew what he was saying. I wondered if it was some sacred prayer that Forrest had taught him, or if he was simply giving voice to what was inside him now. The sound that came from him rose and fell, gentle waves on the sea of night. He lifted his hands as if in supplication. Or perhaps celebration. What did I know? I felt as if I were trespassing, witness to something never meant to be shared, and I quietly retreated.

In the morning, we loaded the canoe and prepared to enter Saint Paul. We could see homes crowning the bluffs upriver, some of which looked huge and magnificent.

"Do you think princes and princesses live there?" Emmy asked, gazing up at the mansions.

"Rich people, for sure," Albert said. "Rich

people always find the places where they can look down on everyone else."

"I want to be rich someday," Emmy said. "And live in a big house like that."

Albert said, "Do you know what a house like that costs?"

Emmy shook her head.

"Your soul," he said. "Come on, let's hit the river."

We paddled a good part of the morning. The face of the river changed. Trees gave way to industry, and rows of neat little houses marched up the hills, and then a cluster of stone towers came into view, the tallest buildings I thought I'd ever seen, crowded shoulder to shoulder, and atop one of the hills that backed them rose the dome of a great cathedral. We slid under the span of a bridge that seemed impossibly high overhead, and finally Albert guided us into a narrow channel between a long island and the south bank, and we drew the canoe up on the opposite side of the river from all the imposing architecture of the great downtown.

Once we'd disembarked, Albert pulled a piece of paper from his pocket, and I recognized it as the scrap on which Forrest had written the name of the person he said would help us. I wasn't sure that we needed any real help, except we could all use a good bath. We hadn't cleaned ourselves well since we'd left Sister Eve, and even to one another we were beginning to smell like things dying or already dead.

" 'West Side Flats, Gertie Hellmann,' " Albert read. " 'Ask anybody.' "

I looked over his shoulder and saw that, in addition to the name, Forrest had drawn a crude map of the river with an *X* marking where we would find the West Side Flats, which was, I figured, exactly where we were.

"What now?" I asked.

"I'm going to find Gertie."

"What do we do with the canoe?"

"You stay with it, all of you. I'm going alone." He looked to Mose. "Don't let anything happen."

Mose gave a solemn nod, and my brother climbed the riverbank and disappeared.

In my experience, railroad tracks and rivers are like brothers. They follow each other everywhere. Above the spot where we'd landed our canoe ran a couple of sets of rails, and while we waited for Albert to return, a slow-moving freight train rolled past, heading downriver. The cars were empty and some of the doors had been left open. Occasionally, we caught sight of a man or two sitting idly inside. We stared at them as they passed, and they stared vacantly back. I wondered where they were going, or if they knew or even cared.

When the last car had gone by, three figures revealed themselves on the far side of the tracks, kids, like us, hands stuffed in their pockets, looking down with great interest at where we stood beside our canoe.

"You Indians?" the tallest of them asked. He had dark, unkempt hair, big ears, and wore clothes nearly as soiled as ours. I put him at about my age.

"Do we look like Indians?" I called up to him.

"He does," he said, pointing to Mose. "And you got a canoe."

"We're vagabonds," I said.

"Vagabonds. What country do they come from?"

"Here."

"Hell, we got Arabs here and Mexicans and Jews, but I ain't never heard of Vagabonds. You got names?"

"Buck Jones," I said. "That's Amdacha. And this is —" Emmy had never taken a different name, and I hesitated, trying to think of something appropriate.

"Emmy," she said.

"I got a sister named Emma. That's almost the same," the tall kid said. "Me, I'm John Kelly. This here is Mook, and that's Chili." He looked upriver. "Did you canoe down here?"

"That we did."

"From where?"

"You're a curious bunch," I said. "You live around here?"

"We all live on the Flats."

"Do you know Gertie Hellmann?"

"Everybody knows Gertie. Why?"

"We're looking for her."

"Won't have any trouble finding her." He eyed our canoe with great interest. "Never been in one of those. Tippy?"

"Not if you know what you're doing."

"Could we take a ride?"

"Maybe another time."

"Gonna be here awhile?"

"Don't know yet."

"Buck Jones," John Kelly said. "Like the movie star." Then he grinned. "My ass. See you around, Buck Jones."

He turned, headed away, and the other two followed.

Albert showed up a few minutes later. "Back in the canoe," he said.

"We're not stopping?"

"Just going downriver a ways."

We canoed another half mile, to the end of the island, where the narrow channel opened once again onto the broad current of the river. All along the bank, shacks had been constructed, and several of what I would later learn were called shantyboats lay moored there as well. We came at last to a large brick building with MORGAN'S BOATWORKS painted in white on the side. A couple of long wooden docks jutted into the river, where a number of vessels were tied up. A few had masts, a couple were sleek-looking speed-boats, and one was a stern-wheel towboat. A man stood knee deep in the brown river water, bent toward one of the larger sailboats, eyeing a hole above the waterline, which had been hastily patched with plywood. Albert guided us to within a few feet of the man, who turned when he heard the splash of our paddles.

"I'm looking for Wooster Morgan," Albert said.

"Found him." He was nearly bald, but a black handlebar mustache curled flamboyantly along his upper lip. He wore a blue work shirt with the sleeves rolled above biceps like bowling balls.

"I just came from Gertie Hellmann's place. She said we could leave our canoe with you."

"She did, did she? Well, we don't want to make a liar out of Gertie. Lift 'er up and we'll find a place to store 'er."

Wooster Morgan waded from the water and watched as we unloaded our things and my brother and Mose lifted the canoe onto their shoulders. "This way," he said, and he waved us to follow.

Inside, the boatworks was one great room with all kinds of lathes and grinders and a whole world of tools I'd never seen before and whose purpose I couldn't begin to guess. There was also a good deal of welding equipment, and from the rafters hung thick chains with hooks big enough to lift a whale. A small craft sat up on blocks, its hull fit with runners — an iceboat, I would later learn. The place smelled of grease and acetylene and beneath that, the sweet scent of new sawdust. As Albert's eyes took in all that machinery, I could see that he thought he'd just stepped into heaven.

Wooster Morgan set up a couple of sawhorses and, once the canoe had been laid across them, asked our names. We gave him the ones we were using those days.

"Did Gertie tell you the rules of my boat hotel?" Morgan asked.

"No, sir," Albert replied.

"You got one week. Normally I'd charge you a buck, but seeing as how you're friends of Gertie's . . ." He looked us over and smoothed his mustache. "A handshake from each of you fellers, and a kiss on the cheek from the little angel will do for now."

We walked through the West Side Flats, seven or eight square blocks of houses built so close together even Emmy would have had trouble squeezing between them. In truth, many of the constructions didn't seem any sturdier than the thrown-together shanties of Hopersville. All of them had outhouses in back, and I saw no indication of running water anywhere. There was not a blade of grass to be seen, and the few trees in evidence were scrawny, struggling things. It seemed to be all squalor, out of which had arisen a community. A vibrant community judging from all the people we saw. Women hanging wash on the line, calling to one another across ragged fences. Scruffy kids playing in the dirt yards. Men with horses and wagons going about their enterprises — ragmen, icemen, tinkers. A few automobiles, but not many. When we turned up a street called Fairfield, a row of shops lined both sides — butchers, dry goods stores, grocers, a couple of barbershops, a blacksmith, all with customers coming and going, giving one another cordial greetings as they met and passed.

At the Lincoln School, we'd had indoor plumbing, showers, and a roof over our heads that generally didn't leak. We'd had grass, plenty of it, and trees. We'd been given three meals a day and a bed to sleep on. In truth, we'd known a great many comforts. But in this crowded, chaotic community, I could see in abundance two precious things that had been withheld from us at Lincoln School: happiness and freedom.

"There." Albert pointed toward a two-story dilapidated corner building with GERTIE'S painted on a window.

The door stood open, and we followed my brother inside. The space was cramped and crowded with tables. Chairs had been upturned and sat on the tabletops, their legs toward the ceiling. The air smelled of something savory.

A stepladder stood in one corner of the small café, with a man atop it, seeing to the repair of a hole in the ceiling. When he heard the clomp of our feet on the wooden floor, he turned and stared at us. He wore workman's gloves, overalls, and boots that looked as if he'd walked to Africa and back in them. He climbed down from the ladder and came to where we stood, and I saw the damage to his face, scarring on the right side so severe it nearly closed up his eye. Although that old wounding seemed to give him no trouble, it was painful to look at. He tugged off his gloves, fisted his hands, and put them on his hips while he took the measure of each of us. Then he spoke, and I realized that, despite appearances, this was no man.

"Hello, there," she said. "I'm Gertie."

CHAPTER FIFTY

"First things first."

Gertie walked us into the kitchen, where a woman stood at a stove, eyeing the contents of two huge, steaming pots, the source of that wonderful aroma I'd smelled on entering the establishment.

"Flo," Gertie said. "We have some guests."

The woman turned. Her blond hair was limp from the steam of the pot and her face flushed, but this took nothing away from her beauty. Her eyes were startling blue and her smile immediate and enormous.

"Children?"

"According to Norman here," Gertie said, "Forrest sent them."

"Forrest? How is he?" Flo said with surprise and delight. "And where is he?"

"Out of work and in Mankato," Gertie replied, giving us no time to answer for ourselves.

"Back in Minnesota," Flo said. Her smile was beginning to seem like a permanent fixture. "Will we see him?"

Although the question was directed to us, it was once again Gertie who gave an answer.

"He's sticking around home for a while, but if I know Forrest, he'll be up here eventually to see his brother."

Flo's blue gaze, warm as a summer sky, ran across us all. "And you're our guests until . . . ?"

"They're on their way to Saint Louis. Just stopping for a breather," Gertie said. "I'm putting them up in the shed for the night."

Flo wore a flowered dress that reached to her calves. She hiked the hem up a bit, crouched so that she was eye-level with Emmy, and said, "You're just about the cutest thing I've ever seen. What's your name?"

"Emmy."

Which made me roll my eyes. When would she ever learn?

Flo glanced up at me.

"Buck," I said. "Buck Jones."

"Like the movie star. And you?" This to Albert.

"Norman," he said.

"And what about you?"

Mose stared down at her, and even if he'd had a tongue, I believe he could not have spoken, he seemed so starstruck.

"His name's Amdacha," Albert said. "He's Sioux."

"Just like Forrest and Calvin," Flo said.

531

"Calvin?" I said.

"That's Forrest's brother. He didn't tell you?"

"No, ma'am. He just sent us up here to Gertie."

"That's probably because he wasn't sure Calvin would be around. This is the busy season on the river. And your parents?" Flo asked.

"We're orphans, every one of us," Albert said.

"I'm sorry." Her smiled flagged a bit. "These are surely difficult times we're living through."

My stomach growled. I hadn't eaten for almost two days, and the smell from the pot was impossible to ignore.

"Hungry?" Flo asked.

"I could eat a horse," I said.

"They're with us just for tonight," Gertie said brusquely. "We'll feed them and they'll sleep in the shed. They'll work it off helping us at dinner."

"All right." Flo nodded her agreement.

"Come along," Gertie said. "Let's get you set up. Then we'll put a little food in your stomachs and then —" She looked us over with stern eye. "Then a shower."

Our showers were taken in a stone building, public baths on the other side of the river, at the edge of the downtown, a place popular with the lower class who had no indoor plumbing. Judging from the crowd, there were a lot of folks in the same boat.

It was late afternoon when we returned to the Flats. Gertie's hadn't opened yet for the evening meal, but a couple of men were sitting at a table. When we stepped inside, they turned and stared at us, as if we were trespassing.

"Gertie's not serving yet," one of the men said.

He was tall, broad-shouldered, with lanky brown hair, and the dark shadow of a beard across his lower face. His eyes were sky blue, just like Flo's, but there wasn't a hint of welcome in them.

The other man was an Indian, and right away I knew it was Calvin, Forrest's brother. He was younger than Forrest by at least a decade and wore his hair in a braid that reached just below his shoulders. His aspect was different from his companion's, especially when his eyes, the color of hickory nuts, settled on Mose, whom he studied intently.

It was Albert who replied for us, and he spoke defiantly: "We're working for Gertie tonight."

"She didn't say anything about you," the broad-shouldered man shot back.

"That's because it's none of your business what I do here," Gertie said, entering from the kitchen. "What you do on your boat is

533

your affair, Tru. What I do here is mine. And I don't like that tone, especially with my employees."

The man she'd called Tru had a glass in front of him. The color of the liquid inside and the slight head of foam told me he was drinking beer. From his tone and the surly look he gave us, I figured it wasn't his first.

Flo came in behind Gertie and looked us up and down with approval. "Cute as bugs in a rug." Then she pulled up a chair at the table where Calvin and the surly man sat. "No luck, Tru?"

He took a long swallow from his beer. "Wooster Morgan says it'll be at least a week but more like two. Claims he's got to locate the engine parts. The Berenson tow'll go to Cooper, that bastard. God only knows if I'll be able to snag anything anytime soon after that."

"You can't fix it?"

"Maybe. If Morgan gave me use of his equipment."

"Which he's already said will happen when hell freezes over," Calvin offered with a calm smile.

"Oh, Tru, I told you not to let your temper get the best of you." She put her hand gently on his arm. "Something will come along."

"I hope I still have a crew when it does. Mac Cooper's already put out the word he'll take every hand willing to work for him."

"Loyalty counts for a lot," Flo said.

"With Hoover in the White House, money counts for more," Tru replied.

"Calvin, it was your brother who sent these kids here," Flo said, then introduced us one by one.

"How is Forrest?" the Indian asked.

"Fine when we left him," Albert said.

"And where was that?"

"Mankato."

"Must've run out of cows to punch. Give you any sense what his plans were?"

"No, sir," Albert said.

Calvin sat back and said, "If we can't get the *Hellor* fixed, maybe I'll pop down to Mankato."

"The *Hellor*?" I said.

"The name of my brother's towboat," Flo said.

Brother and sister. I could see it then.

"It's really the *Hell or High Water*," Flo said. "We just call her the *Hellor* for short."

"But not for long if I can't get that damn engine repaired and back to shoving tows," her brother said.

"Going to sit there and drink until we open for business, Tru?" Gertie said, hands on hips, her eyes drilling the surly man.

"I'd suck on a dead catfish before I'd eat your swill, Gertie."

"Suit yourself, but it's Flo's lentil soup."

"I'll come back," Tru said and finished his

535

beer. "Let's go, Cal. See what might be shaking down at the landing."

After they'd gone, Flo said, "He's really a good man. He's just caught between a rock and a hard place."

"He's been caught there since I've known him," Gertie said. She studied us, then she said, "You kids cleaned up good. Now get yourselves set. We're going to have a busy night."

It was, in its way, my first official employment, and my first evening on the job turned out to be like no job I would ever have after it.

CHAPTER FIFTY-ONE

Gertie served only one offering for each meal. That night it was the lentil soup and bread, take it or leave it. Which made serving pretty easy. Gertie's was a bare-bones operation, no fluff or frills, no tablecloths, no fancy framed photos or paintings on the walls, just a place that served up good, homemade fare at a decent price. Flo dished up from the kitchen; Emmy and I delivered the food; Albert cleared the tables; Mose washed the plates, flatware, and glasses; and Gertie took the cash and kept things moving.

Everyone knew Gertie and Gertie knew everyone. Most of her clientele were men, a lot of them clearly down on their luck. "I'm not running a charity kitchen here" was a line I heard her deliver with some frequency, but I never saw her send a man away hungry.

Although she opened her door for business at five o'clock sharp, she didn't have a specific closing time. Business ended for the night when the soup was gone, and it was no problem emptying those pots.

After we'd cleaned the place up, and the bowls and flatware were put away, Flo brought out a loaf of bread, a block of cheese, cold sliced beef, tomatoes, and lettuce and made us all sandwiches. We sat at a table near the front window. It was dusk, and evening light came through the glass in a wave of gold. Outside, the street was quiet, the hustle of the foot traffic and horse carts and the few automobiles ebbed to a gentler flow.

"You work hard," Gertie said. "And you don't complain. Could've used you a long time ago."

"Everybody was asking about Elmer and Jugs," I said. "Who are Elmer and Jugs?"

"Until two days ago, they were doing just what you all did today. Right now, they're sitting in the county jail across the river."

"What happened?"

Gertie said, "Got drunk and mixed it up with the wrong people. Fifteen days before they're free again." She looked each of us over carefully. "How about you taking their places? You in any hurry to get to Saint Louis?"

Albert said, "What'll you pay?"

"Room and board and a dollar a day."

"For each of us?"

Gertie smiled. "Don't need you that bad. A dollar for the kit and caboodle."

Albert gave each of us a look and saw no

objection. A dollar a day for the four us would, after fifteen days, be enough to carry us some of the distance to Saint Louis. He held out his hand to Gertie. "Deal."

The door opened, and Tru and Calvin returned and swung a couple of chairs up near our table.

"Nothing left," Gertie said.

"Those sandwiches look good," Tru said.

"I'll fix you both something." Flo left the table and went to the kitchen.

"So, what did you find out?" Gertie asked. Although her voice was sharp, I had the sense she was hoping to hear something good.

"If I can get the *Hellor* on the river by next week, Kreske has a tow of grain that he'll give me. Perkins was supposed to push it, but he got busted with a hold full of hooch bound for Moline. The Kreske tow goes to Cincinnati, and there's a load of phosphate I can push back here."

"Can you repair the *Hellor* in time?"

"I don't know. What do you think, Cal?"

"Up to you and Wooster Morgan. You make nice with him, he might let me use his equipment. Even then . . ." He gave a noncommittal shrug.

"Truman Waters go crawling to anyone?" Gertie said. "That I'd like to see."

The door opened again, and a kid rushed inside. I recognized him. John Kelly, one of the kids who'd spoken to us from the tracks earlier that day.

"Gertie," he said, out of breath. "Baby's coming, and Ma's having real trouble."

"Did she send you?"

He shook his head. "Granny. She thinks we need a doctor." He glanced over and saw me. "Hey, Buck."

"You two know each other?" Gertie asked.

"Met this afternoon," John Kelly said.

"You." Gertie drilled me with her eyes. "Come with us." She stood up and said to everyone else, "Don't eat me into bankruptcy. Flo!" she called toward the kitchen. "I'm leaving. Mrs. Goldstein's in labor."

Flo stepped through the kitchen doorway, wiping her hands on an apron. "You don't know anything about delivering babies, Gertie."

"Not knowing something never stopped her before," I heard Tru say under his breath.

"We'll be back when things are good at the Goldsteins'." Gertie marched out the door with John Kelly and me trying to keep up.

We didn't go with her to John Kelly's house. At the end of the street, she ordered, "You two go to Dr. Weinstein. You know where he lives, Shlomo?"

"Yeah, over on State. But Ma says we can't afford no doctor, Gertie."

"You let me worry about that. You just make sure he comes."

"Shlomo?" I asked after we'd parted ways

with Gertie. "I thought your name was John Kelly."

"That's just my nickname."

"Nickname? Mook and Chili are nick-names."

"It's complicated. I'll explain later. Come on." He began to run.

John Kelly — across my whole life I've never thought of him as Shlomo Goldstein — pounded on the door of a house on State Street, which was opened eventually by a thin woman. Although it was near dark and she looked bone-tired, she managed to ask with great patience, "What is it, boys?"

"My ma's having a baby and it ain't going so good."

"Your ma?"

"Rosie Goldstein on Third Street."

"What is it, Esther?" A man, looking even more tired than the woman, stepped into view at her back.

"This boy's mother is having a baby, Simon, and he says there's some difficulty."

A pair of spectacles were perched at the end of the man's narrow nose. He looked over his glasses, appraising me and John Kelly. "Who's with her now?"

"My granny and my big sister."

"No midwife?"

"Just them. But Gertie's on her way. She told us to fetch you."

"Gertie Hellmann? Why didn't you say? Mother, get my bag."

The Goldsteins lived in the upper of a ramshackle duplex with a black waterline two feet up the outside walls.

"That?" John Kelly said, when I asked. "Flood. Happens almost every spring on the Flats."

I could hear the tortured cries of Mrs. Goldstein as soon as we entered the house. Two woman greeted us, the downstairs neighbors, who were spinster sisters, Eva and Bella Cohen. "Thank you for coming, Dr. Weinstein," Eva said. "We offered help but something's not right."

"Stand aside, good ladies," the doctor said and mounted the stairs.

"You boys," Bella said. "Stay down here. Your sister, Emma, is inside, Shlomo. We'll fix you something to eat."

The Cohen sisters fed us rice pudding, me and John Kelly and his little sister, Emma. I'd never tasted it before and it was quite good, but not good enough to distract us from the cries coming from above. Even when I was wounded and spent time in a field hospital in France years later, I never heard screams like those that came from John Kelly's mother as she struggled to give birth that long July night on the West Side Flats of Saint Paul. They went on for hours, and Bella eventually sang Emma to sleep on the ratty sofa and covered her with a knitted afghan and told John Kelly and me that we should try to get some rest. But John Kelly couldn't sleep. He watched the ceiling as if he expected at any moment the baby would drop right through it.

"Do you have a deck of cards, Miss Cohen?" I finally asked.

"Yes, Buck," Eva replied. "I'll get it."

I said to John Kelly, "You know Crazy Eights?"

"Sure. Don't everybody?"

So, we played Crazy Eights well into the early hours of the next morning, when the woman's screaming finally stopped and another kind of screaming began, higher and weaker.

Bella Cohen, who'd been rocking in a chair, nodding off occasionally, clasped her hands dramatically and said, "The baby is here."

John Kelly threw down his cards, leapt to his feet, and ran up the stairs outside the Cohens' flat. I thanked the sisters for their kindness and followed him up. At the top of the landing, I encountered Gertie, who looked as pale as the rice pudding we'd eaten. In her arms she held a bundle of sheets, which had probably been white once but were now deeply mottled with ruby-colored stains.

"A boy," she said.

I stared at the sheets, speechless. I had no

idea about childbirth, and what I saw in Gertie's arms terrified me. "She's dead?"

Gertie shook her head and smiled wanly. "No, Buck, just a very difficult delivery. What's called a breech birth. The baby was turned all wrong."

"Is it always that . . . that noisy? And messy?"

"Not always, I think."

"Have you seen a lot of babies born?"

"Honestly, Buck? This was my first."

"I hope I never see it." I was still staring at the bloodied sheets.

"It's a boy," Gertie said, looking over my shoulder at the Cohen sisters, who'd come up the stairs behind me.

The sisters laughed and said something to each other in a language I would come to learn was Yiddish. "The sheets," Eva said. "Let us take care of the washing."

"Thank you," Gertie said, and gave them over. "One more thing, Buck. Shlomo has newspapers to deliver. Would you go with him? It's been a rough night for his family, and I expect he might appreciate the company."

I said I would, and Gertie thanked me and went back into the Goldsteins' flat. A few minutes later, John Kelly came out looking like somebody had just lifted a piano off his chest.

"I gotta go," he said. "I'll be late delivering

my papers."

"Mind if I come?"

"You're a mensch," he said and threw his arm over my shoulder as if we'd always been the best of friends.

CHAPTER FIFTY-TWO

There were no streetlights on the Flats, but our way was lit by moon glow. We crossed an arched, stone bridge over the Mississippi. Below us, the river was rippled with silver, but in the distance, it tunneled black into the vast dark of night. We made our way along empty streets that ran between the imposing buildings of downtown Saint Paul. I'd visited Saint Louis many years before, which I remembered was also full of looming architecture, but I'd been a resident of Lincoln School for a long time, outside a one-horse town you could practically spit across, and I found the endless, empty corridors of the city unnerving.

There was a lot to be absorbed that night, and we were quiet as we walked. But finally I asked a question that had been nibbling at me the whole time we'd sat with the Cohen sisters.

"Where's your dad, John Kelly?"

"He's a junk dealer. Off all the time collecting stuff. I see him once a month or so, when he comes back to sell. He's in South Dakota right now."

"Who takes care of things while he's gone?"

"We all pull together, but Pop says I'm the man of the house. What about you? Where are your folks?"

"Dead. Long time ago."

"Sorry."

"Why do you call yourself John Kelly?"

"Safer. Easier."

"What do you mean?"

"The cops, most of 'em, are Irish. They find out you're Jewish, they're liable to give you grief. Hell, maybe even kill you. Just look at Gertie."

"Her face, you mean?"

"Yeah. Cops did that."

"Why?"

"Like I said, they find out you're Jewish, their billy clubs come right out. Way I understand it, Gertie tried to help some poor schlub the cops were trying to beat to death, and they did the same to her."

We went up an alley and came to a loading dock, nearly empty now, that ran along the back of a building. A bull of a man stood alone there, chewing on the stub of a cigar.

"Where the hell you been, kid?" he snapped.

"Hard night," John Kelly said, trying to sound tough.

The man threw a bundle of newspapers tied with twine at John Kelly's feet. "You get those papers out fast, see. I don't want no complaints."

"Ever had any complaints from my customers?"

"Don't crack wise with me, kid. I'll bounce your ass all over town."

"All right, all right," John Kelly said.

He lifted the paper bundle by the twine and we wove through downtown, then up a long, steep hill, and finally entered an area near the cathedral, where great houses rose, the biggest I'd ever seen. Streetlamps burned brightly on every corner, and under one of them, John Kelly paused, pulled out a jackknife, and cut the twine. He tried to gather the papers under one arm, but it was hopeless.

"I got a canvas bag at home makes carrying these a lot easier. So rattled tonight I forgot it."

"Give me half," I said.

We did his route together, tramping up one street and down the next, the houses all white columns, gingerbread trim, fancy shutters, and ornate wrought-iron fences, everything screaming wealth, and I thought about the world as I knew it then. There seemed to me two kinds of people — those with and those without. Those with were like the Brickmans, who'd got everything they had by stealing from those without. Were all the people sleeping in the great houses on Cathedral Hill like the Brickmans? If so, I decided I'd rather be one of those without.

We'd delivered the last paper, and there was a faint suggestion of light in the eastern sky, when a gruff voice hailed us. We stopped under a streetlamp and a big cop strolled out of the shadows of an overarching elm.

"What're you two hooligans up to?"

"Delivering papers," John Kelly replied.

"That so? Where are they?"

"All done. We're going home."

"If you're a paperboy, where's your bag?"

"Forgot it. A lot of excitement tonight. A couple of hours ago, my ma birthed a new baby brother for me."

"Yeah? What's his name?"

"Don't know yet. I had to leave before Ma decided."

"What's your name, kid?"

"John Kelly."

"You?" the cop said, sticking the sharp chisel of his chin in my direction.

"Buck Jones."

"Like the movie star, huh?"

"Yes, sir," I said. "My ma, she's kind of sweet on him."

"He's not like that," the cop said. "None of them are, kid. Where's home?" he asked John Kelly.

"Connemara Patch."

"All right, then. Get along with you now. Don't be dawdling."

"Connemara Patch?" I asked after we'd distanced ourselves from the cop.

"It's where a lot of Micks live." He glanced back over his shoulder. "If I told him my name was Shlomo Goldstein from the West Side Flats, we'd both be wearing bruises now."

We parted ways on Fairfield Avenue, which was already beginning to bristle with activity, mostly carts and horses and tired-looking men shuffling to an early shift somewhere, the lucky ones with jobs.

"What are you doing this afternoon, Buck?" John Kelly asked.

"Nothing, I guess."

"Not nothing. You're going to do something with me," he said with a devilish look in his eyes. "I'll come find you."

He walked off, whistling, his hands stuffed in the pockets of his faded dungarees. The big brother. The man of the house. My new best friend.

When I got to Gertie's, the smell of food drew me to the kitchen. I found Flo at the big stove frying bacon and eggs in a cast-iron skillet. She looked up, brushed a long, errant strand of blond hair from her face, and said, "Gertie gave me a fine account of last night. That was quite something."

I didn't want to tell her how hard it had been listening hour after hour to John Kelly's mother screaming as she struggled to deliver the baby.

"You helped Shlomo with his paper route?"

"All done."

"Then you must be hungry."

"I'm okay." The truth was, I could have eaten an elephant, but I didn't want to take Flo's breakfast.

"Nonsense. I'll just pop a little more bacon on and crack another egg. Would you like toast? Do you drink coffee?"

We ate together, just the two of us, at the table. It felt intimate and special.

"Where's Gertie?" I asked.

"She took some blintzes to the Goldsteins."

"Blintzes?"

"It's kind of a Jewish pancake, stuffed and rolled."

Some of the men my father delivered hooch to were Jewish, but I didn't know much about what that meant.

"Is everybody on the Flats Jewish?"

"Not quite everybody."

"So you and Gertie are Jewish?"

"Not me. Confirmed Catholic. You ask Gertie if she's Jewish, she would probably say no."

"She stopped being Jewish?"

"I don't think you just stop being anything. She doesn't go to synagogue anymore."

"Synagogue?"

"It's like church for Jewish people."

"Do you still go to church?"

"Sometimes."

"You haven't given up your religion?"

"You're certainly full of questions. Are you religious yourself, Buck? Is that where all these questions are coming from?"

"Religious?"

I let the word sit on my thinking for a bit. For me at that moment, religion was the hypocrisy of the Brickmans' Sunday services. They'd painted a picture of God as a shepherd watching over his flock. But as Albert had bitterly reminded me again and again, their God was a shepherd who ate his sheep. Even the loving God that Sister Eve believed in so profoundly had deserted me time and again. I didn't believe in one god, I decided. I believed in many, all at war with one another, and lately it was the Tornado God who seemed to have the edge.

"No," I finally said. "I'm not religious."

Gertie walked in then, returning from delivering the blintzes. "I just saw Shlomo," she said. "He seemed pretty beat. You look like you could use a good sleep, too. When you're finished eating, get some shut-eye. Don't worry about helping with the breakfast crowd. We'll do just fine without you."

"You could use some sleep, too," Flo said.

Gertie waved off the suggestion. "Later."

I carried my plate and fork to the sink, rinsed them, and when I turned back, watched with surprise as Flo took Gertie into her arms, held her tenderly for a moment, then kissed her long and lovingly.

Chapter Fifty-Three

We breathe love in and we breathe love out. It's the essence of our existence, the very air of our souls. As I lay on the bunk in the old shed behind Gertie's, I thought about the two women and pondered the nature of the affection I'd witnessed. Flo was a beautiful flower, Gertie a tough mother badger, and I tried to make sense of the love they shared. I hadn't known that women could love women in the way I'd fallen in love with Maybeth Schofield. With every turn of the river since I'd left Lincoln School, the world had become broader, its mysteries more complex, its possibilities infinite.

Gertie had roused my brother and Mose and Emmy to help with breakfast, but I'd been allowed to stay abed. The smell of the shed reminded me of the old tack room where Jack, the pig scarer, had imprisoned us. It was twice as large as the tack room and held two bunks, where Elmer and Jugs slept when they weren't locked up in the county hoosegow. Mose and Albert had shared one of the bunks. Emmy had taken the other, but she'd given it up to me. I could hear the sounds from the Flats, the call of a ragman — "R-a-a-gs! R-a-a-gs! Newspapers! Bones!" — the creak of wagon wheels, the whinny of horses, the occasional grumble of a gasoline engine and rattle of an undercarriage as an automobile negotiated the ruts of a street still unpaved. The voices coming from Fairfield Avenue often spoke in Yiddish, but because the West Side Flats was the first place most immigrants landed in Saint Paul, there were also occasional shouts in Spanish and Arabic and other tongues foreign to my ears, and I felt as if I'd come a million miles from Fremont County.

I slept, but fitfully because I could sense the buzz of activity all around me, and it seemed that I was the only bee not active in the hive. I finally rose, relieved myself in the outhouse back of Gertie's, then headed off to see what was up with everyone else.

I found Emmy and Flo in the kitchen preparing lunch fixings.

"Morning, sleepyhead," Emmy said brightly.

"Where's Norman?"

"Gone long ago, Buck," Flo replied. "Seems your brother has a talent my brother is greatly in need of."

"Irritating people?" I said.

"Is that any way to talk about your brother?"

"Your brother never irritates you?"

"All the time. But we forgive them, don't we?" Flo nodded toward a knife and pile of carrots and said, "Wash your hands, and then help me with some chopping."

While I worked I asked, "So what is it that your brother wanted with Norman?"

It was Emmy who chirped in, "He's going to fix Tru's boat."

"He's going to try," Flo cautioned. She took a bowl of cornmeal batter and held it while Emmy began spooning the batter into the waiting pans.

"Albert can fix anything," I said. "What about Mose?"

"Mose and Calvin went along to help."

"And Gertie?"

"Shopping for dinner. We'll be serving beef stew tonight."

When I'd finished chopping the vegetables, Flo relieved me of my duties but said, "We start serving lunch in an hour and a half. Back by then, Buck."

I asked if she might have a sheet of paper and an envelope so that I could write a letter. She gave me both, along with a No. 2 pencil, which she'd sharpened for me. I walked to the arched bridge over the Mississippi River, sat down, and thought about Maybeth Schofield.

Not a day had passed since we'd left Hopersville that Maybeth hadn't been on my mind. I'd often spent the long hours on the river reliving our kisses, holding tight to that final image of her waving to me sadly from the back of the pickup truck as her family headed toward Chicago, and imagining what kind of life I might have had if I'd gone with them. I knew in my heart I could never have abandoned my own family, but the tantalizing possibilities of that different choice still tormented me.

Dear Maybeth, I wrote. *I'm in St. Paul for a couple of weeks, staying with Gertie Hellmann and her friend Flo on Fairfield Avenue. I hope that your travels are going well. I look at our stars every night, the two that point north, and I think of you.*

I tried to decide if I should say something about the kisses we'd shared but decided to let Maybeth, when she wrote, broach that subject first. If she said something in her letters, which I hoped would await me in Saint Louis, then I'd let loose on my end and pour out to her all the stirrings of my heart. But in the meantime, I thought it best to keep things simple. So, I finished with *I'll write more later. Please give my best to your parents and Mother Beal.* I thought a long time about how to sign it and finally settled on *Yours always, Odie.*

Yours always. Safe code, I thought, for *I*

love you.

I folded the letter, put it in the envelope, and addressed it: *Maybeth Schofield, 147 Stout Street, Cicero, Illinois.* I decided not to include a return address, since I didn't expect to be in Saint Paul when Maybeth wrote back. I didn't know where the post office was, and it was almost time to be back at Gertie's to help with serving lunch, so I slipped the letter inside my shirt to keep it safe from my brother's prying eyes and questions and returned to the Flats.

Mose had returned as well, but not Albert or Tru or Calvin.

Working on the boat engine, Mose signed. He didn't have time to explain anything more before Gertie threw open the door and put us to work.

In two hours, the bean soup and corn bread she'd prepared for the lunch crowd were gone, except for the bit that Flo held back to feed us and herself and Gertie. We sat around a table near the front window, eating together, kind of like family.

"How's it going with the *Hellor*?" Gertie asked Mose. "Did Wooster Morgan agree to help?"

He signed, *Said he'd be damned if he'd help out Truman Waters. But Albert talked to him. He likes Albert. Agreed to let him use the equipment and tools. I think he believed Albert was pissing in the wind, but Albert's making good progress.*

I translated and Gertie shook her head. "Truman is one stubborn son of a bitch. But I'll give him this. He cares about the *Hellor* and his crew."

Flo said, "He made a solemn promise to Pap that he'd take care of that boat."

"Pap?" I said.

"Our dad. When he died, he passed the *Hell or High Water* down to Tru. We've been river people for generations. Taking care of the *Hellor,* that's kind of a sacred duty for Tru."

Gertie gave a derisive snort, and in response, Flo said gently, "In every sinner, Gertie, is the possibility of a saint."

When the kitchen had been cleaned, Mose headed back to the boatworks. Gertie, who looked well and truly beat, finally agreed to Flo's insistence that she lie down for a while. Flo asked Emmy if she'd like to help her bake the biscuits that were going to accompany the beef stew she'd be serving that evening. I was thinking of catching a little shut-eye, like Gertie, when John Kelly stepped in and said, "You wanna do something fun?"

I'd never hopped a freight before, but John Kelly was a pro.

"They all slow down, see, while they rumble through the Flats."

We waited near the arched bridge where an iron trestle crossed the Mississippi. We'd just missed a train, but John Kelly said another was bound to come along any minute.

"How're your mother and baby brother doing?" I asked.

"Aces," he said. "Ma's strong like an ox, and it's easy to see that Mordy takes after me. He's got lungs on him like a ragman."

"Mordy?"

"Mordecai David. But Mordy fits him good," the proud big brother said. "God's truth, though, I don't know if any of us'd make it without Gertie. She's made sure there's food pouring in so Granny can take care of Ma and Ma can take care of Mordy." He pointed down the tracks. "Here she comes."

The engine rumbled passed us, hauling a long line of boxcars. Occasionally we saw shabby men looking out at us through open doors. An empty car came abreast of us, rocking a little as the weight of it pressed down upon the rails. John Kelly yelled, "This one!" and launched himself up and through the open door. I stood there eyeing all those big, groaning iron wheels, thinking that if I slipped, I could end up looking like a loaf of sliced bread with strawberry jam.

"Come on!" John Kelly hollered.

I had to run to catch up, and when I leapt, John Kelly caught me and pulled me safely in beside him. "Where are we going?" I asked, breathless.

"Just to the yards across the river. But if we caught the right train, hell, we could go to Chicago or Saint Louis or Denver or you name it. Trains go everywhere from here."

As the train slowed on the other side of the river, we disembarked among a network of rails and idle cars. John Kelly had no trouble, but I stumbled and fell, and the letter that I'd written to Maybeth Schofield and had stuffed inside my shirt slipped out. I brushed myself off and picked up the letter.

"What's that?" John Kelly asked.

"What's it look like?"

"Maybeth," he said, reading over my shoulder. "Some girl you're sweet on?"

"Something like that," I said.

"Want to mail it?"

"Sure. But I need a stamp."

"Easy as pie," he said.

He led me downtown to an enormous gray stone building with turrets everywhere and a big clock tower, the most impressive structure I thought I'd ever seen. It was the federal courthouse and also served, John Kelly explained to me, as the main post office for the Upper Midwest. It was imposing and, because it was a courthouse, was sure to be filled with all kinds of representatives of the law. John Kelly marched right in as if he owned the place, and although I was full of trepidation, I followed.

The interior was all marble and mahogany, and within it was a constant flow of bodies. I wove among the stream of people coming and going, their faces intent, sometimes tearstained, always preoccupied. The law was a force formidable and heartless, yet here I was under its very nose. I tried to make myself small and unnoticeable.

John Kelly led me to the postal area, where several lines had formed at the windows. We stepped into one, awaiting our turn. Two uniformed cops strolled past. Although I knew logically there was no way they were looking for me specifically, I bent my head anyhow to hide my face.

I was still staring at the polished floor, when a huge hand clamped onto my shoulder, and a deep voice spoke: "My God, it's you."

When I saw who it was, my mind reeled. Because standing before me, drilling me with his one-eyed glare, was Jack, the pig scarer, the man I'd shot dead in a barn in Fremont County.

CHAPTER FIFTY-FOUR

I stood in the grip of a one-eyed demon risen from the grave, and I was absolutely paralyzed.

"Hey!" John Kelly said, mustering all the gruffness a thirteen-year-old kid was capable of. "Let him go!"

Other people stared, and as much as I feared the pig scarer, I feared attracting attention even more. There were cops in the building, and the last thing I needed was interference from the law.

"I . . . I'm sorry," I mumbled.

"Sorry?" Jack said. "What for? You saved me, Buck."

His left arm was in a sling, but his face, far from being a mask of outrage, held a genuine look of pleasure.

"Saved you?" I said.

"Everything okay there?" a man in the next line asked.

"Old friends," Jack told him. "Isn't that right, Buck?"

"That's right," I said carefully.

Jack suggested affably, "Let's go somewhere we can talk."

We made our way outside and to a park across the street. The whole way my insides felt like jelly and my brain kept telling me to run, which I might have done except that I was immensely curious about how this man had risen from the dead. We sat on a bench in the shade of an elm and Jack told us his story.

"I woke up in the barn," he explained. "Blood all over my shirt, a hole in my chest." He used his good right arm to unbutton his shirt and show me the sewn-over wound. "Doc says that bullet's so close to my heart he can't never pull it out safe. Says another half an inch and I'd be a dead man for sure." He rebuttoned his shirt, looked up where sunlight broke through the tree branches and fell on his face in splashes of gold. "That half inch was nothing short of a miracle," he said in a hushed voice. He gazed back down at me with his one good eye. "I'm the last fella on earth deserving of a miracle, Buck, but there she is."

"What are you doing here?" I asked.

"I'm a reformed man. I took an ax to that still your brother built for me, then I got myself cleaned up good and came to Saint Paul to find Aggie and Sophie."

"Have you found them?"

"By God's good graces, I have," he said, beaming. "We're all staying at her sister's place till Aggie's got things together and we can head back home. Another day or two, probably. But hell, imagine running into you like this. Where's the rest of your bunch?"

Just before I'd shot him dead — or thought I'd shot him dead — I'd seen the possibility of a good man in Jack. Then he'd turned. I knew some of that dark shift was caused by the alcohol, but I had no idea what other factors might underlie what seemed the dual nature of the man. So I held off telling him the truth. Instead, I said, "We split up after we left your place. We thought it was safer if we all went our own ways."

"I'm sorry to hear that, Buck. They were your family. A man loses his family, he's lost everything. Little Emmaline, she's okay?"

"She's fine." I couldn't help thinking about the mattress in Jack's attic that had been cut to shreds in what I'd imagined was a fit of murderous rage. "So what about Rudy?"

"Rudy?" Jack shook his head sadly. "I read him all wrong. I thought he was after my Aggie and Sophie, but that was the booze twisting my thinking. Turns out he was just worried that I might do them harm. After he delivered them to Aggie's sister, he headed for Fargo. Has family there." A sudden darkness crossed his face. "You know, Buck, I feel terrible about the way I treated you all. Kept you locked up like animals. And I'm ashamed to say I took your money. Used it to keep the farm from going into foreclosure, which was a big reason I'd been drinking so much. At the time, I figured I was just taking cash you'd stole yourselves from those folks in Lincoln, but that still didn't make it right. I don't know how I can repay you."

I thought about the money I'd given to Mr. Schofield and the good I hoped it had done. And here was Jack before me, a changed man, and I understood that the money he'd taken had played a part in that change. And, honestly, I was so relieved to have the weight of the guilt over that dead man lifted off my shoulders that I felt almost giddy.

"Like you said, it wasn't ours to begin with. I'm glad it did some good."

Jack had been so focused on me that he hadn't even seemed to notice my companion. Now he smiled at John Kelly. "Who's this?"

"This here is . . ." I began, but because things had turned so quickly in his barn that once again offering the truth didn't seem like the most judicious choice, I hesitated.

It was John Kelly who piped in with "Rico."

"Rico, huh? Well, Rico," Jack said, shoving out his hand, "pleased to meet you."

John Kelly gave the man a good, firm handshake and winked at me.

One-eyed Jack stood. "I've got things to do, so I'll be on my way. You ever find yourself down in Fremont County, you're always welcome in my home." He didn't leave us immediately but stood a moment with his good eye closed and his face lifted, as if breathing in some sweet aroma. He touched his chest on the place where I'd put the bullet and he smiled. "Life's stranger and more beautiful than I ever thought possible. Thank you, Buck, for that gift."

He shook my hand and he walked away.

"Rico?" I said as we started back toward the bridge across the river to the Flats.

"You never seen *Little Caesar*? Edward G. Robinson? Rico? He's one tough mug."

My time with Jack made me late in getting back to Gertie's, and Mose and Emmy were already hard at work. Gertie threw me immediately into helping prepare for the meal crowd that night, and I didn't have a chance to say anything to the others about my encounter with the undead man. Dinner was a busy affair, but when we sat around a table together afterward, slopping up the stew that had been set aside for us, I braced myself to tell them about Jack. Before I could, however, Albert, Tru, and Calvin arrived, all in high spirits.

"Genius," Tru declared, clapping my brother's shoulder. "We've got us a bona fide mechanical genius here. Flo, give this man some food. And, Gertie, I think we need beer to celebrate."

Flo rose from her chair immediately, but Gertie didn't move. She cast a dour eye on Tru Waters. "What's the deserving occasion?"

"I believe we got 'er licked," Tru said. "The *Hellor*'s going to be ready to push tows down the river in a day or two, mark my words."

Gertie looked to Calvin for confirmation. "The kid's got the knack," he said. "Even Wooster Morgan was impressed. Wants to hire Norman for the boatworks."

"Over my dead body," Tru said. "This kid's joining my crew."

Flo brought out beef stew, and Gertie brought out two glasses with foamy heads.

Tru said, "A glass for Norman, Gertie."

She eyed my brother, who told her with a very un-Albert-like impish grin, "A beer would sure hit the spot."

I knew Albert had been involved with Volz in bootlegging back at Lincoln School, but I'd never seen him consume any alcohol. He did that evening, and plenty of it, raising glass after glass.

I'd intended to tell them about Jack that night, but the beer had got to Albert, and he stumbled onto the bunk he shared with Mose and immediately began to snore up a storm. It had been a long day for Emmy, and she fell asleep almost the moment her head hit the pillow. Albert's snoring made it impossible for Mose to sleep, and he finally stood and stepped out into the moonlight. I'd hoped that learning I hadn't killed Jack would end my insomnia, but my brain was so full that, yet again, sleep seemed impossible, and I finally got up and joined Mose outside.

There was a smell to the Flats, the odor of slow decay that was due in part to the annual spring floods that lifted the Mississippi out of her banks and set her flowing among the ramshackle houses, so many of which, like the home of John Kelly, carried the high-water mark from the most recent occurrence. In spring, everything was soaked through and through and slowly rotted in the summer heat that followed. I stood with the reek of decay all around, and I saw that a light was on above Gertie's place, and I watched, along with Mose, as silhouettes passed back and forth across the drawn shades.

I like them, Mose signed, his hands milk white in the moonlight and graceful. *They remind me of Emmy's mother. Good hearts.*

"Forrest knew what he was doing when he sent us here," I said. "His brother's a lot like him."

Good people. Then he signed, *I like it here. Albert likes it here.*

I'd known Mose a long while. More often than not, I understood from the expression on his face and the way his hands moved what kind of tone his words would have carried had he been able to give them voice. What I interpreted now scared me a little.

"What does that mean?" I asked cautiously.

Tru wants us to join his crew. He's offered us jobs.

Although I'd heard Truman Waters say as much, I'd thought he was just blowing smoke, exuberant because, thanks to Albert, his towboat was going to be in service much sooner, and undoubtedly with a great deal less expense, than he'd anticipated.

"He was serious?"

Dead serious, Mose signed.

"Both of you?"

Both of us. Cal says we should take him up on it. Says finding a job these days is near to impossible.

"You like Cal."

He's my people.

"I thought Albert and Emmy and I were your people."

Still are. There's room in my heart for all of you.

"What about Saint Louis?"

I don't know Saint Louis. But I'm getting to know the Flats, and it wouldn't be a bad place to settle down. Gertie and Flo love Emmy, and she's taken to them. And you've got a friend here now, best friend, the way you talk.

Albert had always been my best friend. But he was changing. I'd seen how proud he was to be sitting next to Truman Waters, drinking with the man as if they were almost equals. Since his near death from the snakebite, he was becoming someone different, and I felt a deep sadness, as if I was seeing the end of us somehow, or at least the end of what we'd been to each other.

The growl of Albert's snoring had ceased inside the shed, and Mose signed, *Breakfast comes early. Better get some sleep.* He put his hand on my shoulder in a way that felt shockingly patronizing, as if he were an adult urging a child to bed. And that simple gesture nearly broke my heart.

I pulled away from him, and he returned to the shed alone.

I felt like crying, but that would only have confirmed Mose's assessment that I was yet a child. Instead, I turned everything inside me to anger. The Flats, I understood, was just another promise that would somehow be broken. We'd been lulled into a sense of the possibility of belonging, but if we stayed, I knew it would destroy us, or at least destroy our need for one another. It would end what we'd been for each other. It would end our search for our true home. I didn't know how I would do it, but I vowed to see to it that the Flats wasn't the last stop on our journey. We had started for Saint Louis, and by God, I'd see to it that we got there.

CHAPTER FIFTY-FIVE

"Tell me about Saint Louis and Aunt Julia," I said to Albert the next morning.

We sat at a table in Gertie's eating breakfast before my brother and Tru and Cal headed off to the boatworks. The sun was barely up.

"Why?" he said, sipping black coffee and looking badly hungover from his night of drinking with Truman Waters.

"It's been a while, and I forget sometimes."

Which was true but not the reason I'd asked. I wanted to get him back on track, thinking about Saint Louis as our ultimate destination and our real family there as the true purpose of our journey. I planned to segue into memories of Aunt Julia and our mother and father, and tug at Albert's heartstrings until the resonant music of longing brought him to his senses.

He hung his head and stared at his plate, and I was afraid that instead of reminiscing he was contemplating puking into his scrambled eggs.

Emmy proved to be immensely helpful. Bright-eyed, she asked, "Is Saint Louis really big?"

"Uh-huh." Albert gave a nod so faint I thought maybe he was afraid his head was going to fall off.

"What do you remember about Aunt Julia?" I asked. "I only remember that she was really nice to us."

Albert put his fork down and closed his eyes. When he spoke, it was with great effort. "I remember she was pretty. And she smelled like flowers. Lilacs. We only visited her once and that was after Mom died, but I remember she was nice to us."

"I remember her house was huge and pink."

"And near the river," he said.

"Do you remember the street?"

He shook his head. "Some Greek name, but I can't recall what. I remember there was a confectionery on the corner, and she gave us both a few pennies to buy fudge."

"I remember that fudge," I said.

"Best I ever tasted," Albert said.

I saw what I thought was a wistful look in his eyes as he recalled these things.

"Mose told me you're going to work for Tru," I said carefully, looking to Mose for confirmation. He had a forkful of eggs almost to his mouth, but he paused long enough to give a nod.

"Are you?" I asked.

573

"Sure, why not?" Albert said.

"Because it's dangerous to stay here."

"What are you talking about?" he said.

That's when I hit them with it: "I saw one-eyed Jack. He's alive."

Albert's bleary, bloodshot eyes grew suddenly focused. "You're lying."

"Am not."

Mose put his fork down and signed, *Why didn't you tell us?*

"I didn't have a chance. But I'm telling you now. We need to leave."

The door was thrown open, and Tru and Cal walked in, full of early morning exuberance, Tru especially.

"Ah, there he is," he said, slapping my brother so heartily on the back that Albert looked as if he was going to toss up what little he'd been able to get down that morning. "We have a big day ahead of us, Norman."

Mose signed, *Talk later.*

The men pulled chairs up to our table and sat with us, and Gertie and Flo fed them. Tru did most of the talking, laying out his plans to push a tow downriver the following week. "You have a lot to learn," he said, addressing this to both Albert and Mose. "It'll be hard work, but you'll be learning life on the river, and I swear to God, boys, there's no other life like it."

Flo was pouring coffee, and she smiled and explained to us, "We grew up on the river,

574

Tru and me. We've been up and down the Big Muddy more times than I can remember."

"Nothing like watching the sun come up on the Mississippi, Norman," Tru said. "The water like fire all around, and the whole river empty except for you and your tow. I swear, standing in the wheelhouse on such a morning, you know what a king must feel like when he's looking out from his castle across all the land he owns."

"You don't own the river, Tru," Cal reminded him.

"Feels like it sometimes." He put his hand on my brother's shoulder. "You'll see, Norman." Then he smiled at me. "We'll find something to keep you busy too, Buck."

I looked at my brother, his eyes bloodshot, his face pale, nodding his head like some stupid lackey at everything he was hearing, and in that moment, I hated Truman Waters, the man who was stealing my brother away.

In the afternoon, I set out to mail Maybeth's letter, but first I visited the boatworks, where the *Hell or High Water* was docked. When I stepped onto the towboat's deck, I spotted Mose and Cal in the wheelhouse. Through the open door to the engine room came the clank of metal on metal and the voices of Albert and Truman Waters as they discussed things. Engine parts lay on the deck, some cleaned and gleaming, others still steeped in grease and reminding me of the innards of a slaughtered animal rotting under the hot July sun.

"Cal!" I heard Tru holler from inside. "Bring us the starboard piston rod!"

But up in the wheelhouse, Cal hadn't heard.

"Cal!" Tru called again. When no reply came, he swore loudly, then stepped from the engine room onto the deck, caught sight of me, and to my surprise, smiled as if he were quite glad to see me. "Hey there, Buck. Came to help?"

"Just to have a look-see."

"Well, come on in and take a gander." He beckoned me with a greasy hand.

The engine room was a cramped space filled with the great machinery that was the heart of the towboat, a long boiler tank to which was attached a web of rods and pistons and cylinders and pumps. Albert was on his back, staring up into that steel web, covered in grease, a big crescent wrench in his hand, and wearing maybe the fattest, happiest grin I'd ever seen. It was clear to me this was my brother's element, the world of machines. His ordeal with the snakebite had shaken him, and he'd seemed lost in a way, but I understood that in the bowels of that towboat, he was finding himself again. I wanted to be happy for him, but my angry heart had put up a wall. He was so intent on his work that he didn't notice me.

I left the *Hellor,* headed across the arched bridge, but stopped halfway to study the Mississippi, which was shit brown under the afternoon sun. A big island called Harriet lay west of the bridge, and above the island's public beach stood a great bathhouse with no bathers anywhere in sight. The Mississippi in those days had become a foul run of sewage, and although the city would eventually grow into a better steward of that precious resource, in 1932 not even the bravest of souls would dare bathe in the water.

I stared up at the Heights, where fine homes overlooked the squalor of the Flats, and I wondered why Flo and Gertie and Tru and Cal and John Kelly and all the rest of them were content to live with just enough to get by.

I looked down at the boatworks, at the idled *Hellor.* Although I'd spent a more than a month on the river, the towboat seemed alien to me, big and clumsy. Give me a canoe any day, I thought.

Somewhere downtown a clock struck four, and I realized I needed to get back to Gertie's to help with the dinner crowd. I hadn't mailed Maybeth's letter yet. As it turned out, I never would.

CHAPTER FIFTY-SIX

"Gonna hold a little celebration on the *Sweet Sue* tonight," Tru announced after dinner that evening. "You're all welcome to come."

"*Sweet Sue?*" Emmy asked.

"My shanty boat," Tru explained to her. "It's where Cal and me live."

When we finished cleaning the eatery and the kitchen, we trooped down to the river, where a line of weather-beaten, floating shacks sat drawn up to the bank. They were, if possible, poorer-looking than the ramshackle constructions that housed folks on the streets of the Flats, but I thought maybe they had one slight advantage in that when the floods came every spring, the shanty boats rode the rising waters and stayed high and dry. People — whole families — sat on the decks and hailed Tru and Cal as they passed.

Tru pulled bootlegged beer from his icebox and handed it out liberally. The adults drank, but Albert judiciously passed on the offer, accepting like Emmy and me and Mose, the alternative sarsaparilla. Tru had a steel barrel on his deck, cut down to half its original height. As dusk gave way to hard dark, he built a fire in the barrel. Kerosene lanterns glowed on the boats along the riverbank, and we found ourselves in a tiny community within the larger gathering that was the Flats.

Emmy and Flo and Gertie sat together on empty, overturned crates, Mose and Cal next to them. Tru had corralled my brother and was chewing his ear off with talk of adventures on the Big Muddy. I sat alone, apart, fuming silently, until Cal rose and crossed the deck and settled down beside me.

"You're an onion in a petunia patch, Buck. And every time you look at Tru, it's like you're throwing rocks at him. He's really a good man."

"He drinks too much."

"Not when he's pushing a tow. He's sober and all business then, one of the best pilots on the river."

I drank from my sarsaparilla and made no reply.

"Here's something you might find enlightening. The cops who beat up Gertie, they got the living daylights beat out of them. They claimed not to know who done it, and maybe that's the case, but everyone on the Flats knows who made those two cops pay. Who do you suppose that was?"

"Tru?" I said grudgingly.

"He's devoted to Flo, and because she loves Gertie, he's devoted to her as well. And don't let Gertie fool you. She loves Tru."

"They've got a funny way of showing it, the kind of talk they throw at each other."

"You ever eat a walnut? Crack that hard shell and there's sweet, soft meat inside."

Flo called out gently, "Buck, would you play us a tune or two on your harmonica?"

"Don't feel like playing," I said.

"Then a story," Emmy insisted.

"A story, Buck," Truman Waters said and lifted his beer as if in encouragement.

"A story?" I said. "Sure, I'll give you a story."

There were once four Vagabonds.

"The fairy princess, the giant, the wizard, and the imp," Emmy said brightly. "And they're on an odyssey to kill the Black Witch."

"Exactly," I said.

They'd traveled long and hard, and although the Black Witch had sent many foes to battle them, they were still unharmed because together they were invincible. There was magic among them that made them strong, and they knew that nothing could stand against them, not even all the evil powers of the Black Witch.

Although they didn't understand it, this was their weakness. Their absolute certainty of themselves.

But the Black Witch understood it, understood that sending an army against them was useless, and she understood that there was another way to destroy them.

I paused for effect, and the gathering on the deck of the shanty boat was silent, until Emmy cried in distress, "What way?"

She sent a little fly to whisper in their ears as they slept. What the fly whispered to the giant was this: You are strong and do not need the others. And to the wizard: You are smart and do not need the others. And to the fairy princess: You are magical and do not need the others. But when the fly tried to whisper in the imp's ear, the imp slapped at it and crushed it dead.

The next morning, the giant rose and looked at his friends and thought, What do I need with the others? I'm strong enough on my own. And the wizard opened his eyes and thought: What do I need with the others? I'm smart enough on my own. And the fairy princess, who'd always been kind, awoke and thought: My magic is powerful. What do I need with the others?

The imp alone understood the dark plot the Black Witch had hatched. "Comrades," he cried. "Don't be fooled. The only way to stand against all the evil in this land is to stand together."

But the whispering of the little fly had done its job, and the other Vagabonds were deaf to the pleas of the imp.

The giant said, "I'm going to kill the Black Witch myself. I don't need your help."

The wizard said, "I'm going to kill the Black Witch."

The fairy princess said, "No, I will kill the Black Witch."

The three boastful Vagabonds eyed one another with suspicion and then with anger. They began to fight among themselves, and in the end, they destroyed one another. Only the imp, who'd stood sadly by and watched and could do nothing to stop them, survived.

He knew he could never kill the Black Witch by himself. For the rest of his days, he wandered the land alone, cursing the Black Witch and mourning his fallen companions.

After a few moments of silence, in which could be heard only the crackle of the fire burning in the cut-down barrel, Truman Waters barked, "Well, hell, that's not a very happy story."

"Not all stories end happily," I said.

My dour tale had the effect I'd hoped, putting a dark cloud over the celebration on the *Sweet Sue.* Gertie stood and said, "We should all get to bed. Dawn comes early and hungry folks along with it."

We trooped back to Gertie's place, and Albert and Mose and Emmy and I settled ourselves in the shed for the night. Albert lit a candle and we sat on our bunks.

"Okay, imp," Albert said, "tell us everything about one-eyed Jack."

I recounted our chance meeting in the post office and my talk with Jack in the park.

Mose signed, *A bullet in his heart and he's still alive?*

"He was dead," Albert said. "I could have sworn it."

"Only looked dead. The bullet missed his heart by half an inch."

"He didn't hate us, Odie?" Emmy asked.

"In fact, he was thankful, swore we'd changed his life. But here's the thing. If Jack, who wasn't even looking for us, found us, the Black Witch and her toady husband can find us here, too. We need to get back on the river and on our way to Saint Louis and Aunt Julia."

In the flicker of the candlelight, I tried to read the faces of the others. I thought that once upon a time — not that long ago — I could have told you everything about each of them just from what I saw in their faces. But they seemed strangers to me now, their thoughts a mystery.

"Well?" I said.

"I'm staying," Albert said. "I'm going to work for Tru."

Mose nodded and signed, *I'm staying.*

Emmy said gently, as if she were afraid of hurting me, "I want to stay, too, Odie. I like

Flo and Gertie."

"Jack found me," I said. "In a city of a million people, Jack found me, and he wasn't even looking. The Brickmans are looking for us, looking hard."

Albert said, "Next week, Mose and I will be going down the Mississippi on the *Hellor.* Maybe you and Emmy can come along. That should keep us safe for a while."

"For a while. But the Black Witch will never give up. You know that."

"I don't know that. And neither do you. The Brickmans will forget about us eventually."

"Not the Black Witch. She never forgets."

"Okay," Albert said. "You insisted this was a democracy. All those in favor of staying, raise your hands."

I knew the outcome even before the others cast their votes, and when Albert snuffed out the candle, I lay fuming, unable to sleep.

I got up and left the shed and aimlessly walked the streets of the Flats, the houses dark on every side, the storefronts empty, the night air unmoving, hot and heavy. My shirt clung to the sweat on my back, which might have been from the humidity or the effort of the walk or the way everything inside me was twisted and uncertain. Something terrible was on the horizon, I could see that. Why couldn't the others?

Then it hit me. The horrible truth I'd been

unwilling to face. DiMarco's murder. The shooting of Jack. Albert's snakebite. The relentless pursuit by the Brickmans. This was all my doing, all my fault. This was my curse. I saw now that long before the Tornado God descended and killed Cora Frost and decimated Emmy's world, that vengeful spirit had attached itself to me and had followed me everywhere. My mother had died. My father had been murdered. I was to blame for all the misery in my life and the lives of everyone I'd ever cared about. Only me. I saw with painful clarity that if I stayed with my brother and Mose and Emmy, I would end up destroying them, too. The realization devastated me, and I stood breathless and alone and terribly afraid.

I fell to my knees and tried to pray to the merciful God Sister Eve had urged me to embrace, prayed desperately for release from this curse, prayed for guidance. But all I felt was my own isolation and an overwhelming sense of helplessness. Gradually, however, as I knelt on the West Side Flats under the glaring moon, a dark and cold understanding settled over me. When I finally brought myself up from the dirt of that unpaved street, I knew exactly what I had to do.

CHAPTER FIFTY-SEVEN

"Hey, Buck Jones!" John Kelly jogged toward me in the dark. "Gonna help me deliver papers?" He clapped me on the back in greeting, then saw my face. "You okay?"

"I'm leaving," I said.

"Going where?"

"Saint Louis."

"What about the others?"

I thought about my brother and Mose and Emmy. They believed they'd found their home. They were happy. If they came with me, I knew I would somehow destroy that happiness.

"I'm going alone."

"How're you gonna get there?"

I considered the canoe stored at the boatworks. It was a familiar vessel, a friend in a way, but I was pretty sure I couldn't handle it alone on a river as big and as unknown to me as the Mississippi.

"You said trains go to Saint Louis from the rail yard."

"Sure," John Kelly said, warming to the idea. "You can hop a freight."

"Do you know which one?"

"Naw, but I bet if we ask around the yard, someone'll be able to point us right."

"We? You're not coming."

"No, but I ain't gonna desert you till I know you're off safe. We're pals."

"Thanks," I said, truly grateful. "I've got to grab something from Gertie's, okay?"

I slipped into the shed and went to the bunk on which Emmy slept, slid my hand under the thin mattress, where for safekeeping, I'd put both my harmonica and the envelope containing the letter I'd written to Maybeth. I put these precious items into my pants pocket. I stood above Emmy, who'd had always been as cute as a fairy princess. In our long odyssey, she'd become far more than the orphaned daughter of Cora Frost. She'd become my sister. My sweet, little sister. I was tempted to lean down and plant a kiss on her forehead but was afraid of waking her. I turned and stared where Mose shared a bunk with Albert. His face was peaceful in the way that reminded me of the old Mose, the big Indian kid with a ready grin and a huge, simple heart. All that he'd learned about himself and all that he'd come to understand about the world he was born into had made his grin less frequent, but it was still there sometimes, and his heart would always be huge, I was certain, though never again quite so simple.

And then I considered my brother. There had been only one constant in my whole life, and that was Albert. He was at the beginning of all my memories, beside me on every road I'd traveled, had saved me from a thousand perils, knew my heart better than any other human being. Sister Eve had told me that what my brother wanted, his deepest wish, was to keep me safe. That had been his life, a long sacrifice for me. And I loved him for it. I loved him with every atom of my being, with a love so fierce it threatened my resolve. I wanted to lay my head on his shoulder, as I'd done a million times, and have him put his arm around me and tell me everything was all right and I was safe and we would always stay together, because that's what brothers did. Leaving Albert was the hardest thing I'd ever done. I kissed my fingertips and touched them lightly to his chest over his heart, wiped away my tears, and stepped outside, where John Kelly was waiting.

"South," one of the men gathered around the small fire in the rail yard told us. "Any train goin' that way will head you toward Saint Louie." He pointed to where the rails and the river tunneled side by side into the night. "Make sure if the train turns east or west you hop off and catch another 'un. Stay south, son. Just stay south."

We stood together, John Kelly and me, waiting for a train to rumble through, and it wasn't long before one came slowly over the bridge from the direction of the Flats, heading the way the guy at the fire had pointed. John Kelly shook my hand, a man-to-man kind of parting.

"Good luck to you, Buck Jones," he said.

"Thanks, John Kelly. But promise me something. My brother and the others, they're going to ask you about me. I'd appreciate it if you kept your mouth shut."

"You got it, partner. This is just between us." He looked past me. "Open car coming. Better get ready."

As the boxcar rolled past, I swung myself up through the open door, and when I was settled, poked my head out and signaled John Kelly that I was all right. He was a small silver statue in the moonlight, his hand lifted in a frozen goodbye.

I leaned back against the wall and stared through the broad, open door toward the Flats across the river, where all was dark. There were no streetlights yet, but there would be one day, and one day the roads would all be paved, and better houses with indoor plumbing would replace the ramshackle structures. The devastating spring floods would remain a constant, however, and in thirty years, the city of Saint Paul would decide, in the best interests of all its citizenry, to raze every building, while those whose lives had been shaped by the Flats could do nothing but stand by and weep as almost every remnant of their history vanished.

But I knew none of this in the summer of 1932, just shy of my thirteenth birthday, watching everything I loved move steadily away from me into the past. The train rolled slowly out of Saint Paul, gradually picking up speed, and as the engine thundered into the night, I knew that, more swiftly than was possible with any canoe, it was taking me to the place Sister Eve had told me was always in my heart, where all my questions would be answered and all my wandering would cease.

It was taking me home.

■ ■ ■ ■

- PART SIX -
ITHACA

■ ■ ■ ■

CHAPTER FIFTY-EIGHT

Sleep was impossible. I sat in the boxcar all night, staring at Old Man River, who was a constant companion. Towns came and went, but the river was always there, and the moon, too, a white, unblinking, all-seeing eye. I remembered Mose's assurance to Emmy: *Not alone.* And I told myself this again and again and was grateful for the company of the river and the moon.

Near dawn, I finally fell asleep on the boxcar floor. I must have slept hard, because when I awoke, the train had stopped moving. I sat up, aching from the unforgiving wood that had been my mattress, and peered out the open door. We were in a rail yard not un-like the one I'd left the night before, though this one had tall grain elevators, like castle towers, rising beside it. Far up the line of cars, a man walked briskly along, looking under every freight car and peering into those with open doors. A bull, I figured, thinking of the stories I'd heard of the beatings at the hands of the cruel railroad police who patrolled the yards. I eased myself down from the boxcar and hightailed it.

The rail yard and much of the town lay below a high bluff. I found a small diner on a dingy street near the tracks, where the smell of frying bacon reached out, set a hook in my hunger, and reeled me in. In her dream state, Emmy had told me that I'd know when the time was right to use the money in my boot, and I was hungry — and lonely — and decided it was time. I took a stool at the counter. The woman back of it was thin, blond, tired-looking, but with a nice smile when she saw me sit down. She reached out and plucked a couple of bits of straw off my shirt.

"Where'd you sleep last night, hon? In a haystack?"

"Something like that."

"Hungry?"

"You bet."

"What'll it be?"

"Eggs and bacon," I said. "And toast."

"How do you want those eggs?"

"Scrambled, please."

"Please," she said, still smiling. "Wish all my customers were that polite."

"Where am I?" I asked.

A man who sat a few stools away said, "Dubuque, Iowa, son." He winked at the woman behind the counter. "No haystack,

Rowena. This boy slept in a boxcar or my name ain't Otis."

"That right, hon?" Rowena said. "Are you riding the rails?"

I didn't know how they might feel about that, so I didn't answer.

"Where are your folks?" Rowena asked.

"Dead."

"Aw, sweetie, that's a shame."

"How long since you ate, son?" the man asked.

"Last night. I ate pretty good."

"Right," the man said, as if he thought I was lying but understood. "His breakfast is on me, Row."

"I couldn't," I said.

"Look, son, I got a boy your age at home. If he was out there on his own, I'd want somebody to give him a hand."

"Thank you, sir."

"Sir," he said with a smile. "Somebody raised you right."

I left the diner full, not just from the food but also from the kindness of those strangers. I couldn't help wishing Albert had been with me to share the experience, something we could talk about warmly over a fire at night. I missed him terribly, and besides that, good things are made even better when you share the story of how they came to be. But whenever I thought about Albert — or Mose or Emmy — a cloud came over my happiness because I wasn't certain if I would ever see them again.

I caught a freight train south and, because I'd hardly slept the night before, quickly nodded off and didn't waken until late afternoon. When I looked out the boxcar, I saw that the train was rushing through cornfields, heading straight toward the sun, which was low on the horizon and red in the sky. We were going west. How long I'd been traveling in the wrong direction, I didn't know. I kicked myself and swore out loud and prayed that the train would stop soon. But it didn't. It rumbled on past sunset and then moonrise and finally slowed as the lights of a city appeared on the horizon.

The train rolled to a halt amid a large network of rails and idled freight cars, and as soon as I was able, I leapt to the ground. I tried to get my bearings, to see if there were any cars coupled to engines pointed in the direction I'd just come from, but it was a maze of tracks and it was night and I was lost.

A hundred yards away, at the edge of the yard, I spotted the glow of a small fire. I thought of the welcoming fires in Hopersville and of the man beside the fire in the Saint Paul rail yard who'd pointed me in the right direction and had advised me in a friendly way just to stay south. I crossed the yard to a shallow gully where a small thread of water ran and followed it to a culvert where the fire had been laid.

There were two of them, shabby-looking men, one asleep on a blanket and the other sitting up, bent toward the flames, a bottle in his hand. That bottle should have made me think twice. I approached slowly, not wanting to startle anyone, but the man with the bottle turned suddenly in my direction and tensed as if for a fight.

"Sorry," I said. "I didn't mean to scare you."

He eyed me up and down, then relaxed. "Take more'n a snot-nosed kid to scare me."

The moment I heard the animal growl of his voice, devoid of any humanity, I understood that I'd made a terrible mistake.

The man on the blanket roused himself and sat up.

"Company, George," the man with the bottle said.

George eyed me, too, and it was clear from his squint that he'd been sharing whatever was in the bottle. "Only a kid, Manny."

"Yeah," Manny said as if that was good thing. "Have a seat, kid."

"I was just passing through." I took a step back.

"I said have a seat."

George stood and began circling around to my back.

I took another step away.

George wasn't as drunk as I'd hoped. He moved coyote quick and clamped my arm in an iron grip. I tried to pull free, but he was stronger than he looked and pinned my arms behind me. I kicked back at him with a booted foot and connected with his shin, but he didn't let go. It only made him mad, and he shook me like a rag doll and snarled, "Do that again, kid, and I'll break your neck."

Manny rose and went through my pockets. "What's this?" He pulled out my harmonica and the envelope containing the letter I'd written to Maybeth Schofield. He blew one sour note on the harmonica and laughed cruelly. He threw the envelope onto the fire, and I watched it turn brown and burst into flames. He leaned close to my face, and his breath, fouled by whiskey and the long absence of any oral hygiene, hit me.

"Got any money, kid?"

I thought about the two five-dollar bills hidden in my right boot, but I was damned if I was going to give it to them.

"Unh-uh," I said.

The man patted me down roughly all over. "He ain't lyin', George. He's got nuthin for us."

"Not nuthin," George said and gave a grunt like a pig.

"Right," Manny said.

I saw in the face of the man before me the

same repellent hunger I'd seen in Vincent Di-Marco that terrible final night at the quarry when he told me about Billy Red Sleeve. I tried to break loose of George's grip, but his hands were iron manacles. I kicked out at Manny, but he danced back, and George released the grip of one of his hands and gave my head a blow that made my ears ring.

"Over by the fire," Manny said.

George dragged me there and shoved me to the ground, and both men stood over me, ugly as jackals. Whenever I'd thought about Billy Red Sleeve, I'd tried not to let my imagination wander into the horrible specifics of what might have been done to him before DiMarco put an end to his suffering, but in those few seconds with the two leering men above me, images came to me so brutal I felt my stomach fold in on itself in a way that threatened to make me puke. And maybe that would have been a good strategy. But I did something else instead.

"I have money," I said quickly.

"The hell you do," Manny said.

"I swear. Ten dollars."

"Where?" George demanded.

I reached to my right boot and unlaced it. The men watched me closely. I slid the boot off, reached inside, and drew out the five-dollar bills. The men's eyes went bright with a different kind of hunger, and Manny grabbed for the cash, but I jerked my hand out of his reach and held the bills over the fire.

"I'll burn them," I threatened.

"The hell you will," George said.

"Give me back my harmonica, and I'll give you the money."

"Do like he says, Manny."

As soon as I had the harmonica in hand, I threw the bills on the fire, where they fluttered like dry leaves onto the eager flames. The two men stumbled over themselves trying to save the burning cash, and in that confusion, I sprang up and sprinted away from the culvert, carrying the boot and my harmonica. I ran for the maze of tracks and the idled cars and, when I finally risked a glance over my shoulder, saw that I was alone. But still I ran, until I came to an open car and swung myself up and inside and lay panting.

It took a while for the full effect of the encounter to hit me. Then I began to cry, trying to keep my sobs quiet. I'd thought I was alone before, but now I understood how truly abandoned I was. An emptiness opened inside me that could have swallowed the whole universe.

"Albert," I whispered. "Albert."

CHAPTER FIFTY-NINE

I pulled into Saint Louis two days later. The city had been my goal for so long I'd anticipated feeling something momentous when I arrived. Instead, I stood in yet another alien place, amid a spiderweb of tracks spun in the shadows of a jagged line of tall buildings, all of it laid out under a sky as gray as an old nickel.

I had no idea where to go, how to begin my search for Aunt Julia. I hadn't been in Saint Louis since we'd visited following my mother's death, which was half my lifetime ago. What was familiar to me by now was the Mississippi, so I made my way to the river. I found a city of shacks, a Hooverville beyond my imagination with a populace a hundred times greater than I'd seen in Hopersville. Shanties covered the flats for a full mile downriver, hovels built between hillocks of debris, all of it looking so tenuous I thought that if the gray sky cracked open and rain poured out, everything before me would simply wash into the river and be swept away.

I walked along makeshift pathways, amid an overpowering smell and sense of decay. In my imagining across the whole of my journey, Saint Louis had been a distant, golden promise. All that way, I thought with sinking hope, and everything I'd gone through, and for what?

"Hey, kid!"

I looked up. The darkness of my thoughts must have shown on my face, because a man with a beard like Spanish moss on his cheeks eyed me from beneath the brim of a worn fedora the same dismal color as the sky.

"On the bum, kid? Hungry?" He pointed downriver. "Free kitchen under the bridge. The Welcome Inn."

"Thanks."

"You get used to it," he said.

"What?"

"If you don't know now, you soon will." He stepped inside a shack no bigger than a piano crate and covered in tar paper.

I found the Welcome Inn, with a long line of forlorn people looking for whatever might be handed out to them, women and kids among them. Although I was plenty hungry, I couldn't bring myself to join that queue yet, and I wandered down to the edge of the river.

The surface of the water was oily and iridescent, and a foul, unnatural odor came off it. On the far side, industrial chimneys sent up columns of smoke that fed the dirty gray of the sky, and God only knew what those enterprises were pouring into the Mississippi. Up in Saint Paul, the water had been abysmal, and it had flowed past a hundred other towns and cities since then. With that beggared gathering of humanity at my back and the Mississippi looking so sick in front of me, it seemed that the place I'd come to was its own kind of hell.

"I should have gone with Maybeth," I said aloud. At the sound of her name my heart nearly broke. But I brightened as I recalled our promise to each other to write as soon as we could. The letter I'd written hadn't been mailed; maybe Maybeth's luck had been better.

I asked three people in that Hooverville before anyone was able to direct me, and a short while later I found myself in the downtown post office, which was not nearly so grand as the one in Saint Paul but just as busy. I waited in line, and when I got to the window, asked about general delivery.

The clerk eyed me over the lenses that sat on the end of his nose. "What's the name?"

Ever since running from Lincoln School, I'd been careful not to give my real name, in case word of my infamous deeds spread.

"Well, son?"

But this was for Maybeth, so I said,

"O'Banion. Odysseus O'Banion."

"Odysseus? Let me check."

He was gone for a bit, came back, and shook his head. "Nothing, son."

"How about Buck Jones?"

"Like the cowboy star?" He smiled. "You go by a couple of pretty famous monikers. Let me see."

I had no better luck with that name. I was just about to leave when another thought occurred to me. "I'm trying to find my aunt. She lives on a street with a Greek name and there's a fudge store on the corner."

The clerk looked up at the ceiling and thought, but I could tell I was ringing no bells. The man behind me in line, however, a fellow who, judging from his girth, hadn't been hit too hard by the Depression, spoke up, saying, "I know that one. Candy store, corner of Ithaca and Broadway, in Dutchtown, but it closed last year. Another victim of these hard times."

The clerk wrote directions on a slip of paper, and when I left the post office, I walked with renewed energy in my step. I had a destination again. I was almost home.

The white lettering on the glass read EMERSON'S FUDGE HOUSE. There was nothing behind the big window but empty shelves and an empty counter. I walked up Ithaca half a block, and there it was. Straight out of my memory. A three-story brick home set behind a tall, wrought-iron fence, and painted pink, just as I remembered. But it was much smaller than I recalled, and long overdue for a fresh coat of paint. The lot next to the house was vacant, a sea of weeds, and the weeds had begun to creep through the fence and infest the grass of the lawn, which needed cutting. The shades on all the windows were drawn, and the feeling the whole picture gave me was not welcoming. I opened the gate, and the hinges cried out for oil. I went slowly up the walk and mounted the stairs and knocked at the front door. It was eventually opened by a slender Negro woman in a silky red dressing gown. She was pretty but looked desperately in need of sleep and more than a little unhappy to see a kid standing on her doorstep.

"What?" she said even before I could speak.

"I'm looking for someone," I said.

She put a fist on her hip in a challenging way. "Yeah? Who?"

"My aunt Julia."

Her eyebrows, which were penciled on, rose and the tired look vanished. "Julia?"

"Yes, ma'am. My aunt. She used to live here."

She eyed me up and down and gave her head the faintest of shakes, as if having trouble believing I was real. "You wait right here, sweetheart."

I couldn't tell if her sudden sugary tone was sincere or if she was mocking me. She closed the door, and I stood on the small stoop and studied the sky, which was no longer gray, but had taken on a sickly green cast, the kind I recalled only too well from the day the Tornado God had torn through Fremont County and killed Emmy's mother. Around every corner of my journey, the Tornado God had seemed to be waiting, and I was afraid that its ultimate purpose all along had been to deny me a happy ending.

The door opened again, and I didn't recognize the woman who stood there. But her eyes were blooms of wonder and her words were a hush as they escaped her rubied lips: "Oh, my God. It *is* you." She reached out, touched my cheek with her hand, and whispered in amazement, "Odysseus."

CHAPTER SIXTY

We sat in a room at the back of the house that reminded me of the cozy parlor in Cora Frost's farmhouse. There was a little fireplace with a mantel above it, on which stood an antique-looking clock. A filled bookshelf ran along one wall. Vases with colorful flowers were set about the room to brighten it. Aunt Julia had asked the woman in the silky red dressing gown to bring us sandwiches and lemonade. The sandwiches were ham and cheese and the lemonade had ice chips in it. I hadn't eaten at all that day and was tempted to gulp my food. But Aunt Julia was refined in her manners, and I didn't want to offend her, so I ate as carefully as she.

In my whole life, I'd laid eyes on her only once. Mostly, Aunt Julia had been a name that came from my mother's lips in the stories she'd told of her childhood. Even so, I'd imagined a reunion of great emotion, of warm hugs and lots of tears. It hadn't been like that. She'd invited me inside and had led me to this small room at the rear of the house, where we sat across the coffee table from each other, our talk awkward.

"How . . . how did you get here?"

"I rode the rails."

"Like a hobo?"

"Like practically everybody these days."

"Oh, my." She frowned, then smiled. "But safely. You made it safely. All the way from . . . ?"

"Minnesota."

"From the school there? The Indian school?"

"Yes, ma'am. That place."

She nibbled at her sandwich, then her eyebrows, which had been painted on just like the other woman's, bent toward each other. "But you can't have finished your education. You're only twelve."

"Almost thirteen."

"Still."

"I ran away."

She sat back a little and her spine stiffened. "Well, that doesn't sound good."

"They were mean to us there."

"School can be hard."

"They beat us."

"Oh, come now, Odysseus."

"A boy died. Billy Red Sleeve."

That gave her pause. As if in afterthought, she said, "Where's Albert?"

"He stayed in Minnesota."

"At the school?"

"He found a job in Saint Paul."

As soon as I'd entered the house, the green sky had split open, and now a heavy rain beat against the windows. I thought of all those people in Hooverville and imagined everything they had sliding into the river.

Aunt Julia turned her eyes toward the storm outside and seemed lost in what she saw. "Well," she said, looking at me again with a brightness clearly false. "What are your plans?"

I swallowed the bite of sandwich I'd been chewing, which wasn't easy because my throat had gone dry at what I was about to propose.

"I thought I could live with you."

"With me? Here? I'm afraid that won't be possible, Odysseus."

"I don't have anywhere else to go." This was true, but I confess that I did my best to make it sound as pathetic as I could.

"Of course you don't," she said with real sympathy and in a way that sounded as if she were chastising herself for her insensitivity. "Well, I suppose then. Just until we figure what to do with you."

"Thank you, Aunt Julia."

She studied me in silence for an uncomfortably long time and finally said, "Last I saw you, you were half as tall. That's how I've remembered you. You've grown. Almost a man."

Almost a man. She sounded proud when she said that, as if she'd had a hand in shaping me. And I understood that she thought she had. For all those years since our only meeting, she'd been sending money to the Brickmans to see to my well-being. She had no way of knowing that, until we'd stolen it, the money had done Albert and me no good.

She stood up, went to the door, and called, "Monique!"

The woman in the red silk dressing gown returned. Although they spoke in low voices, I heard Monique say, "With this weather, it's going to be slow tonight."

They spoke further, and Aunt Julia finally declared, "The attic room then."

The minute I stepped into the attic, I was dragged back in my memory to Jack's farmhouse and the space in his attic with the cut-to-shreds mattress. This place wasn't in that kind of disarray, but it still gave me the feeling of being shunted away from prying eyes, as if I were a fugitive. Which, I admit, I was, but I didn't appreciate being treated as such by my aunt.

"You'll be fine here," she said with the same false brightness she'd maintained since my arrival. "See, you have a window."

Which overlooked a neglected backyard, an

old stone patio directly below me, and an alleyway along the back of the property, all of it dreary in the downpour. There was also a narrow bed in the room, a chest of drawers, a standing lamp, and the smell of must.

"Who stays here?" I asked.

"No one for a long time." A note of sadness soured her bright tone. Then something dawned on her. "You have no bag, no suitcase?"

"I didn't have time to pack."

"We'll have to do something about that," she said. "Tomorrow, maybe. Today just rest. I imagine you're tired."

"I need to use the bathroom."

Right away, I could see that concerned her.

"There's one on each floor below you, but I'd rather you didn't use them. They're for . . ." She paused to consider her explanation. "They're for my other guests."

"Other guests? Is this a hotel?"

"Not exactly, Odysseus. I'll explain later. There's a toilet in the basement. Use the back stairs."

Swell, I thought. For me and the spiders.

"Just make yourself at home. Have you eaten enough?"

"Yes, ma'am, I'm fine."

"Please don't call me ma'am. It makes me feel old. Aunt Julia will do."

She descended the stairs, and I heard the attic door close, and I was alone again. The

611

room was stuffy, so I opened the window just a crack. Rain came in, puddled along the sill, and dripped onto the wood floor, but at least there was fresh air. I still had to pee, but instead of going all the way down to the basement, I opened the window further and relieved myself into the downpour outside. I lowered the window again but left an opening so that I had some air coming through, then sat on the bed, feeling no less alone than I had in the empty boxcars. But in those boxcars I'd had no mattress, and the one beneath me felt gloriously soft, and Aunt Julia had been right — I was tired. Very soon, I was asleep.

I woke to the sound of laughter, a woman's, high and shrill, coming from directly below me. The attic room was dim, nearly dark, but I could still hear the rain beating against the window. When I stood up from the bed, my feet touched water. I went quickly to the standing lamp, turned it on, and saw that the storm had driven a good deal of rain into the room.

I had nothing with which to dry the floor, so I went down the attic stairs and into the hallway. The laughter had ceased, but I heard the murmur of voices coming from behind a closed door. Before I could move, the door opened. A man stepped out, dressed in a nice suit but with his tie undone. After him came a woman, young and pretty and blond, wearing a pink chemise that just barely covered the tops of her thighs. Her hair was disheveled, her lipstick smeared. The man didn't notice me. He bent to the woman and planted a long, wet kiss on her lips.

"Next week, Mac?" she said.

"Maybe sooner if you're lucky."

"I'm feeling lucky." She gave his butt a playful slap.

The man headed down the hallway to the main staircase without looking back. When he was gone, the woman's posture changed, melted, and she slumped against the doorjamb. She ran a hand over her left side and made a face as if she'd touched a tender place, then she saw me. Her posture didn't change, but a quizzical look came to her face.

"You're him. Julia's boy."

"Her nephew," I said.

"Right, right," she said. "You need something?"

"Rain came in my window. I need a towel."

"Let's see what we can do for you, hon."

She went to a small closet in the hallway, reached in, and pulled out a fluffy, white towel. "Do the trick?"

"Yes, thank you."

"Polite. I like that. What's your name again?"

"Odysseus."

She held out a hand. Her nails were painted

a deep, enticing red. "Dolores. Pleased to meet you."

She was still holding my hand when Aunt Julia appeared, coming from the stairway where the man had just descended. When she saw me with Dolores, her face darkened and her step quickened.

"I told you to stay upstairs, Odysseus."

"He just needed a towel," Dolores said.

"Rain came in my window," I explained.

"Well, close the damn window. And, Dolores, you need to get yourself put back together."

"Sure thing, Julia." She winked at me and vanished into her room.

"Upstairs," Aunt Julia said and followed me.

In the lamplight, she stood assessing the puddle that spread across the floor from below the opened window.

"It was stuffy," I said. "I just wanted some air."

"Give me the towel." When I handed it over, she knelt and began to mop up the rain.

"I can do that."

"It's not your fault, Odysseus. I should have thought." She sat back on her knees and said, "I'm sorry I was short with you. I just wanted the right time to explain everything."

"That's okay."

She stared at the soggy towel in her hands. "There's so much you don't understand."

"I'm okay."

"Tomorrow," she said and returned to her mopping. "Tomorrow we'll talk."

She left me alone again, insisting gently but firmly, "You'll stay in your room the rest of the night."

She didn't lock the door, but I couldn't help feeling that, except for the fact I had a mattress instead of a layer of straw, the attic room wasn't so different from the quiet room at Lincoln School.

CHAPTER SIXTY-ONE

In the night, I had to pee. Once again, instead of going all the way to the basement to relieve myself among the spiders there, I opened the window and peed onto the old stone patio far below, then slept until morning. I got up late and now needed the kind of relief an open window couldn't provide. I headed down the back stairs, as Aunt Julia had instructed, hearing as I went the sounds of women in the kitchen.

The basement surprised me. It wasn't at all the nest of crawling insects I'd imagined but was tiled and brightly lit and housed an appliance I'd heard of but had never seen — an electric wringer/washing machine. At Lincoln School, washing the clothes and linen had been done by hand, all of it the work of the girl residents. The wet things had been hung outside on long lines to dry, even in the bitterest winter cold, a circumstance that, by the time the work was finished, often had the girls crying because their fingers were iced to a point near frostbite. In the basement, drying racks, empty at the moment, stood in three lines, enough to accommodate, I reckoned, all the sheets from all the beds in the house. No need to hang anything outside in the cold or, on a day like this one, to worry about rain delaying the work.

To my great relief, the toilet was clean and modern and even had a small shower stall. I took care of business. When I came out, Dolores was dropping laundry into the tub of the washing machine. She turned, and her face was plain, no makeup, but still pretty. In fact, even prettier.

"Good morning, sleepyhead," she said.

"Morning."

She took stock of the clothes I wore. "Have those ever been washed?"

"Not for a long time."

"I guessed from the smell. If you slept in those, I probably should wash your sheets, too."

"I didn't."

"Strip off your things and I'll throw them in with the rest."

"I don't have anything else to wear."

She smiled, as if she found my reply somehow quaint, and said, "Wait here, sweetie."

She came back downstairs a few minutes later with a pink terry-cloth robe. "You can wear this till everything is dry."

I stripped in the bathroom. Dolores was no

taller than I, and the robe, which I assumed was hers, fit me nicely. She took my clothes and tossed them into the washing machine tub, which was filled with hot water and soap and was already agitating.

"We'll let those wash for a while. Hungry?"

"Yes, ma'am."

"Ma'am? Hell, I'm not much older than you. Why don't you take a shower, then come up to the kitchen."

The kitchen, when I got there, was abuzz with activity. Several women, all young like Dolores, many still dressed in their nightwear, were busy making breakfast. I decided this was a women's residence of some kind. I'd heard of such places in cities. The young women treated me with a kind of sisterly jesting, which made me feel welcome, and then I sat with them at a big table in the dining room and we ate together. Some of the food was familiar — scrambled eggs, ham, toast with raspberry jam — but there were grits and also fried green tomatoes, which I'd never had before and fell immediately in love with.

"Is breakfast always like this?" I asked.

"We used to have a cook," one of the girls, a redhead named Veronica, said. "But we had to let her go."

"Same with our laundress and maid," Dolores said. "This damn economy." She looked to Monique. "All of ten customers last night,

618

right? Worse than a Sunday."

"The storm," Monique said.

Dolores looked out the window at the rain, which still fell heavily, casting a gloom over the morning. "Won't be any better tonight if this downpour continues."

Aunt Julia appeared and the talk quieted. It was clear to me that she held a unique position in this women's residence. She was obviously surprised to see me and her eyes shot questioningly around the table.

"He was up and we invited him," Dolores said.

"And the robe?"

"Mine," Dolores said. "His clothes are washing."

Aunt Julia glanced out the dining room window at the wet and the gloom. "I'd hoped to take you shopping today, Odysseus, but with this rain, I'm afraid that will have to wait. Ladies," she said, taking the only empty chair at the table, "today is a day for catching up on housekeeping."

I was put to work in the basement, helping Dolores with the washing, which was mostly bedding. Since the laundress, who had also been the housekeeper, was let go, the women rotated that particular responsibility, which, for reasons not then apparent to me, had to be done every day.

"You remind me of my brother," Dolores said as we hung sheets on the drying racks.

"Does he live around here?"

"Mayville. Little town outside Joplin. You're what? Thirteen, fourteen? That's what he'd be."

"When was the last time you saw him?"

"The day I left home. Five years ago. About your age."

"What do you do here? Do you have a job?"

She held up in her work and gave me an odd look. "Do you know what this house is, Odysseus?"

"A women's residence, I figure."

"Yeah," Dolores said. "A women's residence. Exactly."

The rain showed no signs of letting up, and in the afternoon, when the work had been done, Aunt Julia told me to go to the attic and she would be up shortly. Upstairs, I stood at the window and stared beyond it and thought about all those people down on the river flats. The paths they walked would be nothing but mud by now, and waiting in line for food at the Welcome Inn, they would be soaked to the bone. I knew I was lucky and felt guilty because although the attic was stuffy, there was a good roof over my head, and my stomach was full, and I had an aunt who cared about me.

I heard her mounting the stairs. She came carrying a silver tray on which sat two glasses of lemonade and a plate of gingersnaps. She set the tray on the bed and patted the mattress. "Come, sit," she said.

"Is this your house?" I asked after I'd sipped a bit of the lemonade and had taken a bite of a cookie.

"Yes."

"You must be rich."

"It cost me more than you can imagine, Odysseus."

"I was only here once," I said.

"Still, you found your way. The last time I saw you was just after Rosalee died." She was talking about my mother. "When Zeke came to tell me the news." That was my father. Ezekiel O'Banion. "Do you recall?"

"Not much. I remember that you gave me and Albert a few pennies to buy fudge."

She smiled and said, as if I'd brought back a good memory for her, "That's right."

"What was she like? My mother?"

"You don't remember?"

"Not really."

"Rosalee was a wonderful big sister, and she was a fine mother to you."

"But what was she like?"

"For someone who couldn't hear, she was awfully talky. I remember when Mom and Dad sent her off to Gallaudet, oh, did I cry my eyes out. When she came back to visit at Christmas, seeing her was the best present I could have asked for."

"Gallaudet? What's that?"

"A school for deaf people. But she didn't

621

stay there long. Dad died the next year and Mom took a job teaching school, which paid nothing. Rosalee came home to help make ends meet. I'd always had a flair for fashion and made my own clothes, so I went to work in a dress shop in town, saving whatever I could. Then Mom died. Zeke had been in love with Rosalee since they were kids, and marrying him seemed like the best thing for her. Me, I wanted to get out of that suffocating little Ozark town in the worst way. So I left and ended up —" She looked around her and held out her hands, indicating the stuffy room and the house it was in. "Ended up here."

"You bought this place?"

"The man who owned it before I did was put away in prison."

"What for?"

"He killed a man. Before he went, he deeded me the property."

"You were married?"

"Just . . . good friends. But that didn't answer your question about your mother. Rosalee was smart and read everything and was kind, and all I ever wanted when I was a kid was to be just like her."

"Why . . . ?"

"Why what?"

"After my father died, why didn't you bring Albert and me back here to live with you?"

"It was a long time before I learned about

your father's death. I was told that you were both being well cared for in a school in Minnesota. I sent money to help with things there, and, well, that was really the best I could do under the circumstances."

"I would have been happy living here in this room. Albert would have been happy, too."

"I thought it was better that you were with other children."

"That place was hell," I said.

"Oh, come now, Odysseus. It couldn't have been that bad."

"There was a room that used to be a prison cell, and they put kids in it who didn't do exactly what they were supposed to do. They called it the quiet room." The words were bitter as they came from my lips. "It was cold in the winter and hot in the summer and there was a rat who lived there. That rat was the best thing about the room. Before they put you in there, they usually beat you with a strap. A man named DiMarco gave the beatings, and he loved it."

"You were put in there?" she asked.

"I practically lived there."

"They really beat you?"

I saw that tears rimmed her eyes, and I softened my tone. "All I'm saying is that I wish I could have been here with you."

She cried and hugged me, and even though everything I'd said was God's truth, I felt terrible for having told her.

"I'll make it up to you, Odysseus. I swear I will."

"Just let me stay."

She wiped her eyes. A smile appeared, like the first ray of sunshine that day, and she said, "Of course, you can stay. Everything's going to be better from now on, I promise."

Not only did the rain not let up, it fell more heavily, fell as it must have in the days of Noah. I sat at the window with its dreary view, and because I had nothing else to do, pulled out my harmonica and began to amuse myself with riffs on some of my old favorites. Before I knew it, several of the girls had crowded into the attic room and were making requests. Finally Dolores asked, "Do you know 'Shenandoah'?"

When I played it, I saw the sad look in her eyes, and I thought about Cora Frost and Emmy and what that song had meant to them, and for some reason, it made me like Dolores best of all the girls. That, and the fact she reminded me a little of Maybeth Schofield.

Aunt Julia joined us, and after she'd listened to "My Wild Irish Rose," she smiled and said, "Your father used to play."

"His," I said, holding up my Hohner. "The only thing I have left from him."

"Girls," Aunt Julia said. "Odysseus and I

need some time alone together." When they'd cleared out, she sat beside me on the bed. "You haven't told me how you got here. I'd like to hear the story."

So I told her everything, laying on her shoulders every crime and every sin. She heard the truth about DiMarco, Emmy and the kidnapping, shooting Jack, Albert and the snakebite, Maybeth Schofield, the Tornado God, and why I left Saint Paul. When I'd finished, had completely unburdened myself, she did something so unexpected it left me speechless. She got down on her knees in front of me, took my hands in hers, and as if we'd changed places, sinner and confessor, begged, "Forgive me."

CHAPTER SIXTY-TWO

Late that night the rains finally passed and the next day, after breakfast, Aunt Julia called for a taxi and sent me shopping with Dolores.

"She's young and knows what you'll look good in" was her explanation. But when I was in the taxi, Dolores said, "Julia never goes out. It's like that house is a prison for her. She holes up in her room and all that comes out is the sound of her sewing machine."

"Sewing machine?"

"The rest of us buy our clothes, but Julia designs and makes everything she wears, always very chic. I'd love to have her skill."

I hadn't noticed this about Aunt Julia. I was twelve years old and had lived a long while in a rural area where high fashion was anything not made from a seed sack.

"Have you been staying with her long?" I asked.

"Staying with her?" She looked at me as if I'd spoken Arabic, then shook her head. "You've got so much peach fuzz on you yet,

Odysseus. My guess, it'll all be coming off real soon."

"Call me Odie."

"Then call me Dollie. And I've been instructed to buy you lots of new everything."

"I don't need shoes," I said. "My Red Wings are practically new."

"I know about Red Wings. They're expensive. Where'd you get the money?"

Because we were having a good time together, I told her how I'd come by that pair of wonderful boots in the dry goods store in Westerville, Minnesota, elaborating a few details, as storytellers do, and leaving out enough of the real circumstances so that she had no idea I was a kidnapper. Or a murderer. By the end, I had her laughing up a storm. And the taxi driver, too, who'd been listening in.

"You tell a good tale, Odie," she said. "Ever think about writing them down?"

"Someday, maybe."

She'd directed the driver to a department store in downtown Saint Louis called Stix, Baer & Fuller, which took up an entire city block. I'd never seen so many goods in one place, and oddly, the effect of it was to put a damper on my high spirits. The store wasn't crowded. I didn't know if this was because it was still early on a weekday, or if it was the economy everybody spoke of in curses. Dollie said her instructions were to see to it that

I had several of everything — pants, shirts, underwear, socks, shoes. I tried on a couple of things, then told Dollie I didn't want to do it anymore.

As if I'd spoken heresy, she said, "You don't want new clothes?"

The truth was, I didn't care. The pants and shirt and underwear and socks I had on were clean now and perfectly good, and I told her so. But there was another truth at work as well.

"Can I show you something, Dollie?" I said.

"Sure. What?"

"Not here. It's kind of a walk."

"I suppose I could use some exercise."

Several blocks later, we stood above the flats along the riverbank, looking down at where a thousand shacks had been thrown together and people waited in line for food in front of the Welcome Inn. Because of the heavy rains the day before, I'd been genuinely concerned about what might have happened to those people and their makeshift shelters. I didn't see a sign of anything having been washed into the river and swept away, but everyone in Hooverville was slogging along pathways deep with mud, and despite the bright sunshine that had come with the passing of the storms, they walked hunched, as if the deluge was still beating down on them.

"You think I don't know about this?" Dollie said, her voice tense, her words edged with anger.

"I just wanted you to understand why I couldn't let you buy all those new things for me. I don't think I could wear them without feeling guilty."

"You think I should feel bad about wearing this?"

Her dress was a blue print with white dots all over it and tan buttons and matching piping along the broad collar. I thought it was pretty and she was pretty in it.

"Do you have any idea what I have to do to be able to wear clothes like this?" Now her eyes flashed and everything in her face was drawn taut. She told me, in graphic detail and with words hurled like a drunken sailor, exactly what she did.

I stood stunned, thrown into a world I could never have imagined. But now I understood all the signs that should have told me where I'd landed when I arrived at the house on Ithaca.

"Aunt Julia, too?"

"Yes, your precious Aunt Julia, too. Wake up, Odie. It's a fucked-up world."

"I'll walk back," I said.

"Fine. I can only imagine what Julia will say. Thanks for nothing, kid."

She stormed away, and I was left alone, staring down at the only world that seemed familiar to me anymore, because the one I'd awakened to that morning felt alien and so wrong.

I wandered into Hooverville, muddied my boots among the hovels, and studied the people standing idly against doors that were constructed of cardboard or scavenged wood or often simply tattered blankets hung in an attempt to keep the weather out. I saw struggle on every face. And disappointment. And hopelessness.

And then I saw something that, in the midst of all the darkness of that moment, gave me hope — a handbill posted on a telephone pole, with a bold headline that read SWORD OF GIDEON HEALING CRUSADE.

The tents had been set up in a place called Riverside Park, which turned out to be a long walk from Hooverville. I heard piano music coming from the big tent and found Whisker there, tickling the keys. He seemed overjoyed to see me, a smile as broad as the Mississippi across his thin face.

"Buck Jones, as I live and breathe." He didn't just shake my hand. He wrapped his skinny arms around me in a warm hug. "Where's the rest of your crew?"

"We had to split up," I said.

"Sorry to hear that. Still got your harmonica?"

I showed him and then asked about Sister Eve.

"Last I saw her, she was headed to the cook tent. Sticking around, son?"

I told him I didn't know, then hurried to the cook tent but didn't find Sister Eve there either. Dimitri crushed my hand in his eager grip and nearly knocked my lungs out with a hearty slap to my back.

"Where's the big Indian?"

I didn't want to go into it with everyone I met, so I gave him the same nonexplanation I'd given Whisker. When I asked about Sister Eve, he directed me to her dressing tent, but she wasn't there either. I thought about how, in New Bremen, she'd told me that wherever she went, she sought out a quiet place a little removed from all the crusade activity so that she could listen to God.

On a rise overlooking the river stood a pavilion that, from a distance, appeared empty. I found Sister Eve sitting on a bench there, in full sunshine, her eyes closed. To me, a kid desperate for some kind of salvation, her face seemed to glow.

Because she appeared so deep in reverie, I said in a whisper, "Sister Eve."

She opened her eyes. As if she'd been expecting me all along, she said simply, "Odie."

We talked. I told her everything that had happened since we'd fled New Bremen and ended with my final discovery about Aunt Julia.

"You believe that's the whole truth of who she is, Odie?"

"She's . . ." But I couldn't haul up a word harsh enough for what I felt about Aunt Julia. "She's not what I imagined at all."

"What did you imagine? That she would be a saint and take you in?"

"Well . . . yes."

"And hasn't she taken you in?"

"She stuffed me away in the attic."

"Did you ever pray about making it safely to Saint Louis, Odie?"

"Sure, I guess."

"But what you've found here wasn't the answer to your prayer?"

"Home, Sister Eve. I prayed for home. Aunt Julia's house isn't home. It's not what I prayed for at all."

"I told you once that there's only one prayer I know absolutely will be answered. Do you remember?"

Because it had sounded simple and so soothing, I'd never forgotten it. "You said to pray for forgiveness."

"Do you think maybe Aunt Julia might be in need of forgiveness? And do you think you can find it in your heart to offer that? From what you tell me, under the circumstances, she's tried her best."

The view of the river from the pavilion was deceptive, the foul color of the water hidden under the reflection of the blue sky. I stared

632

at it, wanting to forgive, but my heart was stone.

"I can't live in that house," I said.

"You can rejoin the crusade, if you like. Whisker has certainly missed you and your harmonica."

Her words were the salvation I'd been seeking. I said yes, yes, and hugged her with such gratitude.

"I need to be sure about Emmy," she said, darkly serious. "She's special, Odie."

I believed I understood what she meant. Alone on the bum from Saint Paul, I'd thought a lot about Emmy, stringing oddities together. How she'd been waiting for us in her room at the Brickmans', already dressed as if she understood that she'd be leaving. How she'd known before the distraught man had threatened Sister Eve with his shotgun that "Beautiful Dreamer" would save the day. And how, long, long ago, she'd known the importance of those five-dollar bills in my boot. I believed I finally saw what Sister Eve had seen from the moment she first took Emmy's hand.

"You see the past," I said. "She sees the future."

Sister Eve gave a little nod but said, "Maybe even more special, Odie." She folded her hands and composed herself. "What I'm going to say may sound impossible. But I've seen impossible things before, so here goes.

Those fits she suffers? I think they may be her attempt at wrestling with what she sees when she looks into the future. I think she might be trying to alter what she sees there."

That knocked me over. "She changes the future?"

"Maybe just tweaks it a little. Like a good storyteller rewriting the last sentence."

I let that sink in and thought about Emmy's fits. She'd had one before Jack grabbed us, and when she'd come out of it, she'd said, "He's not dead, Odie." And when she'd come out of the fit before Albert's snakebite, she'd said, "He's okay." And after her fit on the island where we found the skeleton, she'd said, "They're all dead," and also, "I couldn't help them. I tried but I couldn't. It was already done." Was that because she'd seen the tragic history of Mose's people, but it was the past so she couldn't change it?

I stared at Sister Eve. "I was supposed to kill Jack? And Albert was supposed to die from that snakebite? But Emmy changed things just enough?"

"I've heard that time is fluid, Odie, like this river in front of us. I was given the gift of moving backward on it. Maybe someone with a different kind of gift can glide forward, ahead of the rest of us. And if that's possible, why isn't it possible that things can be changed, just a bit?"

"You held her hand after her fit in New

634

Bremen. What did you see?"

"It was like peering into a fog. I asked her, and she didn't seem to know what I was talking about. If what I'm thinking is true, it may be that she doesn't fully understand it herself. At least not yet. She's still so young, Odie, and I want to be sure she's safe."

"Flo and Gertie will take good care of Emmy," I assured her. "And Albert and Mose are there, too. They'd never let anything happen to her."

She seemed comforted. "Good," she said. "Good. So." She tilted her head and studied me. "What now?"

"I guess I need to go back and let Aunt Julia know I'm leaving."

"Would you like me to go with you?"

"Maybe a ride," I said. "It feels like I've been walking all day."

"I can handle that."

We strolled together to the tents, where we found Sid talking with Whisker at the piano. Sid gave me a sour look.

"Whisker told me you were back. Like a bad penny." He eyed Sister Eve. "Not sticking around, is he?"

"He'll be rejoining us, Sid, and that's that. I need the key to the DeSoto. I'm giving Buck a lift."

"Where to?"

She glanced at me for an answer.

"Ithaca Street," I said. "It's in Dutchtown."

"Five minutes from here," Sid said. "Know where that is, Evie?"

"I'm sure Buck can tell me."

Sid reached into his pocket and brought out the key, which he dropped into Sister Eve's open palm. He gave me one final look of concern. "Christ, you better not bring trouble with you this time."

"Hope, Sid," Sister Eve said gently. "That's what people bring when they come to us."

We located Aunt Julia's house easily. "I'm not surprised you were able to find it," Sister Eve said, smiling at the pink exterior. "Would you like me to come in?"

"I can do this, but it might take a while. I'll join you at the crusade when I've settled things here, okay?"

She looked at me for a long moment, her eyes soft but intense. "You believe you've been looking for home, Odie. This is where your belief has brought you. That doesn't mean it's the end of your journey."

"Wherever I go from here, I want it to be with you."

"All right, then." She kissed me softly on the cheek.

I walked to the door and rang the bell. Dollie opened it, still unhappy with me, I could see.

Her voice was ice. "Your aunt's waiting for you."

I followed her to the attic room, where I

636

found Aunt Julia sitting on the bed. Flanking her on either side was an array of photographs, most in frames. The room felt cool and fresh. Once the rain had stopped, I'd kept the window wide open, both for the breeze and for the convenience of relieving myself in the night without trudging down several flights of stairs.

"Thank you, Dolores," she said. "That will be all."

Dollie left, the air chill in her wake.

I stood before Aunt Julia, fully prepared for her to be angry with me. Angry for not accepting the gift of new clothing. Angry for storming off. Maybe most angry because I'd learned the truth of who she was from Dollie, and she'd had no real chance to prepare me.

The thing was this: I'd already forgiven her. I didn't care anymore about what she was, how she kept the roof over her head and saw to the needs of the girls who lived in the pink house. I'd killed a man. Two, I'd once thought. I'd lied more times than I could remember. I'd stolen, or as good as. I'd sinned a thousand times over. Whatever my aunt was, I was no better.

So, I was prepared to accept whatever harshness was about to befall me. But Aunt Julia surprised me. She took one of the photographs and held it up for me to see.

"Do you know who this is?" she asked quietly.

"A baby."

"What baby?"

I gave a shrug.

"You, Odysseus."

I couldn't recall ever seeing a photograph of myself. Albert and I came to Lincoln School with nothing, no photos or anything else that might be a guide to our past. She handed the photograph to me, but looking at it was like staring at a picture of an exotic animal. I felt that it had nothing to do with me.

She lifted another photograph from the bed. "And this?" It was of a very young child astride a rocking horse. "That's you at three. And here you are at four," she said, pointing to another. "And at five. This is the final one I have of you. You were six. It was taken the only time you visited me here. Until two days ago, the last time I ever saw you. I keep them in my room."

She took the baby picture from me and seemed entranced by the smile on that child's face — my face, although it didn't feel that way to me.

"My parents sent you those?"

"Rosalee. Almost every year."

"I don't see any of Albert."

She didn't seem to hear, she was so lost in the baby photo and whatever deep meaning it had for her. "I remember the day you were born. Remember it as if it were yesterday."

"You were there?"

"Oh, yes. It was here in this room. You were born on this bed."

Well, that was certainly news, such a huge revelation that I didn't know what to say.

"I named you Odysseus because Rosalee and I had grown up listening to our mother read Homer's epic story to us. You know your namesake, Odysseus?"

"A Greek hero. Cora Frost, a teacher at Lincoln School, told me about him."

"He was a great leader, and I knew that you would be, too, someday. But also I named you that because you were born on Ithaca Street. It seemed a sign."

This was too much. "My mother named me," I declared.

She gazed at me silently. A buzzing began in my head like a swarm of flies going round and round, looking for a way out.

In the end, I gazed right back at her, and a look of understanding must have dawned on my face, because she nodded and said in a whisper, "Yes."

Chapter Sixty-Three

"This was no place to raise a child," Aunt Julia explained.

No, not Aunt Julia. Mother. I tried the word in my head, but it sounded all wrong.

After her remarkable revelation, she couldn't be still. I took her place on the bed while she paced, glancing at me periodically to gauge my reaction as she talked. Which must have been hard, because I was stunned to silence and sat looking as senseless as a scarecrow.

"Rosalee had a child already. I knew how good she was with Albert. Much better than I could ever be with you, especially here. Oh, I suppose I could have left and tried to make a living for us some other way, but I had no skills, no training. This" — she lifted her hands to embrace the room, the house, the whole circumstance — "this is all I know. And, Odysseus, they were so good to you, and Albert was such a good brother."

"So . . . who?" I finally asked.

"Who?"

"My father."

That stopped her pacing. She stood a few moments with her face downcast, her body so still it might have been carved from granite. "I wish I could tell you." She brought her eyes to bear on me, gauging my reaction. "In a place like this, Odysseus, despite precautions, a baby sometimes happens." She opened her hands toward me like a beggar hoping for alms. "But that's the past. He's not important now. What's important is that you're here and I'm going to take care of you, if that's what you'd like."

"Why?"

"Why what?"

"When my father was killed . . ." But I stopped myself, because that was wrong. He wasn't my father. "When my uncle was killed," I corrected myself, but felt that, too, was all wrong, "why didn't you send for us then?"

"I've told you already. I didn't know for a long time what had happened. And when I found out, it seemed best to leave you where you were. I talked with people who know about such things, and they assured me Lincoln School was an excellent institution."

"I grew up a white kid among Indians."

"Was that so bad?"

"What was bad was how they treated us all."

"I didn't know any of that, Odysseus. I swear to you. I received a letter from the superintendent every year telling me how well you were doing."

"The Black Witch."

She'd resumed her pacing but paused once again. "What?"

"That's what we all called her, the superintendent, Mrs. Brickman. The Black Witch because she was so horrible to us."

She hung her head, and the nervous energy that had fueled her movements seemed finally to have been exhausted. "I'm sorry, Odysseus. I truly am. But you're here now. I can make things better."

"I'm not staying. I have friends in Saint Louis."

"Who?"

"It's called the Sword of Gideon Healing Crusade."

"What is it? A church?"

"Something like that."

Aunt Julia — I still couldn't think of her as Mother — came and gathered up the photographs and sat beside me on the bed. For a long time, she said nothing. Then: "Can you ever forgive me?"

There it was again, just as Sister Eve had said, all boiling down to forgiveness.

"Maybe," I said. "There's so much to think about. I just need some time. Then I might be ready to come back. You understand?"

"I do." She reached out and took my hand.

We are creatures of spirit, I have come to believe, and this spirit runs through us like electricity and can be passed one to another. That's what I felt coming from my mother's hand, the spirit of her deep longing. I was her son, her only son, and the photographs in her lap, the money she'd sent, her naïve willingness to believe the lies of the Black Witch, all told me that she'd never stopped loving me.

I didn't leave right away. I hadn't eaten since breakfast, and Aunt Julia asked Dollie to bring up sandwiches and lemonade. In that attic room where I'd come into this world, we prepared to share what I figured would be our last meal together, at least for a while. But after we'd taken only a few bites, Dollie returned.

"Some people are here to see you, Julia."

"Not now, Dolores."

"Oh yes, now."

It wasn't Dollie who'd spoken. The voice came from below, unseen, but I knew it well. Dollie stepped aside, and Thelma Brickman appeared on the attic stairs, and behind her came Clyde Brickman.

"Odie O'Banion," the Black Witch said, the words dripping from her lips like poisoned honey. "And Julia. It's so good to see you both again."

Dollie had been sent away and had closed the attic door behind her. The Brickmans and Aunt Julia and I, along with a profound sense of the looming Tornado God, filled that small room.

"You look so lost, Odie," the Black Witch said. "And, Julia, your face is one big question mark."

I was less afraid than surprised and angry. I spat out, "How did you find me?"

"I still know people from my time in Saint Louis years ago, Odie. When you vanished with Emmy and all the papers in our safe, I thought it possible this was where you might be headed, so I sent a telegram and hired a man to watch Julia's house."

Aunt Julia looked at me, understanding in her eyes. "The Black Witch?"

I nodded.

"Do you know, Odie, I've never minded that epithet," Thelma Brickman said. "Fear is a powerful tool."

"What are you doing here, Thelma?" Aunt Julia demanded.

"You know her?" I said.

"Julia and I go way back, Odie," the Black Witch answered for her. Then her voice changed, became full of that twang Albert had told me he'd sometimes heard from her when she'd been drinking, the voice of someone raised in the backwoods of the Ozarks. "I still recollect when I first came to you, Julia. Do you? Brought to you by that brute my pappy sold me to. Was you bought my freedom. And for a while, we was like sisters." Her voice changed again, became smooth and seductive. "You refined all the rough edges of a hillbilly girl, taught me about etiquette and books and the ways to please a man. You remember that, Julia?"

"What I remember, Thelma, is that you weaseled your way into my life, then tried to strike a deal with the local constabulary to steal my house."

"You were the one who encouraged me to have ambition." An animal look came over Thelma Brickman's face. "I rose up from nothing, from dirt and filth and the kind of people who sold their children. That's why I was a whore. You came up from something different, Julia. So, what's your excuse?"

Aunt Julia glanced at me but gave no reply.

"You have no idea the hell I went through after you kicked me out," the Black Witch went on. "I finally ended up working in a shithole of a brothel in Sioux Falls when a lonely man named Sparks asked me to marry him. He ran a school for Indian kids across the state line in Minnesota. A sweet opportunity I couldn't let pass."

"And is this Mr. Sparks?" Aunt Julia asked.

Clyde Brickman hadn't spoken a word, but I could tell he was nervous. His eyes jumped around the room and back toward the closed door, as if he was afraid any moment someone would come bursting through.

"Mr. Sparks suffered a fatal heart attack a year after we wed," Thelma Brickman said. "This is Clyde, my second husband. He ran a gambling operation in Sioux Falls and was one of my regulars. I needed a good right hand at the Indian school and Clyde . . . ?" She glanced at her husband. "Well, I could have done worse."

"Minnesota," Aunt Julia said in a way that sounded as if many things were falling into place for her. "Did you lure Zeke there, Thelma? Did you set him up in some insane plan to get back at us?"

Zeke. My father's name. "You knew my father?" I asked the Black Witch.

"Your father delivered the liquor to this house. Bootleg liquor even in the days before the Volstead Act. When things went south between Julia and me, he was the one who saw me out the door without even giving me a chance to pack a bag. I left with nothing but the clothes on my back." She'd spoken with venom in her words, but now she smiled, a thin line like a scar burned across her face with acid. "Clyde and I were expecting a delivery of liquor up in Lincoln, one of our side enterprises, and who shows up with his

646

two boys in tow? When he recognized me, I was afraid he was going to spill the beans about my past."

"So you shot him?" I wanted to strangle the Black Witch, and I tried to jump from the bed, but Aunt Julia restrained me.

"We'll never know who pulled that trigger, Odie." Then she turned her cruel smile to Aunt Julia. "One of Zeke's boys looked so much like you, Julia, it made my spirit sing. I insisted that we take Odie and his brother under our protective care at Lincoln School." She eyed me with cold glee. "Every pain you suffered there, every stroke of the leather strap was such a joy to me, because it was like a stab at your dear aunt's heart. Now," Thelma Brickman said, composing herself. "The reason I'm here. Where is Emmy?"

"Where you'll never find her," I shot back.

"I don't care about you anymore, Odie. I'm willing to let bygones be bygones. All I want is Emmy."

"Emmy hates you."

"In time, I'll make her love me."

"You can't make someone love you, Thelma," Aunt Julia said. "Love is a gift. It's given."

The Black Witch ignored her. "The police haven't stopped looking for Emmy's kidnappers, Odie. If they get their hands on you, you'll spend the next several years in a place much more difficult than Lincoln School, I can guarantee you. But I'm offering you a chance to save yourself. And your brother and Moses. All I want is little Emmy."

"You're not getting her."

"Then I have no choice but to turn you over to the police."

"Albert has the ledger," I said.

"You mean the ledger in which Clyde kept track of the donations our local citizenry made to Lincoln School? Sheriff Warford knows all about that ledger, Odie. He'll be happy to help us explain all this to the Saint Louis police. You can save yourself a lot of trouble. All I want is Emmy."

"She's lying, Odysseus," Aunt Julia said.

But I knew that already. She wouldn't be satisfied until she'd destroyed us all.

"Why do you want Emmy so bad? She hates you," I said. "And she's not perfect like you want her to be. Sometimes she has fits."

The Black Witch leaned toward me and spoke in a low voice, as if sharing a secret. "I know about those fits."

I stared into her eyes, two coals of evil, and wondered how she could possibly know.

She said, "In the hollow where I grew up, we had a neighbor who lived off by herself, a hag everybody swore was a seer. They said that when she looked into the future, if she had a mind to, she could tinker with what she saw there. Emmy had one of her fits while she was with me. When she came out of it, she said 'You won't fall, Odie. He will but not you.' I asked her about it later, but she didn't remember. After we found Vincent Di-Marco's body in the quarry, I put two and two together and came up with a most remarkable possibility. If I'm right about her, she's special, Odie. Am I right?" When I didn't answer, she smiled in a way that made my skin crawl. "All she needs is the proper person to guide her, to make certain her gift isn't squandered."

"You're not that person," I cried.

"Oh, but I am. I had her once, Odie. I'll have her again."

"She was never yours."

"Well then," she said, as if bringing the discussion to a definitive close, "I guess we'll just have to let the police sort that out."

"You're not going to the police," Aunt Julia said.

"Who's going to stop me? You?"

"Yes."

"How exactly do you propose to do that?"

"I'll kill you if I have to. Leave, Odysseus," Aunt Julia said. "You know where to go."

"I'm not leaving you," I said. Then added, "Mother."

She gazed at me, and in her eyes I found what it was I'd been searching for all along, searching for without understanding. Bone of my bone, flesh of my flesh, blood of my blood, heart of my heart.

"Mother?" Thelma Brickman said, then grinned like a rattler. "Well, no wonder you two look so much alike." She drew a small, silver-plated handgun from her purse. "I'm taking your son, Julia."

Clyde Brickman, who'd stood the whole time in cowardly silence, said, "For Christ's sake, what do you think you're doing, Thelma?"

"Shut up, Clyde. If you were half the man I'd hoped, I wouldn't have to do this. Odie, if you don't come with me, I'll shoot Julia, mother or no."

"And go to the electric chair," I said.

"For defending myself against a woman who brutally attacked me? I don't think so."

"She didn't attack you."

"That's not what Clyde will say. And you kidnapped a little girl, Odie. God only knows what despicable things you've done to her. Do you think anyone would believe a story told by a depraved boy whose mother was a whore?"

That's when I went for her.

I don't recall hearing the report from the gun, but I still remember the sting of the bullet in my right thigh and tumbling to the floor before I reached the Black Witch. In the chaos of that small room and the confusion of my mind as it processed the stunning realization that I'd been shot, I felt the air around me swirl as if a great storm were passing, and I was sure the Tornado God had descended.

But it wasn't the Tornado God. It was my mother. She rushed past me and threw herself at the Black Witch. They struggled, reeling across the room. Then they were at the open window, writhing as one fiercely grappled with the other. And in the next instant, they were gone.

I tried to rise, but my wounded leg would bear no weight. Clyde Brickman ran to the window and stood looking dumbly down. I crawled across the floor, leaving a trail of blood, and grabbed the windowsill to pull myself up. Brickman, whose heart had never been as black as his wife's, lifted me so that I could see what he saw. Together on the stone of the old patio three stories below, the two women lay unmoving, their bodies as entangled as their lives had been.

CHAPTER SIXTY-FOUR

They let me sit beside my mother's hospital bed, my wounded leg bound thick with gauze. She hadn't returned to consciousness. The doctors weren't sure she ever would. Dollie was there with me, keeping vigil. The hospital wards were crowded, but because Aunt Julia had money and some influence, we were in a private room.

The Black Witch was well and truly dead, her head smashed like an egg against the patio stone. A fortunate circumstance had saved my mother from the same fate. She'd landed atop Thelma Brickman. In her departure from this world, the Black Witch had done something almost redeeming. She'd cushioned the impact of my mother's fall. The doctor had called it a small miracle.

I'd been at her bedside for hours when Albert entered the room. Mose and Emmy and Sister Eve were with him. When I saw them, I broke into tears.

"How . . . ?" I tried to ask.

Albert knelt and put a comforting arm around my shoulder. "We finally got John Kelly to spill the beans and came downriver on the *Hellor* as fast as Tru could make her go."

From the doorway, I heard, "Lucky the river was high and clear." Truman Waters poked his head in, and I saw that Cal was with him.

I looked at Sister Eve with some bewilderment. "You found them?"

"They found me. The same way you did. All those posters Sid insists we put up everywhere we go."

"She took us to Aunt Julia's house," Albert explained. "The women there directed us here." He looked at Aunt Julia, who lay so still it was as if she were already dead. "I was afraid we might be too late."

"I have so much to tell you," I said.

A nurse pushed through the gathering and demanded that everyone leave.

Emmy put her hand on mine and said, "But he's our brother."

In the end, the nurse shooed Cal and Tru away but allowed the rest to stay.

I shared everything with them. When I told them the truth about my lineage, I watched Albert's face closely and didn't see at all the surprise I'd imagined. "You knew we weren't really brothers?"

"I've thought about it from time to time.

You just showed up one day. I was only four years old, so what did I know? But now I understand why you drive me crazy sometimes."

I didn't laugh.

"Listen, Odie, you're the biggest part of every memory I have. You *are* my brother. The hell with everything else. I love you so much it's nearly killed me sometimes. Until the day I die you will be my brother."

Mose stepped in and signed, *And mine.*

Emmy smiled and said, "And mine. We will always be the four Vagabonds."

The others took turns sitting with me while I kept vigil at Mother's bedside. Once, when it was just Albert and me, I shared with him what Sister Eve and I had discussed about Emmy and her fits.

He looked at me as if I were insane. "You're saying she kept your bullet from killing Jack? And the snakebite from killing me?"

"Think about it. It required such a small shift of circumstances. A fraction of an inch for the bullet to miss Jack's heart. A little extra time for you so the antivenom could arrive."

He mulled that over. "She had one of her fits on the *Hellor* on the way here. When she came out of it, she said, 'She's not dead now.' I asked her who wasn't dead, but she just gave me that blank stare, you know the one, like she's not really there. Then she slept. I had no idea what she meant."

"A slight twist of Thelma Brickman's body as she fell, Albert. That's all it took." I put my hand on my mother's hand. Although the current was weak, I still felt the electricity of life coming through. "It gave her a chance at least. And here's something else. The Black Witch knew about Emmy and her fits. She told me Emmy had one while she was with the Brickmans."

"Did she tell you what Emmy saw?"

"Not exactly, but I figure it was me and Di-Marco at the quarry. When I went over the edge, I landed on that little tongue of rock just below. It wasn't much but enough to keep me from falling all the way."

"So, you're saying Emmy put that rock tongue there?"

"Or just put me in the place that when I fell, it was directly below me. If I'd been to the right or to the left even a little, I would have missed it."

He thought this over a moment, then said, "If she saw the future, she would have seen the tornado coming. Why didn't she do something to save her mother?"

"I don't know. Maybe she tried but couldn't. Maybe the tornado was just too big for her."

He shook his head. "You know how crazy all this sounds?" I could see his engineer's brain trying to accept a possibility that no mathematical calculation could ever prove. And, in truth, he never admitted to me that he believed the things I told him about Emmy. But he must have seen desperation on my face that night, because he said, "Whatever happens, Odie, we'll still have each other. We'll always be brothers."

Sister Eve sat with me. It had been nearly two days since she'd first come to the hospital. My mother's condition hadn't changed.

"I pray," I told her. "I pray with all my heart. It doesn't seem to help. Do you think there's any chance Emmy could have another one of her fits?"

Sister Eve smiled. "She doesn't really understand this gift she's been given, Odie. Not yet. She will someday. I would love to help her in that, but it's up to her."

"Maybe you could just hit me on the head and I'll get a gift of some kind, too. One that'll help my mother."

She smiled again, gently. "I don't think it works that way. And you've already been given a gift."

"What gift?"

"You're a storyteller. You can create the world in any way your heart imagines."

"That won't make it true."

"Maybe the universe is one grand story, and who says that it can't be changed in the telling?"

I wanted to believe her, and so I imagined this:

My mother finally woke. Her eyes slowly opened, and she turned her head on the pillow. When she saw me, her face lit with a brilliant radiance and she whispered, "Odysseus, Odysseus. My son, my son."

Epilogue

There is a river that runs through time and the universe, vast and inexplicable, a flow of spirit that is at the heart of all existence, and every molecule of our being is a part of it. And what is God but the whole of that river?

When I look back at the summer of 1932, I see a boy not quite thirteen doing his best to pin down God, to corral that river and give it a form he could understand. Like so many before him, he shaped it, and reshaped it, and shaped it again, and yet it continued to defy all his logic. I would love to be able to call out to him and tell him in a kindly way that reason will do him no good, that it's pointless to rail about the difficulty of the twists in that river, and that he shouldn't worry about where the current will take him, but I confess that even after more than eighty years of living, I still struggle to understand what I know in my heart is a mystery beyond human comprehension. Perhaps the most important truth I've learned across the whole of my life is that it's only when I yield to the river and embrace the journey that I find peace.

My tale of the four orphans who set sail together on an odyssey isn't quite finished. Their lives went far beyond the rolling farmlands and high bluffs and river towns and remarkable people they encountered on their meanderings that summer. Here is the end of the story begun many pages ago, an accounting of where the greater river has taken all the Vagabonds.

Clyde Brickman, in his full confession to the Saint Louis police, maintained that it was Thelma who'd shot Albert's father, the man I think of as my father, too. It didn't matter. Brickman still went to prison, not just for his part in that killing but also for the embezzling he'd been party to with his wife while they ran the Lincoln Indian Training School and the bootlegging and all the additional crimes revealed by the ledger and other documents Albert had taken from the Brickmans' safe. When asked why he'd held on to all those letters, Brickman said he'd thought that someday he would try to repay the money he and his wife had stolen from the Indian families. I considered it just another lie meant to mitigate whatever sentence might be handed down, and I hated him all the more.

During World War II, while fighting in

Europe, I received word from Sister Eve that Brickman had died of consumption. Near his end, he'd sent for her and for Emmy, and they'd visited him as he lay in his prison hospital bed. He asked their forgiveness, which they freely gave. He made one request of them before his passing: to intercede on his behalf with me and Albert and Mose and beg our pardon, too.

Of all that we're asked to give others in this life, the most difficult to offer may be forgiveness. For years after that fateful summer of 1932, there was a heavy stone of anger in my heart with the name Brickman etched upon it. For me, the journey that had begun in a small canoe didn't end until, with the gentle urging and guidance of Sister Eve, I was finally able to let go of my enmity. In that moment of release, I also let go of any need to believe in a Tornado God, and I began to have my first inkling of this great river we are all part of and to see how right Mose had been when, comforting a grieving Emmy on the banks of the Gilead, he'd told her she was not alone.

I didn't return to Saint Paul with Albert and Mose, nor did Emmy. We chose Saint Louis, I with my mother and Emmy with Sister Eve, who would guide her in so many necessary ways to a full understanding of her remarkable gift.

There's no single road to redemption. My

mother did come out of her coma, but ever after her legs were useless. When Lucifer bit Albert and the doctor had advocated amputation of the affected limb, I'd darkly imagined the beggar's life my brother might have led. When I learned the truth of my mother's injuries, I fell into despair imagining much the same tragic outcome. I selfishly urged her to embrace a profound belief in God so that Sister Eve might help her to be healed, but like Albert, she simply could not. Instead, she reached into a deep well of courage inside herself and proved to be every bit the woman I'd hoped I might find when I headed for Saint Louis. Though bound to a wheelchair, she set about creating a new kind of life. She'd been designing and making her own clothes forever, and she determined to do the same for others. She bought the empty fudge shop on the corner of Ithaca Street and turned it into a dress shop where she sold her creations. Three of the young women who'd been in her charge stayed with her — to my great relief, Dollie among them — and she taught them her craft. It was a slow go at first, but my mother was not above a little bit of blackmail, and she tapped the wealthiest of her former clientele to buy dresses for their wives. Eventually, her reputation as a designer spread. By the end of the Great Depression, gowns from Maison de Julia were all the rage among women of the Saint Louis elite.

At eighteen, Albert enrolled in the University of Minnesota to pursue a degree in engineering, multiple degrees it turned out. But every year, once the upper Mississippi River was clear of ice, my brother and Mose worked on the *Hellor* with Truman Waters and Cal. I often joined them, and Emmy did, too. On one of our early spring trips downriver together near the end of those days, Mose, on a whim, tried out for the Saint Louis Cardinals as a walk-on. He made the farm team, and a year later they brought him up to the majors. Emmy had once predicted that he would be a famous ballplayer, which was not precisely true, but he twice led the league in RBIs. They called him the Silent Sioux Slugger, and the baseball cards that bear his image and stats are highly prized now.

When World War II commenced, like millions of other young men, Albert and I donned uniforms. Despite his gimp leg, which was the legacy of the snakebite, my brother's mechanical genius was an asset too valuable to let pass, and the navy took him. He rose quickly in rank and was finally put in charge of the powerful engines of an aircraft carrier. Near the end of the war, that great vessel was sunk, victim of kamikaze attacks. Although the carrier was abandoned, Albert stayed aboard, seeing to the safe evacuation of as many of his engine room crew as possible. My brother had been a hero to me his whole life, and he died a hero's death. In Albert's honor, my firstborn son proudly bears his name, and in a leather case on a shelf above my writing desk, I still keep the Navy Cross given for my brother's sacrifice.

Mose played three full seasons with the Cardinals, but early into his fourth a fastball caught him in the head, in much the same way the paperweight he'd thrown years earlier had clipped Clyde Brickman. The blow damaged his left eye, and the brief career of the Silent Sioux Slugger was over. But that didn't end Mose's love of the sport. A year later, he returned to Lincoln School, where the administration had changed dramatically and the idea of "Kill the Indian, save the man" had been abandoned in favor of a more humane approach to housing and educating Native American children. Herman Volz, that kind old German who'd done his best to mitigate the darkness during the Brickmans' reign, was still there when Mose arrived, but he died in his sleep a couple of years later. Mose coached the school's baseball and basketball teams. He married Donna High Hawk, the sweet Winnebago from Nebraska who'd once served me Cream of Wheat in a chipped bowl and who later taught home economics to the girls at Lincoln School.

Because of his time with the Cardinals and

because his teams at Lincoln School did so well, Mose acquired a national reputation, his image once gracing the cover of *The Saturday Evening Post.* He parlayed his fame into an advocacy for Native American rights, particularly the welfare of children. The Lincoln Indian Training School closed in 1958. Shortly after that, Gallaudet University hired Mose as a coach and he moved his family to Washington, D.C., and was a not infrequent visitor to legislators' offices, where, with the words that flowed from his eloquent hands, he worked at raising the consciousness of the nation's lawmakers. I visited him and his family many times across the years and was always happy to see that Mose's journey had brought him to a place of understanding and of peace. He died of leukemia in 1986, with his wife and children at his bedside. Donna told me later that the final words Mose signed to her were these: *Not alone.*

As I told you in the beginning, this is all ancient history. There are not many left who remember these things. But I believe if you tell a story, it's like sending a nightingale into the air with the hope that its song will never be forgotten.

My great-grandchildren, when they visit, beg for stories about the four Vagabonds and their battle against the Black Witch. The tale I like telling best is the love story of the imp with

664

his magic harmonica and the princess with the unlikely name of Maybeth Schofield, and how, after a long separation and many trials, they married and lived happily ever after on the banks of a river called the Gilead. Because that beautiful princess passed away quietly long before any of them were born, to these children she's just part of a lovely fairy tale.

When they've gone away, back to their home in Saint Paul, I often rest in the shadow of the sycamore. I'm not alone in the house I built here. My sisterly companion is a woman to whom I made a promise under this same tree seven decades ago, a promise to return to the place where, for a moment on our odyssey in that distant summer, we'd been at peace. She is near the end of her own remarkable journey, which she foresaw long before anyone else. She's still subject to fits, which she calls episodes of the divine, but has had to accept that some things — like the circumstances of her mother's death and Albert's — are far beyond her reach and ability. Even so, she has dramatically changed the lives of many. In the pale evening light, she walks from the house and sits with me beside the Gilead and takes my hand. Our skin is blotched and wrinkled, but the love that binds us is eternally young. Brother and sister in spirit though not in blood, we are the last of the Vagabonds.

In every good tale there is a seed of truth,

and from that seed a lovely story grows. Some of what I've told you is true and some . . . well, let's just call it the bloom on the rosebush. A woman who can heal the afflicted? A girl who looks into the future and wrestles with what she sees there? Yet are these things more difficult to accept than that all of existence came out of a single, random moment when cosmic gases exploded? Our eyes perceive so dimly, and our brains are so easily confused. Far better, I believe, to be like children and open ourselves to every beautiful possibility, for there is nothing our hearts can imagine that is not so.

ACKNOWLEDGMENTS

I am indebted, as always, to my agent, Danielle Egan-Miller, and her team at Browne and Miller Literary Associates for their editorial comments, their business acumen, their enthusiasm, their support, and their friendship across so many years. I've been blessed.

I owe so much to my editors at Atria Books, Peter Borland and Sean deLone, who opened their arms to a pretty rough manuscript and generously applied their expertise. Thanks for helping to shape that early draft into the story I believe it was always meant to be.

For assistance with the historical backdrop of this tale, I owe thanks to the Blue Earth County Historical Society and the Gale Family Library at the Minnesota History Center. Also a big thank-you goes out to Clare Pavelka of Red Wing Shoes for her dogged efforts to track down boot facts long ago buried in the dust of time.

Sadly, the stories of the ill-treatment of Native American children forced into government boarding schools are as numerous as the blades of grass on the prairies. For the story I've told, I am particularly grateful to the account of his own experience offered by Adam Fortunate Eagle in his fine memoir, *Pipestone.*

Finally, to the baristas at Caribou Coffee and the Underground Music Café, where this story was written: Thanks for your smiles in the dark hours of every morning, the caffeine you supplied to start my engine, and your patience as I occupied a chair and table way beyond any reasonable time limit. I couldn't have done it without you.

AUTHOR'S NOTE

The river voyage upon which Odie O'Banion and his fellow Vagabonds embark in the summer of 1932 is a mythic journey. The reality of the Great Depression landscape that serves as its backdrop, however, was etched into the memory of my parents and the parents of those children who, like me, were born in a time of plenty following World War II. My father was a native of Oklahoma. I grew up listening to his stories of the Dust Bowl years, of foraging for wild greens to supplement meals, of watching mud rain from the skies. My mother was born in Ellendale, North Dakota, to a struggling family who could not afford to feed another mouth. At the age of four, she was sent to live with relatives in Wyoming, who eventually adopted and raised her.

The Great Depression was hard on almost everyone, but it was particularly devastating to families. In 1932, the United States Children's Bureau reported that there were at least 25,000 families wandering the country. During the height of the Great Depression, an estimated 250,000 teenagers had left home, willingly or not, and had become itinerant.

When I began to consider the story I wanted to write, which, quite honestly, I envisioned as an update of *Huckleberry Finn,* the Great Depression appealed to me as the perfect, challenging setting. It was a time of desperation in our nation, with the best and the worst of human nature broadly on display. To create this setting as realistically as possible, I read countless first-person narratives, pored over reams of microfilmed newspapers from the day, and studied the vast photographic records of the time. As much as possible, I tried to hold to the economic and social truths of the period.

Particularly important to both that historic era and the story I created were the shantytowns that sprang up in cities across the nation. They were called Hoovervilles, a derisive jab at Herbert Hoover, president in the early years of the Depression. (A Hoover shoe was one with a hole in its sole; Hoover leather was the cardboard inserted to cover that hole.) These makeshift communities were built of scraps and were populated by those dispossessed as a result of the worldwide financial collapse. The people who lived there were the objects not only of charitable relief efforts but also of concerted efforts at eradication. The Hooverville in Saint Louis, which I included in the story, was the largest in the country, with a population of more than 5,000. The federal government cleared out this encampment in 1936, but small clusters of shacks endured until well into the 1960s.

I love the works of Charles Dickens, and in part, my decision to open *This Tender Land* in a fictional institution called the Lincoln Indian Training School was a nod to his powerful novels of social inequity. The history of our nation's treatment of Native Americans is one of the saddest litanies of human cruelty imaginable. Among the many attempts at cultural genocide was a horribly ill-conceived program of off-reservation boarding schools initiated by Richard Henry Pratt, who famously declared that its purpose was to "Kill the Indian, save the man." Beginning in the 1870s and continuing until the mid-twentieth century, hundreds of thousands of Native children were forcibly removed from their families and sent to live in boarding schools far from their reservation homes. In 1925, more than 60,000 children were being housed in 357 of these institutions in thirty states. Life in an Indian boarding school wasn't just harsh, it was soul-crushing. Children were stripped of their native clothing, hair, and personal belongings. They were punished for speaking their native language. They were emotionally, physically, and sexually abused. Although touted as a way to assimilate children into the white culture and teach them a productive trade, in truth, many of these schools functioned as a pipeline for free labor, offering up the children as field hands or domestic help for local citizens.

For *This Tender Land,* I read dozens of personal narratives of life in these institutions, but I relied heavily on *Pipestone: My Life in an Indian Boarding School,* a memoir by Adam Fortunate Eagle, which recounts his days as a resident of the Pipestone Indian Training School in southwestern Minnesota. For some, Adam Fortunate Eagle may be a familiar name. He was one of the leaders of the Indian occupation of Alacatraz, which began in November 1969 and lasted for nineteen months, galvanizing Native activism across the nation.

In the early part of the twentieth century, a wave of Protestant revivalism swept the country, promulgated by the likes of William J. Seymour and the Azusa Street Revival, the evangelist Billy Sunday, and the charismatic faith healer Amy Semple McPherson. Although by the 1930s, much of the religious fervor had died down, revival tent crusades, like the Sword of Gideon Healing Crusade in my story, continued to be popular in the South and Midwest. In truth, I owe a great debt of gratitude to Sinclair Lewis and his novel *Elmer Gantry,* a scathing look at the religious hypocrisy he saw in his day. I have always been fascinated by Sharon Falconer, the story's tent evangelist, a woman of deep and honest religious passion but also of worldly experience. My own Sister Eve is largely constructed on the framework of Lewis's intriguing character.

Though much of my research was conducted in libraries and museums — hours in the Gale Family Library at the Minnesota History Center and in the Blue Earth County Historical Society's History Center and Museum — I spent a great deal of time personally exploring the actual landscape of the story. I kayaked and canoed the waterways that Odie and his companions follow in the novel, and I walked much of the same ground they would have walked. I stood at the confluence of the Blue Earth and Minnesota Rivers, where the citizens of the fictional Hopersville erect their makeshift shelters, and I sat on the rock where Odie and Maybeth Scofield share a kiss. I roamed the streets of the West Side Flats in Saint Paul, and despite all the remarkable changes in the landscape since the days in which the Vagabonds sought respite there, I was still able to see in my mind's eye just where Gertie's restaurant would have been and the boat works and the home where John Kelly's baby brother might have been born.

In the end, here's the truth behind the writing of my novel: Although I tried to be true to the spirit of the time and to use as much as possible the factual guideposts from my research, *This Tender Land* is simply a story. As the narrator, Odie O'Banion, freely admits near the novel's end, "Some of what I've told you is true. The rest . . . well, let's just call it the bloom on the rosebush."

ABOUT THE AUTHOR

William Kent Krueger is the award-winning author of the *New York Times* bestselling *Ordinary Grace,* winner of the Edgar Award for best novel, as well as eighteen Cork O'Connor novels, including *Desolation Mountain* and *Sulfur Springs.* He lives in the Twin Cities with his family. Visit his website at William KentKrueger.com.